DESIREE

WELCOME

TO

TREELESS

PARK

CHENTAL-SONG BEMBRY

Text copyright © 2019 by Chental Song Bembry
Cover art by Aaron C. Fisher
Cover art copyright © 2019 Chental Song Bembry

Summary: Twelve-year-old Desiree Davenport, whose parents get divorced right before seventh grade, adjusts to life in a new city and a new school while fitting in as a cheerleader for USA Little League Football. Challenges arise when she befriends the stars of the football team, who bully one of their teammates, Chauncey Willis. Desiree dives into the mystery of why the twins bully Chauncey and must choose between holding onto the close relationship with her friends and standing up for what is right.

First paperback edition March 2020

Text formatting and copy editing by Word-2-Kindle

The text of this book is set in 12-point Goudy Old Style

ISBN 9781710377965 (paperback)

Published by Sweet Song Publishing, a subsidiary of Sweet Song Productions LLC

Other books, authored and illustrated by Chental Song Bembry:
The Honey Bunch Kids – Copyright © 2010
The Honey Bunch Kids: School's In Session (Book 1) – Copyright © 2011
The Honey Bunch Kids: School's In Session (Book 2) – Copyright © 2012

To learn more about Chental Song Bembry, go to:
www.chentalsong.com

To keep up with the latest in the "Desiree Davenport" series, visit:
www.desireedavenport.com

Follow Chental Song Bembry on:
Twitter: @chentalsong
Instagram: @chentalsong
LinkedIn: Chental Song Bembry
Facebook: Chental Song Bembry
YouTube: Chental Song The Author

Books coming soon from Chental Song Bembry:
Passion and Purpose
Desiree Davenport: Invasion of the Friend-Snatcher

I dedicate this book to the following:

To my mother, Holly, for being my Number One cheerleader.

To my grandmother, Tula, for completing my family.

To my grandfather, Willie, for your amazing contributions to science.

To the rest of my family (my aunts, uncles, and cousins) for your love and support.

To Rashad and Phil, two amazing football players with a real passion for the sport, for being my inspirations.

To my pastor, Rev. Dr. Soaries, and my church family for supporting me from the beginning.

To all of the children who may not like to read, I wrote this book especially for you. ☺

A Message to My Readers

To My Dearest Readers,

I wrote *Desiree Davenport: Welcome to Treeless Park* with you in mind. I wanted to tell a story that highlights the very best of people in a community who care about each other: a story that allows you to see yourselves, your families, and your friends in each of my characters. I encourage you all to stay true to yourselves and to never let anyone silence your voices. Don't blend in with the crowd. Be different; be a change-maker. When you recognize that something is wrong, come up with a solution to fix it. I encourage each and every one of you to rely on your interests, passions, and talents to create and develop something positive. Always be kind to everyone, and remember to help others. Once you start something, don't stop until you've seen it through to the very end. The best part about creativity is that you can use your imagination to uplift and inspire others, and that's what I hope this book does for you.

Over the past three years, I've had so much fun bringing this story to life. Desiree, her mom, Rashad, Gumbo, the du Bois family, Corinne, Chauncey, and the rest of the people of Treeless Park are my dearest friends, and I hope you fall in love with them just as much as I have. A few chapters in this book are written from the twins' perspectives. I thought it was really important to show their thought process as well – not just Desiree's. I thank God for allowing me to share this story with you all. If you remember anything from this message, remember these words: Be genuine, be exceptional, follow your dreams, and always walk with your head up.

Sincerely,
Chental Song Bembry

Table of Contents

1

A New Start

Screeeeechhh!!! Skrrrrttt!!!

My entire body lurches forward as my mother jams on her brakes. Swerving the steering wheel with one hand and shielding me with her other, she narrowly escapes colliding with a speeding ambulance. Its lights flash as it whizzes through the intersection, never slowing as it passes us. We didn't hear it, and we definitely didn't see it coming.

Heart racing, I lean back in my seat and face my mother's frightened expression. Neither of us speaks. A few seconds pass before I realize I'm not even breathing.

"Desiree, are you all right?" my mother asks, finally breaking the silence. I nod, still too shaken to utter a word.

My mother takes a deep breath and proceeds through the intersection. I chew on my bottom lip and stare out at our new surroundings through the smudged windshield. The bright sky, lit up by the hot rays of the midafternoon sun, highlights it all: crowded streets, brick buildings, and a few closed-down stores. This is different.

Clutching my copy of *A Raisin in the Sun* by Lorraine Hansberry, I glare at the moving truck driving ahead of us. Inside of that truck are things I know all too well: My queen-sized bed with the beautiful tulip carved into the footboard;

a plastic toy chest overflowing with toys that I can't bear to part with; boxes of clothes; and my hot pink roller skates that I used to ride up and down our block with Priya and Tatyana: my best friends since third grade.

"Mommy, do we really have to move?" I ask in a meek voice. Towards the end of June, my mother sat me down and explained that she and my father were getting divorced. Looking back, I should have seen it coming. My parents used to argue all the time. I'd heard about divorces tearing up other kids' families, but I never thought it would happen to mine.

"Your father wasn't good at managing our money," my mother says tiredly. "I've told you this before."

My heart aches as I think back to our house in the development on 5 Pepper Court. That house had an amazing front porch with an open backyard. It was complete with lush, green grass, and a long driveway that welcomed us home each time we rolled up.

"Besides, this new place is a lot closer to my job at the unemployment office, and it's what I could afford for now," my mother says, and I nod my head silently.

After everything we've been through, I really have to hand it to my mother. She's been so strong, even though I know she's hurting, too. It's just the two of us now, and I'm worried about her.

I reach for the radio buttons and turn on my mother's favorite Motown song, *You're All I Need to Get By*, by Marvin Gaye and Tammi Terrell. I'd much rather listen to Beyoncé, but if this song can lift my mother's spirits, I'll listen to it all day. "Mommy. Your song's on."

My mother doesn't answer me right away, and I know her mind is somewhere else. Finally, she forces a smile. "Oh, yeah. I love this one, baby," she says, but she doesn't sing her heart out to the chorus like she usually does. I sigh as she follows the moving truck past a sign that reads, "Welcome to Treeless Park. We Are Family." A lonely ache swells in my chest. No offense, but these people aren't my family.

The moving truck stops in front of a little store called "Manny's Fish Market." I turn to my mother with a confused frown. "Why are we at a fish store?"

"I told you: We live in an apartment now." My mother points to a few windows above the fish store. "It's upstairs."

My face feels like stone, but I keep quiet. I know my mother is doing her best for the both of us, and it's not fair for me to start complaining. Even though I'm livid.

While my mother climbs out of our Audi to speak with the movers, I tap my phone and search for a message from my father. Sadly, I find nothing, so I stare at the charm bracelet on my wrist. I received the bracelet from my father on my birthday this past June, when I turned 12. Wearing this bracelet makes me feel like he's always with us, even though I know he's off living his life not too far from here.

I reluctantly climb out of the car, fanning myself against the humid July weather. New Jersey always gets ridiculously hot in the summer and freezing cold in the winter. At times like this, I wish we lived in California.

My mother leads me towards Manny's Fish Market, which smells just like - wouldn't you know? - fish. "Whoo! This store is *stinkin'*!" I wail a lot louder than I meant to.

"Shh! Girl! The man is standing right here!" my mother hisses. I whip around and meet eyes with a man sweeping up in front of the store. His stained apron holds a name tag that reads "Manny." I gulp, instantly feeling embarrassed. Welp, Manny heard me.

"That's okay. Welcome," Manny says, his voice revealing a Spanish accent. My mother drags me around to the back of the store and explains that he's the landlord.

We stop in front of a dirty white door that my mother opens with a silver key. The door opens and we climb a small flight of stairs that creak like nobody's business. At the top of the stairs is a second door, which my mother unlocks with a different key. I push my way into our new home, which smells just like somebody set off a fish bomb and looks like a gray dungeon.

There's a small kitchen with a refrigerator and stove, but no dishwasher. I notice a little space that I think is supposed to be our living room. There's a bathroom the size of a coat closet down the hall and two bedrooms across from each other. I take a careful step inside the smaller bedroom and look around, disappointed to find a little closet and a small window with a torn shade.

"Oh...!" my mother cries from the living room area. She sounds really disappointed. "Manny promised me he'd have this place painted *before* we moved in!"

I can hear my mother's footsteps behind me as I walk over to the window. I place my hand against the hot glass, staring down at the sights that make up Treeless Park. "Did you tell grandma and everybody else where we've moved to? Does Daddy know where we are?" I ask my mother.

"Everybody knows where we live. You'll see them all eventually, when we're settled. I promise," my mother insists. I lower my eyes in silence and my mother sighs. "Wait here. I have something for you." She disappears from my room and returns with her black purse. She reaches into it and unveils a pink leather journal.

There's a strap that snaps where the journal opens. It reminds me of Nancy Drew. She always has a journal, which she uses to keep track of her observations. I've always loved mysteries, so this journal is perfect. Plus, writing is my favorite hobby. But when I think about my parents splitting up and the looks of this place, writing is the last thing I want to do.

Bzzz! Bzzz! Bzzz!

I jump and glance down at my phone, but then I smile when I see whose name is flashing on the screen. It's Priya.

"Talk to your friend," my mother says with a smile. "I'll be outside unloading the car. Come down in a few minutes, okay?" She *creak, creak, creaks* out of my room while I answer Priya's call.

"Hey, hey, Desiree!" Priya sings, and I can picture her purple braces shining against her teeth. "I've got Tatyana on the other line." Priya puts me on "Hold" and loops Tatyana into the call.

"What's up, Girl?" Tatyana asks through a mouthful of something crunchy. It's probably pretzels, her favorite snack. "How's the move? Tell us everything!"

I cringe. When I first found out about my parents' divorce, I felt scared and embarrassed to tell my friends. Their parents get along; why couldn't mine?

"I hate this," I confess to my friends. "My family's all busted up and I'm so far away from you guys."

"Where do you live now?" Priya asks.

"This city called Treeless Park. We live in an apartment now." I scratch my arm nervously and force out the next few words. "It's above this fish store and it stinks."

"Ew!" Tatyana snaps, and I wince at the disgust in her voice. "If I didn't have dance practice in twenty minutes, I'd jump on my bike and come rescue you."

I glance around my new room with its dingy walls and creaky floors. I'd never want my friends to see this place. My throat gets this funny, lumpy feeling and it hurts to swallow. "How am I gonna make it through the seventh grade without you guys?"

"It'll be hard," Tatyana says sadly, "but listen, Priya and I *always* got your back."

"Totally," Priya says. "Anytime you need us, just call!"

My mouth breaks into a smile and I lean closer against the window. Then suddenly, I notice something weird outside. "I'll...talk to you guys later," I say, hanging up with my friends.

Down below and across the street, I see two boys wearing helmets and sitting on red bikes. They're staring at me. These nosy creeps! When I twist my face into an ugly scowl, one of the boys smirks at me. He and the other boy ride off and I narrow my eyes suspiciously.

I walk outside to greet my mother, who's reaching into one of my bags and unveiling an outfit that I hoped I wouldn't see until next week.

"Look!" my mother says. She holds up my cheerleading uniform that came in the mail last week. The uniform colors — blue and white with black trim — make me cringe. Thanks to my mother signing me up for USA Little League Cheer, I'll be wearing this uniform until December.

"Mommy, I don't really want to be a cheerleader. I don't even know anything about football."

"Desiree, why don't you just give it a chance?" My mother folds up my uniform and puts it back in the bag. "I think cheer will be a nice way for you to make some friends in this neighborhood."

"Um, excuse me. Do y'all need some help?"

My mother and I freeze. Standing by our car is a boy with white spots all over his face, arms, and legs. I blink in stunned silence. What happened to his skin?

"Do y'all need help carrying some stuff inside?" the boy asks. "I'm picking up some fish for my mom, but I can do that after. I live right around the corner. It's not a problem."

My mother twists her face into a pained expression. She doesn't like using other people's kids. However, the boy continues to hang by the car and my mother finally gives in. "Thank you, young man. We really appreciate your help."

"No problem," the boy says. "It's just people helping people. That's how we do around here in Treeless Park."

What is this, The Twilight Zone? I wish he'd shut up.

My mother walks off to guide the movers, leaving me alone with Chatterbox. His brown and white skin looks so interesting against his black t-shirt. "Hi," Chatterbox says to me with a slight smile.

"Hi," I mutter. Chatterbox reaches for the bag with my cheer uniform, and I panic. I don't want anyone to know about me and this cheer thing. "Hey, don't touch that bag!"

"I...I was just trying to help."

I shake my head and clutch my bag tightly. "I'll carry this one myself."

Chatterbox rubs one of his spotted arms. "I'm not going to give you any cooties. I just have vitiligo."

"What's vitiligo?" I ask.

"It basically means I'm losing my brown color." He scratches his wooly hair. "Don't worry. It's not contagious."

I want to punch myself in the face. I was only embarrassed about cheerleading, not afraid of his skin.

I let go of the bag with my cheerleading uniform and Chatterbox lifts it with ease. "So, you're a cheerleader." He gives my uniform a closer look and grins when he sees the team name stitched on the front. "The Pirates, huh?" I nod and give a light shrug. These people around here are so nosy! "Then I'll see you around," he says. "Next month, I'll be —"

"Desiree! Where are you guys?" my mother calls.

I exchange a quick glance with Chatterbox, who hurries upstairs with the bags. I shove my Lorraine Hansberry book into a smaller bag and carry it upstairs, where Chatterbox looks around curiously. He's *really* nosy! My heart slams against my chest as I wait for him to comment on the fish funk, but he never does. It's like he's used to it, or maybe he doesn't care. Either way, I'm more than grateful.

Chatterbox carries the remaining bags up to our apartment. When he's finished, we walk outside and see the bicycle creeps, staring us down like two lions waiting to attack. I start to yell for my mother, when suddenly, one of them shouts, "There he is! Get him!"

Chatterbox runs off. "Hey! What's your name?" I call after him, but he doesn't answer me. The bicycle creeps speed after him, and in less than 10 seconds, they're all gone. I stand by the moving truck with my mouth hanging open.

"Desiree!" my mother calls, walking outside with the movers. She glances around and asks where Chatterbox went. When I tell her about the bicycle creeps, she stares into the distance and shakes her head. "I was gonna pay him."

At 4:30 p.m., the movers finish arranging our furniture. My mother thanks them for their services, and after eating pizza, we unpack and set up our things until the dungeon starts to look like something.

"Whew! Girl, let's take a break!" my mother exclaims as we flop down on our peach leather couch. The two of us sit in silence and take in our new surroundings. This is really it.

I curl up in the corner of the couch, feeling lonely. Suddenly, my mother touches my hand. "Desiree...do you know why I love Motown so much?" She stares at the ceiling, her voice soft and low as she speaks. "Your grandfather was so strong, Desiree. He was a chemist and grew up in a time that wasn't ready for him. The adversity he faced..." My mother's voice cracks and I see a tear roll down her face.

"My father used Motown as a way to get him through his toughest days. When I listen to Motown, I think of *him*. I know this place isn't what you're used to, but it's what we have for now. Most of all, we have each other."

My mother squeezes my hand and wipes her tears. We sit there together until the sun goes down, and that night, before I go to sleep, I hang up my cheerleading uniform and flip through the empty pages in my journal. I'm definitely skeptical about this new life, but after being reminded of the story of my grandfather and all that he endured, I know that I have to hang in here – for myself, but most importantly, for my mother.

2

First Day Jitters

BEEP! BEEP! BE–
 I roll over and tap the "Snooze" icon on my phone before it finishes beeping. Through a forced peek of my left eye, I'm able to make out the glowing 6:30 A.M. on the screen. Darn. It's September third: the first day of seventh grade.

 Most kids are probably thinking about the clothes they bought that they didn't need and couldn't afford, only to impress people they don't know or even like. Today, I'm more concerned with how my clothes will *smell*. After hanging in a fishy closet for a month...my God.

 "Desiree? Are you up yet?"

 I glance to my left and see my mother standing in the doorway. She's dressed in her favorite pajamas that I gave her for her birthday – the satin ones with the little buttons and a million tiny clouds across the shirt and pants.

 "How did you sleep?" she asks softly. I stare at her pajama clouds, wishing I could sit on one and just float away.

 "Fine, I guess." I go to my window and stare out into the dark sky. The rain pours steadily as big drops beat against the ground. "Mommy, can you please drive me to school?" I beg.

"Desiree, we already agreed that you'd ride the bus."

I dig my ever-growing fingernails into my palms and groan until my chest hurts. There's only one kind of bus in Treeless Park, and that's the public bus. "But..."

"It won't be so bad," my mother insists. "You and I spoke with the driver last week, and she promised to keep a close eye on you and the other kids, remember?"

Yeah. I remember that bus driver's wide smile, which was lost in a sea of chapped lips and missing teeth.

My mother leaves my room, so I sigh and stare out the window. My mind flashes back to a month ago, when I saw those bicycle creeps staring at me from across the street. Strangely, I haven't seen them or Chatterbox since then.

I turn to my closet and slide my cheerleading uniform to the end of the rack. We've been having indoor practices five days a week, but now that school's starting up, it'll only be three days a week. And I'm glad, because I'm sick of Coach Robin yelling at me for not keeping my legs straight during splits. What part of I'M NOT FLEXIBLE doesn't she get?

Shoving all my boring clothes next to my cheerleading uniform, I finally spot something cute: my hot pink mini dress with lime green sequins trimming the edges. I yank the dress and matching leggings down from its hanger and push my arms through the sleeves.

"Desiree!" my mother calls from the living room. I can smell a faint trail of vanilla incense burning. Thank goodness. "Did you find something to wear, Desiree?"

I love my mother, but she'll run my name in the ground if I let her. Let's go, Desiree. Finish your food, Desiree. Show me your cheers, Desiree! I mean, I like my name, but I wish I had a nickname. You know, one that's catchy and clever.

I slip into my hot pink cowgirl boots and head to the bathroom down the hall. I wash my face, brush my teeth, and style my curly hair into two, long, braided ponytails. Aunt Nadine has always said when I wear my hair like this, I look like a doll. People say I look like the Rudy Huxtable character from *The Cosby Show*.

"Desiree!" my mother suddenly shouts. "Hurry up! The bus is at the corner!"

I sprint out of the bathroom, knocking the toothpaste and lotion off the sink. I race into my room and glance around like a maniac. WHERE IS MY BACKPACK?!

I wheel around and spot the sequined, hot pink bag hanging from the doorknob. I swing it over my shoulder and dash into the kitchen, where my mother hands me an egg-and-cheese English muffin wrapped in a napkin. Then I race out of the apartment, down the steps, through the backdoor of Manny's Fish Market, and out into the pouring rain.

"Wait for me!" I yell. But it's too late. My stomach sinks in disappointment as I watch the bus pull off down the street without me, leaving a thick trail of smog in its path. I didn't want to take that bus, anyway. I'll get a ride from my mother, just like I wanted. Heh.

I hold my breath as I trudge back upstairs. When I get inside, my mother rushes over to me with big, concerned eyes. Now she's dressed and ready for work.

"Oh, Desiree...look at you!" she cries. Here it comes: *My poor baby. Hop in the car. I'm driving you to school.* "What happened? Why weren't you watching the clock?"

"I was watching the clock!" Lie. "I—I was trying to get ready and I..." *had a too-long fashion show in the bathroom mirror.*

My mother sighs and slings her purse over her shoulder. "All right, I'll drive you." She rapidly glances at her work tablet and sucks her teeth. "I'm supposed to be at work early to train this new girl. I'll get there when I get there."

I stare at my mother sadly. It's my fault I missed the bus; my mother shouldn't have to be late for work. "That's okay, Mommy. I can just walk."

My mother stares at me like I'm crazy. "Walk? Girl, it's raining and you don't even know where you're going."

"Yes, I do! We've driven past the school plenty of times. It's not far. I'll put the address in my phone's GPS."

My mother stares at me with huge eyes and finally runs a hand through her hair. "All right, well, be safe, you hear me? I'll stay on the phone with you until you arrive." I nod and give my mother a tight hug. "And remember, I signed you up for aftercare. I'll pick you up at a little after five o'clock."

"Okay, Mommy," I say, and we hurry through the door together.

3

The Walk

Once my mother pulls off in her Audi, I get her on the phone, open my umbrella, and start walking to school. I stick my earbuds in, open my texts, and shoot a quick message to Priya and Tatyana. They're probably on the bus right now.

Me: Happy 1st Day of 7th grade! Missed the bus. Walking ☹

Tatyana: Bust!!!

Me: Yup. And it's raining.

Priya: OMG!! Get there safe. Wish u were still on our bus ☹

I close out of our group chat, open my GPS app, and type in the address to Treeless Park Middle School. It's just a 15-minute walk from here, so I walk along the sidewalk, shifting my bulky umbrella from hand to hand as I pass by the familiar surroundings. Every store has a clever name.

Across the street from my apartment is a restaurant called The Crunch Bowl. They probably sell fried foods, which I love, but I don't really want to go there. When my family was still together, we always went to this restaurant called Sweet Song's, where a red carpet stretched from the sidewalk to the main entrance. The walls were lined with mirrors and the ceilings were decorated with beautiful chandeliers.

On Friday nights, people danced to music from a live band. Sometimes local talents performed. The food was amazing, too, but the real reason I miss Sweet Song's is because it was the place that my family loved to eat at together.

"Are we ever going back to Sweet Song's?" I asked my mother after she brought up The Crunch Bowl.

"It's too expensive now, baby," she answered sadly. "Maybe in a few months."

"Daddy pays the child support, doesn't he? Let's pay with that."

My mother laughed and shook her head. "That's not how you use money, Desiree."

I push this conversation to the back of my mind and lift my boots around a puddle of dirty water. I check my phone. Nine minutes left.

At the end of the block, I turn left and approach this hair salon called Pump It Up. I peer through the glass windows at the cute arrangement of sinks, salon chairs, hair dryers, and shampoo shelves. I imagine it wouldn't be so bad to get my hair done in there. It looks so fancy, but since my mother has named herself the only person allowed to go near my head with a flat iron, I can forget it.

Next door is the Flipsy Wiggle Dance Academy, which sounds like the kind of place my mother would absolutely love. She loves dancing to songs with hot beats. I, on the other hand, am pretty shy. My father wasn't too crazy about dancing either – another topic he and my mother would sometimes argue about.

I keep walking and eventually notice two clothing stores: a cutesy-cutesy one for girls called Glimmer Glamour and another store called Living Large. My cousin Tyrell should shop there. He's so big.

As I reach the intersection, I see a corner store across the street called Get It and Come On. Ha! It means, *Get what you came for and get out.* I like this store the most.

"Hey, Mommy, I'm almost at the Get It and Come On," I say into the microphone on my earbuds.

"Oh, great, because I'm at work and this new child is already here," my mother grumbles through the phone. "I've got to go, but just text me, okay? Love you."

"Love you, too." As I hang up with my mother, I see something under the store's awning that makes my stomach turn.

A group of boys are fighting. One boy grabs another in a headlock, gripping him tighter and tighter as he struggles to escape, while another one jumps on his back. I look closer and freeze when I make out who the boys are: It's the bicycle creeps and the Chatterbox. They're beating him up.

My mind wants to run but my legs won't let me. I become a statue, standing there with my eyes glued to the scene. My phone suddenly vibrates and I hear the chorus to the song *Level Up* by Ciara. My mother is texting me, probably wishing me a great first day of school.

I don't have a chance to check the text, because the bicycle creeps turn away from the Chatterbox and glare straight at me. My blood goes cold, and suddenly, I feel very afraid.

4

The Nickname

"Hey! Girl!" one of the bicycle creeps shouts at me with a smirk. "I see you looking over here!" He sounds crazy. He releases his grip on the Chatterbox, who hustles off into the rain.

"Yeah, Spots! You'd better run!" the other creep screams.

Oh, heck no. I've gotta get out of here *now*. My eyes dart around crazily as I look for another route to school, anywhere to escape these creeps before they get *me* next!

Suddenly the rain picks up speed. It's pouring harder and everything around me is a blur. My eyes blink rapidly as splashes of water cloud my vision. A powerful gust of wind blows, flipping my umbrella inside out. I try to fix it but I can't. The wind yanks my umbrella right out of my hands and blows it into the middle of the street. I watch in horror as a garbage truck barrels right over it. Now my only option for shelter is the Get It and Come On.

I can feel the creeps staring at me as I hurry across the street and underneath the awning. *Please do not talk to me,* I pray silently, squeezing my eyes shut.

"Hey. You with the ponytails," one of the creeps says. I keep my eyes shut. Maybe if I ignore them, they'll leave me alone.

"Hey!" The voice gets louder. I open my eyes and see one of the creeps standing right in front of me. Where'd the other creep go? "I said, 'You with the—'"

"I *heard* you!" I shoot back, glaring this creep dead in his face. He's wearing a leather jacket and some black sunglasses. He removes the glasses, and that's when I *really* get a good look at him. He's got light brown skin, hazel eyes, and a head full of waves. He's really cute. I pull my English muffin out of my pocket.

"What'cha got?" Leather Jacket asks, craning his neck to examine my food.

I shoot him a sideways glance and unwrap my breakfast. "None of your business."

"Man, would you leave her alone?" the other creep asks with a laugh. He emerges from the street carrying my dismantled umbrella and shoots me a charming smile. "Hi. How're you doing?"

I don't know how to respond. On one hand, I don't want to talk to this guy, either, but on the other hand, I can't stop staring up at him. This boy is *foooiiiinnee!*

He's got the same light brown complexion as Leather Jacket, but I could care less about his complexion. His features are just very striking, like a model's. His square face holds a set of thick eyebrows and huge, piercing, light brown eyes. There's a mole on his nose, which rests above a pair of full lips. His dark, curly hair sits high above his head like a crown. I tear my eyes away from his prince-like face and notice that he's wearing a varsity jacket with a football on the sleeve.

"I'm good, thanks," I answer, trying to appear calm.

"I'm good, thanks," Football Jacket mimics in a nasally voice. He laughs. "Girl, how come you talk like that?"

I glare at him. "Talk like what?"

Football Jacket cringes with a slight smirk. "You talk all...proper and stuff."

I narrow my eyes. "Oh, so that's a bad thing?"

Football Jacket gets flustered. "No, no, I mean..." I just nod my head and he clears his throat. "Anyway, here's your umbrella," he finally says, handing me the busted thing. "That garbage truck straight rolled right over it, like it was making a pizza." He snickers. "Ha! Pizza umbrella."

"That thing didn't have a chance!" Leather Jacket chimes in. "It went *crack-crack*."

"I know. I saw," I snap, shoving the dismantled thing into a nearby trash can.

Football Jacket looks at me like I'm a mutant. "Yo, what's your problem?"

"I don't have one." I glance between him and Leather Jacket. "Why were you guys beating up that kid?"

"You mean Spots?" Football Jacket sneers angrily.

"Do you have to call him that?"

"Yeah, why not?" Leather Jacket asks. He slaps a high five to Football Jacket and they crack up. I take a step back. These guys are mean.

"Hold up..." Football Jacket says, staring at me with a slight smile. "Haven't we seen you around before?"

Leather Jacket snaps his fingers. "Oh, yeah! We saw you moving in across the street a few weeks ago."

I rub my arm nervously. I don't want them knowing where I live. "That wasn't me."

"Girl, please. Nuh-uh," Football Jacket says, giving me a knowing look. "We saw you in the window and you made that face." He scrunches up his face.

Leather Jacket laughs. "Yeah, and we saw Spots trying to steal your stuff out of your car!"

"What? No! He wasn't stealing anything!"

"That's what *you* think," Leather Jacket says, but I'm still unconvinced. Would a thief really say something like, "People helping people?"

"The point is, stay away from Spots. He's bad news," Football Jacket informs, pointing an index finger in my face.

Leather Jacket nods, unwraps a wad of gum, and shoves it into his mouth. "Yeah, that's all you need to know, Ponytails."

"My name isn't Ponytails," I snap.

"We know." Football Jacket crouches down to tie his shoelaces. "Your name's Desiree."

"How'd *you* know?" I demand, feeling surprised, flattered, and creeped out.

"We heard your mom yelling at you while she was unpacking y'all's car," he tells me, standing up. "But I'm not going to call you Desiree. Nah, I have a better name for you."

"*What?*"

Football Jacket shoves his hands in his pockets and steps closer to me. His eyes glaze over my face and then my pink cowgirl boots. "I'm going to call you...Pony Boots. Yeah. 'Cause you've got them cute ponytails and them girly-girly boots on," he says, smiling.

"Ha! Good one, bro!" Leather Jacket laughs like it's the funniest thing in the world.

My face heats up. "You are *not* calling me Pony Boots."

"Yeah, I am. I just did." Football Jacket shrugs like this is all a big joke. I glare at him, struggling to ignore his charming smile and find some sort of flaw.

"Well, I'll just call you..." My eyes land on his ears, which stick out on each side of his head like a pair of leaves.

I notice that one of his ears has a small bump on the lobe. "I'll call *you* Big Ears."

I expect Football Jacket to back down, but he just smiles wider. "My name's Rashad. Rashad Maurice du Bois."

"And I'm Antwan Philippe du Bois, but I go by Phil," Leather Jacket says. I scoff. These guys are so arrogant. Phil jerks a thumb at Rashad. "He and I are fraternal twins, if you couldn't already tell."

I glance between Rashad and Phil. They definitely look and act like brothers. I should have noticed it sooner.

"Hey, do you know what 'fraternal' means?" Phil continues, still smacking on his gum. "It means we don't look alike, but we're still—"

"I *know* what it means!" I say, rolling my eyes. Thankfully it's not raining anymore, so I get on my way. To my surprise, the twins start following me.

"Hold up! Where are you going?" Phil asks.

My neck snaps to the right as I shoot him an annoyed look. "To school."

"Cool. Us too, Pony Boots," Rashad says.

"Do *not* call me 'Pony Boots' and leave me alone!"

"Alone?" Rashad circles in front of me and walks backwards, so now, we're facing each other. "Why do you want to be alone?"

I'm speechless. *Don't look in his eyes, Desiree. Don't do it, Girl!* "Why do you keep talking to me?"

Rashad continues walking backwards. He doesn't even stumble. "I don't know. There's just something...different about you." He puts his earbuds in. "I can't put my finger on it yet." He smiles even bigger, showing off a pair of dimples and pearly-white teeth. I can't help but stare at him.

I quickly look away before Rashad catches me and shove my earbuds in to finish my Ciara song. He's probably used to girls grinning up in his face, but I'm not going to give him that satisfaction.

Beyond the fast drums and hot beat of *Level Up*, I can hear the twins asking what song I'm listening to. Instead of giving them anymore of my time, I just ignore them and lead the rest of the walk to school.

5

Phil's Point of View: The New Girl

"Yo, Pony Boots! Girl, what'cha listening to?" Rashad calls for the fourth time in a row. I gave up after the first try.

Desiree mashes her earbuds deeper into her ears and walks faster, like her boots are a pair of jets and she's taking off. I laugh around the wad of gum stuck to the inside of my cheek and shake my head. "No offense, bro, but that girl ain't thinking about you."

Rashad acts like I didn't just spit facts. "Pony Boots!" he calls again.

I give him a hard shove. "Dude, leave her alone. You're making a fool out of yourself."

Rashad shoves me back. "No, I'm not," he snaps loudly. Desiree glances over her shoulder and gives Rashad the weirdest look. He grins at her like I've seen him grin at Mom after she's heard him mutter under his breath about doing the dishes. When Desiree finally turns around, Rashad glances back at me and starts whispering. "Look, she just moved here and she's new to the school. She doesn't know anybody…"

"You don't know that," I say, raising an eyebrow. "A lot can happen in a month, Ra, and pretty girls get friends fast."

"Not always. Some of them are shy." Rashad shifts his gaze to Desiree. "Besides, we've never seen her hanging around anybody."

Wrapping my gum around my tongue, I think back to last month, when Rashad forced me to ride bikes with him every afternoon. "C'mon, P. Just for a half hour," he pretty much ordered, tossing my red-and-black helmet in my lap. I groaned – not because I didn't like riding bikes, but because I had some serious business planning to do before school started. Still, it was Ra, so I reluctantly closed my marble notebook and followed him outside. We rode up and down the street, with Ra in front and me trailing behind. A couple times we saw Desiree walking up the sidewalk with her mom and carrying groceries up to their apartment. I don't think she ever saw us.

Rashad nudges me in the side, snapping me out of my thoughts. "Look, if she's already popular, then where's her crew, Phil? We're the ones walking her to school this morning."

"Dude, we're *following* her, and chill with the *Pony Boots*. That name is straight up wacked."

"It's not wacked; it's original. You're just jealous you didn't think of it."

"Whatever," I mutter, just to put the argument to bed. When my brother is set on something, there's no changing his mind.

We walk in silence for a little while, until Rashad clears his throat. "Hey, P?" he asks me. He's been calling me "P" since we were seven. He thought "Ra" was a pretty cool name and wanted to shorten my name, too. So he came up with "P." He said it was better than "Ph." He was right.

"Yeah?" I ask him.

Rashad shoves his hands in the pockets of his varsity jacket. His eyes flick to Desiree and he looks almost worried. "You think she's stuck up?"

I turn away from Rashad and study Desiree: small and innocent-looking in her dress, boots, and sparkly backpack. This girl is definitely different.

I look back at Rashad, who stares at Desiree with his head tilted to one side. I can't tell what he's thinking. A few seconds pass before he chuckles and shakes his head at me. "Never mind. Forget I said anything."

My eyes narrow skeptically behind my sunglasses, but I decide to let the conversation go for now. "Fine."

Rashad nudges me in the side. "Hey, P. *Football Smashup* after dinner? I beat you last time, so *I* get to use the good controller."

"You know the summer's over right?" I ask. "Besides, Dad's gotta look at our books first. You know how he is."

"I got this. Dad needs to chill," Rashad mutters.

I look at Rashad like he's crazy. "Oh, so you're gonna tell Dad that he *needs to chill?*"

Rashad smiles. "Uh, no."

We bust out laughing and I shake my head. "Look. Dad's expecting more 'A's' from us this year and I'm gonna make sure we get them."

"I hear you, P," Rashad says, and we finish the walk in silence.

6

Homeroom 1105

After a few minutes of walking with the twins, I spot a familiar three-story brick building up ahead and breathe a sigh of relief. At the entrance, I see some cracked steps that lead up to a pair of double doors. To the right is a flagpole so tall it seems to touch the sky, and to the left is a sign with faded letters that spell out: *Welcome to Treeless Park Middle School.*

I text my mother to let her know that I've arrived safely. When she types back, **Have a great day, Sweet! Hugs,** I close her message conversation and open my father's. The last time we texted was last week, when I told him I'd be starting my new school today. He wrote back, **Wish I was there to see you off, baby,** but I'm not sure if he meant it. He never texted me this morning to see if I woke up on time or asked for any pictures of my first-day-of-school outfit. I slide my phone into my pocket and squeeze my charm bracelet.

The twins push themselves in front of me and through the doors. "Come on, Pony Boots! Keep up!" Rashad orders.

"It's *Desiree*, Big Ears!" I shoot back. Rashad makes a funny face at me, while I just roll my eyes and walk inside.

The school lobby is full of kids laughing and talking with each other excitedly. Before I can even process what's happening, the twins grab my wrists and drag me through the crowd. I grimace. "Hey! Let go of me!"

"How do you expect to find out what classroom you're in?" Rashad demands. He and Phil lead me to a bulletin board, which is decorated with construction paper and school-themed stickers, like pencils and apples and stuff. I quickly scan the alphabetized list and find my name.

Desiree Davenport: Homeroom 1105

That's all I need to see. "Well, I'm out of here," I state, pushing past the twins.

Phil frowns and turns away from the board. "Whoa! Can you wait for us?"

I scrunch up my face in annoyance. "For what?"

Rashad looks offended. "We walked you to school."

My eyes narrow. "You *followed* me." Rashad rolls his eyes and I keep going. "Listen, I've got to go. See you guys around."

Rashad looks me up and down in silence for a moment. Finally, he smirks, like I'm joking with him or something. "Oh. Be like that, then. Just don't get lost, now, you hear?"

I glare at him, ready to fire off another "Big Ears" remark, but I take a deep breath and walk off without another word. The twins are much taller than me, so they're probably in eighth grade. It's a safe bet I won't see them too often. Thank goodness.

As I search for my homeroom, I get distracted by a mural that wraps across an entire hallway and around a corner. I follow the mural's vibrant colors and find myself walking past classrooms filled with lab tables, instruments, art easels, and theater props.

I turn another corner and slow my pace, carefully observing the walls. They're painted an ugly mustard yellow color, and some of the paint is chipping. I look at the green lockers, which are long, thin, and slightly dented in some parts. Even the floors in this area look busted. Some of the tiles are cracked and others are straight up missing. As I pass by the gym, the faint smell of cheese and armpits fills the air, and I start breathing through my mouth to avoid the funk. Being here makes me miss my old school, and I wonder how Priya and Tatyana's first days of seventh grade are going.

Rrrriiiinnngggg!!!

Upon hearing the morning bell, my body tenses. I speed walk around the first floor until finally, I make it to Homeroom 1105. The door is wooden with a tarnished knob. I reach for it, but before my fingers even touch the metal, the door swings open.

A tall, thin woman wearing a fitted blue dress stands in my path. Her face is flawless, with smooth skin and a set of perfectly glossed lips. I notice her dark brown hair, which is slicked up in a big, tight bun. I know that thing must hurt. Her piercing eyes stare down at me as I clutch my backpack straps. She must be the teacher.

"Can I help you, young lady?" she asks sternly. I hear a faint Spanish accent in her voice.

"Yes, um..." I'm so nervous, I can barely get my words out. "My name is Desiree Davenport and I'm in this class..."

"You're late. Come in and sit down," she orders, ushering me inside. Heart racing, I keep my head down, avoiding eye contact with anyone. Out of the corner of my eye, I spot an empty seat in the second row. I look up and my heart skips a beat when I see who's sitting in the front row. Jesus, *no.*

"Pony Boots! You made it! Girl, what took you so long?" Rashad exclaims, leaning back in his chair. "I knew you'd get lost."

Snickers erupt throughout the room. I want to teleport the heck out of here. "I wasn't lost," I hiss, glaring through

Rashad's huge, light brown eyes. He bites his bottom lip and stares at me, smiling.

Next to Rashad, Phil leans forward in his seat and laughs at me. "Hurry up and sit down. We saved you a seat," he says, gesturing to the empty desk behind Rashad. I turn to face the teacher, who's staring down at me with a look that could kill.

I hurry up and drop into the empty seat behind Rashad. My seat happens to be next to a girl I recognize from cheerleading. She has light brown skin and coarse hair that's braided with colorful beads.

I put my head down, waiting for this crazy day to end. Suddenly, I hear the door open.

"Are you in my class, too?" the teacher's voice snaps. "Well, take a seat. School is in session."

As I lift my head to see who it is, my heart stops. Ooh. It's Chatterbox.

My eyes instantly cut to the twins, who smirk and give each other a low-five beneath their desks. I don't know exactly what's going on here, but I know one thing's for sure.

Something just isn't right.

7

A New Nickname

"Young man, what is your name?" the teacher demands. Everyone gets real quiet while Chatterbox stands at the front of the room. His lips are pressed into a pout and his eyes are fixed on the floor, almost like he's trying to read the fine print on the tiles. His button-down shirt is untucked and his pants are dirty and wrinkled from the fight at the Get It and Come On this morning.

"My name's Chauncey," he mumbles in a low voice.

The teacher doesn't hear him because she twists up her face and snaps, "Chunky? Your name is Chunky?"

This makes the whole class crack up, like it's showtime at the Apollo and Chauncey is the act on display. The laughter is loud and mean, bouncing off the walls and around the room like a symphony, but I don't laugh. I don't think this teacher is funny at all. Well...maybe a little. Heh.

Chauncey furrows his brow in frustration. "My name's *Chauncey!*"

Phil faces the rest of the class. He stands up, whips off his sunglasses, scrunches up his face really ugly-like, and puts his hands on his hips. "Howdy. My name's Chauncey the Bless-ed and I got the best, ding-dang ribs West of the

Mississippi!" he screams with a gruff, Southern accent, shaking his head back and forth like a bobblehead.

Rashad laughs like a lunatic. "Man, why you mocking Granddaddy?"

I try to suppress my giggles. These guys are crazy.

"ENOUGH!" the teacher shrieks, silencing us all. In front of me, the twins hiss like two snakes, their shoulders bouncing up and down with quiet laughter. "I apologize, Chauncey," the teacher says.

Chauncey scrambles to the back of the room and tries to make his way past each desk. However, the desks are too close together, so he ends up bumping into each one along the way. There's a chorus of "Hey!" and "Watch it!" and "Man, look what you did!" as he accidentally knocks over notebooks, pencil cases, and binders. Next to me, my cheerleading teammate watches the calamity unfold in disgust.

"Ew! He came all late, bumping people's stuff with his big self!" she spits with pure menace. I give her a look. Chauncey isn't really "big." He's just stocky. Our eyes meet and that's when her expression changes. She gives me a big, friendly grin and whispers, "Wow! I love your dress!"

I force a smile and turn away from her before she can say anything else to me.

"Settle down," the teacher orders as Chauncey makes it to his seat in the back row. "Welcome to the seventh grade here at Treeless Park Middle School. My name is—"

Errrr....

We all hear the sound of crying wood and then...

BOOM! CLACKITY-CLACK-CLACK!

I turn around to find the wooden ledge of Chauncey's desk rattling against the floor. The whole class dies.

"What—what is going on?" the teacher sputters.

"I'm...I'm sorry, Ma'am. I put my stuff on top of the desk and it just broke," Chauncey mumbles, confused.

"Yeah, right. He probably sat on it!" Rashad crows.

Chauncey glares at him. "No, I didn't!"

"That's enough!" the teacher shouts. She instructs Chauncey to sit at an empty desk by the window. Thankfully, he doesn't break that one. "As I was saying," the teacher continues, "my name is..." She turns to the dry erase board, uncaps a stubby, black marker, and prints her name in tall, intimidating letters that spell out: **MS. HERNANDEZ**.

"When I call your name, please say 'here' and raise your hand," Ms. Hernandez says, grabbing the attendance sheet off her desk. "If you have a nickname that you'd like to be called — one that's *appropriate* — please tell me now."

Ms. Hernandez calls all the kids with "A" and "B" last names and then goes through a couple of "C's."

"Corinne Corelle?" she calls out. My cheerleading teammate shoots her hand in the air, waving it like it's on fire. "Here, Ms. Hernandez!" Her words sound funny. They sound like, "He-oh, Ms. Hoh-nandez!" It's baby talk. I never got to hear her voice during cheer practices — probably because her voice was always drowned out with the rest of ours.

"Desiree Davenport?" Ms. Hernandez calls. I raise my hand shyly and tell her I'm here.

"She forgot to tell you her nickname, Ms. Hernandez," Rashad announces. Oh. My. God. He stands up, points at me, and starts talking in a flawless, thick, Jamaican accent. "It's *Pony Boots*! Yes, mon! See arr in arr pretty, pink dress wid arr ponytail and arr girly-girly boots dem pon arr feet? Watch dem, nuh! She shaaarp, eeh?" He grins at me like a loon.

Everybody, including Ms. Hernandez, busts out laughing. Even Corinne can't contain herself. I glare at her and she quiets down. I didn't laugh at her baby voice, and I wish Rashad would shut up. I look over at Phil. He looks mortified.

"That's not my nickname!" I protest. If I don't come up with something clever now, Rashad will never stop teasing me. I think back to Corinne's baby voice and remember how Tyrell used to say my name when he was little. He couldn't pronounce "Desiree," so he just said "Dizzy."

"My nickname is *Dizzy*," I blurt out. Ms. Hernandez writes that down on her attendance sheet. Rashad whips around, shooting me a raised eyebrow and a smirk. I glare at him while Ms. Hernandez continues down the "D" list.

"Okay...the du Bois twins," she says.

"Ms. Hernandez, it's *doo-Bwah*," Phil corrects. Ms. Hernandez makes a note on her attendance sheet and Phil raises his hand. "I'm Phil." He faces the class. "As many of y'all already know, I'm an entrepreneur. I sell gum." He turns back to Ms. Hernandez. "Everybody calls me *Gumbo*."

Rashad raises his hand. I brace myself for an arrogant introduction in another accent. Surprisingly, he speaks in his normal voice. "I'm Rashad. Some people call me 'Ra-Ra.'"

Ms. Hernandez shoots him a dry look. "And I will call you 'Rashad.'" Rashad smirks and shrugs his shoulders. Ha! I snicker to myself as Ms. Hernandez finishes calling the roll. "And last but not least, Chauncey Willis," she says as she reaches the end of her attendance sheet. She stares at Chauncey as he sits at his new desk, and I know exactly what she's thinking: He'd better not bust *that* one up next.

8

Mission Possible

M s. Hernandez spends the rest of the morning telling us her classroom rules: treat everyone with respect, homework must be neat and handed in on time to receive full credit, and late work will not be accepted unless you have a valid excuse. She tells us that we will report to homeroom every day for math, science, language arts, Spanish, and history. We'll change classrooms for our gym period and electives, which include music, theater, art, keyboarding, and home economics.

"There's no reason to be bored here at this school," Ms. Hernandez says. "We have a variety of clubs, after-school activities, and a talent showcase at the end of the month."

The whole class immediately comes to life. We all sit up straighter in our chairs and lean forward, begging Ms. Hernandez for more details on the talent showcase.

"Quiet down!" Ms. Hernandez orders. "Please keep in mind: The talent showcase is not a competition. This is simply an opportunity to get to know everyone."

Well, that's just boring. Where's the fun in showing off your talents if you don't even get a prize? Not that I would do it. I'm super shy when it comes to performances, and there's no way I'm making a fool out of myself in front of these people.

"If you'd like to participate in the showcase, I'm passing around the sign-up sheet," Ms. Hernandez continues. "Please write your name and the talent you'd like to demonstrate."

As the sign-up sheet travels around the room, most of the kids put their names down. Except for me, of course. Ms. Hernandez finally collects the sign-up sheet and glances it over. As her eyes travel to the bottom of the sheet, she frowns.

"Who's responsible for this?" she demands angrily, holding up the sheet for everyone to see. At first, I can't tell what she's so mad about, but then I see it. Somebody scratched out Chauncey's name and wrote "Spots" in thick, black ink. They even crossed out his talent (singing) and replaced it with "Bust another desk."

I glance over at Chauncey, who looks like he wants to scream. When nobody owns up to the hateful jab, Ms. Hernandez slams the sheet on her desk and glares at us.

"I'll have you all know that I don't tolerate bullying," she states. "So, whoever thinks they're being funny, know that there's a seat in the principal's office with your name on it."

Chauncey groans and puts his head down on his desk, while the twins glance at each other with shifty smiles. They'd better watch out before Ms. Hernandez starts making phone calls to people's parents. This lady seems like she's no joke.

At noon, the lunch bell rings. I stay at my desk and examine my fingernails while the classroom clears out.

"Ahem!"

My eyes dart up and I see the twins standing in front of me. Rashad drums his fingers on my desk and stares at me with an expectant smirk. I shake my head. "Can I help you?"

"Yeah, you can let us show you where The Caf is so you don't get lost again," Rashad answers, stifling a laugh.

My top lip curls in annoyance. "Please. After you embarrassed me in front of the whole class this morning with your big, Jamaican accent, I'll pass." I finish my statement with my hard eyes boring through Rashad's. His cocky expression dims and he looks disappointed. I turn away and finish examining my fingernails.

"Hey, *Gumboooo*. Hiiii, *Rashaaaad*."

My eyes immediately dart up. Some girl (*Morgan* I think is her name) who sits in the back of the classroom is standing in front of the twins...and making goo-goo eyes at them.

Gumbo gives Morgan a brief *what's up*, while Rashad smiles like a polite celebrity greeting his fan. "Oh, um, hey, Morgan."

Morgan plays with the ends of her hair. "Going to The Caf?"

Rashad glances at me. When he realizes I'm not following him for real, he rubs the back of his neck and shrugs. "Uh, yeah."

"I'll walk with you guys." Morgan's smile widens as she follows the twins out of the classroom. I force down the tiny twinge of jealousy bubbling in my stomach.

You didn't want to eat with them, Desiree, re-mem-ber?

Next to me, Corinne nosily shuffles a pile of papers. I had no idea she was still here. "You coming to lunch, Dizzy?" she asks.

I just stare. I'm still mad about how she laughed at Rashad's "Pony Boots" announcement. "I don't know where I'm going."

"We can go together!" she says with a grin. I shrug, stand up, and follow her down the hall. As we follow a huge crowd of kids to The Caf, I see the twins walking with

Morgan up ahead. They stop every now and then to chat with some guys from other classrooms. I notice a few girls saying hey to the twins and batting their eyelashes at them. Hmm. Looks like they're really popular.

Once Corinne and I make it to The Caf, we stand in the lunch line together. "You're *sooo* pretty, Dizzy!" she says.

"Thanks. You are, too," I tell her, and it's true.

Corinne grabs my wrist and starts examining the sleeve of my dress. "This is just like something I would see in Glimmer Glamour! Do you shop at Glimmer Glamour?"

"I live around the corner from it. What's so hot about Glimmer Glamour?"

"Everything!" Corinne's face lights up as she tells me about the clothes, purses, and accessories I'll find at the store. "I love fashion, if you can't already tell. See my outfit?"

I stare down at Corinne's short, scrawny body, which is wrapped in a green sweater, gray skirt, and yellow-and-white striped stockings. She's wearing a pair of pink boots with brown fur shooting out of the tops.

"Wow...!" I mutter, struggling to find something nice to say about the fashion crisis I'm staring at.

"I made it myself. Do you like it?"

"It's tight!" I do *not* want to hurt this girl's feelings, but her outfit looks wacked.

Corinne giggles, showing off a pair of buck teeth. "Thanks. As soon as you sat next to me this morning, I got so excited!" She pauses and stares up at me. "How come you've never talked to me in practice?"

"Well...how come *you've* never talked to *me?*" I ask.

"I *wanted* to, but you always seemed kind of..." Corinne trails off and scrunches up her face, like it's her turn to insult me nicely. "Like you didn't want to be bothered."

I tense up. It's not my fault that my mother signed me up for a sport that I'm not even flexible enough to be good at. And now this girl who I don't even know is putting me on the spot? I swallow a huge lump that's building in my throat and keep my eyes locked on the kid in front of me with the bad rash on the back of his neck. Ew.

Corinne must sense that she's offended me, because she scurries in front of me with her bugged-out eyes. "Well... the important thing is that we're talking now, right?" I shoot her a sideways glance, which she must mistake for forgiveness because she keeps talking to me. "Are you excited for the first football game? I can't wait to say the chee-ohs."

"The what?" I ask.

"The *chee-ohs*!" Corinne repeats. "Did you sign up for the talent showcase?" When I shake my head no, Corinne looks shocked. "But it'll be so much fun. We could even do a dance routine together!"

No. No. No. "Uh, I don't know. I've always been way, too shy for that kind of stuff."

"You can't be that shy dancing with a poht-noh."

"A *what*?"

"A poht-noh! You know, two people!" Corinne says. "Come on, say yes! I can show you all my moves!" She bites her bottom lip and breaks into a fierce pop-and-lock dance right here in the lunch line. Her entire body bends and twists like lightning. I can't deny it: This girl's got mad skills. Besides, she's very persistent, and she's the only girl in my class who's tried to make friends with me.

I force a smile at Corinne and agree to be her dance partner. She jumps up and down excitedly. "Yes! Yes! Yes! After lunch, I'll tell Ms. Hernandez to put your name next to mine!"

Yay. Not. Wait until I tell Priya and Tatyana.

When we finally reach the end of the lunch line, I spend two dollars on a soggy-looking piece of pizza and milk, while Corinne buys a cheeseburger with an orange ticket. I stare at her ticket in confusion, but then I get distracted by what I see happening at the table up ahead.

Chauncey sits there angrily while the twins flick him in his head. Chauncey swats his arms in the air like he's chasing away a swarm of bees. "Leave me alone!" he snaps.

"Leave me alone," Rashad mocks in a nasally voice.

Gumbo flicks Chauncey near the top of his head. "Hey, Spots. Nice performance today in class. You broke that desk so hard. How'd it go? BOOM! CLACKITY-CLACK-CLACK!"

"We know you signed up for the talent showcase," Rashad says. "Man, you ain't got no talent!"

"Maybe he'll balance a plate of brownies on his big belly and gobble 'em down like a big, greedy magician pig!" Gumbo crows. My jaw hits the floor.

Rashad swipes the pizza, tater tots, and brownie off Chauncey's tray. He and Gumbo play Keep Away with Chauncey's lunch. Chauncey sits there in silence, looking like he wants to yell, cry, and explode all at the same time.

I watch the action with a confused frown, wanting to speak out. However, the twins are very intimidating. They're much taller than me, and if I get on their nerves, they might embarrass me again. The last thing I want to do is make waves at a new school, so I just turn to Corinne. "Why do the twins mess with Chauncey so much? And how come he's not saying anything? He's just taking it!"

"I don't know," Corinne answers. "This is my first year doing chee-oh, but last week after practice, I heard some of the chee-oh parents talking about the football players. They said the twins' names and Chauncey's, too. They play on the same team, so it doesn't make sense why they don't like him."

I raise an eyebrow. "*You* heard all that? How come I didn't hear any of it?"

"Oh, you and most of the other girls had already gone home. I usually stay late because I have to wait for my grandma to pick me up, and we live on the other side of town. Most times, I'm the last one to leave." Corinne's voice trails off sadly. I wait for her to say more, but she just blinks and changes the subject. "Hey! Did you know that Glimmer Glamour gives discounts on weekends?"

I nod and act interested while she blabs on about some funky discounts at Glimmer Glamour, but there's this burning curiosity inside of me that won't go away. My eyes stay locked on the twins as they return Chauncey's lunch and give him one last flick to the back of his head. They strut off to their own table, while Chauncey glares after them with menace.

Watching all of this takes me back to third grade, when I was minding my own business, eating my homemade cheese-and-mayonnaise sandwich in the cafeteria. My original short story about Yuck-Yuck, The Yellow-Toothed Duck had just been voted "Funniest Story" by my class. My teacher, Mrs. Cohen, had presented me with a shiny, blue ribbon and I'd felt on top of the world. I couldn't wait to get home to show my father, who loved crazy stories. All of my classmates seemed happy for me...all but Michaela Johnson.

Michaela stomped over to me in her big, dirty sneakers and slapped my juice box out of my hand. "You think you're so funny and so cute, Desiree Davenport!" she spat. My mother told me that when a person says things like that – *you* think you're so this and *you* think you're so that – it's really because *they* think those things about you.

I stared up at Michaela's twisted scowl, wondering if anyone was going to stand up for me, but no one did. Maybe they were all too afraid of her.

Finally, Priya and Tatyana plopped down in the empty seats across from me. The two of them were already inseparable in Mrs. Cohen's class, so I was surprised to see them at my table.

"Can we sit with you, Desiree?" Priya asked. I nodded while she and Tatyana unpacked their lunches.

"Your story was so funny," Tatyana added. "How'd you come up with the idea?"

Michaela just glared at me and stomped away. She never bothered me again, and Priya and Tatyana became my friends.

Michaela was my first real encounter with a bully, but after I made friends, I stopped noticing other people getting picked on. But I can't ignore what I see happening with Chauncey and the twins. On that hot, July afternoon, Chauncey helped me and my mother move into our apartment. He didn't have to, and he said something that I haven't forgotten: "People helping people."

As easy as it would be for me to just focus on myself and adjusting to this new school, I feel sorry for Chauncey and want to try and help him. I've never been one to butt into other people's business, but I don't like what I see. My mother told me that people act a certain way for a certain reason. The twins obviously have a reason for bullying Chauncey, and I suddenly feel this overwhelming responsibility to find out what that reason is.

The last thing I want to do is make waves in a new school, so I'll have to figure this out peacefully.

9

Locker Blunders

When lunch ends, Corinne follows me back to Ms. Hernandez's classroom, talking the whole way there about the talent showcase. "We need to start practicing right away, Dizzy! You can come to my place and I can come to yours!"

"I'll think about it," I mutter. Corinne is literally killing me. Her big, hazel eyes turn dull, like I've just announced that Glimmer Glamour went out of business. I bite my lip and try a slightly nicer approach. "I mean, the talent showcase isn't until the end of the month. We've got plenty of time to think about our routine and practice schedule, don't you think?"

Corinne is quiet. After a few seconds, she turns to me with her usual bubbly eyes. "Yeah, that's true. Before school ends, let's exchange numbers so we can talk all the time!"

Jesus, be a fence.

We finally make it back to Ms. Hernandez's classroom, where we receive our textbooks and do a writing exercise. "I want each of you to write one page telling me about yourself," Ms. Hernandez says. "Talk about your likes, dislikes, hobbies, and one subject that you want to do better in this year."

I breeze through the first part of the exercise and grimace when I make it to the last part. I hate talking about things I'm not good at, but since Ms. Hernandez wants to be so nosy, I scribble down, *I want to do better in math this year.* When it comes to algebra, I get a headache. Hopefully, I make it out of seventh grade with at least a B in math.

When the final bell rings at 2:30 p.m., I trudge out of Ms. Hernandez's classroom and go to my locker. Earlier today, we received little slips of paper with our assigned locker numbers. I think I remember my slip saying B-32 or something like that, so I head there and start twisting my combination on the knob. Strangely, the locker doesn't open.

"Desiree Pony Boots Davenport!" a voice announces from behind me. I whip around and meet eyes with Rashad. Gumbo trails behind him, polishing his dirty sunglasses.

I keep twisting my locker's knob. "Didn't you hear, Big Ears? I go by *Dizzy* now."

"Oh, yeah. Cute." Rashad smirks and my heart skips a beat. He raps his knuckles on the locker. "Sorry, Pony Boots, but this one's mine."

I freeze. Gumbo laughs while I reach into my pocket and pull out my locker assignment. It reads B-30.

"Sorry," I mutter, my face burning. Thank goodness Rashad can't see me blush. He shakes his head, smiling, and we open our rightful lockers. Gumbo's locker is between ours.

"Yo, Ra! What's up, Gumbo?"

I glance up and see some kid with really nice dreadlocks approaching, and he's got two other guys behind him. They all dap the twins up and glide down the hall. Seconds later, two girls wearing *way* too much lip gloss breeze past us. "*Heyyy, Gumbooo. Hiii, Ra-Raaa,*" they sing.

The twins grin and flick their heads at them. Rashad faces me. "You can call me Ra-Ra, too, you know."

"I'll pass," I state. Rashad narrows his eyes at me, but then he chuckles and puts his books away. I do the same and glance between him and Gumbo. "You guys sure are popular."

"Well, Treeless Park is a small town," Gumbo explains. "A lot of us have known each other since preschool, and we'll all go to the same high school, too."

"So, everyone will get to know *you*, too," Rashad adds, staring at me like he's expecting a big reaction.

I crouch down and stack my notebooks in a neat pile. "Yeah, well, I don't need a whole lot of people knowing me."

"How come?" Gumbo asks.

I let out a frustrated groan. Why won't these two just leave me alone? "Because I already *have* friends back home."

I stand up and face the twins. Gumbo quietly chews on a wad of gum and stares at the floor, while Rashad looks me dead in the eyes. His mouth is pressed in a flat line and his expression deflates in a sad sort of way. Finally, he lifts his lips into a half-smile. "Oh. Well, excuse us," he mutters, with a short laugh. He turns back to his locker and I try to deny the guilty feeling crawling up my throat.

"Hey, Dizzy!" Corinne's voice suddenly chirps from behind me. I turn around and see her grinning at me.

Gumbo glances at Corinne and clears his throat. He opens his leather jacket, revealing an assortment of wrapped gum. "Wanna buy some gum, Corinne? I'll give you a First-Day-Of-School discount."

Corinne scoffs and turns away from Gumbo. He closes his jacket and glares at Corinne, but she just shoves her flip phone in my face. "We almost forgot to exchange numbers! Here!" She grins while I pound my number in.

Next to me, Gumbo snorts. "Dizzy, make sure you push those buttons real hard so she'll have your *numb-oh*."

Corinne's hazel eyes flare as she glares at Gumbo. "Nobody was talking to you," she snaps in a deep voice. She puts her number in my smartphone and grins. "I'll see you later, Dizzy!" She flounces off.

Rashad closes his locker. "Heading home, Dizzy?"

"No. My mom signed me up for aftercare."

"Man," Gumbo says. "You could've walked with us."

I frown. "Don't you guys ride the bus?"

"Sometimes." Rashad glances between his locker and his shoes. Then he looks at me and laughs a little, like he's about to reveal something embarrassing. "It's just that..."

"Nothing." Gumbo elbows Rashad in his stomach.

Rashad glares at his brother and turns to me with an exasperated eye-roll. "Never mind. We'll see you later, Dizzy."

"Yeah, see ya, Dizzy," Gumbo says, still glaring at Rashad. I give them both a suspicious stare as they walk off.

I close my locker and head to aftercare, which happens to be in The Caf. I walk inside and see plenty of other kids in here. I dump my bag on the empty table closest to the doors. Then I open my backpack and whip out my journal, ready to make a new entry about my first day of school. There's so much to write about; I don't even know where to begin.

Just as my pen hits the paper, I glance up and see a familiar person sitting alone at the table across from mine. He reaches into his blue backpack and pulls out a marble notebook covered in football stickers. Our eyes lock and I slowly close my journal.

It's Chauncey.

10

Chauncey

Chauncey and I have an awkward stare-off for what feels like an eternity. I wasn't expecting to see *him* up in here. Should I smile? Wait, no. Maybe I'll just wave? Argh! If only things hadn't ended so weird between us when the twins chased him away from my apartment that day.

Are you going to say something? my mind screams as I stare Chauncey down. I can't tell what he's thinking. His eyes seem empty, like he's not even here.

I open my journal again. My pen hovers above the paper, just begging to leak my thoughts, but my hand doesn't move. I can't write anything now. Not when I already told myself that I would find out why the twins bully Chauncey.

I sigh, stand up, and carry my things over to Chauncey's table. He stares at me as I gesture to the empty chair across from his. "Can I sit with you?"

Chauncey is quiet for an uncomfortably long moment. He finally shrugs and flicks his hand towards the chair. I force a tight-lipped smile and sit, fighting the urge to forget this whole mission and leave him alone. I don't need this.

Wait, Desiree, my brain whispers. *You'd have an attitude, too, if you spent your first day of school getting beat up and bullied.*

I sink my teeth into my bottom lip and give Chauncey one of my best smiles. "Thanks," I say. Chauncey just stares. I glance at my fingernails, wondering what happened to the chatterbox who carried my bags that day. That's when I realize something awful: I never got the chance to thank him. No wonder he's so clammed up.

"So...um..." I begin. Chauncey blinks. "Thank you for helping me and my mom carry our bags upstairs." My eyes lower in shame. "You didn't have to do that."

Two more blinks. "Oh. You're welcome," he finally mumbles. Using a spotted finger, he traces invisible squiggles on the table. "I would've helped y'all some more if it weren't for..."

I lean forward with interest as Chauncey's voice trails off. "Are you talking about Phil and Rashad?" I ask. Chauncey glances up at me and returns his eyes to the table. He nods once. Finally, I'm making progress. "I'm really sorry," I offer.

Chauncey just shrugs and I examine his face. His spots are all different sizes and seem to crawl around his mouth and eyes, like they're eating away at his color. His arms and hands are mostly white, with a few specks of brown here and there. I tear my eyes away from him and glance at his football-stickered notebook. "You play football with the twins, don't you? You guys are teammates. Why do you beef?" I press. Chauncey just coughs and rubs his nose.

This guy's giving me nothing. He reaches into his bag and fishes out a dull pencil with a chewed eraser. He slams it on the table and opens his notebook. Taped to the inside of the cover is a photo of a football player. He looks like a professional, with a shiny helmet, big shoulder pads, and the number 96 on his chest.

Chauncey flips to a random blank page in his notebook. I glare at him. What's his problem?

"All right! It's study time!" the aftercare monitor bellows from the front of The Caf. I think she's one of the librarians, too. She crosses her big legs, showing off a pair of ugly, green shoes. "Please start your homework."

Lady, please! It's the first day of school. There *is* no homework. I cringe in disgust, glaring at her fat toes just popping through the fronts of her shoes like two packs of Vienna sausages.

For the rest of aftercare, Chauncey ignores me. I act like I don't care and read *A Raisin in the Sun*. At a little after 5:00 p.m., I get the "**I'm outside**" text from my mother. I gather my things and sneak a final look at Chauncey. "Bye, Chauncey," I say. He just looks at me, does something that I think is a wave, and goes back to his notebook.

My jaw locks angrily as I push my chair away from the table, creating an extra-loud SCREEEECH! The aftercare monitor gives me a stern look, but I don't even care.

I sign out on the aftercare monitor's attendance sheet, walk outside to my mother's car, and toss my bag in her backseat. "Hi, Baby!" she sings as I drop into the passenger seat. As usual, my mother is playing another Motown song. This time, it's *Can't Hurry Love* by The Supremes. "Whoo! Girl, I am *exhausted*. Today was such a busy day at work, you wouldn't believe it," my mother continues. She looks professional in her black blazer with her hair pulled back in a bun. "But enough about me. Tell me all about your first day of school!"

As my mother drives us home, I think back to all the not-so-terrible things that happened today. I could tell my mother about how I didn't have to walk to school alone, how I met Gumbo and Rashad, who both look like models, and how I think Rashad might like me.

I could tell her about how I'm dancing in the school talent showcase with Corinne, who's half my height but has a ginormous personality. I could tell her that the boy who helped us move in is named Chauncey, that he, Corinne, and the twins are all in my class, and how my teacher seems pretty cool and I think I'll make mostly good grades this year.

But despite all of these seemingly good things that happened today, I'm disappointed.

Disappointed that Rashad and Gumbo are bullies.

Disappointed that I allowed Corinne to force me into doing the talent showcase with her.

Disappointed that I tried helping Chauncey today and got absolutely nowhere.

Disappointed that my parents are divorced and that I'm stuck here in Treeless Park.

"Nothing happened today," I mutter, blinking back tears. My hands tremble as I fumble around in my pocket for my phone. I stick my earbuds in and crank up the volume to Ariana Grande's latest album, while my mother drives us the rest of the way home in silence. She grips her hands tighter around the wheel – something I know she only does when she's either stressed out or hurt. I think I've caused her to feel both, and I hate myself for that, but at the same time, adjusting to this new life in Treeless Park is harder than I thought it would be, and I just can't help how I feel.

11

Old Friends, New Worries

"Desiree! Talk to us, Girl. What's the tea with your new school?"

At the sound of Tatyana's voice, I flop back on my bed and smile. Thank God she and Priya answered the phone.

"I still can't believe your mom let you walk," Priya says. "Were you scared?"

"It wasn't as bad as I thought it would be," I say, and it's the truth. In reality, the walk was quick and the only scary part was seeing the twins fight Chauncey in front of that store, but I leave this detail out. I clear my throat and change the subject. "So, guys, tell me all about *your* first day of school."

"It was awesome," Priya blurts out. "Tatyana and I are in, like, every class together except for two."

"Wow," I mutter. Even though we're all on the phone together, I feel small and far away. "That...sounds awesome."

"Oh, Priya, don't forget we have to tell Mr. Mitchell that we want to be partners," Tatyana says.

"Partners?" I grip my phone tighter. "For what?"

"Nothing, it's just for a small science project due Friday," Priya says quickly. To Tatyana, she says, "You want to get the glitter and I'll get the hot glue?"

"For sure," Tatyana says. "I'll ask my mom to stop by the art supply store tomorrow after dance practice."

I sit in silence. Partners? Projects? Hot glue? My friends' first day runs circles around mine.

"Hey, Desiree, tell us about *your* school," Priya says.

"What kinds of people have you met so far?" Tatyana asks.

An image of Chauncey pops into my brain. I could tell my friends about the bully mystery I'm trying to solve, but I don't want to. Keeping it a secret from everyone makes me feel cool and a little bit brave. Maybe I'll share more after I crack the case.

I tell my friends about Corinne and how she's on my cheer squad and convinced me to do the talent showcase with her.

"What's the prize?" Priya asks eagerly.

"Well, there isn't one," I mutter. "It's just a way for people to get to know each other."

Tatyana snorts. "That's stupid." I cringe and she asks, "What about the boys there?"

"Yeah, the ones at our school are all gross and immature," Priya says, laughing.

I scratch my leg nervously. I hadn't planned to tell my friends about Chauncey *or* the twins, but I guess it beats listening to them brag about being science partners. "Well, there are these fraternal twins in my class," I start.

"Are they cute?" Tatyana asks.

"Yes. They look like models."

"Well, which one do you like?" Priya asks.

"The one who wears a football jacket," I answer.

"Ooooh," Tatyana squeals. "What's his name?"

"Is he on Instagram?" Priya presses.

"Let's find out." I search Rashad's name on Instagram and find his profile. I click on his most recent picture, which is a shot of him dressed in a football uniform with the number four on his jersey. Then I tell my friends his username.

"Wow! He *is* cute!" Priya exclaims.

Tatyana chimes in. "Cute? He is *foooiiine!*"

I bite my bottom lip and try not to smile. "Yeah, he gave me this nickname and kept talking to me. I think he likes me." Just then, Tatyana busts out laughing. My face grows hot. "What's so funny?"

"Desiree, come on. You know that fine, light-skinned boys like Rashad only look at light-skinned girls like me."

My entire body feels like it's on fire, and it takes everything in me not to hang up on Priya and Tatyana. "That's not true," I snap. "What do *you* know?"

"Name a young, famous couple that looks like you and Rashad," Tatyana shoots back.

I rack my brain for an example, but I can't think of one. "What does that have to do with anything?" I quip, wishing that Tatyana would just shut up.

"Face it, Desiree," she says. "You may not see complexion, but other people do."

"Well, I think all of this talk about complexion and couples is stupid," I hiss. "Why are people so obsessed with commenting on how people look together, anyway?"

"I agree with you, Desiree," Priya chimes in, "but unfortunately, Tatyana's right."

"Girl, I'm not trying to insult you," Tatyana says.

"But you are," I shoot back.

"Listen, it's all we see in the media. When it comes to most couples, the girls are usually lighter than the boys, or they're another race completely. Rashad might think you're pretty – he might even like you – but face it, Desiree: You're just too dark to be his girlfriend." There's a long pause.

"Don't waste your time with him, because you'll just get your feelings hurt," Tatyana finishes.

I don't say a word. I can't.

"Well...Tatyana and I should really get started on our science project," Priya finally says in a small voice. "It was great talking to you, Desiree."

"Yeah. Text us soon, if you can," Tatyana says.

My eye twitches, which only happens when I get really ticked off, but I press my palm against it before it gets out of control. "Bye." My finger taps the "End" button and my phone returns to its home screen. Just then, a message from Corinne pops up.

Corinne: Hey Dizzy! Let's wear costumes for our dance routine! I can make us some! ☺

I imagine myself standing onstage next to Corinne in an outfit made of peacock feathers, colorful ribbons, and a whole bunch of other things that just don't go together. After listening to Tatyana insult me over the phone, I'm not in the mood for Corinne or this talent showcase. Instead of responding to her text, I let my thumb hover over the screen and hit "Delete."

12

New Discoveries

The next morning, I wake up on time and zoom through my morning routine. I settle on a white button-up blouse with a pleated skirt, dark stockings, and buckled shoes. At first, I didn't want to wear this outfit because I thought it made me look too stiff, but my mother insisted I looked classy. Examining myself in my closet mirror, I have to say that my mother was right.

Today, the skies are clear and it's 75 degrees, so all I need is a denim jacket. I say bye to my mother as she chats on the phone with my grandmother, who talks excitedly about some big party coming up at her senior housing development.

I strut outside to the bus stop, where surprisingly, the twins are standing. Rashad scrolls through his phone, while Gumbo pops a piece of green gum in his mouth and tosses the wrapper on the sidewalk. I frown as I walk up to him and Rashad. "Don't you know that littering is gross?"

"Well, 'good morning' to you, too," Gumbo says with a snide smile. When I don't smile back, he rolls his eyes, picks up the gum wrapper, and throws it in the trash.

Rashad cracks up. "Hey, Dizzy," he says through his charming smile. I smile back, but deep down, I'm still thinking about Tatyana's comments and wondering if Rashad really feels that way.

"Dizzy, how's the fish hut?" Gumbo asks, cackling like a hyena. I glare at him. He thinks he can just talk about where I live? Rashad catches my expression and gives Gumbo a look.

"For your information, Phil, I don't smell anything anymore." BIG LIE. I place a hand on my hip and glance between the twins. "What are you guys even doing out here?"

"What do you mean? We live right there," Rashad says, jerking his thumb behind him. Hold up. He's pointing to the restaurant that my mother kept trying to make me eat at over the summer: The Crunch Bowl.

"We live right upstairs," Gumbo says. "Our family owns The Crunch Bowl, and we own the building, too."

My mouth drops open as I stare at the twins' smug smiles. They're obviously very proud of their restaurant. I'd be, too, if my family owned a business.

"That's cool," I say, fighting off a small twinge of jealousy. "You rich boys must be waiting for your limousine." I laugh lightheartedly, but the twins don't crack a smile. My mouth twists in an awkward shape and I quiet down.

"We're not rich," Gumbo corrects in a slightly annoyed tone, "and we're just waiting for the bus."

"How come you didn't ride the bus yesterday?"

"'Cause we only had enough money for lunch, and Phil didn't want to spend his gum money on bus tickets for the both of us," Rashad confesses with a tight smile. "Our parents say we have to stay together, so..."

Gumbo scowls and shoves his brother in the shoulder. "Man, shut up and stop telling our business!"

Rashad shrugs, rolls his eyes, and faces me. "Well, hey, you should come by our restaurant sometime," he suggests, smiling so that his dimples cave in.

"Yeah, we've got all kinds of stuff on our menu," Gumbo adds. "You'd really love it."

I stare at my shoes and think back to Sweet Song's, where my family often ate before we got so broken up. Until I see any sign of my parents getting back together, I don't really want to eat out at any restaurants. No offense to the twins, but I just wouldn't feel comfortable. "I don't know, guys...I'm really more of a Sweet Song's kind of gal." As soon as the comment leaves my mouth, I regret it. I glance up at the twins, who aren't smiling anymore. Now they look disappointed. My heart slams against my chest. I didn't mean to insult them.

"Oh." Rashad's dimples disappear and he sounds like I kicked him in the stomach. "You've been to Sweet Song's?"

"It was right near my old house," I say in a shaky voice. The twins stare at me sadly, so I lick my lips and try to smile at them. "Have *you* guys ever been to Sweet Song's?"

Rashad scratches one of his big ears. "Yeah," he says, but Gumbo gives him a funny look and I know he's lying.

"Well..." I rack my brain for something nice to say. "I'd still love to come to *your* restaurant. Maybe today."

Rashad shakes his head and offers me an embarrassed smile. "Nah. You don't have to."

Everyone is quiet for way too long. I've got to say something to bring the lighthearted mood back in the air.

"So, uh...I heard you guys play USA Little League Football," I say. "You any good?"

This does the trick. As soon as the question leaves my mouth, the twins' eyes light up like a pair of glowsticks.

"We're the best," Rashad says, his dimples returning. "I'm the starting quarterback: Number Four." He pops the collar on his varsity jacket, revealing his last name in cursive.

"And I'm a wide receiver: Number Twenty-Four," Gumbo adds, smacking extra-hard on his wad of green gum. "I've got the best stiff-arm in the league." He hops into a pose, extending his right arm like a superhero. "You should definitely come to our games and bring your friends. We usually play better with a crowd hyping us up, you know?"

"Yeah, our head coach, Coach Marino, puts us in the games a lot," Rashad says. "You'll definitely hear our names."

I didn't expect to be hit with all this bragging. "Well, I cheerlead, so I *have* to be at every game," I mutter.

The twins look thrilled. Rashad slaps his brother on the arm and exclaims, "We've got a personal cheerleader!"

"Rashad's right!" Gumbo tells me with a bright smile. "You can make up a bunch of cheers just for us!"

Wait, wait! I didn't bring up football to talk about making up cheers for anybody, but since I *did* accidentally offend the twins with my Sweet Song's remark, letting them grin about their football stardom is the least I can do.

"I'll...I'll think about it," I say, nodding my head slowly. The twins smile and nudge each other excitedly, like we're all part of some big, secret thing together.

I suddenly hear the rumble of the bus approaching from the far end of the street. Thank God.

"Look, guys, I'll have to hear about your football some other time," I announce, leading the way onto the bus.

13

Gossip Gone Wrong

As much as I hate to admit it, keeping up with school, my Chauncey mission, and cheer practices is *HARD*.

The first football game of the season is this Sunday and Coach Robin has taken our practice to another level. I honestly believe this woman is trying to kill us!

We rehearse every cheer, stunt, and dance routine until my throat stings and my dogs are barking *big* time. On Friday, when I come in last during our cool-down running exercise, Coach Robin glares at me from under her blue visor. "Let's go, Davenport! Get your mind out of La-La Land and focus! Another lap for you!"

Lungs burning, I force my legs around the gym again and glare at my coach. What she'll never understand is that my mind was actually on Chauncey, who's still not talking. Every time I've tried to bring up his beef with the twins, he's just ignored me. Ugh!

The twins haven't been any help, either, since all they've done is nag me about making up cheers, and Corinne always ends cheer practice with the same question:

"Do you want to come over to my place so we can start practicing for the showcase?"

I keep brushing her off and reminding her that we still have a month. I mean, this isn't *Dancing with the Stars.*

Dealing with everything makes me think about Priya and Tatyana. On Saturday afternoon, I call Priya to find out how their science project went. I'm still mad at Tatyana after hearing her stupid comments about Rashad.

"Hey, hey, Desiree!" Priya says when she answers the phone, but this time, I don't smile. Instead of one ring, it took her *three* to answer. "I've got Tatyana on the other line." Priya puts me on "Hold" and I sit in uncomfortable silence.

"'Sup, Desiree?" Tatyana asks once she joins the call. "Priya and I were just reliving our *amazing* science project. We made this diorama of an underwater ecosystem and got an A!"

"Congrats." I try to sound supportive and not completely jealous. "Well, um, my first football game is tomorrow. I'll finally get to cheer for real."

"That's cool," Tatyana says, but she sounds bored. "How's that Lite-Brite football star?"

My jaw locks. I'm not about to listen to Tatyana's complexion comments again. "His name is *Rashad.*"

"Did you learn anything new about him?" Priya asks.

I clutch my ponytail. I don't want to tell them anything else about Rashad, but after listening to their big science project victory, I want to outdo them. "Rashad comes from a family of entrepreneurs. They own a restaurant."

"That is so cool!" Priya exclaims. "What do they sell?"

"Oh, I don't know. I haven't been inside."

"Well, what's the name of it?" Tatyana asks skeptically.

My chest tightens. Any time Tatyana asks for the name of something, she's about to do a Google search. I want to tell her a fake name, but that'll only end up making me look stupid. I sigh and reluctantly say, "The Crunch Bowl."

There's a second of silence. Tatyana's probably clicking away on her phone screen. She suddenly gasps and lets out a huge laugh. "Omigosh! Priya, you *have* to see this!"

"Text a pic to the group chat!" Priya urges. *No. No. No.* My throat feels like it's closing up. I glance down at my screen and see the picture from Tatyana. It's a shot of the outside of The Crunch Bowl, and it definitely doesn't look as fancy as some of the restaurants in my old neighborhood.

"Ew," Priya snaps. "*That's* the restaurant?"

"That ain't no restaurant!" Tatyana crows. I listen to her laughter with a guilty ache in my chest. The twins were so proud of The Crunch Bowl, and thanks to my big mouth, my friends are mocking it. I shouldn't have said anything.

"Why would you like this Rashad guy?" Priya asks.

"Yeah, he's cute, but..." Tatyana trails off with another huge laugh. "This place looks like a DUMP!"

My body feels hot with anger and embarrassment. "Come on, guys. You don't have to say all that."

Tatyana sucks her teeth. "Girl, bye. You just like him."

My face is blazing. If I'm being honest, I've definitely had a crush on Rashad since the moment I met him, but the appearance of his family's restaurant shouldn't have anything to do with whether or not he's "good enough" for me to like.

I start to tell Priya and Tatyana off, but I'm too slow. "Talk to you later, Desiree," Priya says, giggling.

"Yeah, and don't let the Lite-Brite drag you into the dump," Tatyana says.

My eye twitches. "His name is *Rashad*, Tatyana, and their restaurant is called The Crunch Bowl!" I snap, but no one hears me because the line goes dead.

14

Game Day

The next day, Sunday, September 8th, is the day my cheer squad and I have been waiting for: GAME DAY.

All of our stretches, drills, workouts, and cheers have finally come down to this moment. It's 1:15 p.m. and we're dressed in our uniforms behind the regional high school. We are ready to cheer our Pirates to victory! Our opponents are another team in the Central Jersey League – the Tigers – and according to Coach Robin, they're going *D-O-W-N!!!*

I group up with my cheer squad and we stagger ourselves in front of the bleachers, which are *packed*. USA Little League Football is a big deal around here. "Desiree!" my mother yells from her seat on the top row. She's grinning and waving like a parent who's watching their kid perform in a Thanksgiving Day Parade.

I wave back and study the rest of the crowd. There are posters and foam fingers *everywhere*. Down front, I see a woman and little girl holding up posters that say: *DU BOIS STRONG* and *#4 AND #24 MAKE THE PIRATES SOAR!*

At the start of the game, my squad and I get the crowd all fired up with our signature cheer:

Let's go, Pirates!
Show 'em what you've got!
Let's go, Pirates!
Can't be stopped!

When we're not cheering, we're dancing to hip-hop music blasting from the speakers and doing stunts. I can't lie: I love being pushed up high in the air. I feel like I'm flying, but it's also pretty scary. I mean, what if they drop me?

Just like the twins said, the announcers really do call their names a lot. I can't believe I'm saying this, but this game is a lot of fun to watch.

Twenty-two guys on the field, two goalposts, and one mission: SCORE. THAT. TOUCHDOWN. At the start of each play, our center snaps the ball to Rashad, our star quarterback, who only has a few seconds to either throw or run with the ball before the Tigers' defense tries to sack him. I think he's toast, but then, our offense steps up, giving him a little more time. Gumbo weaves around our opponents and finds an open space on the field. Rashad fires the ball to Gumbo, who makes a crisp catch and zips into the end zone. He scores touchdown after touchdown, sending the crowd into a fit of roars.

"*Beautiful* pass by Rashad Maurice du Bois to his brother, Phil!" the announcer exclaims from his seat in the press box. "Look at him go! It's a sixty-five-yard run! Touchdown by Antwan Philippe du Bois!"

I think the coolest part of this game is watching how well the whole team plays together. Especially the twins. They are *so* in sync with each other. It's like Rashad knows exactly where his brother is going to move on the field. He makes one completed pass after another, and when Gumbo makes those catches, you'd better believe the Tigers are in trouble.

During the second quarter of the game, Coach Robin suggests that we make up a cheer just for the twins. At first, I don't do it because, knowing the twins, they'll probably think it was their idea, but then Coach Robin gives me a dirty look and I have no choice. We shake our pom-poms and chant:

Pass that ball!
Run that ball!
Do it all, du Bois!
They can't catch you!
They can't stop you!
Do it all, du Bois!

The twins give me two big thumbs up and I return the gesture. A cheerleader can't diss her own football players.

Out of the corner of my eye, I notice how Corinne giggles and shakes her pom-poms like a natural-born cheerleader. I give her a look, envying her flat stomach. I'm small, but my stomach is sort of chubby and rolls up a few times when I sit down.

I tap Corinne on the shoulder and gesture to the field. "Seems like the twins are the stars of the team, huh?"

Corinne glances around with shifty eyes and motions for me to come closer. "Girl, listen to this: On Friday, before my grandma picked me up from cheer practice, I heard some of the parents talking. Apparently, the twins' daddy is the Team Parent for the football team. Plus, he sponsored all the uniforms."

I look at my cheer squad and the football players. The words "The Crunch Bowl" are stitched in small print on all of our backs. My eyebrows shoot up as I glance around the field. "Is their dad out here today?" I wonder aloud.

Corinne nods. "He usually stands on the sidelines with the coaches." She points to a tall, stocky man wearing a polo shirt and some cargo shorts. The man turns around, and that's when I see his square face. He's got the same light brown skin and dark, curly hair as the twins.

During the rest of the second quarter, Coach Marino swaps out Rashad for the other two quarterbacks. They're not as good as Rashad. They don't score any touchdowns for us.

At halftime, the Pirates lead 35-7. My cheer squad performs a halftime show to a Rihanna song. We dance, hit a few splits – which I'm still awful at, but whatever, Coach Robin – and shake our pom-poms for the next 10 minutes. When we're done, the Pirates are ready to take the field again.

"Coach Marino, put me in the game!" one of the Pirates pleads. He's got sad eyes and the number 96 on his back. It's *Chauncey*. I didn't even know he was out here. He grips his fist around the coach's sleeve and tugs a few times. "The game's almost over and I haven't played yet."

Coach Marino pats Chauncey on the back, like that's supposed to make him feel better. "Your time's coming, all right?" he says and walks off to tend to the other players.

"Back up, Spots. You ain't playing," Gumbo sneers.

"You ain't even good enough to be out here," Rashad adds. I watch in shock as the twins' father refills the water cooler, completely oblivious to what's happening.

Coach Marino tells his team to get in the huddle. The team shouts, "One, two, three, Pirates!" Chauncey, defeated, retreats to the bench. He kicks the grass and sits down angrily.

In the fourth quarter, Coach Marino puts Chauncey in as a wide receiver. Unfortunately, he doesn't get to do anything because the ball never comes his way. With Rashad on the field as the quarterback, he and Gumbo dominate every play. With just 10 seconds left in the game, Rashad fires an off-balance pass to Gumbo, who surprises everyone by making the wobbly catch. In a split second, he's darting to the end zone, weaving in and out of our opponents' defense like lightning. It's nothing but cleats and mud. Nobody can catch him and it's the Pirates' final touchdown. The kick is good and the game is over. We *won* 42-14!

As a cheerleader, I'm obligated to put on my biggest smile and jump up and down with the rest of my squad so it looks like I'm just *ecstatic*. In reality, I am. This game was amazing, and I had no idea football could be so exciting.

After we shake hands with the Tigers, Coach Marino leads the football players to the bleachers, where the other cheerleaders and I are already standing. The twins find me in the crowd and give me high fives. "Nice game," I say.

"Nice cheering," Gumbo says with a grin. I smile and shrug. If the twins want to think I'm the one who came up with the *Do it all, du Bois* cheer, that's fine by me. They honestly deserve it.

I look around for Rashad, but he's already walked away and is now standing by his father, who's whispering something in his ear. Whatever he's whispering must be pretty intense, because Rashad keeps nodding his head furiously. Meanwhile, Chauncey hangs in the back. Nobody's talking to him.

"Hello, everyone," Coach Marino announces. His dark hair, peppered with strands of gray, sticks out from under his cap, and he looks pretty fit. "My name is Christopher Marino and I'm the head coach of the Pirates football team. My football career started forty years ago, right here on this ball field in Treeless Park, when I was all you guys' age." He points to the grass and gives the football players a proud smile.

Some of the parents nod, while I exchange a surprised look with Corinne. *Forty years ago?* This man is old.

"I grew up playing USA Little League Football, played ball through college, and spent a few years as a defensive back for the New York Giants," Coach Marino continues. Rashad grins up at his father, who gives him an excited nudge. Coach Marino goes on. "Let me tell ya: I had a great time playing for the pros, but when I got hurt and couldn't play anymore, I decided I wanted to give back to where I came from." He puts one of his hands to his heart and straightens his cap. "So, for the last twenty years, I've been blessed to be the head coach of the Treeless Park Pirates, and boy, did they show up today! Forty-two to fourteen! Come on! Let's clap it up!"

Coach Marino grins and leads everyone in a round of applause. I clap normally, but then Rashad grins at me with his dimples and I clap like there's no tomorrow.

"This is a great way to start the season," Coach Marino continues. "Our goal is to finish with a strong regular season record and claim the title of Central Jersey League Champion. From there, we've got our eyes set on the Eastern Regional Championship and then the USA Little League National Championship in Florida! That's football players *and* cheerleaders!"

Oh. My. Gosh. *Florida???*

When I was nine, my mother sent me to Atlanta for a tennis camp, where I burned up in the hot sun and got so delirious during a match that I had to forfeit and drop out of the tournament, but I've never been to Florida. It's, like, number four on my bucket list.

"Hold on, hold on," Coach Robin suddenly interrupts. "Let me just remind my girls that we also have our eyes on a Florida competition! If our routine takes first or second place in the Region, we'll be down in Florida competing in the USA Little League National Cheer and Dance Championships!"

Wait, *what*? I look around to see if anyone else looks as surprised as I do, but strangely, the rest of my squad looks like they've heard all of this before.

"What is she talking about?" I whisper to Corinne.

"Didn't you hear during the summer?" she questions. "Coach Robin told us at the first meeting!"

"That's right! Our girls are just as talented as our guys," Coach Marino says, giving Coach Robin a supportive smile. "And we all have what it takes to make it to Florida in December. I want to commend you all for your performance in today's game."

The crowd goes wild. The twins stand there, grinning like two kings as they take in the coach's words. Mr. du Bois makes a big show of shaking the twins' shoulders, while their mother and sister wave their posters.

"I'd like to thank our Assistant Coaches, Dan Pertly and John Carter," Coach Marino says, "and thank you to our Team Parent, Mr. Antwan du Bois."

Mr. du Bois lifts his cap in acknowledgment. He looks just like Rashad, with the same, smug grin and everything.

"I look forward to a great season, and I can't wait to see our Pirates shine in Florida this December," Coach Marino finishes.

As the crowd disperses, I look around for the twins and Chauncey, but Corinne distracts me by tapping my shoulder. "Do you want to meet my grandma?"

My spine stiffens. No offense to Corinne or her grandma, but I don't really have time for all that right now.

"Sorry, Corinne, but maybe next week, okay?" I offer hastily. Corinne nods sadly, which makes me feel really guilty. I hope she doesn't think I'm intentionally brushing her off.

I hustle away from her and over to a clear spot on the field, where Mr. du Bois gives the whole football team a round of high fives. When he gets to Chauncey, Chauncey reaches down to grab his helmet instead, leaving him hanging. I watch the scene in shock, wondering if the Pirates can really work together to make it to Florida in December.

15

New Friends, New Problems

Once the field is almost empty, my mother makes her way down the bleacher steps and wraps me in a giant hug. "Ooh, Baby, you were so good!" She whips out her phone and forces me to strike a pose with my pom-poms. Out of the corner of my eye, I see the twins and their family coming at us.

"Excuse me, Miss!" the twins' mother says.

"Yes, hi, can I help you?" my mother asks politely.

"We wanted to catch you before you left today," the twins' mother continues. She's got a smooth Jamaican accent. Hmm, so Rashad was mimicking his mother that day in class. "My name is Olivia du Bois and this is my husband, Antwan." She gestures to Mr. du Bois. He smiles and shakes our hands.

"Hi. Antwan. Team Parent. Nice to meet y'all," Mr. du Bois says. He's got a raspy, Southern accent. I see where Gumbo got it from. "How about that game?" It's clear where the twins get their personalities from.

"Yes, it was a great game! I'm Giselle." My mother puts a hand on my back. "And this is my daughter, Desiree."

"Yes, Antwan and I have heard so much about this pretty cheerleader! We recognized her down on the field."

Mrs. du Bois grins at me. "The boys told us that you're classmates. They talk about you all the time. Desiree *this* and Desiree *that.*"

My mother turns to me in surprise. I'm a little embarrassed because I haven't told her anything about the twins since I met them.

"Well, it's a pleasure to meet you boys, as well!" my mother says to the twins. "That was some football you fellas played today."

"Huh! Wasn't it?" Mr. du Bois pushes the twins forward. "These two kings have been dominating this game since they were seven. Give 'em ten years, and we'll all be sitting around, watching them on ESPN."

My mother and I stare at Mr. du Bois, not really knowing how to respond. Mrs. du Bois laughs sheepishly and says, "All right, Antwan, ease up a little."

Mr. du Bois cracks up and pulls Mrs. du Bois close. "I love this woman right here. She keeps me in line."

Mrs. du Bois smiles and says, "Yes, I certainly try." The twins look embarrassed.

My mother sort of laughs. "Well, you all certainly have an incredible goal," she says, glancing back at our car in the parking lot.

"We ain't reach the mountaintop yet. These boys have a lot of work to do." Mr. du Bois nudges Rashad. "With today's win, my boy is *well* on his way to becoming the Number One Varsity quarterback with *the* most completed passes in the Eastern Region. Isn't that right, Son?"

"You know it, Dad," Rashad says confidently. Mrs. du Bois smiles with sleepy eyes. I notice that she's really pretty.

Suddenly, the twins' little sister pipes up. "Me, too, Daddy?" she asks, tugging on her father's shirt. I tense up. As an only child, I've never had patience for other people's little sisters or brothers. I wish she'd sit down somewhere. No one was even talking to her.

Mr. du Bois picks her up and plants a big kiss on her forehead. "You, too, Baby Girl." He plays the airplane game with her and a small twinge of jealousy burns in my chest. My father and I used to play that game when I was little.

I stare at my mother, hoping she can sense that I'm ready to get out of here. Unfortunately, she's still talking to Mrs. du Bois. A lonely feeling washes over me, so I take a few steps back and turn away from everyone. Just then, Rashad taps me on my shoulder and I face him. He's got an eyebrow raised and he stares at me with a half-smile.

"What?" I ask skeptically.

Rashad tilts his head to one side. "You're an only child, aren't you?"

I shift uncomfortably in the grass. Why is he obsessed with asking me so many personal questions? "Maybe." I lift my chin in the air. "What's wrong with being an only child?"

"Nothing." He pulls his elbow behind his head in a long stretch. "I could tell by the way you reacted to my little sister." He smiles. "You think she's annoying, don't you?"

"What? No, she's cute." Sheesh, he caught me. I look him in the eyes. It's *my* turn to ask questions. "Your mom said you talk about me all the time. What have you told her?"

Rashad's eyebrows shoot up. He stifles a laugh and glances at the ground. Then he cups a hand around his ear. "Huh? What'd you say?" he asks. He looks embarrassed.

I make a big show of glancing around the field. "Get Gumbo over here." I stand on my tiptoes and spot Gumbo chatting with a huge crowd of people. "Who's he talking to?"

"Our relatives," Rashad says with a light shrug. "They come out every weekend during football season to watch us play. You know, for extra support."

I shrink back and twirl one of my ponytails. "Really...?" My brain retreats to three years ago, when my mother signed me up for tennis. When I played in tournaments, both sides of my extended family used to pack up on the sidelines with lawn chairs to cheer me on, but since the divorce, we haven't seen any family. The twins have no idea how fortunate they are to have that kind of support. Or maybe they do. Maybe that's why they're so confident. Must be nice.

"Desiree...? Oh, Pony Boots?" I snap out of my thoughts and see Rashad frowning at me. "You okay?" he asks.

My eyes get this teary feeling. I turn away. "I'm fine."

Rashad gives me a hard stare, but he doesn't say anything. I sidestep away from him and back over to my mother, who's still speaking with Mrs. du Bois.

"Giselle, what does Desiree do until cheer practice in the evenings?" Mrs. du Bois questions.

"Well, I'm sending her to aftercare every day."

"What? You'd better keep your money, Chile, and send Desiree to me!" Mrs. du Bois rubs my back gently and I stare up at her in confusion. What does she mean, send me to *her*? "You know The Crunch Bowl restaurant?" she continues.

"Yes, of course!" my mother responds brightly. "We live right across the street from it!"

My entire body stiffens. No. What's happening here?

"Well, Antwan and I own The Crunch Bowl and we're there every day," Mrs. du Bois goes on. "You can send Desiree home with the boys after school."

NO!!! I need to be in aftercare so I can talk to Chauncey!

"Oh, Desiree and I would really appreciate that!" My mother turns to me and shakes my shoulder. "Desiree! Isn't this wonderful?"

My face feels like it's peeling. I'd never tell Priya and Tatyana. They'd bust a gut laughing at me forever. I force my lips into something I hope is a smile and thank Mrs. du Bois.

"Yes, thank you so much, Olivia," my mother adds.

"You're welcome. We mothers have to help each other," Mrs. du Bois says, smiling. "And please, call me 'Liv.'"

We all exchange numbers and I notice that Rashad's phone is blowing up with all kinds of notifications. My phone is straight up silent. Ain't get a buzz, a beep, a blip – *nothing*.

After we finish talking, I say bye to the twins and they walk off with their family. "You boys keep this up and you'll definitely make it to that Championship in December," their father says.

I look past the du Bois family and notice Chauncey slowly trudging along in the distance. Today was such a big win for the Pirates. Although Chauncey never got his chance to do much, he still deserves to share this moment with someone, but instead of walking away with his family, he's walking alone.

He must have come here by himself.

16

A Lesson from Mom

When my mother and I get home from the game, I change into a big t-shirt with some comfy sweatpants. After shoving my feet into a pair of fuzzy purple socks, I text my cheerleading picture to Priya and Tatyana. I expect at least one of them to answer right away, but they don't. They must be busy doing their own Sunday things.

I text the picture to my father and he replies, **Beautiful baby girl**, which makes my heart soar. **Maybe u can come to one of my games?** I type back. I know it sounds silly, but when I saw how the twins' huge family came to today's game, it made me want the same thing.

Ding!

Heart racing, I glance down at my phone and open my new text notification.

Corinne: Hey! For the showcase, should we dance to Beyoncé or Ciara? You pick! ☺

Sheesh. I'm not even thinking about that showcase. I type back **Ciara** and toss my phone on the bed.

I walk into the kitchen, where my mother makes a pot of spaghetti and meatballs. I set the table. My father used to whistle while *he* set the table. I wonder what he's having for dinner tonight...and if he's having it with someone else.

I go into the living room and search Rashad on Instagram. We don't follow each other, which is fine by me. I mean, I really don't want him seeing how unpopular I am.

I click on his most recent picture, which is a shot of him and Gumbo after today's game. The caption reads, **DYNAMIC DUO.** The picture got over 250 likes and a ton of comments. Some guys wrote things like, **LET'S EAT!!** and **THE GRIND NEVER STOPS!!!**, while a few girls left comments with heart-eye emojis. I leave his page and peer across the street at The Crunch Bowl. Strangely, the lights are off and the place is closed. Hmm...

"So, Desiree," my mother says, snapping my attention away from The Crunch Bowl. "How come you never told me about your little football friends – the du Bois brothers?"

"They're *fraternal twins*, Mommy, and they're just some boys in my class." They're also the boys who chased Chauncey away from our apartment, but I leave this detail out. My mother is so excited to have me sit at The Crunch Bowl every day, and I don't want to cause any confusion.

"Well, they're adorable!" my mother says with way too much enthusiasm. She stirs the spaghetti pot with a smile. "Their family seems to like you a lot."

I shrug. "Yeah, they're nice, I guess."

"And I saw that quarterback – Number Four – staring at you after the game."

My face grows warm as snippets of Tatyana's cruel remarks crowd my mind. I shake my head and stare at the floor. "Mommy, he wasn't looking at me."

"Yes, he was. I think he likes you."

"No, he doesn't."

"Why wouldn't he, as pretty as you are?"

I lick my lips and struggle to find my voice. "Because."

"Because *what?*" My mother stares at me with wide eyes. There's an awkward silence. "Desiree?" she asks.

My hands twitch as I rub my arm, noticing the glow of my copper skin. "Because...I'm too dark...I'm too dark for a boy Rashad's complexion."

The apartment is heavy with silence. My mouth goes dry as I watch my mother turn off the stove. She crosses over to me, her pretty face sunken with disappointment. "Baby, who told you that?"

For a long moment, I don't say anything. It hurts too much to talk about it. "Tatyana said it on the phone the other day when I was on with her and Priya," I finally mutter, lowering my head in shame.

In that moment, my mother grabs my wrist with one hand and my chin with the other. She slowly lifts my head and looks me in my eyes. "Desiree, your complexion is beautiful. Our complexion is beautiful, and don't let anyone make you feel differently." My mother holds my gaze and leads me into the hallway bathroom. We stand in front of the mirror and I let her pull my hair away from my face. "What do you see?" she asks me in a soft voice.

I gaze at my reflection, unsure of what to think. My eyes peel away from the mirror. I can't focus. All I hear are Tatyana's words: *You're too dark.* I've never even considered those words before, and now I can't get them out of my head.

"Let me tell you what *I* see," my mother suddenly says. She gently rubs my face and speaks in a calm voice. "I see a girl with big, brown eyes, a round nose, and *beautiful* skin." My mother wraps her arms around my shoulders and rocks me back and forth. "I love what I see. Do you?"

In that moment, a fire within me ignites, and Tatyana's words fizzle. I return my eyes to the mirror. The girl staring back at me grins, and I nod. I do love what I see. I always have.

"You're kind, smart, loveable, and talented," my mother continues. "Don't ever let anybody's opinions change how you feel about yourself." She pauses and stifles a laugh. "I think Tatyana's a little bit jealous."

"Well, why does she think that way?" I ask.

"Honey, Tatyana didn't make this up. This is called colorism, which is a type of racism."

"What?"

"Listen. A long time ago, there were people who believed and promoted the idea that people with lighter skin were better, smarter, and more attractive than people with darker skin. People were and still are discriminated against because of their darker skin."

I frown. "It sounds so stupid."

"It is. There's beauty in all shades. There are some people whose complexions are darker than ours and they are just as beautiful," my mother states. I nod and she continues. "The main thing is that you have to love yourself and know that you are beautiful. Did you see the twins' mother and little sister? They're the same complexion as we are, Desiree."

I pause. "I hadn't noticed."

"Exactly. Because it's not important, is it? What matters is how a boy treats you and how you treat him."

The corners of my mouth lift into a soft grin as I stare at my reflection and then my mother's. We look so much alike, and I've never been more thankful.

My mother plants a kiss on my forehead and leads me out of the bathroom. "The spaghetti's almost finished, okay?"

"Okay. I'll be right back." I walk into my room, close my door, and stare at my phone. The things Tatyana said to me were wrong, but after listening to my mother, I realize it's not her fault. Maybe I'll call her and Priya up tomorrow and try to get things back to how they used to be.

I sit on my bed, open Instagram, and scroll through pictures of cats and plates of foods I can't identify. Suddenly, I see a post from Tatyana and it breaks my heart.

It's a picture of Tatyana and Priya standing in front of a movie theater. Their arms are wrapped around each other and their smiles are big and carefree. Beneath the picture is Tatyana's caption: **Sunday Funday with bestie!** The picture got 59 likes, but right now, I wish Instagram had a dislike button.

Why didn't my friends tell me they were going to the movies? And what's with this "**bestie**" business? Doesn't Tatyana remember that she has *two* besties, not just one?

Ding!

At the sound of my text tone, I immediately perk up. I scroll through my messages and smile when I see a new one from my father. He's finally responded to my question about coming to see me cheer during one of the football games.

Daddy: Now's not a good time for me to come around just yet, baby girl. I'll let u know as soon as I can.

As I reread his text, my vision blurs and tears sprinkle my phone screen. There's no point in answering him. He doesn't care about me, so why should I even bother?

I see three new messages from Corinne, but I hit "delete" without even reading them. She's the last person I want to talk to right now. I rip off my charm bracelet and throw it at the wall. With the sound of a sharp SNAP, it disappears somewhere behind my bed. That bracelet will never be able to keep my family together.

Unable to fight back my tears, I press my face into my pillow and bite down, stifling my sobs. My friends have moved on, my father doesn't care about me, and it's just me and my mother living above this fish store. I feel so alone and I wish I could just disappear.

As I lay here, feeling like my world has come to an end, my phone rings. I take one look at whose name is flashing on the screen and my heart stops. It's Rashad.

17

On Time God

I stare at my phone in a daze. This is unexpected. I take a deep breath, wipe my tears, and answer the phone. "Hello?"

"Pony Boots! What's up, Girl?" Rashad's voice rings through the phone. Oh, my gosh. I don't know how to respond. *He's* calling *me*? "Oh...the silent treatment, huh? My bad." He clears his throat and puts on a dignified voice. "Good evening, may I speak to Miss Desiree Davenport, please?"

In spite of my sadness, I can't help but laugh. This boy is crazy. I sniff and try to smile. "Hi, Rashad. It's just *Dizzy*."

"I know, but I like your full name." My heart rate quickens as he continues. "Nice cheering today."

"Thanks. You had a great game." I narrow my eyes. "Is that why you called? So you could hear more 'Do It All, du Bois?'"

Rashad laughs a little. "I called 'cause I noticed you looked kind of sad after the game and I wanted to see if you were okay."

My chest deflates. "I'm fine," I say with a short nod.

"Cool, 'cause, um..." Rashad suddenly sounds hopeful, but a little nervous. "I wanted to know if you wanted to come to..."

Just then, he gets cut off by his little sister in the background. "Whee! Daddy, spin me around!" she cries. Her shrieking laughter starts off loud and gradually grows soft, like Rashad is walking away with his phone.

"My bad, Dizzy," Rashad says. "You still there?"

I open my mouth and struggle to calm my trembling lip. That's when a giant sob escapes my throat. I quickly cover my mouth before I start bawling. I know it's wrong to be jealous, but I can't help it. The twins' little sister gets to have her father around, but my father doesn't even care about me.

"Dizzy?" Rashad sounds worried. "What's wrong?"

I force myself to take a deep breath. *You will not cry on the phone with Rashad. You will not do it!* "Nothing's wrong," I lie, but then my body betrays me with a huge round of sniffles and sobs and whimpers. The whole time, Rashad doesn't say a word. I'm so humiliated.

My crying gets louder until suddenly, I hear my mother knocking on my door. "Desiree! Are you okay in there?"

I put Rashad on "Mute" and turn to face my door. "I'm fine," I assure my mother, starting to regain the steadiness in my voice.

After another minute of sniffling, I finally calm myself down and take Rashad off "Mute." He keeps talking. "I'm… sorry you're sad, Dizzy. I wanted to invite you to something, but I'll tell you about it another day, when you're feeling better."

"Oh…okay," I mumble. I'm about to say bye when suddenly, a worried feeling creeps up my spine. "Wait, Rashad, wait!"

"Yeah, Dizzy?"

My hand grips tighter around my phone. "Promise me you won't tell anybody about this. Please."

Rashad is quiet for a fearfully long moment. My insides churn nauseously. I bet he's already telling Gumbo everything. Twins are close that way, and don't even get me started on all the people blowing up his phone. He's probably telling the whole football team, and then, it'll get out to the cheer squad, and then—

"You can trust me, Desiree. I won't tell," he says calmly.

I cough a little, still feeling uneasy. "Not even Phil?"

"We don't tell each other everything," he says, and I can hear the faint smile in his voice. "I'll see you tomorrow. Feel better."

"Thanks," I squeak. We hang up and I get a text message.

Rashad: Whatever you're sad about, it's gonna be okay.

My chest suddenly feels a thousand pounds lighter and I dry my eyes for the final time this evening. **Thanks,** I type back. I hug my phone to my chest, wondering what he wants to invite me to. Out of all the people blowing up his phone, he called *me*, and his call came right on time.

Thank you, God.

18

A Mysterious Misunderstanding

"Desiree, hurry up! It's time for breakfast!"

At the sound of my mother's call, I close my jar of Taliah Waajid Curly Gello and take a final look at my hair. Today I'm wearing a braided side-do that hangs down my left shoulder. Sometimes, you've got to mix it up.

I walk into the kitchen, where my mother fixes my breakfast plate. I sit down, bless my food, and dig in. Last night, Rashad Maurice du Bois called me to cheer me up *and* he wanted to invite me to something. I can't wait to find out what it is.

My mother smiles at me while I eat my breakfast. "So... you talked to Rashad last night." I stop in mid-chew, almost choking on my toast. How does she know *that*? My mother must sense what I'm thinking, because she keeps smiling and says, "I heard you say bye to him when you hung up." I force down the rest of my toast and twirl my fork in my grits. Hmm. She must have been standing outside my door.

"Well...yeah, he called me," I confess, twirling my fork faster. "He wanted to invite me somewhere, but he said we'll talk about it another time." I keep my eyes lowered and pray to God that my mother doesn't get excited and start asking more questions. Thankfully, she just gives me a broad smile.

Once I finish my breakfast, I shove my arms in a light jacket and throw my backpack over my shoulder. Then I give my mother a giant hug and we wish each other great days.

As I walk outside, I realize how embarrassed I am to face Rashad today. After he heard me bawling on the phone, I don't know if he'll keep his promise of not telling anybody.

I try to appear confident by strutting over to the bus stop like I own it. The first person I see is Gumbo, who whips off his sunglasses and waves me down. "Hey, Dizzy!" he calls excitedly. Hmm. He doesn't *sound* like he knows anything about last night. Rashad must have kept his promise after all.

"Hey, Gumbo," I say. My eyes peel over to Rashad, who's already staring at me with an expression I can't read. I clutch my backpack straps and clear my throat. "Hi, Rashad."

Rashad quickly looks at his sneakers and shoves his hands in his pockets. He looks just as embarrassed as I feel. "Hi, Dizzy," he mutters. We turn away awkwardly.

Gumbo frowns. "What's wrong with y'all?"

"Nothing!" Rashad and I shout at the same time. We both look at each other like, *Really?* Gumbo keeps shooting us a suspicious glare, so I smile, reach into my jacket pocket, and whip out two quarters. "Hey, how much gum will this get me?"

This does the trick. Gumbo's skeptical eyes brighten. "Oh! Wow!" he exclaims. Rashad snickers but Gumbo doesn't notice. He opens his leather jacket and examines his stash. Then he glances at my 50 cents. "How do four pieces sound?"

"Deal. Gimme two strawberry and two orange." I hand Gumbo my money and he rewards me with the gum. I pop one of the strawberry pieces in my mouth. My teeth make a weird *crunch* against the gum. Nuh-uh! This is *stale*!

Rashad catches my pained expression and busts out laughing. Gumbo ignores him. "Thanks for your business, Dizzy," he says, putting on his sunglasses. "Just let me know anytime you want to buy more. I've got other flavors."

"Mm-hm," I mumble around the stale wad of gum. Maybe it'll loosen up the longer I suck on it.

"So, Dizzy, guess what?" Gumbo continues. "This morning, our mom told us that you're gonna start coming to our restaurant *every day* after school. Is that for real?"

I think back to the day I accidentally offended the twins with my "Sweet Song's" remark. Even though Sweet Song's will always have a special place in my heart, it can't hurt to try a new restaurant, especially since my father isn't coming around anytime soon.

"Yup, it's for real. I can't wait to see your place today."

I notice Rashad staring at me with his piercing eyes. He looks skeptical, like he doesn't believe me.

"Trust me: You'll love The Crunch Bowl," Gumbo tells me, oblivious to his brother's silence. "And it'll be a great place to come up with some more *Do it all, du Bois* cheers."

I stand there with a smile plastered to my face while Gumbo keeps talking about how much I'll love The Crunch Bowl. The entire time, Rashad never says a word. He stares through me, like he's not exactly sure who I am. His staring makes me feel uncomfortable, so I turn away just as the bus pulls up to the corner. I hand the friendly driver my ticket and find a seat across the aisle from the twins. Gumbo sits on the outside and talks my ear off about The Crunch Bowl's menu and last week's game, while Rashad just stares out the window and acts like we're not even here. What's bothering him?

19

A New Promise

At school, Gumbo leads the way to our lockers, stopping along the way to sell his stale gum. Are these people crazy?

We make it to our lockers, where Corinne is already standing. She's wearing a pink-and-red striped shirt underneath a pair of yellow overall shorts with purple tights and neon green sneakers. The most normal outfit I've seen her in so far is her cheer uniform.

I open my locker, reach into my backpack, and yank out the pack of Nintendo stickers that my mother bought me from the store last night. Smiling, I peel off Pikachu, Kirby, and Mario and slap them to the wall of my locker.

Corinne frowns. "Why do you have those stickers?"

"Don't you like video games?" I ask. Corinne shakes her head like I'm asking her if she climbs volcanoes. That's weird. I've been a Nintendo fan for years. I always had the latest games, and when I lived in my old house, my cousins always came over to play, but after moving to Treeless Park, all of that changed. My games just sit in boxes in my room.

Gumbo stares at Corinne's yellow overalls. "Don't you get tired of looking *and* sounding like a duck, Baby Talk?"

Corinne puts a hand on her hip. "Don't *you* get tired of wearing those ol' nasty sunglasses?"

Oh *snap*. Rashad and I exchange a surprised look and glance at Gumbo, who looks stunned. He nods his head quickly and adjusts his glasses. "All right. I'll remember that." He slams his locker shut and walks off to Ms. Hernandez's class. Rashad laughs and follows his brother. As they approach the classroom door, I see Chauncey trailing behind them. The twins notice him and push him out of the way.

"Watch it, Spots!" Gumbo snaps. He slaps Chauncey's books and folders out of his hands, sending a flurry of papers floating to the tiled floor.

"Come on, man! You're messing up my stuff!" Chauncey cries. He crouches on the floor and scrambles to gather his papers. He reaches for a white square that fell out of his football-stickered notebook, but Rashad grabs it first. I gasp. It's the picture of the mystery football player.

"Hey!" Chauncey shoots up from the floor and tries to reach for his picture, but Rashad holds it above his head.

"Boy, if you don't back up off me, this thing is trash," Rashad snarls. Chauncey tries to lunge for Rashad, but Rashad passes the picture to Gumbo. "Rip it up, man! Do it!"

"No! Stop!" Chauncey lunges for Gumbo, but Rashad grabs him by his shirt collar and holds him back.

"Say we're Number One on the football field and you can have your picture," Rashad demands.

"Just give it back!" Chauncey shouts.

Gumbo shrugs. "Fine, Spots. Have it your way." As his thumbs tighten around the top of Chauncey's picture, my heart plummets. I can't stand here and watch this happen.

"Guys!" I shout. The twins freeze and look at me. I lick my lips nervously, thinking of a way to get the twins away from Chauncey. "Gumbo, Jennifer Jackson's looking for you."

Gumbo raises his sunglasses. "Ooh! For real?"

I nod. Jennifer Jackson is this popular eighth grader who looks like a model. I've never talked to her, but I've seen her around. There's no way she'd ever look twice at another guy, since she's going out with this other eighth grader named Desmond Price. "Jennifer wants to buy gum," I tell Gumbo.

Gumbo grins, flicks Chauncey's picture to the floor, and hustles off. "Ra, come on!"

Rashad follows his brother, giving me a skeptical glare. I wait until he and Gumbo are gone before crouching down next to Chauncey. "Here," I whisper, handing him his picture.

Chauncey just takes it from me. "Thanks. I got it."

Again with his attitude. Part of me wants to forget this whole thing, but I stay put. That picture is important to Chauncey and I want to find out why. "That's a really cool picture," I say. Chauncey doesn't hide the picture like he did last week in aftercare, so I take a closer look. "Who is he?"

Chauncey shoves the picture in his notebook and stands up. "He's nobody. Just leave me alone." Chauncey storms into the classroom, leaving me alone on the floor.

"Dizzy!" Corinne suddenly calls, stepping in front of me. "Don't touch Chauncey's stuff. You'll catch his spots!"

I stand up. "Vitiligo isn't contagious."

"Well...how come you never texted me back last night?" Corinne asks. Thinking back to last night's drama, I groan and explain that I'll be spending my afternoons at The Crunch Bowl. Corinne looks ecstatic. "You're so lucky! The Crunch Bowl is the nicest restaurant in Treeless Park! Everybody goes there after school!"

"Have you been there?"

"I wish. My grandma and I don't have the money to eat out. Do you think they'll make you pay for your food?"

"No. I think free meals are part of the deal."

"Sweet!" Corinne suddenly looks hopeful. "Do you think they'd mind if...I came with you sometimes?"

My teeth sink into the inside of my lip. Corinne tagging along wasn't part of the deal. My mother would probably be mad at me for bringing her, and Mrs. du Bois would feel obligated to feed her. "I...I don't know, Corinne," I respond sadly. "It's not that I *don't* want you to come, but I don't want to take advantage of their family, either."

Corinne's eyes swell with disappointment. As I stare down at her, she suddenly seems so small. "Oh..." she mutters.

The lifelessness in her voice makes me feel terrible. I've got to say something to bring some joy back to her face. "Well, hey. We'd better get cracking on our dance routine, right? How about...I stay late with you every night after cheer practice, and we can rehearse our dance right in the gym until your grandma comes to pick you up?" As soon as the words slip out of my mouth, I regret it. After cheer practice, I talk to my mother, do my homework, and look for messages from my father, but it's too late to take back my offer, because Corinne's face brightens like a candle building its glow.

"That would be amazing!" Corinne exclaims. I lead the way inside Ms. Hernandez's classroom while Corinne hurries alongside me, grinning from ear to ear.

20

The Crunch Bowl

Later, Ms. Hernandez hits us all with a pop quiz on cell division. I didn't study much of that over the weekend, so I'm not surprised when I get an 84. Corinne got an 81 and Rashad got an 83. Gumbo, on the other hand, outdid all of us with a 93. What in the world?

When the 2:30 bell rings, I gather my books and see Corinne staring at me sadly. "Have fun at The Crunch Bowl."

I smile at her. "Thanks. Call me later and we'll talk about some good Ciara songs to include in our routine." Corinne gives me a big thumbs up and skips out of the classroom. On the other side of the room, I watch as Chauncey tucks his books under his arm. He leaves the classroom, staring at me with a curious expression.

"You ready for The Crunch Bowl, Dizzy?" Gumbo asks. When I nod, he removes his sunglasses and gives me a dry look. "For your information, Jennifer Jackson didn't want any of my gum."

I stiffen. "Really? I thought she did."

"No. She didn't," Gumbo says through a phony smile.

I turn to Rashad, who gives me the side-eye. Feeling too stumped to come up with an explanation for myself, I stand up. "Can't wait to get to The Crunch Bowl!"

Gumbo grins. "Yeah, wait until you see the menu."

On the bus, Gumbo tries to convince me to buy more of his stale gum. Rashad ignores us and plays a game on his phone. I want to ask him if he's mad about something, but with Gumbo doing all the talking, I don't get a word in.

We arrive to our stop, pile out of the bus, and walk into The Crunch Bowl. As soon as I step inside, I'm greeted with the aroma of fried and Jamaican foods. The place is *packed* with kids from school. I guess Corinne was right.

When Mrs. du Bois sees us, she smiles and waves me inside. "Antwan! The boys are here with Desiree!" she calls.

Mr. du Bois enters the dining area. He's wearing a stained apron and a hairnet. When he sees me, he smiles like he's known me all his life. "Hey, sweetie, how are you? Welcome to The Crunch Bowl!"

"Hi, Mr. du Bois. Thank you so much." I look around the place, which looks like a diner. I see booths, a cake display window, and a counter with bar stools. There's an electronic jukebox in the corner that some little kids are messing with.

"So, Dizzy, what do you think?" Gumbo asks. He stands in front of me with a huge smile, like The Crunch Bowl is the best restaurant to grace the world. Rashad stands off to the side and stares at me with uncertainty looming in his eyes.

The Crunch Bowl isn't a hole-in-the-wall like Priya and Tatyana said. The place is very clean and has a nice vibe to it.

"I love it," I say, throwing an extra-big smile at Rashad. He chews on his bottom lip and turns away. I sigh while Gumbo guides us to a big, circular booth near the register. I sit in between Gumbo and Rashad. Mr. du Bois hands each of us a menu.

"Hmm..." Gumbo purrs, studying the menu.

Rashad raises an eyebrow at his brother. "Why are you looking at it like you haven't seen it a million times?"

Gumbo ignores Rashad. "I think...I'm gonna go with the fried chicken sliders today."

"Man, you eat that *every* day," Rashad mutters.

I turn to him. "What are *you* gonna order?"

Rashad gestures to the menu. "The fried mac and cheese balls with a vanilla milkshake."

Gumbo gives Rashad a look. "Go easy on the milk products, Bro. Remember last week?" He rubs his stomach and gives me a look. "Dizzy, he sounded like a machine gun."

Rashad glances at me and turns red. "Phil, shut up!"

Gumbo just shrugs and leans back in the booth. "We're even now. Remember what you said about how I didn't want to share my gum money?"

I try to smile. "Hey, Rashad. I think I'll have what you're having," I say. Rashad doesn't crack a smile. He keeps glaring at Gumbo, who just smiles.

Moments later, Mr. du Bois comes over to take our orders. He collects our menus and we wait for our food to arrive. My eyes wander around the restaurant, where pictures of the twins and the Pirates football team hang on the walls. "Are you guys close with your teammates?" I ask.

"They're like our brothers," Rashad says.

Mr. du Bois arrives with our food. Everything looks and smells delicious. Even the milkshakes – thick and topped with fluffy whipped cream, chocolate sprinkles, and a cherry – look too good to eat.

"Go ahead, Dizzy. You take the first bite," Gumbo urges. I turn to Rashad, who nervously glances between my eyes and my plate. I slice open the first mac and cheese ball. The melted cheese oozes onto the plate and I pop a bite into my mouth. What I don't expect is for the flavors to hit my taste buds all at once – and *man* is it bomb!

The noodles are covered in a white cheese sauce that makes me want to break into a two-step. The crispy shell tastes amazing with the sweet sauce sitting beneath it. I munch on everything, feeling like I could sprout wings and fly right out of this joint.

"Oh my God," I mumble once I swallow the first bite. "This is the best thing I've ever eaten in my entire life."

Gumbo grins so wide, his face practically splits in half. Rashad, on the other hand, studies me with a straight face. "Is it really good enough for a 'Sweet Song's kind of gal' like you?"

I drop my fork and stare at Rashad's hard expression. *This* is why he's been freezing me out. Last week, I insulted his family's restaurant with my big mouth. Now I'm sitting here eating their food...for free.

"Wow. Well, um..." Gumbo glances between me and Rashad. "I'm sure Dizzy didn't mean any of that stuff, Ra."

I twirl my ponytail so hard, it could pop right off my head. "Of course I didn't mean it, Rashad."

No one speaks. Gumbo drums his hands on the table and stands up. "Uh...I think I'm gonna use the bathroom real quick." He dashes off, leaving me alone with Rashad.

"Rashad, I shouldn't have said what I said, okay?"

"Then why'd you say it?" he asks, sounding more sad than angry. "You don't want to come to our restaurant every day. That's why you were crying last night, isn't it?"

My heart drops. He thinks I meant to hurt him. "No, Rashad. There's more to it than you know."

Just then, Gumbo returns to our table and glances between me and Rashad. "Y'all good?"

As Rashad's piercing eyes stare through mine, I think about my father's charm bracelet that I threw behind my bed.

I blink away tears and share everything: how my parents are divorced, how the three of us used to eat at Sweet Song's all the time, how Priya and Tatyana went to the movies without me, and how my father can't seem to remember that I exist.

"I wasn't trying to insult you guys," I finish.

I lift my eyes to meet Rashad's. The look in his eyes tells me that he understands. "I'm really sorry, Dizzy," he says.

Gumbo smiles. "So, tell us about Sweet Song's."

I smirk at Rashad. "You said you've been there."

"I did?" he asks sheepishly. I smile and tell the twins about the red carpet, chandeliers, and fabulous band.

I pick up my fork and dig into the rest of my food. Just then, a huge burp shoots out of my mouth. Completely mortified, I slap my hand over my mouth and sink low in the booth. The twins stare at me, stone-faced.

Rashad claps slowly. "Oh my God, Desiree. That...was absolutely...AMAZING!" He grins and cracks up.

"Man, Dizzy, we didn't know you had it in you!" Gumbo adds. He and Rashad give me a high five, and we all crack up like a group of crazies. Mrs. du Bois smiles and reminds us to start our homework. Still giggling, I take out my books and sneak another round of high fives with the twins.

This after-school agreement isn't so bad after all.

21

Severed Ties

Five o'clock arrives a lot sooner than I expect it to. When my phone's alarm goes off, the twins and I look up from our textbooks and see my mother entering the restaurant.

"Giselle!" Mrs. du Bois sings, waving my mother over to the register. "Come! Come inside, Girl!"

"Hey, 'Liv!" My mother approaches our booth and kisses my forehead. Then she high fives the twins. "Hey, football boys!"

"Hi, Mrs. Davenport," the twins say at the same time. I dig my fingernails into my palms. I have my father's last name, but my mother's last name is Germaine.

I wait for my mother to correct the twins, but she just smiles and rubs Gumbo's shoulder. "Where's Baby Girl?"

"Brianna's in kindergarten, but after school, she goes to a dance class," Mrs. du Bois says, smiling. "Antwan just left to pick her up."

"Oh, I missed her," my mother whines.

"You'll see her on Sunday at the next game," Mrs. du Bois says. "You should sit with all of us in the bleachers."

"I think I'll take you up on that," my mother says.

Mrs. du Bois rubs my back and then turns to the twins. "You finish your homework?" When the twins nod, she gives Rashad a look. "Your father and I saw your pop quiz grades. An 83 is not so bad, but we know you can do better." Rashad sinks low in the booth. Mrs. du Bois shoos both of them away. "Go upstairs and get ready for football."

The twins gather their books and head towards a door in the back of the restaurant. "Bye, Dizzy!" Gumbo calls. I wave to them, while Rashad gives me a toothy smile and a wink. My heart soars.

My mother and I leave The Crunch Bowl and walk across the street to our apartment. She wraps her arm around my shoulders. "So, who is this 'Dizzy?'" she asks playfully.

"Ms. Hernandez let us give ourselves nicknames on the first day of school," I say. "Remember how Tyrell used to call me 'Dizzy' when he was a baby?"

"I remember," my mother answers with a wistful smile. She nudges my elbow. "So, how was the food?"

I start to smile, but freeze when an image of Corinne pops into my head. It's a shame she wasn't able to come, too. "The food was *amazing*," I tell my mother, and her mouth drops open when I tell her all about the incredible fried mac and cheese.

"I'll have to get a taste next time," my mother says with a laugh. She unlocks the door to our apartment. "I knew you'd make some nice friends here, Desiree."

I silently follow my mother inside, unsure of how to respond. "Friends" used to be a word I reserved for Priya and Tatyana. Now I don't want to talk to them anymore.

My nose crinkles at the fishy smell filling our apartment, so I go to the kitchen cabinets and yank out our new stash of incense.

"Try the cinnamon ones this time," my mother says with a yawn. "How about some chicken Alfredo tonight?"

I'm about to tell my mother *yes*, when suddenly, my phone rings. I reach into my backpack and pull out my phone. It's Priya. I'm usually excited to talk to her, but after seeing her and Tatyana at the movies without me, I'm skeptical.

My top lip sweats. "I'll...be right back." I tread into my room and shut the door. Then I hit "Accept."

"Hey, hey, Desiree!" Priya chirps. "Tatyana's here."

"Hi," Tatyana says, but she sounds guilty. "Sorry we never got back to you last night. Priya and I were..."

"At the movies?" I blurt out sharply. No one says a word. For a moment, I wonder if that was the wrong way to start off the call, but it's too late to backtrack. Priya and Tatyana hurt my feelings and now they know. "I saw your Instagram post."

"Sorry we didn't invite you," Tatyana mutters.

"It wasn't planned," Priya offers. "It was just Sunday and Tatyana and I finished our Honors English homework..."

"Yeah, yeah." I can feel my eye twitching.

"Well...your cheerleading picture was cute," Priya says in a slightly brighter tone. "How was the football game?"

"Did your boy score any goals for Team Light Skin?" Tatyana asks, giggling.

My fingers clench so tightly around my phone, I can feel my bedazzled case digging into my skin. "For the last time, Tatyana, his name is Rashad, and you don't know anything about football! He's the quarterback. He throws the ball to the wide receiver or other open guys on the team. A touchdown is scored when they make it to the end zone. Quarterbacks rarely run touchdowns."

"Well, how's his little food spot?" Priya asks with a laugh. "Have you been inside yet?"

"Priya, no!" Tatyana gasps through a fit of giggles. "We warned her to never get sucked into that hole-in-the-wall!"

She and Priya crack up, while I sit on my bed and try to steady my racing heart. Fury spreads through my entire body like lava, and my mouth is a volcano ready to blow.

"Who do you guys think you are?"

The words spew out of my mouth before I can stop them. There's a long, heavy silence.

"*What?*" Tatyana asks through an outraged laugh.

"Every time I talk to you guys, you either have something rude to say about me or the friends I'm making."

"Friends?" Priya snaps. "What friends?"

Tatyana chuckles. "You mean your little football boyfriend with the dirty restaurant?"

I raise my eyebrows. "And what restaurant does *your* family own, Tatyana?"

"Who cares who owns what, Desiree?" Priya snaps.

"Exactly. Because neither of your families own a business," I snap. "And Tatyana, you're so obsessed with talking about which complexions look 'right' together. You sound so stupid. You act like you're not Black. Black is Black!"

Tatyana sucks her teeth, and I can practically see the scowl on her face. "Girl, bye! Your little town ain't nothing but a dump! And that football player, as corny as he is, will *never* like you!"

"He's so corny that you keep talking about him," I shoot back. "You're both jealous and think you're better than people. Just lose my number!"

My thumb pounds the "End" button and I walk back into the living room, feeling on top of the world. Priya and Tatyana have turned into snakes. I don't need their energy.

I walk up to my mother, who stirs a pot of noodles. "Mommy? Can I stay late after cheer practice for the next few weeks?"

My mother turns to me in surprise as I tell her all about Corinne and the talent showcase coming up at the end of the month. When I'm finished filling her in, she smiles like she's just unlocked a piece of me that was closed off. "That sounds lovely, Desiree," she finally says.

I smile and turn away before my mother can make too big a deal out of this. Then I shoot a new text to Corinne.

Me: I was thinking about our dance routine for the showcase. You know Ciara's "Level Up"?

Corinne responds a few seconds later.

Corinne: That's HOT!! You wanna dance to it???

I just smile and type back, **Yes.** ☺

22

Mission Complication

Throughout the rest of the week, I'm torn between eating at The Crunch Bowl and making progress with Chauncey. The only place I can catch him alone is during lunch. On Wednesday, I break away from Corinne in the lunch line.

"Corinne, I'll be right back," I promise. I start to walk away from her, but she trails behind me like a puppy.

"Where ya going?" she asks, staring at me with her wide, hazel eyes. Today they look extra glowy against her polka-dot navy-and-white sweatshirt and orange leggings.

"I just need to talk to someone." My eyes scan The Caf for Chauncey, who eats alone at a small table near the stage. The twins are standing several spots ahead of us in the lunch line and chatting with some other guys. I'll have to be fast.

I speed walk over to Chauncey. He sees me approaching and gives me a blank stare.

"Hi, Chauncey," I say with a wave. He gives me a half-wave back and lowers his eyes. I sigh and search for the twins in the lunch line. Sheesh, now they're practically in the front. "I won't be coming to aftercare anymore."

I try to block out memories of yesterday, when I'd split an ice cream sundae with the twins at The Crunch Bowl. Rashad and I had cracked up while Gumbo burped a few letters of the alphabet. Mrs. du Bois threatened to tell Mr. du Bois and almost sent Gumbo up to his room.

Chauncey shrugs. "Oh...okay." He turns back to his lunch, ending our conversation.

"Hey, Spots!" a familiar voice snaps from behind me. I whirl around and see Rashad walking in our direction. Gumbo trails behind his brother with a mischievous look on his face. I hastily turn to Chauncey, whose eyes go wide with terror. My head starts to spin and I feel sick to my stomach.

I can't let Chauncey find out that I'm friends with the twins, and I can't let the twins find out that I'm trying to help Chauncey. It would make things too complicated and ruin the peaceful path I'm trying to take with this whole situation.

Heart racing, I walk away from Chauncey. Corinne waves me down from a circular table by the door. She munches on a hoagie. The meat, flopping out of the sides of the hard roll, looks plastic. "Get some lunch, Dizzy!" she says.

I glance at the twins, who play another round of Keep Away with Chauncey's lunch. Chauncey tries to snatch his lunch back, but the twins pass it over his head.

I sit next to Corinne and fold my arms. This food looks nasty. "I'm not hungry." The right thing to do would be to march up to the twins and tell them to leave Chauncey alone, but I'm too afraid to start any confusion with the du Bois family. My mother would probably say something to Mrs. du Bois, and she might get mad at my mother. Plus, it could make things worse for Chauncey. Then everything would be busted up.

I've got to figure this whole thing out on my own and peacefully. To do that, I need Chauncey to open up to me, which I can only do when the twins aren't around.

23

Dance Rehearsal

" Toe touches, ladies! Thirty seconds! Go!"
My ears bleed at the sound of Coach Robin's voice booming across the gym. She sticks her whistle in her mouth and blows, sending all of us into a toe-touching frenzy. The gym floor feels dusty against my legs as I lean over and struggle to meet my fingers to the tip of my right sneaker. I'm still not as flexible as the other girls on the squad, but today, I feel just the teensiest bit looser. Maybe it's the kick from The Crunch Bowl's fried mac and cheese that I ate before practice, or maybe it's the thought of our potential Florida trip in December. Either way, I push my fingers a few inches farther and try not to wince at the pain burning behind my thigh.

"Psst. Dizzy!" Corinne whispers, effortlessly wrapping her fingers around the entire top part of her sneaker. I might have the upper hand when it comes to fashion, but Corinne runs circles around me in flexibility. "It's been three days and you haven't told me anything about The Crunch Bowl! What's it like?"

I groan. The Crunch Bowl isn't the first thing on my mind right now. "It's cool," I say. Coach Robin blows her whistle again and we switch our warm-up to lunges. Corinne keeps grinning like she's waiting for me to spill more tea, so I sigh and say, "The food's good and their family's nice."

"Even *Gumbo?*" Corinne asks. When I nod, she snorts and rolls her eyes. "I can't stand him. He's always bothering me when I'm not even doing anything to him."

I shrug. "No, he's nice. Maybe he likes you."

Corinne just laughs. "Yeah, right."

Coach Robin blows her whistle and it's officially time to start practice. I spend the next two hours watching her braided ponytail sway back and forth as she teaches us a new dance routine for this Sunday's halftime show. Some of the moves are pretty difficult, but now that I know we're competing for Florida, I try to hang in there. Coach Robin must notice my extra effort, because she ends practice by giving me a high five.

"Nice work today, Davenport," she says. I try to smile through my aching palm and mutter a weak "thanks." Coach Robin instructs me to keep it up and then hustles off to scold another girl on our squad for cheering too loud above the rest of us.

Corinne shakes my wrist excitedly. "My grandma comes in a half hour, Dizzy. Let's get started on our showcase routine!" Her eyes suddenly go dull and she backs away from me. "Unless you changed your mind about staying late."

I glance at the Exit sign on the other end of the gym. Technically, there's nothing stopping me from calling my mother to come pick me up. It's 8:02 p.m. and I'm pretty worn out, but I made a promise to Corinne, and I'd feel awful if I broke that promise.

"We have a routine to rehearse," I say with a smile. "But I'm not much of a dancer, so you'll have to teach me all your moves."

For the next half hour, Corinne's tiny body twists and cranks like a machine as she shows me how to do The

Shoot, The Floss, and even a few portions of Ciara's *Level Up Challenge* dance. By the time she's finished schooling me, my whole body is *drenched*.

Corinne gathers her braids into a ponytail and holds them away from her neck. "Not bad for your first lesson."

I text my mother to let her know I'm finished dancing for the night. She responds, **OK. Be there in 5!** Then I take a long sip from my water bottle and stare at Corinne in surprise. "Who taught you how to dance so well?" I ask, fanning myself against the stuffy gym air.

"Well..." Corinne looks at me with a shy smile. "I learned from my mother. She used to dance with me all the time."

I almost choke on my water. Corinne's never mentioned her mother, and what does she mean "used" to dance with her all the time? Where is she now?

Corinne's phone rings in her flower-print duffle bag. She rushes over to check it and then slings the bag over her shoulder. "Wanna meet my grandma? She's outside."

I follow Corinne outside and over to the curb, where an old car is parked. Sitting in the driver's seat is a woman with kind eyes. For a grandmother, she doesn't look very old at all. If I had to guess, I'd say she's in her fifties. This confuses me, since both of my grandmothers turned 72 this year.

"Hi, Grandma!" Corinne grabs my wrist and pulls me closer to the car. "This is Dizzy! She's in my class and on my cheer squad and we're doing the talent showcase together!"

I stand there with an uncomfortable smile glued to my lips. "It's, um, nice to meet you, Ms. Corelle."

"Ooh, aren't you pretty?" Ms. Corelle says, beaming at me through the car window. She's wearing hospital scrubs. "Are you the nice friend that my Corinne's been telling me so much about?"

My brain rewinds to my argument with Priya and Tatyana. It's so funny, but up until now, *they* were my friends. They were the ones who said they'd always have my back when I needed them, but they were also the ones who went to the movies without inviting me, posted a picture on social media, and were sneakily putting me down every time I got on the phone with them.

"Yes, I'm Corinne's friend," I tell Ms. Corelle.

Corinne hops into her grandmother's backseat and waves goodbye to me just as my mother pulls up to the curb. I climb into my mother's Audi and watch Ms. Corelle peel away in her car.

"How was your dance rehearsal?" my mother questions. She turns down the radio and I smile when I hear what song is playing: *Signed, Sealed, Delivered* by Stevie Wonder. My mother sure loves her Motown.

"It was great," I say, and I tell my mother all about Corinne's mad dance skills. The entire way home, I bob my head to Stevie Wonder, but in the back of my mind, I'm thinking about Corinne and where her mother might be.

24

Phil's Point of View: Confessions

That Thursday night, after practice, Rashad and I eat a quick dinner and finish our homework. I take a shower. We go to our room, get ready for bed, and I turn out the light. We never go to sleep right away. Instead, we stay up for a little bit and talk (usually about strategies for our upcoming game or how I can sell more gum) until one of us starts snoring. But tonight, Ra does something different.

"P, turn the light back on," he orders.

I frown at his dark figure. "What? Why?" Rashad jumps out of his bed, breezes past me, and turns on the light himself. Then he crouches on the floor and starts doing push-ups. "What the heck are you doing?" I demand.

"Push-ups," he mutters through his exercise. "This is part of my workout routine."

"Since *when?*"

"Since tonight." He does about twenty push-ups and grabs the small basketball sitting by my bed. He grins and gestures to the mini basketball hoop hanging on our door. "C'mon. Let's get a quick game in."

"Dude, it's after ten. I'm not *getting a quick game in.*"

"Why? Scared you'll lose?"

"To you? No! Just go to bed!"

Rashad laughs crazily and does a few high knee jumps. "I can't sleep, P. I'm *wide* awake." He tosses the ball through the hoop and pumps his fist. "Two points!"

Suddenly, there's a knock at our door. Rashad opens it and we see our little sister, Brianna, standing there in her PJ's and holding her favorite doll. "You're being too loud, Ra-Ra. Miss Giggle Pie can't sleep," she whines.

Some normalcy returns to Rashad's face. "Sorry, Bri. C'mon." He picks Brianna up and carries her back to her room.

I grin and wave at Brianna. "Night, Boogs," I say. Sometimes I call her "Boogs" because no matter how hard she tries, she's always got a little something in her nose.

Rashad returns to our room and shuts the door. He goes over to the mirror and starts dancing and muttering the verses to some rap. I give him a weird look and he starts examining his hair. What the heck? Then, out of nowhere, he blurts out, "Hey, do you think Dizzy likes The Crunch Bowl?"

Dizzy? I raise an eyebrow, wishing he'd sit down and shut up already. "What's not to like?"

Rashad steps closer to the mirror and runs a hand across his head. "I know Dizzy *said* she liked it, but...I don't know. I was just wondering."

"She orders the same thing every day," I remind him.

"Hmm." Rashad starts doing sit-ups and working up a funk.

I cringe. "Dude, did you even shower?"

"Nah, I'll do it in the morning." His sit-ups get faster and faster. "What...does Dizzy like...to get from...The Crunch Bowl again?" he pants.

"Deodorant," I snap, waving his B.O. away with my hand. "Seriously, why are we talking about Dizzy right now?"

Instead of answering me, Rashad just sits up and takes a moment to catch his breath. He wipes a hand across his face, which is sweaty and flushed from his random workout. Then he takes a swig of water from the bottle on his nightstand and burps. "Dizzy always gets the fried mac and cheese with a vanilla milkshake, right?" He stands up and touches his toes. "I just hope Dad doesn't burn the mac and cheese. It'll taste bad and then she really won't want to come back."

"She explained everything that happened with her parents and her old friends. What are you talking about?"

"I dunno. Maybe I'll ask Dizzy if she wants to order something else, just to be safe." Rashad stretches his quad muscle. "P, can you hook me up with some gum? Dizzy always sits next to me at The Crunch Bowl and I don't want my breath to be stinkin' while I'm talking to her."

"Just brush your teeth. Look, I'm not giving you free gum. Everybody's breath is funky sometimes."

Rashad looks offended. "Not Dizzy's." He starts doing jumping jacks and I stare at him like he's a crazy person.

Suddenly, it hits me.

"You can't sleep 'cause you've got Dizzy on the brain," I tell Rashad. He freezes and stares at me like he's busted. I sit up straight. "I knew it. You *like* Dizzy."

Ra hesitates, then laughs nervously. "No, I don't." He scratches his ear.

"Liar. That's why you kept begging me to ride bikes with you every day last month. You were looking for Dizzy." Rashad's jaw locks and I know I've got him. "You started calling her *Pony Boots* and haven't stopped. Now, it's after ten and you're up working out, stinkin' up the room, and saying all this random stuff about Dizzy *this* and Dizzy *that*."

Rashad blinks. He glances around our room. He scratches his ankle with his sock. I expect him to come up with some excuse, but he just chews his bottom lip. "Well... *you* like Jennifer Jackson!" he accuses.

My face gets warm as I think about Jennifer — a beauty with big eyes and full lips. But it's hopeless because she's already fourteen *and* she's going out with some other dude. Plus, she doesn't even know me. "No, I don't like Jennifer. Don't you remember how mean she was when I thought she wanted to buy my gum?"

Rashad smiles. "Oh, yeah. Heh. Dizzy told you that. Remember that time when Dizzy thought my locker was hers?" He laughs to himself. "She started blushing. She's so crazy."

I raise an eyebrow as Rashad rummages through our closet and pulls out his football helmet. Then he goes back to the mirror, puts his helmet on, and stares at his reflection in silence. "What is *wrong* with you, Ra?" I demand. Rashad removes his helmet and stares at his reflection thoughtfully, but he doesn't answer me. Now I'm really ticked. "*Rashad.*"

Rashad stays quiet. I'm about to roll over and forget him, when finally, he asks, "You think she'd even like me, P?"

"*Who?*"

"Dizzy," Rashad says, sounding a little embarrassed. "She's really pretty, dresses real nice, talks all proper..." He trails off, sulks to the closet, and puts his helmet away.

I study Rashad carefully. This is my *brother* — the starting quarterback of the Pirates who's never afraid to show any opponent who's boss; the same dude who makes time to memorize our playbook inside and out; the one who can always pull new tricks out of his bag to secure the win, even when it looks like our team's going out cold in the last quarter of a game.

But right now, he's afraid of what Desiree Davenport thinks of him and it's really interesting. I've never seen him like this before.

"Listen, Ra. You're a great athlete and a leader and you inspire our whole team, including me," I say.

Rashad stares at me. He's quiet for a little bit. "I inspire *you?*"

I nod. "All the time."

My brother blinks, but he finally looks calmer. "Well... thanks, P," he says after a few seconds. I grab the football sitting at the end of my bed and pass it to him. He catches it like nothing and smirks. "I am pretty great, aren't I?"

I shrug. "Eh, sometimes you hesitate with the ball when you could've *been* thrown it." Ra busts out laughing and I continue. "But yeah, you're all right, and Dizzy probably thinks so, too."

25

A Surprise Invitation

I don't know what I'm expecting to see when I walk outside to the bus stop on Friday morning, but Gumbo's sly smile is *not* it. "Just ask her!" he urges, shoving Rashad's shoulder. I slow my pace as Rashad swats at his brother and shoves his hands in his pockets. He's smiling, but he also looks embarrassed.

I walk up to the twins. "Hey, guys."

"Hey, Dizzy." Gumbo pushes Rashad forward. "*Rashad* wants to ask you something."

"Nuh-uh," Rashad tells me, scratching his ear. The last time I saw him scratching his ear was when he lied about having been to Sweet Song's.

Gumbo sucks his teeth and gives his brother a look. "Man, if you don't stop playing..."

"Would you back up off me?" Rashad asks, pushing Gumbo away from him. My heart pounds a mile a minute as Rashad faces me with a nervous smile. "Well, the other day, I kinda overheard you talking to Corinne about video games, and Phil and I have some good games at home, so... um..." Rashad trails off and rubs the back of his neck.

Gumbo sighs in exasperation. "Ra wants to know if you want to come over tomorrow and play video games."

I turn to Rashad. "Really?" All this time, I had no idea he was paying so much attention to me.

"Yeah," Rashad says, smiling. "Unless you're busy."

A light bulb goes off in my brain. Aside from getting some video games going, this could be the perfect chance to learn more about the twins' beef with Chauncey. I text my mother about Rashad's video game invitation. She writes back, **Yes, that's fine.** ☺, and I tell the twins I'm good to go.

Rashad grins. "Cool. Can I come by at six?"

"I...thought we were playing at your house."

"We are, but I'm gonna come and get you."

I raise my eyebrows. "Oh! It's just across the street."

"Yeah, but my dad said I need to walk you over."

I stare at Rashad with an eager smile. "Sure," I finally say. Gumbo nudges his brother in a *See? I told you!* kind of way. I smile at the ground and pretend not to notice.

When the bus arrives to our stop, we climb on and hand the driver our tickets. Gumbo rushes to the back and tries to convince two kids from our gym period to buy his stale gum, while Rashad and I find seats together in the front. "So...last weekend, when you called me," I start, trying to sound casual, "you wanted to invite me to play video games?"

Rashad smiles. He looks so much different than the mean Rashad that threatened to ruin Chauncey's picture. "Nah, that was something else," he says. His breath smells like hot chocolate. "I'll tell you about it on Sunday after the next game." I bite my bottom lip and try not to smile too hard, while Rashad whips out his phone. "Are you on Instagram?"

My face feels like wood. "No, uh...well, yeah, but..." I stammer. Rashad raises an eyebrow at me and I sigh. "I don't really have a lot of followers or likes, okay?" I admit sheepishly.

Rashad looks disgusted. "Oh. Well, forget it, then."

My face heats up. "Wait, what? Are you serious?"

Rashad cracks up and nudges my elbow. "I'm just kidding, Pony Boots. You're cool in real life." I blink in stunned silence as Rashad finds my profile and scrolls through my posts. "If I follow you, will you follow me back?"

I nod, whip out my phone, and we follow each other. *Ding!*

I gasp. It's a message from my dad.

Daddy: Good morning baby girl. Do u have lunch plans tomorrow? U + me = pizza date.

My face breaks into a smile so wide, I'm certain I'm growing a third row of teeth.

Me: Tomorrow is PERFECT!!! ☺ ☺ ☺

Daddy: Can't wait. Have a great day princess. <3 <3

I let out a long giggle. Rashad stares at me in surprise and cracks up. "You're crazy, Desiree Davenport," he says.

Feeling on top of the world, I give Rashad a pass for calling me by my full name, again. I wave my phone in the air like a champion. "My dad's taking me out for pizza tomorrow afternoon."

"Nice." Rashad gives me a fist bump and smirks. "You can tell me about it after I beat you in *Mario Kart* tomorrow night." He laughs and I give him the stink eye.

Seconds later, Gumbo slinks his way to the front of the bus and shoves a handful of quarters into his pocket. "In case anybody was wondering, I just made a couple of sales."

"Well, nobody was wondering," Rashad digs.

Gumbo ignores the jab and turns to me. "I got mango-flavored today. You buying any?"

I groan to myself and hand Gumbo a quarter. I guess I'll be starting off the day with cracked teeth. Mm.

At school, the day passes by pretty quickly. Ms. Hernandez smiles at me when I volunteer to read the answers to my science homework, and Corinne socks Gumbo with a dodgeball when he calls her a duck during gym class. At lunch, the twins enjoy their usual game of Keep Away with Chauncey's food. Nobody ever tries to stop them. As much as I want to speak out, I hold back. I'm going to stick with my plan and get my interrogation in tomorrow at the video game party. Then I'll really be on track to solving this thing.

I scarf down more fried mac and cheese at The Crunch Bowl and try not to cry when Coach Robin works us to the bone during practice. Then, Corinne helps me sharpen my dance moves. I'm still not as good as she is, but my moves are definitely getting more fluid. Corinne's a great teacher.

"This routine's gonna be fire!" Corinne insists as we leave the gym. "Wanna hang out at my place this weekend?"

I stiffen. I already have plans with my father and the twins. No offense to Corinne, but if I'm going to learn more details about the twins' beef with Chauncey, I'll need to be at that video game party – alone.

"I'm, uh, busy this weekend," I say sadly.

Corinne looks disappointed. "Doing anything fun?"

I shake my head. "Not really." Corinne keeps staring at me, but I just smile and wave goodbye as we get into our cars. Corinne had all of these questions about my visits to The Crunch Bowl. If she found out about the twins' video game invitation, I know she'd just lose her mind. I don't want her to feel left out, so I don't tell her anything.

26

Just Say a Little Prayer

I've always believed that Saturday mornings are meant for sleeping in until you can't stand the taste of your own tongue. Today, that's not me. It's 8:00 a.m. and I'm up and about.

I smell the faint trail of breakfast cooking, so I head to the kitchen. My mother slides three, golden pancakes and eggs onto a plate and hands it to me. For herself, she has the same.

"Has your father told you what time he's picking you up?" she asks as we eat. I struggle to meet her skeptical gaze. When I first told her about my father's planned lunch date, she didn't look impressed, especially when I revealed that he never confirmed a time to meet.

"Um...not yet," I admit softly. My mother stares at me with a combination of anger and disbelief flaring in her eyes. "But Mommy, it's still early. He has time to let me know."

My mother doesn't say anything. She just slides another pancake onto my plate.

I spend the next few hours catching up on my homework and browsing Instagram. My thumb lands on a few new posts from Priya and Tatyana, but I just unfollow them.

At 1:00 p.m., I reread my favorite parts of *Nancy Drew: The Hidden Staircase*. Within a half hour, I can feel myself getting too sucked into the story, so I close the book and change into a pink sweater dress with a matching headband, belt, and my hot pink cowgirl boots. My father's always said how pretty I look in pink, and when he sees me today, I want him to be blown away.

At a little after 2:00 p.m., I get down on my hands and knees to look for my father's charm bracelet under my bed. At first, I can't find the bracelet behind my dirty socks and stretched-out scrunchies, but then I finally spot it laying against the wall closest to my bed frame. I start to reach for it when suddenly, I hear a familiar *Ding!*

I stand up and reach for my phone on my nightstand. My insides soar when I see **Daddy** flashing on the screen, and I quickly glance over his message looking for any sign of a pickup time, but that's not what I find.

Daddy: Hey baby girl. So sorry but something came up & I have to reschedule our lunch date. Will call u soon.

There's a few pink and red heart emojis included with the message, but I act like I don't see them.

Me: R u coming to my 2nd game tomorrow? 1:15 pm.
Daddy: Not sure baby but I'll let u know tomorrow morning.

I delete my father's text conversation and slam my phone on my nightstand. If that charm bracelet weren't already under my bed, I'd yank it off my wrist and snap it until each and every charm came loose. Let it stay there.

"Desiree? Let me see your outfit." My mother enters my bedroom and grins when she sees my pink ensemble. "Beauuutiful! Is your father on his way?"

I lick my bottom lip because it's the only thing I can do to keep from crying. "Daddy has to reschedule."

My mother's eyes flash with pity and then outrage. "He called you?"

I flick my head towards my phone. "Texted."

"Has he called you since we've moved here?"

If I open my mouth again, I know I'll start crying, so I just shake my head. My mother wraps me in a tight embrace, and before I can stop them, the tears start rolling. It's not fair. Priya and Tatyana's fathers are always there for them, but mine can't seem to show me that he cares even a little bit.

"Hey." My mother pulls away from me and wipes my eyes. "This face is too pretty to look this sad. What time did Rashad invite you over tonight?"

I sniff up a clump of snot. "He's picking me up at six."

"Girl, we've got to get you *ready!*" My mother leads me back into the kitchen, where we have a lunch of chicken salad sandwiches and lemonade. Once the table is cleared, I finish my homework, change into some jeans and a pink top, and let my mother help me style my hair into a gorgeous twist-out that hangs just below my shoulders. "Beautiful," she says, spraying some curl-sealer throughout my head. She walks away to talk to one of her old college friends over the phone, while I study my reflection in the mirror.

Smiling, I grab my phone off the sink and pop my earbuds in. Then I scroll through my songs and choose "I Say a Little Prayer" by the legendary Aretha Franklin. My mother got me hooked on this song yesterday, and I sing along in a smooth voice as I apply my lip gloss. Once I'm finished, I sing louder, dancing out of the bathroom and down the hallway. I start to belt out the next verse, but then I spin around and almost choke. *Rashad Maurice du Bois* is standing in my living room. He heard me singing. He saw me dancing.

My face heats up as I messily remove my earbuds and wrap them around my phone. The entire time, Rashad bites his bottom lip and stares at me with an amused smile. "Uh, hey, Dizzy," he says through a small laugh. "You look nice."

Heart racing, I quickly glance at the kitchen clock. It's 6:00 p.m. and Rashad is right on time. I was too busy playing *American Idol* to hear the doorbell ring. I want to die. I wonder if the apartment stinks like fish...and if Rashad smells the fish.

I grab my purse and cross over to Rashad. He smiles and waves to my mother. "Bye, Mrs. Davenport."

My mom waves at us and goes back to her phone call. I'll share my mom's real last name with Rashad another time. As Rashad leads me downstairs, I stare at the back of his curly head of hair and sigh sadly. Why does this handsome boy who's so nice to me have to bully Chauncey?

Once we're outside, I expect Rashad to hurry across the street so we can get the games going. Instead, he stops outside of Manny's Fish Market and stares at me, smirking.

"What?" I ask timidly.

"How'd it go?" Rashad breaks into a two-step.

"Ugh, stop!" I'm embarrassed times infinity. We stroll alongside each other and he raises an eyebrow at me.

"I see you, Desiree Davenport. You're different. You know, from when I first met you."

"Uh, I haven't changed," I protest.

Rashad goes on. "I'm gonna tell you something and I hope you don't take this the wrong way." I knew it. The apartment stunk. He smelled the fish. "You're chill and you talk a lot more, which is cool, 'cause you've always got something interesting to say, and you smile more, too." Thank God! I thought he smelled the fish. Rashad clears his throat. "I like your hair."

I turn away and twist one of my curls so he doesn't see how big I'm grinning. "Thanks," I say, following him to the traffic pole. He presses the button and I sigh. "So...what are your hobbies outside of school?"

"Well, I'm mainly into football, but Phil and I started playing instruments last year," Rashad answers.

I raise my eyebrows. "Really? What do you play?"

"I play the trombone. Phil plays the saxophone."

"What made you guys choose those instruments?"

"Our dad's from New Orleans. He's teaching us about jazz so we can know our roots." I nod and he smiles at me. "Have you always done cheer?"

"Actually, I grew up playing tennis."

"Oh, yeah. Tennis is cool. Look at me." Rashad swings an imaginary racquet. "Venusss! Serenaaaa! Cocoooo!"

I laugh. "Yeah, tennis is more of a solo sport, unless you're playing doubles."

"Well, that's what I like about football. You're on a team and it gives you a chance to learn how to be a leader and how to be accountable. Me being the quarterback, the guys on my team depend on me to know the plays and how to throw that ball."

"Right. Well, what'd you do today?"

"Phil and I did conditioning drills with our dad."

"Conditioning drills?"

"They're exercises to help you build skill and agility," Rashad explains, his voice suddenly taking on a more serious tone. "All the top athletes do 'em to stay in shape."

The light turns green and we cross the street. "But you guys do conditioning during practice, don't you?" I ask.

"My dad says that isn't enough and that you can't make it to the pros by just doing the bare minimum."

"How often do you guys do extra conditioning?"

"Every Saturday for two hours. Today was Footwork Day, so my dad had us doing stuff with the sprint ladder, cones, speed parachute...all that stuff."

As we finish crossing the street, my mind wanders to Chauncey. I wonder if he does conditioning with *his* dad? "Does everybody on your team do conditioning on Saturdays?"

"Yeah, some of the guys join us, but not everybody can come out because they do other things on Saturdays." He leads me to the back door of The Crunch Bowl. "I almost forgot to ask you: How was pizza with your dad?"

Jesus, take the wheel. My stomach churns as I stare up at Rashad. I feel so embarrassed. "No...we didn't go," I mutter.

Rashad stares at me sadly. "I'm sorry, Desiree."

I shake my head quickly. "It's fine."

"You sure?" Rashad presses. "You seem pretty down about it." When I don't answer, he gestures to my apartment. "If you don't feel up to video games tonight, I understand. I can walk you back home." He takes a few steps towards the traffic pole, but I grab the sleeve of his jacket.

"Scared I'll beat you in *Mario Kart*?" I ask with a smirk.

Rashad stares at me in surprise. When he realizes that I'm not backing down, he laughs and opens the back door to The Crunch Bowl. "Oh, you got jokes! We'll see."

"Yes, we will," I say, grinning as he leads me up the stairs to his family's apartment.

27

Video Games and Super Soakers

The du Bois' apartment is bright and very spacious, with a nice, open living room that holds a coffee table, flat screen television, and a giant, fluffy couch. To the left is a beautiful dining room table that leads into the kitchen, where I can smell the comforting aroma of spices, meats, and desserts. In the corner is a smartphone that sits in a stereo system, which plays *Every Little Thing* by Bob Marley. The music relaxes me, and I start bobbing my head to the beat.

"Ma! Dizzy's here!" Rashad yells, slamming the door.

Mrs. du Bois' voice rings from the kitchen. "How many times have I told you and your brother not to slam that door?" She emerges from the kitchen and smiles when she sees me. "Hello, Miss Pretty Girl! How's your mom doing?"

"Hi, Mrs. du Bois. My mom's fine. She said 'hi,'" I say.

Mrs. du Bois wipes her flour-stained hands on the apron around her small waist. "I was just cooking."

"I helped, too, Mama!"

I glance past Mrs. du Bois and see the twins' little sister, Brianna, skipping over to us. There's flour all over her clothes and a glob of strawberry frosting on her cheek.

Rashad scoops the frosting off Brianna's cheek. "Say 'hi' to Dizzy, Bri," he says, sticking the frosting in his mouth.

"Hi, Dizzy!" Brianna squeaks. She stares down at my pink boots. "Oh! Ra-Ra! Is this Pony Boots?"

Rashad gives me a sheepish smile and clears his throat. "Uh, Phil's setting up the games in the den. Follow me."

"Uh-huh," I mutter slyly. After we remove our shoes, I follow Rashad down the hall and past a cinnamon-scented bathroom and a few bedrooms. On the wall is a beautiful portrait of the entire du Bois family posed in front of a Christmas tree. Rashad stands in front of his father with a calm, dimpled smile. They look so much alike.

"Where's your dad?" I ask Rashad.

"Downstairs running the restaurant. He'll be up later," Rashad explains. We enter a carpeted room filled with sports balls and toys. There's a flat screen hanging on the wall and a red bean bag chair in the corner by the window. Gumbo sits on the floor. He's wearing a red t-shirt and basketball shorts.

"Hey, Dizzy," Gumbo says, popping a game into the console.

"Hey, Gumbo." I gesture to his face. "No sunglasses today?"

Gumbo rubs the end of his basketball shorts. "I don't wear 'em at home." He turns on the console and the words FOOTBALL SMASHUP appear on the flat screen in monstrous letters.

Rashad frowns. "We're playing Mario Kart today."

"What about Football Smashup?" Gumbo demands.

"Dizzy didn't come here to play that," Rashad snaps.

Hmm...Football Smashup would give me a chance to talk about Chauncey. "Actually, Football Smashup sounds fun," I say.

"Yes! Let me get the good controller. I know it's under your bed." Gumbo makes a face at Rashad and dashes out of the den.

Rashad turns to me with a raised eyebrow. "Why'd you change your mind?"

My palms itch with nervousness. If Gumbo is in a good mood, I'm sure he'll be more open to talking about Chauncey. I can't tell Rashad this, so I just smile and say, "Because I thought it'd be fun to learn more about football. I'm a cheerleader, aren't I?"

Rashad looks skeptical, but then his expression relaxes and he smiles. "Whatever you want, Desiree Davenport."

I grin and stare at my socks.

Gumbo returns with the good controller. His eyes catch something out the window and he laughs. "Guys, over here." We all walk over to the window and see Chauncey approaching Manny's Fish Market. Gumbo opens the window and screams, "Hey, Spots!"

Chauncey turns to the window and I duck. If he ever knew I was up here at the twins' place today, he'd never talk to me again.

Rashad snickers and yells, "Spotty, Spotty, Spots!" He turns to me. "Why are you hiding down there?"

"Yeah, Dizzy! Say something," Gumbo urges, laughing.

"I...need to wash my hands." I shoot up from the floor, hustle into the hallway bathroom, and run my hands under some cold water. I can't speak out against the twins yet. I need to keep the peace so I can keep their trust and question their motive for bullying Chauncey.

I turn off the sink and return to the den, where the twins still hover by the window. "Oh, oh!" Rashad exclaims. He taps Gumbo on the back. "Go get some water from the fridge."

Gumbo laughs and scurries out of the den. My chest feels like it's about to explode. "What are you guys doing?" I follow Rashad as he rushes to the closet. He yanks the door open and tosses out a bunch of sports equipment.

"Chauncey's coming out of the fish store," Rashad says hastily. "We need...oh! Oh! Here it is!" He spots an orange Super Soaker lying next to a teddy bear and grins crazily. As he bends down to grab the Super Soaker, that's when I hear it: *Prrt! Prrrfft!* Rashad freezes and slowly looks at me.

I scrunch up my face. "Ew! I heard those!"

Rashad stands up straight and laughs a little. "Um, excuse me," he mumbles. I fan the air and he leans into the hallway. "P! Where you at, man? Hurry up!"

Gumbo rushes back into the den holding a gallon of water. He laughs and fills the Super Soaker. "You think it'll reach?"

"We're about to find out," Rashad says with a laugh. "Here he comes!" He clutches the Super Soaker and aims it out the window.

My stomach drops. "Guys, this is dumb!" I say, but it's too late. Chauncey exits the fish store.

"Yo, Spots!" Rashad shrieks. His fingers tighten around the Super Soaker and he pumps the valve like crazy, sending an endless stream of water across the street and right at Chauncey's face. Chauncey flinches and shakes his head back and forth. His arms clutch tightly around his paper bag as he hustles down the sidewalk.

"Nuh-uh. Let me get him." Gumbo snatches the Super Soaker from Rashad and sprays Chauncey from behind. "Look at Spots run," he mutters, laughing. He gives one more pump, but the Super Soaker is empty. "Aw, man. We're out."

"It's cool. Spots is gone now, anyway," Rashad says. He and Gumbo crack up and close the window, while I struggle to calm my racing heart. That was *crazy*, and I start to ask the twins what in the heck they were thinking, but then Rashad smiles at me like the same, considerate boy who escorted me across the street. All traces of menace are gone from his face. "Dizzy, you can sit in the bean bag chair, okay?" He tosses the Super Soaker back in the closet and drags a red bean bag chair from the corner to the middle of the room.

"Okay..." I mutter cautiously. We all sit down, and I listen to the twins teach me the rules of *Football Smashup*. "I, um, learn better by watching first," I say. They shrug and get the game going, while I sit up straight and clear my throat. It's time to grill these twins like steaks. "So, guys. Are you ready for the second game tomorrow?"

"We stay ready," Gumbo says, staring at the screen.

"And we'll win, too, as long as Coach keeps us in the game," Rashad says.

"Well, what about your teammates who *don't* play as much?" I press. "Like...Chauncey?"

Rashad snorts. "Spots? He doesn't deserve to play. He's never been good. He's a scrub!"

"Well...how long have you all been teammates?"

"Rashad and I started playing USA Little League Football when we were seven," Gumbo explains. "But Spots joined the team last year and messed up *everything*."

Finally, I'm getting somewhere. I lean forward with interest. "What did he do? Why don't you guys like him?"

Rashad pauses *Football Smashup* and frowns at me. "Why do you keep talking about him so much?"

"Yeah, do you like him or something?" Gumbo asks, laughing. Rashad stares at me in surprise, while my face heats up in humiliation. This isn't how my interrogation is supposed to be going.

"No! I don't like Chauncey," I state.

"Yeah, Phil, that's ridiculous," Rashad snaps. He resumes the game while I sit there and fan my burning face.

A half hour later, Mrs. du Bois brings us a huge plate of assorted appetizers from The Crunch Bowl. She frowns and picks up the empty water jug. "What are you doing in here with this, huh?"

"Ra was thirsty," Gumbo says. I don't say anything.

After Mrs. du Bois leaves the room, Rashad pauses the game and turns to me. "Here, Dizzy, take my controller."

For the next 15 minutes, I try my hardest to learn the game's controls. I'm not very good and sometimes, I struggle with moving my player around. Thankfully, the twins remain patient and explain the stuff I don't understand. By the end of the lesson, I'm enlightened. Football is way more interesting than I thought.

At 7:30 p.m., Gumbo pops *Black Panther* into the DVD player. The movie starts and Brianna skips into the room. She's dressed in some strawberry-print pajamas and singing at the top of her lungs. "Twinkle, twinkle, little star! How I wonder what you are!" she screams. I tense in annoyance as she skips in front of Rashad. She grabs his hands and jumps up and down. "I'm an airplane, Ra-Ra, and I'm gonna *flyyyy* to the stars! Twinkle, twinkle, little star..."

Goodness. Fighting the urge to claw my eyes out, I glance at Rashad to see his expression. He looks calm. "Shh..." he whispers, pulling Brianna into a sitting position. He smiles and wraps an arm around her. "You are so sleepy."

"Nuh-uh," Brianna says, but she's rubbing her eyes.

Rashad points to the TV. "Watch the movie with us, okay?" Brianna nods, sucks her thumb, and rubs Rashad's ear. I raise an eyebrow. Rashad doesn't even look phased.

Gumbo catches my curious expression and shakes his head with a tired smile. "She does that to Ra *all* the time," he whispers.

"And he lets her?" I whisper back. Gumbo just nods and I sit back in surprise. I definitely don't have the patience for all that.

An hour later, Mr. du Bois comes upstairs. He high-fives the twins and kisses Brianna, who's now fast asleep in Rashad's lap. I feel like an intruder because I'm not part of their family, but then Mr. du Bois squeezes my shoulder. "Hi, Sweetie, how are you?" he whispers.

"Hi, Mr. du Bois. I'm good," I say softly. He leaves the room, carrying Brianna over his shoulders. A lonely ache burns in my chest. When I was little, I'd often wake up to my father carrying me to my bed. Brianna has no idea how lucky she is.

I doze off near the third act of *Black Panther*, and when I open my eyes, the credits are rolling and the twins are fast asleep on the floor. I hear muffled voices and light footsteps approaching the room, but I'm just too sleepy to stay awake. I close my eyes again and feel the presence of someone strong standing over me. Before I know it, the person is picking me up and carrying me over their shoulder. At first, I'm afraid, but then I wrap my arms around the person's neck. It's my father. I knew he felt bad about cancelling our pizza date. He came to see me after all. Wait until I tell Rashad.

"Hi, Daddy," I murmur sleepily. My father rubs my back.

I rest my head against my father's shoulder as he carries me through the living room. Through my sleepy eyes, I can see a blurry image of Mrs. du Bois smiling and waving goodbye to me.

My father holds me tighter as he carries me out of their apartment, down the steps, and outside. I'd forgotten how comfortable I used to feel in his arms.

He carries me up the steps to my apartment, where my mother opens the door and thanks him for bringing me home. He gently places me on the couch and tells my mother that he'll see us tomorrow at the game.

As I sit there rubbing my eyes, my mother shakes me gently until I'm fully awake. When I look up, I realize it was never my father after all.

It was Mr. du Bois.

28

The Big Invitation

"Do not seek revenge or bear a grudge against anyone amongst your people, but love your neighbor as yourself! I am the Lord! Leviticus nineteen-eighteen!"

At the sound of Pastor Soarbrook's commanding voice, my mother nods her head and cranks up the volume on her phone. My mother and I haven't found a new church home in Treeless Park just yet, so on some Sundays, we watch the live broadcasts of the 11:00 a.m. services at our old Baptist church. That church is huge, with three floors and over 6,000 members. As Pastor Soarbrook continues his sermon, I gently swing my legs under the kitchen table and eat my egg-and-cheese English muffin. I'll need all the protein I can get to cheer for the Pirates at today's football game in a few hours.

Ding!

I grab my phone, hoping to find a text from my father. Yesterday, he promised to text me about coming to today's game, but instead of **Daddy** on my screen, I see **Rashad**.

Rashad: Hey. Don't leave right after the game today. Wanna ask u something.

I stare at Rashad's message in surprise.

Me: Ok ☺ Good luck today!

Rashad: Thx.

I try to force down the smile building on my face. My mother gives me a knowing look. "Is that Rashad?"

My eyes lower in embarrassment. How do mothers *always* know everything *all* the time? "Um, yeah," I mutter. Before she can ask too many questions, I blurt out, "The video games were fun. We watched *Black Panther* afterwards."

My mother smiles and collects my empty breakfast plate. "Go shower and get dressed. Use deodorant."

I stand up and glance at my phone. Still, nothing from my father, but instead of dwelling on the negative, I reread Rashad's text. I wonder what he wants to ask me.

At 12:30 p.m., my mother and I arrive to the football field behind the regional high school. We hop out of our car and I rush over to Coach Robin and the rest of my cheer squad on the grass. Meanwhile, my mother finds a seat in the bleachers with the du Bois family. Today, their posters look bigger and more colorful than they did last week.

"Dizzy!" a familiar voice chirps from behind me. I spin around and meet eyes with Corinne, who grins like she hasn't seen me in years. "How was your weekend?"

My tongue feels like sandpaper. If Corinne ever knew about yesterday at the du Bois' place, she might try to get on the bottom during our preps and drop *me*. "It was cool," I say.

I look for the twins and spot them huddled with their team. In the center of the huddle is Coach Marino, who talks with a lot of emphasis and sharp hand movements. "All right, team, listen up!" Coach Marino bellows. "It's the second game of the season and we want to come out strong, just like last week. Offense, be alert. Quick on your feet, good hands. Defense, move like a tornado on those guys. We play as a team; we play as one. Who are we?"

"Pirates!" the football players scream in unison.

"I am so proud of each and every single member of this team," Coach Marino continues. "Now let's get out there and show 'em what we're made of: grit and perseverance!"

Mr. du Bois and the assistant coaches hover nearby, while Chauncey tries to push his way into the mix. The twins shove Chauncey to the back of the huddle and I stare at him curiously. Compared to the other football players, he looks so out of place, like he's not even part of the team.

Today's opponents are the Bisons, and within the first few minutes of the game, I can tell that their star quarterback is pretty good. To my relief, our defense came to *eat* and Rashad's aim is crisp. With each offensive play, he drives the ball right into Gumbo's hands. Gumbo shoots down the field like a rocket and drives in the touchdowns. I sing *Do it all, du Bois* and *Ra-Ra-Ra* so many times. I'm sure I'll be chanting these words in my sleep tonight.

During my cheer squad's halftime routine, I see Chauncey tugging on Coach Marino's sleeve. I bet he's trying to get in the game. Coach Marino leans down and says something in his ear. When he walks off, the twins push Chauncey out of their way so they can get a drink from the water cooler. Chauncey sulks over to the bench. He sits there angrily until the fourth quarter, when he finally gets on the field. He doesn't get to do anything good. At all.

Thanks to Rashad's slick handoff to our running back, the Pirates win 35-28. I grin and laugh with my cheer squad and look for the twins amongst the celebration. They're jumping up and down with their teammates and shouting some chant that ends with, "Fight, Pirates, fight!" Chauncey sulks, alone, on the bench. It's like no one even notices him.

"This is so exciting! We're two-and-oh!" Corinne exclaims, breaking into a fierce Floss dance. I'm about to join her, when suddenly, the twins approach us with their helmets tucked under their arms. They look tired, but happy.

"Hey, guys. Great game today," I say.

"Thanks." Rashad flicks his head to the left. "Can I talk to you for a sec?"

"We're all already talking," Corinne says with a laugh.

My spine stiffens. Rashad suddenly looks uncomfortable. "I...need to talk to Dizzy alone, actually."

Corinne blinks twice. Her eyes flash with confusion and surprise. "Oh..." she mutters.

Rashad leads me away from Corinne and Gumbo. Once we're out of earshot, he takes a deep breath and grins at me. "All right. Remember last week when I called you and..."

"I bawled my eyes out?" I finish with an awkward laugh.

Rashad tries not to smile and glances around the field. "Shh. Nobody's supposed to know, remember?" I grin and he continues. "My family's coming over for dinner tonight, so I was wondering if you and your mom wanted to join us at around six p.m.?"

My heart does backflips. "Really?"

"Yeah. On Sundays after the games, my family comes over to our place for dinner and everybody brings a dish. It's a tradition."

I don't know how to respond. First video games and now dinner invitations? Since my parents are divorced, spending time with the du Bois family brings back memories of being with my own family.

"Well, do you want me to bring something, too?" I ask.

Rashad smirks. "Just your appetite. My dad's family is Creole and my mom's family is Jamaican, so it'll be a mix of Louisiana and Jamaican cuisines. There'll be plenty of food."

That. Sounds. *Delicious.* I start to accept Rashad's invitation, when suddenly, I spot Chauncey coming at us. My chest feels like it's going to explode. If Chauncey sees me grinning in Rashad's face, I'll be busted harder than a crystal vase on concrete.

I take a few baby steps around Rashad and use his tall frame to hide from Chauncey. Rashad stares at me with a confused frown. "What are you doing?" He leans over and sniffs his armpit. "Do I stink?"

"No!" I say, trying to smile. Chauncey crouches in the grass to tie his laces. Panicking, I run around the opposite side of Rashad to avoid being seen. I feel like a lunatic.

Rashad swivels around in frustration. "Why are you acting so weird?"

Heart pounding, I rack my brain for an explanation. "Um, well...this is pretty embarrassing, but it's something I ate." I rub my stomach for emphasis.

Rashad's expression relaxes. He laughs, but not in a mean way. "Desiree Davenport, you are *crazy*, Girl," he says, smiling. "You might want to try some ginger ale."

I glance past Rashad's smile and over at Chauncey, who's now standing up. I've gotta go *now*. "Dinner sounds great, Rashad," I say hastily. He grins and I take a few steps back. "Just let me ask my mom if she had other plans for us."

Heart pounding, I hustle away from Rashad and over to my mother, who's speaking with Mrs. du Bois. I glance behind me. Chauncey is walking away, so I breathe a sigh of relief. I tap my mother on the shoulder and share Rashad's dinner invitation. Mrs. du Bois' eyes light up. "Oh, yes, Giselle! You and Desiree should come by. Do you like Jamaican food?"

"Girl, my mother was born and raised in Kingston!" my mother exclaims. She and Mrs. du Bois talk excitedly about their Jamaican heritage for a moment. When they're finished, my mother puts her hand on my shoulder. "Desiree can join you all, but I have a lot of work to catch up on before tomorrow."

Mrs. du Bois gives my mother a sympathetic nod and tells me that she'll see me in a few hours. She, Mr. du Bois, and the rest of their family walk with the twins to the parking lot. Rashad turns to face me and I give him a big thumbs up. He smiles and makes the *I'll call you* gesture with his hand.

"Dizzy!" Corinne suddenly calls from across the field. My top lip sweats as she approaches with her grandmother. "What did Rashad want to talk to you about?"

I take a step back. I can't tell Corinne about a dinner that she wasn't invited to. It would be too much. My teeth sink into the inside of my cheek. "Rashad was just...confused about something on our science homework."

Corinne frowns. "But he can just ask Gumbo."

Jesus, take the wheel. Why is she being so nosy?

I can't think of anything else to say, so I just grin and wave goodbye. "Can't wait to finish our dance routine!"

Corinne starts to answer, but I'm already hightailing it away from the field with my mother before she can say another word.

29

Dinner with the du Bois

I've always been a fashionista, but tonight, nothing in my closet seems right for dinner with the du Bois family.

Standing on my tiptoes, I impatiently yank through sweaters, dresses, and a few skirts that are slowly becoming out of season. When did my style get so dry?

"Desiree! It's five forty-five!" my mother calls from down the hall.

I reach into the back of my closet and grab my shimmery pink top from two years ago. The sleeves are a little short on me now, but the sparkly fabric makes my brown eyes pop. I pair the top with black leggings and my pink cowgirl boots. Brianna will probably get a kick out of them again.

I meet my mother in the bathroom, where she slicks the front of my hair down with a glob of Taliah Waajid and braids the rest in a side ponytail. I look elegant and *very* ready for a big dinner, but I also feel sorry for my mother. "Mommy, are you sure you don't want to come?"

"No, baby. I have too much to do here," my mother says with a soft smile. "Go and have some fun. I think it'll be good for you. Besides, you and I will have our girl time soon. I was thinking...a hair day at Pump It Up?"

I nod with a huge grin. That sounds right up my alley.

At 6:00 p.m., Rashad arrives to pick me up. He looks very handsome in an olive green polo shirt, but I'm too shy to tell him.

We say bye to my mother and head down the apartment steps. Once we're outside, Rashad grins at me. "My mom told us you're Jamaican. You got a favorite dish?"

My lips stretch into a huge smile. When I was younger, my grandmother introduced me to our Jamaican culture. We'd often visit our relatives during the holidays. There was always tons of food. "I love cocktail patties," I say.

Rashad quickens his pace. "Then we'd better hurry before my cousin eats 'em all."

I crack up and follow Rashad across the street to The Crunch Bowl. Just like last Sunday, the restaurant is closed. "Do you close the restaurant every Sunday?"

"During football season, yes. The games usually take up the whole day, and then we've got our family that comes over for dinner. In the off-season, we'll all go back to church and let the staff open the restaurant later in the afternoons."

I nod silently. That definitely makes sense.

Rashad leads me through the back door of The Crunch Bowl and I hear the lively roar of laughter, chatter, and music. I freeze.

Rashad faces me. "You okay?"

No, I'm not. I'm actually intimidated to spend time with their big, poster-waving, extended family. "I'm...a little nervous," I finally admit.

"Don't be. You'll fit right in." Rashad smiles and extends his hand to me. My top lip sweats as I slowly slip my hand in his. My entire body goes hot and my heart starts pounding like rapid fire.

Rashad Maurice du Bois is holding my haaaannddd!!!

As Rashad leads me upstairs, I can't help but stare at his towering frame. "How tall are you?" I ask shyly.

"Phil and I are five-foot-eight, and Dad says we're not done growing yet." Rashad grins at me and I start to grin back, when suddenly, an image of Chauncey pops into my head. It feels like he's staring right at me. If he saw me holding Rashad's hand right now, my mission would be *over*.

I reluctantly slide my hand out of Rashad's. His eyes go dull with disappointment. "What's wrong, Girl?"

"Uh...my...palm was sweaty," I say.

Rashad gives me a weak smile. "Oh."

We enter the apartment, which smells *amazing* and is packed with all the relatives I've seen sitting in the bleachers. I notice Mr. du Bois laughing and slapping the shoulders of some of the other male relatives, while Mrs. du Bois forces Brianna to share her toys with two little girls. Humming from the stereo is another Bob Marley song: *Redemption Song*. The TV is set to a football game between the Dallas Cowboys and the New York Giants.

"Where's Phil?" I ask Rashad, but he's not listening. Instead, he's staring at the TV with a huge grin on his face. I look at the screen and see one of the Cowboys – Number Four – darting around the defense with the ball tucked under his arm. He scores a touchdown, causing every guy in the apartment to go crazy. Rashad is the loudest of them all.

"I take it you're a fan?" I ask with a laugh.

"Dizzy, that's *Dak Prescott*. He's the quarterback for the Dallas Cowboys," Rashad says with a lot of emphasis. "He played for Mississippi State and was a fourth round pick in the 2016 NFL Draft. His stats are *crazy*. He's got a seventy-five percent completed passes rate, and he's passed over nine hundred yards this season."

My eyebrows shoot up. "Wow. He sounds amazing."

"Girl, he's a *legend*. When I grow up, I'm gonna be a pro quarterback, just like Dak. Don't get me wrong; there are so many great quarterbacks in the NFL. You've got Russell

Wilson, Drew Brees, Lamar Jackson, Aaron Rogers..."
Rashad pauses and gives me a sheepish smile. "Sorry, I'm
talking too much, aren't I?"

I smile and shake my head. "No way. A cheerleader's got
to learn her football." Rashad grins and I raise an eyebrow.
"Phil's a wide receiver. Who are some of his favorite players?"

Rashad's eyes light up. "Ah, my brother's a huge fan
of Mohamed Sanu. He graduated from high school in New
Jersey and has some *crazy* good hands. Aside from Sanu,
Phil also likes Cole Beasley, Julio Jones, Larry Fitzgerald,
and Golden Tate. They're some sick dudes on the field."

I stare at Rashad in awe. He and Gumbo are very
passionate about their sport. It's inspiring. "So, do you wear
Number Four because of Dak?"

"Nah. Four was my uncle Levon's number when he
used to play ball with my dad. My dad was Number Twenty-
Four, like Phil."

I nod and glance around the sea of relatives in the
apartment. "Is your uncle Levon here?"

Rashad nods and points to a tall man standing next to
Mr. du Bois. They look so much alike. "That's him. He was
an amazing quarterback and wanted to go pro, too."

"Well, what happened to him?"

Rashad blinks and stares at the floor. "We, uh, don't
talk about it much," he mumbles. I chew on my bottom lip
and nod a few times. A moment passes before Rashad sighs
and smiles at me. "Well, what's your dream, Pony Boots?"

I tense up. As an avid reader and writer, my dream is
to become a journalist and write books. I've never shared
my dreams with anyone besides my parents, but tonight,
standing in the du Bois apartment across from Rashad, it
feels okay.

Suddenly, Gumbo pushes his way through the crowd.
"Hey, Dizzy!" His hair is kind of wet. "Sorry, I was bathing."

My face twists up. Rashad glares at his brother. "Dude! Too much information!"

Gumbo rolls his eyes. Then he smiles and drapes an arm around me. "C'mon and meet the family, Dizzy."

The twins lead me through their apartment, where I say hello to Mr. and Mrs. du Bois and greet the extended relatives: their grandparents and so many aunts, uncles, and cousins on both sides. I learn that Mr. du Bois' family is originally from New Orleans, Louisiana. Meanwhile, Mrs. du Bois' family is from Montego Bay, Jamaica. I'm not sure where all these people are going to sit when it's time for dinner, but hopefully there's a spot for me somewhere.

The twins lead me into the den, where a fat girl eats a bag of white cheddar popcorn. "This is one of our cousins on our mom's side, Nikita," Gumbo says. "She's our age and goes to a middle school on the other side of town."

I wave and say "hi" to Nikita. She burps, pats her chest with her hand and squints her eyes at me. "What's your name again?" Nikita asks me, crunching loudly on more of the popcorn. Some of the cheddar dust gets trapped in the corners of her mouth and she licks it away greedily.

"Nikita, I told you: Her name is Desiree." Rashad places his hand on my shoulder and I get this queasy feeling in my stomach.

Nikita stares at Rashad's hand on my shoulder. Her chubby face breaks into a sly grin, showing off a pair of beady eyes and a row of tiny, yellow teeth. Oh, she looks just like a big cat. "Oh, yeahhh. I remember *you*, Desiree," she says.

Gumbo reaches for Nikita's popcorn, but she snatches the bag up. "Nikita, you already ate two bags!" Gumbo snaps.

Rashad looks embarrassed. "I...think we're about to bless the food. Come on, Dizzy." He leads me back into the living room.

Mr. du Bois calls for everyone to join hands and say grace. Rashad reaches for my hand. With thoughts of Chauncey still looming in my mind, I hastily hold hands with Brianna and Nikita. When our prayer is over, I find Nikita's white cheddar dust caked into the creases of *my* palms. Note to self: *Never* hold hands with Nikita during grace again.

Gumbo hands me a plate and urges me to stand by the dining room table before the food gets picked over. I feel shy, so I fall back while the relatives swarm the table. They notice me standing behind everyone and smile down at me.

"Go ahead, young lady!" the twins' uncle Malcolm insists. He's on Mr. du Bois' side of the family.

"This gal is too thin," Mrs. du Bois' sister, Violet, says with a playful smile. She leads me right up to the table and fills my plate with rice and peas, jerk chicken, macaroni and cheese, gumbo, collard greens, and of course, the golden cocktail beef patties. I join the twins and Nikita in the den. Nikita's plate is loaded *down*, but I just smile and tell her I like her cornrows. She doesn't answer me, though, because she's too busy pushing food into her face. I look over at Rashad and realize that he's been staring at me. He caught me watching Nikita eat. Feeling embarrassed, I look away and get into my own plate. Hmm, these greens sure are good.

"Ra-Ra!" Brianna sings. She skips into the den and wraps her arms around Rashad. "Did you show Dizzy your trophies? You said you were gonna show Dizzy your trophies!"

Nikita smirks and steals a cocktail patty off Gumbo's plate. Rashad shoots me a nervous glance. "Um..."

"You have trophies?" I question with interest.

"We both do." Gumbo grabs some mac and cheese off Nikita's plate and sticks it into his mouth. "But Rashad's got a few trophies that are just for his quarterback stats."

"Well, bring 'em out," I insist.

Rashad smiles at me and walks down the hall. Minutes later, he returns with a few trophies in his arms. He lines them up on the floor, and I marvel at how gorgeous they all look.

Each trophy is topped with a shiny, golden statue of a quarterback in mid-pass. At each base is the engraving: *Rashad du Bois: USA Little League Football Central Jersey Top Quarterback*, along with the specific year. Rashad reclaims his seat next to me. "You can hold 'em if you want, Dizzy."

I wipe my hands with my napkin and pick up the trophy from two years ago. It's a lot heavier than I thought it would be, so I cradle it in my hands carefully.

"Ooohh...you never let *meeee* touch them, Ra-Ra!" Brianna whines. She starts fake crying.

Rashad grabs Brianna and tickles her. "'Cause you're always eating beignets with jelly and you've got jelly fingers!" Brianna giggles crazily and we all hear a loud *Prrrt!*

Brianna glances at all of us sheepishly and snuggles closer to Rashad. I meet eyes with Rashad, who stifles a laugh. Sensing Brianna's embarrassment, he rubs her back and puts his finger to his lips, as if to say, *Act like you didn't hear it.*

Nikita laughs out loud. Chewed food shoots from her mouth. I duck. "Rashad doesn't let anybody up in here touch his trophies," she says, giving me a sly smirk. "He must be crushing hard on you, Desiree."

My entire body freezes up and Rashad turns red. "Desiree's my *friend*, Nikita," he says through gritted teeth.

"Huh! Your friend who you like," Nikita shoots back.

Now Rashad is fuming. "Mind your business!"

I stare at Gumbo, wishing he'd change the subject. To my relief, he winks at me and turns to Nikita. "Let's get some more cocktail patties, Nikita. You know you want 'em."

Brianna laughs. "She doesn't need any more patties."

Nikita gives her a look. "And neither do you." She stands up and yanks her tight jeans higher above her big belly. "Come on, because you know they go quick."

Gumbo and Brianna follow Nikita out of the den, leaving me alone with Rashad. I set his trophy on the table. "These are all really amazing, Rashad. What's next?"

"Well, our season is off to a good start. If we keep it up, we'll hopefully compete in Florida. That's where Phil and I need to be to network with the best high school scouts."

That's a huge goal. As I think about the relatives in the living room, I can't help but feel a little jealous. "You and Phil are lucky to have a big family that supports you, Rashad."

Rashad smiles and nudges my elbow. "Well, we're lucky to have such a cute cheerleader who supports us, too."

I lower my eyes and try not to smile too wide. Brianna pokes her head into the den. "I heard that, Ra-Ra!"

Rashad gives his sister a tight smile. "I wasn't talking to you, Jelly Fingers."

For the rest of the evening, I enjoy the twins' family as they talk and shout excitedly over the Cowboys game. After we're all finished eating, Mr. du Bois initiates a game of charades that leaves me in stitches. The last time my family was gathered like this was last Christmas. Everyone had fun, except for my parents. The only time they spoke to each other was to complain about why my mother's relatives couldn't just go home after the party.

I notice Mr. and Mrs. du Bois standing in the kitchen together. Mrs. du Bois reaches into the fridge and pulls out a cake. It's heavy, and she struggles with it for a moment, but then Mr. du Bois reaches out and takes the cake from her. They share a short kiss and bring the cake into the living room. Watching them makes my eyes tear up, so I turn away before Rashad catches me crying, again. I wish my family could be like his.

I wish *every* family could be like his.

30

The Hallway Showdown

"Dizzy! You're here!" are the first words I hear the next morning at my locker.

I try to focus on entering my combination, but I'm too distracted by Corinne's big, purple-and-green bow. It's paired with an orange sweater, red jeans, and her classic pink boots.

Gumbo looks Corinne up and down. He claps slowly. "Wow, Baby Talk." He checks the imaginary watch on his wrist. "The circus train should be here any minute now."

Corinne glares at Gumbo and places a hand on her hip. "At least I change my look. You come up in here every day with the same, fake leather jacket and crooked sunglasses!"

Rashad cracks up and shakes his head. He turns to me. "Dizzy, did your mom like the leftovers?"

The air suddenly feels too thick to breathe. I can feel the heat of Corinne's suspicious glare as she slowly glances from me to Rashad. "Leftovers from what?"

Gumbo gives Corinne a snide smile. "Oh, didn't Dizzy tell you? She came over for dinner last night and ate with our family. We sent a to-go plate for her mom."

Corinne turns to me with a raised eyebrow. She looks heated. "You never told me that."

Gumbo smirks. "Did she tell you that she came over to play video games with us on Saturday, too? We had a blast!"

I shoot daggers at Gumbo, wishing he'd shut up. Feeling helpless, I turn to Rashad, but he's too busy thumbing through his Spanish folder for his homework. Meanwhile, Corinne's skinny fingers clutch her books in anger. "You didn't tell me about video games either, Dizzy."

Jesus, take the wheel. This is too much.

"Corinne, I'll explain at cheer practice," I insist.

"You'd better." Corinne flounces off to class in a huff. I glance past her and see Chauncey headed this way. No!

I try to wave him away, but it's too late. The twins already see him coming at us and smile sneakily. "Here comes Spots," Rashad mutters to Gumbo. "You got the picture?"

Gumbo reaches into his science folder and whips out a drawing of a spotted boy. I look closer and see that the boy is wearing a football jersey with the number 96 on it.

I frown. "What are you guys gonna do with that?"

"Put it on Chauncey's back," Gumbo says through a laugh. He points to the boy's face. "Look, I drew the face."

"And I drew the jersey," Rashad says.

My mouth drops open, but no words come out right away. "This isn't a good idea. Why are you doing this?"

Gumbo snorts. "Why not? It's Monday."

"We have to keep Spots in his place," Rashad explains.

"In his place?" I repeat in frustration.

Rashad glances behind him and quiets his voice. "Oh! Oh! Phil, he's coming! Get the tape!"

Gumbo reaches into his locker and yanks out a tape dispenser. He sticks a piece of tape on the drawing and hands it to Rashad, who snickers and hides it behind his back. The back of my neck grows hot with anger. The twins might be my friends, and their family might be everything

I've been missing, but I can't keep quiet about the bullying this time.

"Guys, this is stupid." I try to grab the drawing but I'm too slow. The twins run off and stop Chauncey in his tracks.

"What's up, Spots?" Gumbo asks loudly. A few other kids look on as he grabs Chauncey around his neck.

Chauncey pushes Gumbo away. "Get off me!"

"Jeez, Spots, calm down," Rashad says, stealthily slapping the drawing on Chauncey's back.

Chauncey glares up at Rashad with an angry fire burning in his usually-sad eyes. "At least I've got NFL legacy. Your family's always been nothing but a bunch of wannabes."

My face hits the floor. *Chauncey* has "NFL legacy"? Suddenly, it hits me: the photo of the mystery football player.

Gumbo whips off his sunglasses and shoves Chauncey, who stumbles backwards and catches himself before he falls. "Don't you *ever* talk about our family," Gumbo hisses.

"This fool must be out of his spotted mind." Rashad cups his hands around his mouth. "Hey, everybody! Look at the big, fat cow!" Rashad chants, "Spots. Spots. Spots," until Gumbo joins in, and soon, every kid in the hallway surrounds Chauncey and starts chanting "Spots," too.

I stand by my locker and watch the scene in disgust. All of the voices become one as the word "Spots" grows louder and faster. The whole time, Chauncey stands there looking so helpless. He tries to push past the crowd, but everyone just pushes and spins him around like a ragdoll. My heart cracks in two. This is *so* wrong. Right now, I don't recognize the twins.

Slamming my locker shut, I march up to them and tug on their arms. They whip around and face me. "Guys, this is out of control," I hiss.

"Dizzy, you heard what he said about our family," Rashad snaps, and he doesn't just look angry. He looks hurt.

"I know, Rashad, and that was wrong, but look at what *you* guys started!" I point to the crowd as they shove Chauncey around in circles.

Just then, the first morning bell rings. A collective groan rises from the crowd as everyone backs away from Chauncey and walks to their homerooms.

Rashad walks away and points a finger at Chauncey. "Say something else stupid about our family and you'll be picking your teeth up off that floor." He and Gumbo storm off to Ms. Hernandez's class without another word.

At this point, Chauncey and I are the only two people in the hallway. I walk up to him and remove the drawing from his back. He stares at the drawing, hot anger clouding his face, and shoves it in the trash. "Thanks," he mumbles in shame. His jaw locks as he clutches the books under his arms and walks down the hall.

I dig my fingernails into my palms. Chauncey might be humiliated, but I have to at least *try* and talk to him. "Chauncey, wait! I want to help you!"

At these words, Chauncey stops walking. He turns around and faces me with a skeptical glower. "Why do you even care?"

A lump builds in my throat as I take a small step forward. "People helping people, right? Isn't that what you told me?"

The anger in Chauncey's eyes slowly dims until there's nothing left but sadness. I take a deep breath and walk right up to him. He stares at me like he's trying to figure out who I am. "I don't want your help," he mutters, but his voice wavers slightly, and it's obvious that he doesn't believe his own words.

"I think you need it," I say. Chauncey doesn't answer me and I sigh. "How long have the twins been bullying you?"

Chauncey rubs one of his eyes for what feels like an eternity. "Since last year."

I nod. The twins *were* telling the truth during our video game party. "Well, what happened? Why don't they like you?"

"I don't want to talk about it," Chauncey says, turning away.

"Chauncey, please. For the past two football games, I've watched you stand there and let them insult you. Why don't you tell anyone?"

"I can't, and you'd better not say anything, either."

"Why not?"

"If you start talking, it'll get back to Coach Marino. He'll tell Mr. du Bois, and I may never play at all."

I don't know how to respond. Would Mr. du Bois really make football difficult for Chauncey? How? He treats me like a member of his own family. What am I supposed to do? "Well..."

Chauncey sighs. "Don't say anything, and leave me alone." He goes into the boys' bathroom, leaving me standing in the hallway.

Groaning, I walk into Ms. Hernandez's classroom just before the late bell rings. The twins try to catch my eyes, but I ignore them and take my seat next to Corinne. "Good morning, everyone," Ms. Hernandez announces. "Please take out your Spanish homework."

Out of the corner of my eye, I notice Gumbo scribbling something on a piece of paper. He passes the paper to Rashad, who writes something of his own, whips around, and drops the paper on my desk. I glance at Corinne to make sure she's not looking and open the twins' note. The first half is written in Gumbo's handwriting:

Dizzy,

Are you mad at us? You look pretty mad. Who are you more mad at?

☐ *Me*   ☐ *Rashad*

-Gumbo

I read the rest of the note. It's from Rashad.

Dizzy,

Please don't be mad at me, cuz I wanted to invite you over for video games this Saturday. We can play Mario Kart or whatever you want. Promise.

-Rashad

I stare at Rashad's words with annoyance swirling in my heart. Yeah, it was nice of him to remember how much I like *Mario Kart,* but who cares? I *am* mad at him and Gumbo. The showdown they cooked up against Chauncey in the hallway was awful.

Suddenly, Ms. Hernandez snatches the note off my desk. She reads the twins' message and chuckles. Then she taps her heel on the tiled floor. "Rashad, you and Gumbo can discuss your video game party with Desiree after class."

The twins shift in their seats as giggles erupt throughout the room. I can feel Corinne's eyes burning into the side of my skull, so I stare at my hands. I refuse to look at her. Nope.

"Lunch detention. All three of you," Ms. Hernandez states, letting her sharp gaze fall on me.

Just then, Chauncey returns from the bathroom and hustles to his desk. Ms. Hernandez scolds him for being late and starts taking attendance. I massage my aching temples, thankful that Chauncey wasn't in the room to hear the twins' note.

31

Lunch Detention

At my old school, lunch detentions were reserved for the kids who either talked back to their teachers or were caught fooling around during class time. Today, I'm trapped in the second category, and it's all thanks to the twins.

For the next 45 minutes, Ms. Hernandez is making me sit at Stuart Greene's desk, which is right up against the wall. Rashad sits in the middle of the room and munches on a sandwich, while Gumbo sits on the left side of the room and eats a bag of grapes. I bite into my Granny Smith apple with a loud *CRUNCH!* Ms. Hernandez looks up from her gradebook and shoots me a disapproving glare. I lower my eyes apologetically and she takes a bite of her seafood paella.

Bzzz!

My phone vibrates in the pocket of my jacket, and I glance at Ms. Hernandez to make sure she didn't hear it. Thankfully, she's busy grading papers and eating, so I slide my phone out of my pocket and hold it near my lap. I see a thread of text messages and they're all from Corinne.

**Corinne: Girl, Chauncey is here in The Caf WILDIN'
OUT.**
Corinne: He's going crazy. Having a fit.

Corinne: Lunch monitors trying 2 calm him down.
My lunch feels like it's crawling right up my throat.
Me: OMG. Why's he going crazy?
Corinne: Someone posted 2 vids on IG under
#SpotsOuttaControl. Everybody's looking
@ the vids now & making fun of Chauncey.
Corinne: Check IG. Now!

Heart pounding, I fumble around in my other pocket for my earbuds and stick them into the bottom of my phone. I messily shove one bud into my right ear, open Instagram, and type "#SpotsOuttaControl" in the search bar. The first video was posted three minutes ago by an anonymous account and already has 226 views. I play it and almost throw up.

The camera shakes crazily as it captures footage of Chauncey sitting alone at his usual lunch table in the corner. A crowd of kids swarms him, chucking empty milk cartons and plastic food wrappers at his head while screaming the word "Spots." Chauncey bangs his fists on the table, shoots up from his seat, and spins around to face the crowd. He shrieks, "Leave me alone!" over and over again. Two lunch monitors hustle to the scene and motion for everyone to back away, but that's all I see. The video's over and I'm the 227th viewer.

Swallowing a gulp, I open the second video, which was posted by the same anonymous account a few hours ago. This video has over 400 views and shows the terrifying scene from the showdown this morning in the hallway. I guess everybody spent the morning getting their fill on this video, and when lunchtime rolled around, they just gave it to Chauncey.

Suddenly, Ms. Hernandez knocks over her thermos. It clatters against her desk and splatters brown liquid – Coffee? Tea? – all over her pink blouse. She frantically grabs the thermos, shoots up from her desk, and promises us that she'll be right back. Then she turns on her heel, leaving the three of us alone. The twins glance at me, notice my phone in my hand, and frown.

"Why do you have your phone out?" Rashad whispers.

I hold my phone up. "You guys need to see this."

The twins exchange wary glances and walk over to my side of the room. They hover around my desk and I play the Instagram video of Chauncey getting spun around in the hallway. Gumbo scrunches up his face. "Who posted this?"

"I don't know, but whoever it was posted this, too." Clenching my jaw, I play the second video of Chauncey losing his mind in The Caf. The video loops a few times and the twins watch in silence. I can't tell what's going through their minds right now, but they look stone-faced.

"Chauncey's crazy," Rashad finally mutters, turning away from the video. "That's why he said that stupid mess about our family. He deserves what he gets."

"Besides, we didn't post those videos," Gumbo says, "and we didn't tell whoever *did* post them to do it."

I shove my phone into my pocket. "But guys, *you* caused this. If you hadn't riled everyone up in the hallway, there wouldn't be any Instagram videos right now."

Rashad shrugs and shakes his head. "Dizzy, we can't control what other people do."

"But you can control what you do," I shoot back.

"So, you *are* mad at us, then," Gumbo says. I stare at him, suddenly remembering the note that got me stuck here in the first place. Even though I want to be furious with the twins, I just can't. They're my friends; their family watches and feeds me every day after school; they welcomed me into their home; Mr. du Bois carried *me* home. But I just hate the way they bullied Chauncey with that stupid drawing and caused these Instagram videos.

Instead of answering Gumbo, I turn away from him. Rashad stares at me nervously and kneels right in front of my desk so that we're at eye level. "You can't ignore us, Desiree." When I don't answer, his eyes grow more worried and he drums his fingers on my desk. "So, you hate us now?"

I shake my head tiredly. "I don't *hate* you, Rashad."

"Are you coming over for video games on Saturday?"

I turn away. More video games at the du Bois' place does sound like fun, but not if the evening includes another round of water-filled Super Soakers aimed at Chauncey. "I don't think so, Rashad."

Rashad looks crushed. Gumbo stares at his brother and turns to me. "Aw, come on, Dizzy. We're sorry about the note. We didn't mean to get you in trouble."

Click-click-click.

Our eyes dart to the door. The twins fly back to their desks and sit down just before Ms. Hernandez enters the room. The stain on her blouse is much lighter than it was earlier. She reclaims her seat behind her desk, while the twins and I resume our lunches in silence. I sneak my phone out of my pocket and shoot a quick text to Corinne.

Me: Thx 4 telling me about Chauncey.

Corinne: Ur welcome, but don't get it twisted. U still owe me an explanation about leftovers AND video game parties 2nite @ cheer practice.

I groan and shove my phone back into my pocket, wishing that I could wake up and find out that today was nothing but a bad dream.

32

Spilling the Tea

Coach Robin's long, track pant-covered legs sashay to the front of the gym. She wraps her glossed lips around her whistle and blows, officially marking the start of tonight's cheer practice.

"Good evening, my Pirettes!" Coach Robin bellows.

"Good evening, Coach Robin!" we all shout back. My eyes peel over to the opposite side of the gym, where Corinne stands next to a few taller girls on our squad. I exhale softly and try to shield myself behind Maya Anderson's big belly. I won't have to explain anything to Corinne about leftovers or video game parties at the du Bois' place if she doesn't see me in here tonight.

Coach Robin claps her hands. "Warm up: sit-ups! Everyone grab a partner!"

Oh, come *on!*

I frantically reach out to Maya, but she's already hustling over to acne-picking Carly Cartwright. Panicking, my eyes dart around the gym in search of another partner, but everyone is already paired up...except for Corinne. Of course.

"Thirty sit-ups per partner! Go!" Coach Robin says. She blows her whistle again.

My sneakers feel like bricks as I trudge over to Corinne. "You can go first," she snaps, pointing to the gym floor. I sink my teeth into the sides of my tongue and I lie on the floor with my hands behind my head. Corinne crouches down and digs her sharp, bony knees into my sneakers. "So. How was lunch detention with the twins?" she demands, her voice loaded with ice.

"It was detention. We didn't talk much." My heart pounds as I struggle to lift my body back and forth. Maybe if I did this more often, my stomach would be flat like Corinne's.

"I bet you guys had a lot to say at The Crunch Bowl," Corinne shoots back.

"We didn't say much there, either." In reality, Gumbo did all the talking about new gum flavors he plans to sell. Rashad and I listened and ate our food, but we didn't speak.

"I don't believe you." Corinne digs her knees further into my sneakers and I try not to wince at the pain. "Not after you lied to me about leftovers and video game parties!"

Her accusing voice is like a knife slicing right through my ears. I sit up and meet her eye to eye. "I'm sorry I didn't tell you about that stuff, but there's more to the story than you know."

"Yeah, right," Corinne quips. It's time for us to switch positions, so she lies on her back while I rest my knees on her feet.

"I didn't want to tell anybody, but I'm trying to figure out why the twins bully Chauncey," I say.

Corinne effortlessly completes sit-up after sit-up. "What do you care about *him* for?"

"Because back in my old school, there was this girl who picked on me. I know how it feels," I state. "And plus, when I first moved to Treeless Park, Chauncey carried my bags upstairs to my apartment. He didn't have to do that, you know."

"Hm," Corinne mutters. "What have you found out so far?"

"Bits and pieces. The twins have been bullying Chauncey since last year, but Chauncey's too scared to say anything. He thinks Mr. du Bois will take away his playing time."

"He could be right." Corinne does three more sit-ups with ease and I stare at her with envy. "So, you saw the videos I texted you about?" she continues. "I didn't. I don't have Instagram."

"I saw them both," I say. "I even showed the twins, but they acted like they didn't care. They thought Chauncey deserved it."

Corinne finishes her last sit-up and looks me in the eyes. "Maybe they have a reason."

"Well, of course they do," I say. Coach Robin blows her whistle again and we switch our warm-up to knee-highs. "I'm...really sorry I didn't tell you...about my weekend plans...Corinne," I pant against the rhythm of our exercise. "How can I...make it up to you?"

Corinne lifts her knees four times before cutting her eyes at me. "My birthday's on Friday. I was gonna invite you to my place for a sleepover party."

"Oh! That sounds fun. Are any other girls invited?"

"Just you. The talent showcase is next Monday, so I wanted to finalize our routine." She narrows her eyes at me. "Unless you're too busy eating *leftovers* with the twins' family."

Ouch. I deserved that one.

Just then, Maya and Carly approach me with jealous, turned-up lips. "So, you're going out with Rashad?" Maya demands.

I take a step back and blink a few times. My mouth opens and closes, but no words come out.

Carly squints her eyes at me. "We heard you were at their apartment for dinner. You must think you're special or something."

"Hold up. Y'all are too nosy," Corinne suddenly snaps. She glares at Maya and Carly. "Dizzy *is* special, because Rashad *invited* her to dinner. Come on, Girl." She grabs my arm and leads me away from them. Thank God they're not invited to Corinne's party.

I stare at Corinne curiously and think back to Tatyana. Although Corinne's complexion is lighter than Tatyana's, I've never heard her say I was "too dark" for Rashad to like. She's only been supportive. Hmm...I guess not everyone with light skin thinks like Tatyana. Corinne's cool.

"Thanks, Corinne. I *promise* I'll be at your sleepover," I say.

Corinne's suspicious eyes glaze over my face. Finally, she grins her usual bubbly grin and wraps me in a hug. "We'll have so much fun, Dizzy! There's a *very* special guest coming."

"Really? Who?"

"You'll find out on Friday. I'll text you my address after we practice our routine."

I give Corinne a big thumbs-up. If going to her sleepover party will get our friendship back to normal, I'll do it in a heartbeat.

33

Glimmer Glamour

On Tuesday, after cheer practice, my mother speaks with Corinne's grandmother about the sleepover party. My mother agrees to drop me off at their place on Friday at 6:00 p.m., and Corinne's grandmother will drive me home the next morning after we eat breakfast. Corinne spends all of Wednesday's lunch period going over the party schedule, which she begs me to write on a napkin.

- 6:00 – Dizzy arrives!
- 6:15–7:15 – Party games!
- 7:15–8:00 – Dance rehearsal!
- 8:00–9:00 – Dinner & cake!
- 9:00–11:00 – Makeovers + movie time!
- 11:00 – Sleepover time!

This is going to be boring, but I don't tell Corinne.

I ask Corinne about the "surprise guest," but she insists on keeping it a secret.

When I'm not party-planning with Corinne, I'm sneaking looks across The Caf at Chauncey, who finally got wise and now sits by the lunch monitor. The twins sit at a table and mind their own business. I'm thankful because it's the only time I can get a moment of peace from them, especially from Rashad.

He's been sitting next to me on every bus ride, carrying my books to class, and even sharing his food with me at The Crunch Bowl. I know he's trying to butter me up so I'll come over to play video games again. Instead of calling him out, I keep quiet. I'd hate to embarrass him and ruin what's left of our friendship.

On Thursday evening, I push the twins to the back of my mind and accompany my mother to Glimmer Glamour, where we browse the aisles for the perfect birthday present for Corinne. The store is packed with dresses, tops, and other accessories that sparkle with glitter and shimmery fabric.

My mother glances around the store with a concerned frown. "Does Corinne really want something from here?"

I lead her deeper into the store. "Yes, Mommy. Corinne talks about this place all the time. This is her *store*."

My mother picks up a pack of thin headbands and grimaces when she sees the price tag. "These people must be crazy," she mutters, slapping the headbands back on the rack.

"Mommy, those were too plain. Corinne would want something flashy." Because that's exactly who Corinne is.

"How much is 'flashy' going to cost me?" my mother asks with a laugh. I turn away from her and spot something hanging up high on the wall. It's a sequined dress decorated with a gorgeous swirl pattern of pinks, blues, yellows, and reds. Each swirl is lined with a thick black trim and bedazzled with diamonds. It's cute enough to be fashionable and loud enough to turn heads. It's *perfect* for Corinne.

"Mommy! Up there!" I exclaim, pointing to the dress.

My mother takes one look at the dress and stares at me like I'm crazy. "Would Corinne really wear *that* to *school*?"

"Yes! Mommy, you should see her. She dresses like she's going to a costume party every single day."

"And this is your friend?"

I grin and nod excitedly. "Yeah."

My mother stares at me for a long moment. Then she waves her hand in the air and motions for a sales clerk to come over. The clerk looks about 16 years old, and she's wearing an electric blue weave. Her name tag says "Rashida."

"Y'all need some help?" Rashida asks, smacking on a big wad of blue gum.

My mother nods. "Yes, we'd like that dress up there."

Rashida nods. "Let me get the ladder." She breezes past us, swaying her hips in a pair of cosmic leggings. They look *so* cool.

"Do you sell those leggings here?" I ask Rashida.

"Yeah, girl. They're on clearance. Two for ten dollars." Rashida flicks her head towards a rack by the window. Sure enough, there are plenty of cosmic leggings to choose from.

"Mommy! Those would be perfect for our dance routine! Can we get those, too?"

My mother nods tiredly. Grinning, I snatch up two pairs of leggings and watch Rashida pull Corinne's dress off the rack.

"Giselle!" a familiar voice calls from the opposite end of the aisle. My mother and I turn around and meet eyes with Mrs. du Bois, who sashays over to us. Brianna skips behind her mother, clutching a pack of sparkly hair ribbons.

"Hey, 'Liv!" my mother says. They exchange a round of compliments about each other's hair and outfits, while Brianna wraps her little arms around my waist and twists me back and forth. Since I've been having a tough time with her brothers, receiving her hug makes me feel guilty. I force my lips into a smile and rub my palm on her back. She's too little to be caught up in any drama.

Rashida finally comes down from the ladder and hands my mother the swirly dress. "Y'all need any more help?" she asks.

My mother shakes her head and Rashida flounces off, grinning at something on her phone. My mother smiles down at Brianna. "I see you're out with your pretty baby," she says to Mrs. du Bois.

"And you with yours," Mrs. du Bois says, smiling at me. She pulls Brianna close and rubs her face tenderly. "Brianna and I are taking a quick break from the restaurant. We mothers have to stick *so* close to our daughters, especially after what happened with that little nine-year-old. The poor child didn't even have a chance. My heart just breaks when I think about her."

The corners of my mother's mouth curl down with worry. "What are you talking about?"

"It was on CNN today, Chile. This little girl from Alabama was bullied by her classmates because of her dark complexion." Mrs. du Bois shakes her head sadly and blinks her tearing eyes. "She took her life this morning. Her mother found her."

The store feels like it's spinning. I turn to my mother, whose face is twisted in shock. "'Liv, what are you *telling* me?"

Mrs. du Bois frowns and whips out her phone. She taps and scrolls a few times before showing us a CNN article with the headline: **9-year-old commits suicide after being victimized by racist bullying**. Below the headline is a photo of a little girl. The photo's caption reads: **McKayla Arlington**.

"How does a nine-year-old figure out how to take her life?" Mrs. du Bois asks in a low voice. "And where do these children learn this hatred for dark complexions at such a young age?"

"Girl, when it comes to our children, we have to be like *this*." My mother crosses her fingers. Mrs. du Bois nods sadly and squeezes Brianna's hand, while I try to calm my racing heart. I've heard stories of teenagers and adults who suffered from depression and took their lives, but to do it at nine? It doesn't make any sense.

My mind flashes back to that awful phone call I had with Priya and Tatyana. On that call, Tatyana said something so mean to me: *"You're just too dark..."* I'll never forget it.

As her words replay in my head, I can't help but feel angry. I hate to think about what Tatyana would have said to or about McKayla. Even though Tatyana's words never made *me* want to take my life, there could be another girl somewhere with my complexion who *would* want to. It's just so wrong.

I take a shuddery, deep breath and think about how the twins always call Chauncey "Spots" and how they turned everyone against him during that hallway showdown. Being the subject of some torture like that would be enough to make anybody want to take their life. I need to talk to the twins about this bullying situation before it gets out of control, and I know the perfect place to do it.

I reach into my purse, whip out my phone, and shoot the twins a text.

Me: Hey. Wud luv 2 come over for video games again if u guys r still up for it. Let me know.

For a while, no one responds. I start to panic, when finally, a reply from Gumbo appears at the bottom of the screen.

Gumbo: Hey Dizzy. Sounds gr8!!!

I sigh and stare at my phone in search of a text from Rashad. The video game invitation won't feel complete unless he responds, too. A long moment passes before I see a private message pop into my inbox.

Rashad: Wut made you change ur mind?

My chest tightens. I can't tell him or Gumbo why I really want to come over. They'll find out on Saturday.

Me: We're friends aren't we?

Rashad: Of course. It's just that u were so mad...

I bite my bottom lip anxiously. If I'm going to make this happen, I'll have to act like everything's normal.

Me: Not mad anymore. ☺

Rashad: Cool. See u Saturday. I'll pick u up like last time. ☺

I exhale in relief and put my phone away. To be honest, I feel really bad for keeping my true "video game" intentions a secret from the twins, but it's the risk I have to take in order to get to the bottom of this bully situation. If the twins aren't careful, their bullying could force Chauncey into the same corner as McKayla Arlington, and by then, it will be too late.

34

Real Friends

On Friday evening, I swap my school clothes for a cute party dress with a beaded collar. I put a small curl in the front of my hair and comb the rest into an elegant bun. I scour my bedroom for my sleeping bag, pajamas, and Corinne's birthday presents. I quickly grab a t-shirt and leggings to change into tomorrow morning. Then I snatch my toothbrush and toothpaste from the hallway bathroom and follow my mother outside. We hop into our car and she immediately gets her Motown going. This time, it's a classic: *Ain't No Mountain High Enough*, by Marvin Gaye and Tammi Terrell.

"Whoo! C'mon, Marvin! Sing it, Tammi!" My mother jams on the gas pedal and cranks up the volume. I mindlessly scroll through Instagram's "explore" feed and land on a post from Priya. I haven't heard from her or Tatyana since I told them off last week, but with my thumb hovering over Priya's picture, I can't help but take a closer look.

It's a crisp shot of Priya and Tatyana engaged in a fake sword fight with a pair of pool cues. Behind them is a pool table, and in the corner, I see the edge of a carpet and a giant flat screen TV. It's Priya's fancy basement.

As I stare at the picture, the beaded collar on my party dress feels like it's choking me. I think back to the countless hours I spent in that basement, back when I lived next door.

"You've reached your destination," says my mother's GPS. We're parked in front of a brick building with barred windows and three levels of fire escapes. There are air conditioning units sitting in some of the windows.

I take another glance at Priya's castle-sized basement and fancy pool equipment. All of that stuff was definitely fun while we were still friends, but after learning how stuck-up and jealous she and Tatyana have become, I don't miss that basement for a second. She can keep it *and* the pool table.

"Dizzy!" someone calls. I glance up from my phone and smile when I see Corinne. She's standing in the doorway, waving like she hasn't seen me in years. Her birthday tiara is way too big for her head, but she wears it proudly.

"Happy Birthday, Corinne!" I call excitedly. I push myself out of the car, grab the gifts and sleepover essentials from the backseat, and follow my mother to Corinne's front door. With each step I take, Corinne's smile grows wider, like I'm the gift she's been waiting for.

My mother grins at Corinne and tells her "Happy Birthday." Then she turns to Corinne's grandmother. "Thank you so much for having Desiree."

"It's our pleasure. We'll have her back home safe and sound tomorrow morning," Ms. Corelle insists.

My mother wraps me in a tight hug and tells me to have a great time with Corinne. Then she waves goodbye to Corinne's grandmother, hops into her Audi, and drives away.

I take a last glance at Priya's picture and close out of Instagram altogether. Who needs a big basement with a pool table when the people you used to play with were never real friends in the first place?

35

Anita

"**I**s this for me?" Corinne asks once we shut the front door. She snatches the gift bag out of my hand and rummages through the colorful paper like she's on a mission.

Ms. Corelle shoots me an apologetic glance and clears her throat. "Corinne? Don't you think it's best to show Desiree around before you start opening her gift?"

Corinne freezes in mid-rummage. "Sorry, Grandma." She reluctantly lifts her hand out of the bag, but doesn't let go of the handle. "Come on, Dizzy! I'll give you the grand tour."

Ms. Corelle smiles as I follow Corinne around the apartment, which is smaller than mine and looks like it was furnished a long time ago. There's a living room that joins into a kitchenette, one bathroom, and two bedrooms.

Corinne faces me with an embarrassed shrug. She gestures around her apartment. "I know it's not much, but..."

I don't let her finish. "It's just fine, Corinne, really. Am I allowed to see your room?"

The worried lines in Corinne's face instantly brighten. "I thought you'd never ask." She twists the tarnished knob on the door closest to the bathroom and ushers me into a room filled with brightly colored fabrics and threads. I notice a twin bed pushed up against the wall and an oval mirror hanging above a dresser. Sitting on the dresser is a collection of books by the incredible Maya Angelou. My face lights up. Any friend with a notable book collection is someone I want to be around.

I start to ask Corinne about those books, when suddenly, I spot a white contraption sitting on the floor. My eyebrows shoot up in surprise. "You have a sewing machine?"

Corinne flounces over to her dresser. "Don't you?" I shake my head sheepishly and she smiles. "Girl, I sew *all* my clothes! You should let me teach you sometime."

"Who taught *you?*"

"My grandma's been teaching me since I was little. Why spend money on other people's clothes when you can make your own?"

Her question leaves me speechless. I place my hand against the sewing machine's smooth, white surface and glance around at the sea of colorful fabrics. "Where do you get all your fabrics from?"

"A fabric store downtown. I go there all the time."

"Well, what about the inspirations for your outfits?"

"I read this magazine called *Fashionista, Ooh-La-La,* see what's hot in Glimmer Glamour, and...ooh!" She opens her top dresser drawer and unveils a pack of tattered sketchbooks. "Before I sew anything, I always sketch it out first."

Corinne shoves her sketchbooks in my arms and grins as I flip through her masterpieces. Each page is decorated with unique pencil drawings of shirts, blouses, and poufy skirts. Priya and Tatyana were *never* this creative.

"These are really amazing, Corinne." I smile and gently place her sketchbooks back in the drawer. "And what about those Maya Angelou books?"

Corinne hastily shoves a copy of *And Still I Rise* and *Phenomenal Woman* into my hands. "I love, love, *love* Maya Angelou! Sometimes, when I'm not busy, I'll write poetry." I stare at Corinne in surprise. She likes writing, too? Who knew we had so much in common? "Are you familiar with any of Maya Angelou's poems?" Corinne asks me.

I nod. When I was in the third grade, my mother signed me up for a public-speaking program to help me overcome my shyness. I recited *Phenomenal Woman* by Maya Angelou and won the Honors medal for my entire chapter. Maya Angelou was truly a literary queen.

Corinne rubs my beaded collar. "Dizzy, you always have the nicest clothes." A sad smile plays on her lips. "You remind me a lot of my mother."

"Really?"

Corinne nods. "She's so pretty – like you – and a snazzy dresser." She's quiet for a moment, but then her eyes light up. "You'll meet her tonight, though."

My eyes bug out. "Your *mom*? *She's* the special guest?"

Corinne bites her bottom lip and nods excitedly. "She'll be here soon. For now, let's get this party started!" She digs through her gift bag and unveils the swirly dress from Glimmer Glamour. "*Oooooohhhh!*" she squeals.

"You really like it?"

"I *love* it! Thank you, Dizzy! Wait until my mother sees me in *this!*" Corinne rushes into the bathroom and moments later emerges wearing the swirly dress and a pair of plastic star-shaped sunglasses. She looks *amazing*.

I grin and snatch my phone off Corinne's dresser. "Corinne Corelle! Over here!" I shout, snapping a round of pictures paparazzi style.

Corinne strikes a few poses and giggles like a lunatic when I show her the shots I took. "I look just like my mom in these pictures," she says, swiping through each photo. "Dizzy, can you save these so we can show her when she comes?"

I hold out my phone and make a special photo album just for Corinne's runway shots. "You're the birthday queen."

Corinne wraps me in a hug so tight it reminds me of Brianna. "I'm so happy you're here!" She checks the time on my phone and gasps. "Six fifteen! Time for party games!"

For the next hour, Corinne and I rotate between playing Twister, Pictionary, and Speak Out. After a while, Corinne checks her phone. She frowns and scurries over to the living room window, pressing her palms against the glass.

Ms. Corelle sighs sadly and washes a plastic bowl in the kitchen sink. "Corinne, baby, come away from that window." Her voice is tired, like she's said these words before.

Corinne doesn't budge. "But Grandma, Mom said she would be here by now," she whines in a small voice.

Ms. Corelle walks up to Corinne and wraps an arm around her skinny frame. She leads Corinne away from the window and speaks in a low, kind voice. "Why don't you and Desiree move on to the next activity? Isn't it dance rehearsal?"

The worried lines on Corinne's face seem to relax slightly. "Oh, yeah." She smooths out her swirly dress and helps me up off the floor. "Come on, Dizzy! Let's finish our showcase routine, and when my mom gets here, we'll dance for her! She'll be so excited!"

Ms. Corelle doesn't say anything; she just sets the table. A worried knot forms in my stomach, but I keep quiet and cue up *Level Up* on my phone.

Corinne and I rehearse every pop, bend, twist, and jump until we know the entire routine cold. When I reach into my duffel bag and pull out the matching cosmic leggings, she loses her mind. "Are those from *Glimmer Glamour*?"

I nod eagerly. "We can wear them with plain black t-shirts. What do you think?"

"I *think* you're a genius," Corinne says. She rubs her hand against the stretchy fabric and grins. "This is just like something my mom would wear. Dizzy, what time is it?"

My eyes dart to my phone screen and I gulp. "It's, uh, eight-oh-five," I reveal softly.

Corinne's face falls. "Already?" She checks her phone and hurries back to the window. "But...she isn't here yet."

Ms. Corelle walks over to Corinne and leads her away from the window - again. "Corinne, honey, it's time for dinner. I made your favorite."

Corinne's face lights up. "Chicken stew over rice?"

Ms. Corelle nods and smiles at me. "I hope that's all right with you, Desiree."

"Yes, that's fine," I say. Honestly, chicken stew over rice is something I eat when I'm getting over a cold, but this lady won't hear any complaints from me. I take a seat at the table and put on a big smile as she spoons some clumpy brown liquid onto a plate of rice.

Corinne sits next to me and clasps her hands anxiously. "Grandma, don't forget to set a place for Mom."

"Okay, Corinne. All right," Ms. Corelle says softly.

We join hands and say grace over dinner. Corinne scarfs down her food in minutes, while I pick through my rice and broth in search of the meat. I finally spot a few pieces clumped together with the carrot slices and swallow it all whole. It leaves a weird feeling in my stomach. I hope Ms. Corelle has some air freshener in that bathroom, because...

At 8:45 p.m., Ms. Corelle brings out a vanilla sheet cake with the words "Happy 12th Birthday, Corinne" laced in red icing. She lights the candles and we sing, but when Ms. Corelle gets out the cutting knife, Corinne yelps in anger. "Not until Mom gets here!"

Ms. Corelle sighs and puts the cake back on the counter. "All right. We'll wait a bit longer. Go ahead and start your makeovers and movie time."

To keep Corinne in good spirits, I act like I'm having the best night of my life as we do our makeovers and watch *The Cheetah Girls* on DVD. Corinne knows every word to all the songs, while I just bob my head to the music and let her enjoy herself. Halfway through the film, I get a FaceTime call from Rashad. I hit "Ignore" because there's no way I'm letting him see me in this crazy pink eye shadow, blush, and fake lashes. Instead, I shoot him a text.

Me: Hey. Can't talk right now. At Corinne's bday party.
Rashad: Oh. Phil & I say happy bday. Wanted to know if ur still coming over tmrw.

I shoot him a fast response.

Me: Yes. See u tmrw.

Rashad responds with a thumbs up emoji and I turn my phone off.

"Corinne? Desiree? Come on and get some cake," Ms. Corelle calls from the kitchenette. I shoot up from the floor, while Corinne pouts and stays put.

"But Grandma..." Corinne turns to the window again.

"Corinne? It's ten o'clock at night, honey. We have to cut your cake so you and Desiree can go to bed."

I nervously glance between Corinne and Ms. Corelle. If Corinne's mother doesn't show up soon, Corinne will be devastated. I feel really bad for her, but I'm not sure how much longer I can stay awake.

We finish the night with a few slices of the sheet cake, which tastes amazing. I wash off the makeup, put on my pajamas, and get ready for bed. Corinne hangs by the window and stares out into the night sky. She's still wearing her swirly dress and tiara. I bite my lip and check the time. It's almost midnight and her mother still hasn't shown.

"Corinne?" Ms. Corelle calls from the kitchenette. "It's bedtime. Hang up the dress and put on your pajamas."

Corinne slowly turns from the window and blinks a few times. Her hazel eyes are heavy with sleep. "Come on, Dizzy. You can share my bed," she mutters through a yawn.

I say goodnight to Ms. Corelle and silently follow Corinne into her bedroom. She changes into a pink nightgown and curls herself up in the corner of her twin bed. I lay at the opposite end of her bed with my head next to her feet. "Night, Corinne," I whisper, but she doesn't answer me; she's already snoring.

For the next few minutes, I lay awake and think about Corinne's mother. Where is she, and why didn't she show up to her birthday party? I think back to last weekend, when my father promised to take me out on a pizza date. I'd gotten all dressed up and waited for his call, only for him to cancel at the last minute. I close my eyes and let a few tears slip down my cheeks, feeling sorry for Corinne, but grateful that we're friends. I guess we're not so different after all.

"Shh! Be quiet!"

At the sound of Ms. Corelle's voice, my eyes fly open.

"Come on, Ma. I got here as soon as I could. Move!"

I sit up straight. Who could that be?

"Anita, it's after midnight!" Ms. Corelle says gruffly. "Come back in the morning!" Someone bumps around.

Aw, no. I've got to catch this confusion *right* now.

Moving like a ninja, I slip out of Corinne's bed and creep over to the bedroom door. Then I pull the door open a crack to hear more and peer out into the hallway.

Standing in the living room with Ms. Corelle is a short, skinny woman carrying a few gifts. Her face is pale and swallowed beneath a dark brown weave that hangs into the shoulders of her skin-tight cheetah print dress. Her legs are covered in a pair of red thigh-high boots, the heels of which sink deep into the carpet as she walks towards the couch. "I'm here to see my baby. Now, go get her."

Oh. My. Gosh. It's Corinne's mother???

"Anita, Corinne is asleep!" Ms. Corelle snaps. "She waited for you all night and you never came! Do you ever get tired of disappointing this child?"

"Mama, you know how my jobs are. I clean the motel during the day, and at night, I'm at the hospital checking in the patients."

"Why don't you look for something else so you can spend more time with Corinne?"

"I can't switch jobs right now. I need the money."

"Well, Corinne needs *you!*" Ms. Corelle says. "You live right upstairs, Anita, but Corinne hardly sees you."

"I'm here now." She approaches the bedroom, but Ms. Corelle blocks her. I dip back. I can't let them see me.

"No! It's too late!" Ms. Corelle shrieks. I peek out again and see her face twisted into the angriest scowl. "And take them heels off! Coming in here all late, just steppin' and poppin' and pokin' holes into my good rug!"

I have to wake Corinne up *now.* I rush to Corinne and shake her awake. "Corinne! Corinne, your mother's here!" Corinne's eyes peel open. "She is?" I nod quickly and yank Corinne out of her bed. "Mommy?" she calls, pushing her way through the bedroom door.

Anita locks eyes with Corinne and her hard face melts. "Corinne? Baby? Mommy's here." She pushes past Ms. Corelle and wraps Corinne in a tight hug.

"Mommy, this is my friend Dizzy." Corinne grabs my wrist and pulls me forward. "She's in my class and we do cheer and she dresses real nice, just like you."

My heart pounds as Anita's hazel eyes rest on me. Her red lips crack into a hideous smile. "It's so nice to meet you," she says, breathing her bad breath in my face. Father, God. I jump back and lean into the hallway bathroom. It smells just like Lysol and Ms. Corelle's chicken stew dinner. At least it's better than Anita's nasty breath.

"Mommy, I saved you some cake," Corinne continues. "Are you gonna stay? I'll show you the dress that Dizzy got me, and we've been working on this dance routine for the talent showcase coming up..."

"I wish I could stay, but it's too late," Anita says. Ms. Corelle grunts. Anita glares at Ms. Corelle like a dragon and turns to Corinne with softer eyes. "I'll be back soon, Baby."

"How soon?" Corinne asks. "Will you come to see me cheer at Sunday's game?"

Anita glances off. "If I'm not working."

Suddenly, the fierce honk of a car horn penetrates the silence. "Anita! Come on, Girl! We're already late for the party!" a deep voice shouts from outside.

Anita glares at the door. "Reggie! I'm coming!"

Ms. Corelle frowns. "Where are you going now?"

"Out with a few friends." Anita gives Corinne a quick hug and kisses her cheek. "Happy Birthday, Baby Girl."

Before Corinne can say another word, Anita hands her the gifts and walks out of the apartment. Ms. Corelle sighs in exhaustion and tells us to go back to bed. I follow Corinne into her room and we get under her bed covers.

"Is...Reggie your dad?" I ask in a meek voice.

Corinne doesn't answer me right away. "No. I don't know who that was."

My heart aches as I stare at the ceiling in silence. I reach for my phone on Corinne's nightstand and shoot off a quick text.

Me: Good night, Mommy. I love you.

As I close my eyes and start to drift off, I say a special prayer for my mother and thank God that Corinne has her grandmother in her life.

36

Worm Tooth

The morning car ride home is silent except for the gentle hum of Ms. Corelle's radio. She's playing Gospel.

I sit in the back of her car next to Corinne, who stares out the window. She was quiet all during our breakfast of eggs, pancakes, and grits. I know she was thinking of her mother.

After a rigid 20-minute ride, Ms. Corelle drops me off in front of Manny's Fish Market. My mother meets us outside. I fly out of the car and wrap her in the biggest hug.

"Thank you so much!" my mother calls to Ms. Corelle.

Ms. Corelle waves from her spot in the driver's seat and peels away. Corinne kneels on the backseat and smiles at me through the rear window, but there's sadness behind her smile. I wave back, squeezing my mother's hand.

"I got your text, Baby," my mother says, smiling as we walk upstairs to our apartment. "How about the two of us go to the movies tomorrow evening?" I nod gratefully. I love spending time with my mother. "Did you have a nice time at the party?" she asks.

"Yeah, it was fun." That's all I say. I'll never have the heart to tell my mother about Anita. If my mother knew, she'd probably never let me hang out with Corinne again, and that wouldn't be fair. Corinne and I need each other. We're friends.

"That's nice," my mother says. "Is...Rashad picking you up for video games today?"

My spirits rise. Amongst the confusion with Corinne's mother, I completely forgot about the twins and Chauncey.

"He's coming at six," I say, and he does.

At 5:59 p.m., after I've finished taking notes on energy and matter from our science textbook, Rashad arrives to my apartment. The weather's been unusually mild, so he's got his football jacket draped over one shoulder. He grins as he escorts me down the steps of Manny's Fish Market. "How was Corinne's birthday party?" he asks me.

Say only good things. "Oh, we had fun."

"Cool." His smile dims slightly. "You met her mom?"

My entire mouth goes dry. "I...um...yeah," I squeak.

Rashad nods, and we're both quiet for a long moment. Thankfully, he changes the subject. "I'm glad you decided to come over, Dizzy." He leads me outside and stops on the sidewalk. "I was...starting to wonder if we were still friends." There's a small laugh in his voice, but his eyes look sad.

My heart lurches. I love the du Bois family, and I love the way they make me feel like I'm *part* of their family, but I also care about Chauncey. I put a hand on Rashad's shoulder. "We'll always be friends," I tell him.

Rashad smiles slightly. "Promise?" I nod and he cuts his eyes at me. "Prove it."

I take a small step back and glance between each of Rashad's light brown eyes. How am I supposed to "prove" my loyalty to this friendship? That's when I glance down at the extra, skinny fingernail that's been growing out of my left pinky for as long as I can remember. The nail looks like a worm's tooth, and no matter how many times I clip it, it always grows back. It's so gross, and I've always been super embarrassed about it, but for Rashad, I'll expose it proudly.

I hold my pinky out to Rashad. "Pinky swear."

Rashad stares at my pinky's worm tooth and busts out laughing. "Girl, what *is* this?" he asks, grabbing my pinky.

My face heats up. "It's an extra nail, okay? It looks like a worm's tooth. I know. It's gross." Rashad cracks up even harder. I try to look serious. "Look, I've never liked showing this thing off, so is this enough to prove we're friends or not?"

"Yeah, it is," Rashad says, still laughing. He wraps his extra nail-less pinky around mine and smiles. "I think this worm tooth makes you very unique, Desiree Davenport."

"Thank you, Rashad du Bois," I say. Rashad grins and I really wish I could grin along with him, but I can't. Not yet. "But Ra, good friends are real with each other, right?"

"Of course." Rashad looks serious. "What's going on?"

I take a deep breath and start to talk about McKayla Arlington, when suddenly, I spot Chauncey approaching Manny's from the opposite end of the block.

Thinking quickly, I snatch Rashad's football jacket out of his hand and take off running the other way.

"Hey!" Rashad shouts, but I keep running. I have to lead him away from Chauncey. My lips stretch into a crazy grin as I glance over my shoulder. Rashad is right on my heels, so I pick up my pace. Then, out of nowhere...

"Aah!" I trip over the uneven sidewalk and crash to the ground. I land on my left knee, which forms a circle of blood beneath the thin fabric of my pink leggings. The pain is unbearable, and it takes everything in me not to cry.

37

The Phone Call

"Dizzy!" Rashad yells. He crouches next to me on the sidewalk. "Dang, Girl! Are you okay?"

I glance past Rashad and see Chauncey going into the fish store, unbothered. If it took a little blood to save Chauncey from another round of bullying, it was well worth it. "Yeah...yeah, I'm fine," I tell Rashad.

"Good," Rashad breathes. I hand him his football jacket and he stares at me with a bewildered frown. "Why'd you just run off with my jacket like that?"

The pain in my knee makes my head spin, but I pull myself together and think of an explanation. "I...just wanted to see if I could race you and win." The lie slips out of my mouth like butter, and I feel terrible for hiding the truth from Rashad, but it's what I have to do right now.

Rashad seems to buy my race story, because his face relaxes and he helps me stand up. "You're crazy, Desiree Davenport. You know you can't beat me," he says, laughing. He wraps my arm around his shoulders and helps me as I limp down the sidewalk. "Come on. I'll take you back home."

"No, don't you guys have Band-Aids?"

Rashad hesitates for a second, but finally shrugs. "Yeah. My mom can take care of you." We walk towards his apartment. "You know, the Pirates could use another wide receiver," he says, smirking.

I cut my eyes at him. "Sure. I'll take Gumbo's spot."

Rashad's dimples cave in as he laughs. "Let's not get ahead of ourselves, Pony Boots."

We walk upstairs to his family's apartment, where Gumbo gallops around the living room with Brianna on his back. "Faster, Phil! Faster!" Brianna cries.

Gumbo starts to gallop around the couch, but freezes when he sees me standing with Rashad. "Uh...hey, Dizzy," he mutters with an embarrassed grin. His eyes flick to my knee and he frowns. "What happened to *you?*"

"She tripped," Rashad says. "Where's Mom?"

Gumbo puts Brianna on the floor and yells for Mrs. du Bois, who emerges from the hallway. When the twins tell her that I scraped my knee, she orders me to sit on the couch and rummages through the hallway bathroom medicine cabinet for some bandages and disinfectant wipes. I pull my legging above my scraped knee, and in a few minutes, Mrs. du Bois has my knee all cleaned up.

"Dizzy, you ready for *Mario Kart?*" Gumbo asks. He and Rashad lead me into the den and gesture for me to sit in the bean bag chair, just like last week. We grab our controllers and start a race on the Luigi's Mansion course. Even though this is one of my favorites, I don't let myself get too excited and instead focus on what I *really* came here for.

I clear my throat. "Um, guys? There's something I need to talk to you about."

"What's up?" Gumbo asks, his eyes glued to the screen. He socks me with a red turtle shell and my kart spins out of control, but I don't even care.

"There was a story on CNN about a nine-year-old girl named McKayla Arlington," I continue. "She was bullied because of her dark skin and ended up taking her life."

The twins stare at me with a mixture of sadness and discomfort looming on their faces. "Oh...yeah," Rashad moans. "Our mom told us about what happened to her."

Gumbo nods. "It's really sad. She was just a little younger than us."

My heart pounds rapidly. This is good; they're showing compassion for McKayla's story. "Well, don't you guys think all of this is getting out of control?"

Rashad pauses the game and frowns. "What does this story have to do with us?"

I glance at Gumbo, who stares at me with the same confused expression as Rashad. Right now, they look so identical. "You guys really don't know?" I ask lightly. I have to be so careful with how I phrase my words, because the last thing I want to do is make the twins mad. "Guys, you had the whole hallway chanting 'Spots' at Chauncey, which led to the whole Instagram thing. You sprayed water at him through a window. You pick on him every day at lunch. What if Chauncey did the same thing that McKayla did?"

The twins are silent. Rashad's stomach gurgles and he quickly clutches it. "Chauncey wouldn't do that," he says, but I can see traces of guilt and fear on his face.

"How do you know, Ra?" I challenge. "None of us knows how a person feels until they actually do something."

"Well, our situation is different than McKayla's story," Gumbo says. "We don't beef with Chauncey because of the way his skin looks."

"But you do make fun of his skin," I state.

"We only say that stuff 'cause he has vitiligo, but that's not why we hate him," Rashad says.

"Then why *do* you hate him?" I press.

Rashad's eyes sparkle with skepticism. "Desiree, seriously, what is it with you and Chauncey?" he demands. I keep my mouth shut.

"Come on, Dizzy. Can we just play?" Gumbo mumbles tiredly. Rashad's stomach gurgles louder. He drops his controller and grabs his stomach. Gumbo stares at his brother in concern. "You good?"

Rashad shoots me a nervous glance and nods at Gumbo. "I just need to use the bathroom." He stands up and leaves the den, leaving me alone with Gumbo.

"Is Rashad okay?" I ask softly.

"I think so, but...can we just play video games for the rest of the night?" Gumbo asks.

I lower my eyes and grip my hands around my video game controller. "Fine," I say, and I don't bring up Chauncey or bullying or McKayla Arlington for the rest of the night.

At 8:00 p.m., Mr. du Bois comes upstairs from The Crunch Bowl. He slaps the twins high fives and squeezes my shoulder, just like last week, but tonight, I don't feel as close to their family as I did before.

Suddenly, the house phone rings.

"I'll get it," Gumbo says. He stands up and leaves the den. A second passes before his voice rings out through the apartment. "Dad! It's Coach Marino!"

Rashad shoots up and hustles out of the den. I follow because I don't want to be left alone. As Mr. du Bois takes the phone from Gumbo, I chew on my bottom lip nervously.

I ask to use the bathroom and excuse myself from the living room. As I make my way down the hall, I overhear Mr. du Bois speaking with Coach Marino over the phone. "You see my boys' contributions to the team's wins every week," he states. "The Pirates will have a shot at the Super Bowl because of them. You cannot lessen their playing time."

My eyeballs practically pop out of their sockets. I quickly dip into the bathroom and leave the door open a crack so I can hear more.

"Who's complaining?" Mr. du Bois asks. He pauses for a moment before continuing. "It's always the parents who never come to the games who have so much to say."

There's a long, muffled response from Coach Marino.

"You know what football means for my sons," Mr. du Bois says. "I've been busting my back for this team for the past few years. When nobody else wanted to be the Team Parent, I stepped up. I even invite the other boys to work out with the twins on Saturday mornings. Even after what happened with this team last year, I'm *still* here."

My eyes narrow suspiciously as I press my ear closer to the door. Last year was when Chauncey joined the team. Oh, I've got to hear some more of this.

"This team needs my family as a sponsor. Rashad is on track to achieving his goal of completed passes, and he needs Phil out there making those catches. If we make it to Florida this year, that puts my sons on the radar of the best high schools in the state, not to mention colleges nationwide. We're not interested in giving up opportunities to anybody who isn't serious."

He hangs up, causing the phone to make a fierce BLAM! against the receiver. I flush the toilet and turn on the sink so it sounds like I used the bathroom. When I come out, the whole family looks tense, especially Rashad.

Mrs. du Bois puts a hand on her husband's shoulder. "Antwan, don't let this football get to you," she says softly.

"Olivia, you don't understand." Mr. du Bois points to the twins. "Football is their shot at a better life. We have three kids to put through college, and it's right around the corner for the twins. College is more expensive than when we were in school, Olivia. You know we don't have that kind of money saved. We've put everything we have into The Crunch Bowl."

Rashad groans and collapses against the arm of the fluffy couch. He's sweating bullets and he looks nauseous. "P...get me to the bathroom," I hear him mumble.

Gumbo walks over to Rashad and puts the back of his hand on Rashad's forehead. He struggles to help Rashad stand up and turns to his parents. "Ma? Dad?"

No one answers him. "Do you know how important it is for them to make it to Florida *now*?" Mr. du Bois continues. "Florida will open doors to the best private high schools in the state, which will eventually lead to scholarships to the best colleges. This is about securing their education, Olivia, so they have to be the best." He points to Brianna. "When Baby Girl turns seven, she'll do a sport, too. It's not just about academics anymore. That's why they play instruments. These colleges expect you to bring something extra, and for Rashad, it's even more important. He's on his way to becoming the top quarterback with the most completed passes in the Eastern Region. You know how competitive it is for that high school starting quarterback spot. Rashad has to stand out!"

Just then, Rashad burps loudly. We all turn to him in shock. His face contorts in pain as he takes a shaky, deep breath. Mr. du Bois frowns in concern and crosses over to Rashad. "Ra? What's the matter, Son?" he demands.

A strangled grunt shoots out of Rashad's throat. He slaps his hand over his mouth and flies into the hallway bathroom. The next thing I know, we all hear gagging and splattering noises. I gasp in horror.

Mr. du Bois' eyebrows shoot up. "Rashad!" he cries. He glares at Gumbo. "Boy, your brother's sick and you didn't say anything?" he snaps, hustling into the bathroom.

"Dad, I tried, but you weren't listening!" Gumbo shouts after his father.

Brianna starts crying. Mrs. du Bois puts her on the couch and follows Mr. du Bois to the bathroom. "Lord, if it isn't one thing, it's another," she mutters.

My throat closes up. I hear Rashad clearing his throat and his parents talking in low voices. "Come on, Son. Let me wipe your mouth," Mr. du Bois says.

"Hold his head over the sink," Mrs. du Bois says. "It's all right, my dear. Let me get you something for your stomach, okay? You're putting too much pressure on him, Antwan."

Gumbo sighs and turns to me. "Dizzy, I'll walk you home." Brianna cries harder and extends her arms towards Gumbo. He rubs her back softly. "I'll be right back, Bri. I promise. I'm just going across the street real quick."

As Gumbo leads me out of the apartment, I think about Rashad and the pressure he's under. "Is Rashad gonna be okay?" I ask.

Gumbo rubs his nose. "Yeah. Don't tell anybody, but Rashad always gets a bad stomach whenever he's anxious. He's been that way ever since we were little."

My heart plummets as I think back to my McKayla Arlington conversation. Rashad's stomach was acting funny from back then. "Is it...my fault?" I ask timidly. I wasn't trying to make Rashad sick. I was only trying to help him see why bullying is wrong.

"Well, I think all the stuff you said *did* freak him out a little," Gumbo admits. I cringe and he keeps talking. "But it's not your fault Rashad puked. It was all of my dad's talking." I nod silently and he gives me the side-eye. "So... how much did you hear my dad say?"

"What are you talking about?" I ask lightly.

"Dizzy, look, I know you heard what my dad said to Coach Marino on the phone, okay?"

There's an edge to Gumbo's voice that causes the back of my neck to heat up. There's no point in lying.

As Gumbo and I walk through the back door of Manny's Fish Market and climb the stairs, he stares at me with a worried expression. "What?" I whisper.

"Dizzy...will you please promise me that you'll never tell anybody about tonight?" Gumbo begs. The worry in his eyes makes my heart crumble. Even after the confusion I just witnessed, I still care about the du Bois family like they're my own. They've been so kind to help my mother take care of me. I don't know who I feel sorrier for: Chauncey or the twins.

"I promise, Phil," I whisper.

My words seem to calm the worry in Gumbo's eyes. He exhales. "Thanks. It would mean a lot to Rashad, too, and I hope you don't think any less of him, because...he really likes you, Dizzy."

My face heats up and my heart starts pounding a mile a minute. "He does?"

Gumbo nods with a knowing smile. "He talks about you all the time."

I take a deep breath and try not to smile too wide. "Well, what does he say?"

"Can't tell you. Some things have to stay between brothers," Gumbo says, shrugging. "But trust me: He likes you. He's just too scared to admit it right now." He gives me a salute and heads off down the stairs. "See you tomorrow."

As I get ready for bed that night, my mother asks me about the video game party. I tell her all of the good parts, leaving out the big phone call.

After I'm all settled in my pajamas, I lay awake, thinking about Rashad. I can't imagine the humiliation of getting sick in front of everyone. Priya and Tatyana would tell me to drop him like a hot rock, but that's not me. Deep down, I still really like him, even after seeing him at his lowest.

I reach for my phone on my nightstand and shoot Rashad a text.

Me: Hey. Hope ur feeling better.

Rashad doesn't answer me. I sigh and start to roll over, when suddenly, I get a text from Gumbo.

Gumbo: Hey Dizzy. Ra's asleep. I'll tell him u texted tmrw.

I smile sadly and send Gumbo the thumbs-up emoji. Then I roll on my side, my head swirling with thoughts of that phone call. Will the twins remember any of what I said about McKayla Arlington and Chauncey? Or did it just go in one ear and out the other? The du Bois family has been so kind to me, but after that phone call, I saw a side of them that I know they didn't want me to see, and for Chauncey's sake, I hope I never see that side again.

As I drift off to sleep, my mind swirls with visions of all of the drama I've experienced since moving to Treeless Park. Missing my friends, solving this bully mystery, cheering at football games, keeping up with my homework, spending time with Corinne, and not to mention managing the strained relationship with my father have all been draining, physically and mentally. Sometimes, I think it's all too much for me to handle. After all, who am I to solve anyone's problems?

But tonight, I learned a few things that push me to keep going: Something happened with the Pirates last year, and it still bothers the du Bois family. Whatever it is, the twins haven't forgiven Chauncey.

Rashad Maurice du Bois, star quarterback of the Pirates football team, is gorgeous and charming and has big dreams. He loves his family, but he's flawed. He's a bully.

He's under a lot of pressure to be the best on the field, and he has bouts of anxiety because of it. Tonight, I also learned that Rashad likes me, and I am at a loss for words.

If I remain persistent, I'm sure I can make a difference, because when it comes to Chauncey, I know the twins can be better people.

38

Rashad's Point of View: A Brother's Keeper

It's dark. I'm out on the gridiron, standing eye-to-eye with eleven dudes who look ready to take me down. We take our positions and begin the play. The ball is hiked and I quickly receive it, backpedaling like my life depends on it. My eyes dart left and right in search of Phil, but I can't see him; I can't find P. I glance around for any other open guys, but then I get sacked and everything goes pitch-black. My legs twitch as I struggle to get the defense off me, but it's no use. *Let me up!*

"Ra...Ra..." a voice calls in the distance.

I squirm uncomfortably as patches of light break through the darkness. Suddenly, my eyes shoot open and I find myself lying flat on my back. I'm in my bed and my little sister is sitting on my legs. "Hi, Ra-Ra," she says, blinking her big eyes at me.

I run a hand across my drenched forehead and catch my breath. I try to smile at Brianna. "Uh, hey, Jelly Fingers. What'cha doing in here?"

Brianna holds out a tall cup of orange juice. "I brought this to make you feel better."

I force myself to sit up and try to fight off the crazy headache racking against my skull. Then I take the juice from Brianna and watch as her little face lights up. My sister's my buddy; my *Right-Hand Boogie*. That's a name I made up for her when she was three. She and I have always been real close. Phil thinks I baby her too much, but I don't care. I want to show Brianna that I'm her big brother and that she can come to me with anything. "Thanks, Boogie. How long you been sitting in here?"

"A while. You should drink. I squeezed the oranges myself."

I play along. "What? Girl, you're so strong."

Brianna giggles her crazy, contagious giggle. "I fooled you, Ra-Ra. It's just the juice from the box."

"Oh, you got pranks." I examine the glass and frown when I see some tiny lip prints on it. I give my sister a dry smile. "Seems like somebody was thirsty."

"Nuh-uh," she says, but then she burps. "'Scuse me."

I just smile and take a small sip, wincing as the tangy juice slides down my throat. It's still really raw from last night, but I try to ignore the feeling.

Brianna gets in my face. "Ra-Ra. Tell me something. Did you dream something scary?" she whispers deeply. I turn my head. She didn't brush her teeth yet.

I rub her shoulder. "Yeah, I did. Go brush your teeth, Bri," I whisper back. Brianna hops off my bed, shakes Phil awake, and runs down the hall.

Just then, Mom enters in her pajamas and bathrobe. Her hair is pulled behind her calm face. "Good morning," she says to us. We say "good morning" back and she sits on my bed. "You okay this morning, Baby?" she asks, touching my forehead. "You feel a little warm."

I wince, thinking back to my nightmare. "I'm fine, Ma."

"You sure? Your father and I don't want you out there playing today if you don't feel well."

My stomach gurgles. I shift positions in my bed and cough so no one hears it. "No, I feel great," I tell Mom.

Mom stares at me really hard, like she's searching my soul for a lie. I start praying that she lets it go, and thankfully, she says, "All right. You let us know if that changes, okay?" I just nod. I feel really bad for lying, but I have no choice. Mom walks over to Phil and rubs his head. "The both of you can come into the kitchen for breakfast when you're ready, okay?"

"Yes, Mom," Phil and I say at the same time. Mom smiles and leaves our room. As soon as she shuts the door, I exhale and flop back on my pillow.

"Ra," Phil suddenly says. I glance at him and he sort of smiles. "Dizzy texted you last night. You were asleep."

Wait. WHAT?!

I frantically bolt up and reach for my phone. I scroll through a bunch of texts from other kids and a few Instagram messages from Morgan and some other girls in my class. My cheeks get real hot when I finally see two text messages from Desiree; one from last night and one from a few minutes ago. In both messages, she asks me how I'm feeling.

"She was just checking on you," Phil continues. "How you holding up?"

My gut wrenches as I think back to last night. Phil, Desiree and I had a blast playing *Mario Kart*, but then my stomach started acting up when Desiree brought up Chauncey and McKayla Arlington. Later, Dad and Coach Marino got into it on the phone and my stomach couldn't hold it in any longer. I get nervous when Dad is stressed about football, especially when I'm trying to be the best for him, our family, and my entire team. Worst of all, Desiree

Davenport, the girl who I try to be cool in front of, heard and saw *everything*.

Too humiliated to answer Desiree, I put my phone down and cradle my head in my hands. The raging headache banging against my temples makes me want to scream. "I, uh, feel all right," I mutter to Phil.

"Cool," Phil says, and I can tell he's grinning. "I know you'll show those Bulldogs who's boss on the field today."

The field: The place where Dad and Coach Marino might get into it again; where I'll have to prove just how good a quarterback I really am; where I'll have to face Desiree after everything that happened.

I...I can't do it. But I *have* to. 'Cause if I don't...

"Ra? You okay?" Phil asks me, but I can't think straight because my head is pounding and my stomach is in knots. My heart starts racing and the room starts to spin. I open my mouth and try to answer my brother, but I burp and slap my hand over my mouth. The next thing I know, I'm flying off my bed and to the trash can by our door. Everything comes up.

"Rashad," I hear Phil say. Clutching my stomach, I glance up and see him standing over me with a worried expression. He starts to yell for Dad, but I grab his arm.

"P, no," I moan. "Don't tell Dad."

"Boy, move," Phil snaps. He steps towards the door, but I slam my body against it so he can't get by. "What is wrong with you, Ra? You're still sick and I'm not letting you go out there today and risk getting worse!"

"I have to try. I can't let the team down. They depend on me. What would they think?"

"They'd think you were sick."

"Look, they need me, okay?"

"They'll be all right, Ra."

"Well, what about you? You need me," I shoot back. "Don't you remember how important Florida is to us, P?"

"Florida's a dream, Rashad, but —"

"Florida's *our* dream and it's always been ours," I snap, and Phil doesn't answer me. He knows good and well how many nights we've stayed up talking about Florida and the doors that will open for us once we make it there. "We need to pay for college and I'm the quarterback who's going to get us there," I remind him. "Don't you want to study business?"

Phil glances off and shakes his head. "Ra...you can't carry the burdens of our family and this team, dude."

"Like you're always carrying me?" I challenge. "You're always running behind me and making me look good, and you know it, P. Why can't you let me do what *I* gotta do for once?"

"Boys?" a deep voice calls from down the hall. Phil and I exchange a worried glance. It's *Dad.*

I stare at my brother with a pleading expression. He hesitates and wipes a hand across his face. Finally, he groans and pushes me out of the way. "Move." He snatches the puke-filled trash can and shoves it under my bed. He sprays air-freshener everywhere. Then he goes to our closet, rummages through the pockets of his leather jacket, and pulls out a few pieces of gum. "Here," he says, shoving the gum into my hands. "Chew on these so Dad doesn't smell your puke breath."

I do as I'm told. "I'll pay you back for the gum, P."

"Don't worry about it. Now, shut up. Dad's coming."

Right on cue, there's a knock at our door. It opens and in walks Dad. His tall frame fills the doorway. "Hey, hey. Y'all all right this morning?" he asks. His Southern accent is always thicker when he's around just us. He sniffs the air. "What did y'all spray in here for?"

Phil glances back and forth. "My...cleats were funky. Sorry, Dad."

Dad frowns, but he's laughing. "P, you need to wash them things." He looks at me and his face grows serious. "How about you, Ra? How you feeling today, huh?"

I look at Phil, who chews his bottom lip and glances away. My stomach flips as I think about the trash can under my bed. "I feel okay, Dad." I wring my hands to keep from scratching my ear.

"You sure? You positive?" Dad presses. "I don't want you going out there sick, now."

I lick my lips. "It's cool, Dad. I'm ready."

Dad stares at me for a bit, then turns to Phil. "He telling the truth, Phil?" My brother nods silently and Dad glances between us. Finally, he exhales. "All right. Come on and eat. Your sister's looking at your bacon." He laughs and slaps both of us high-fives. Then he leaves our room and we sigh.

"Thanks, P," I mutter. "I owe you big time."

Phil doesn't crack a smile. "Don't thank me. Let's just get through this game." He walks out of our room, leaving me standing there, alone.

39

Game Day Anxiety

Sunday morning comes a lot sooner than I want it to.
After what feels like minutes of laying with my eyes closed, I wake up to the sun peeking its rays through my window shade. The bright light begs me to get out of bed, but I lie still. I'm still sad about my night at Corinne's place, not to mention hearing Mr. du Bois' argument with Coach Marino and seeing Rashad get sick. Rolling over, I reach for my phone and check the time. It's a little after 9:30 a.m., so I decide to shoot Rashad a quick text.

Me: Hey. U feeling any better?

Rashad doesn't respond. I sigh and push myself out of bed. Today's an away game, so my mother and I have to be out of the apartment a little earlier than usual.

At 11:45 a.m., my mother and I hop into our car and drive 30 minutes to Whispering Woods High School for our game against the Bulldogs. Once we arrive, I hustle over to the grass and search for Corinne amongst the other cheerleaders. I spot her standing alone with her pom-poms sitting in the grass. Her hand reaches up to twirl her beaded braids, and her eyes are wide with uncertainty as she glances around the field.

"Hey, Corinne," I say.

Corinne turns to me and lifts her lips into a smile, but her eyes are dull. "Hi, Dizzy," she mutters. She glances past me and over at the bleachers. I follow her gaze, only to find her staring at her grandmother, who sits in the front. That's when it dawns on me: Corinne is looking for her mother out here, but I don't see her anywhere. I feel so sorry for Corinne.

As my eyes travel around the bleachers, I see my mother sitting with the du Bois family. They all hold their posters, as usual, but today, Mrs. du Bois looks worried.

Swallowing a gulp, I look for any signs of hostility between Mr. du Bois and Coach Marino. Surprisingly, I find none. Mr. du Bois minds his business and fills the water coolers with Lemon-Lime Gatorade, while Coach Marino and the assistant coaches talk strategy with the football players.

Today, Chauncey stands plenty of feet away from the twins, who aren't paying attention to their coaches. Rashad clutches his stomach and takes a few steps towards the bench. Gumbo puts a hand on his brother's shoulder and gestures to their father, who's too busy filling the coolers to notice anything. Rashad quickly shakes his head at Gumbo and tries to stand up straighter, but he fails. My fists clench nervously inside my pom-poms. Rashad's obviously still anxious, and I'm scared that this game won't go well.

At 1:15 p.m., it's game time against the Bulldogs, whose players are a lot stronger and faster than I expected. The first quarter of the game is hard to watch, as the Bulldogs' star quarterback throws nothing but completed passes. Their wide receivers move like lightning around our defense. They score two easy touchdowns and their kicker came to play, too, putting them in the lead 14 to zip.

When we're on offense, Rashad tries his hardest to drill the ball to Gumbo, but his game is off today. He throws the ball too high or too far out of Gumbo's reach. Coach Marino yanks his cap off his head in frustration, while Mr. du Bois claps loudly. "Come on, Rashad! Focus! Just like we practiced!" he yells from the sidelines.

Next to me, Corinne grimaces and folds her pom-poms across her chest. "What's wrong with *him*?"

My eye starts twitching. "It's not his fault. He's sick."

"Well, he should sit down, then," Corinne snaps. I bite my tongue. I know she's probably on edge because of her mother, so I turn away and focus on the rest of the game.

During the second quarter, our kicker scores a 30-yard field goal, getting us on the board with three points. Finally! Sadly, the Bulldogs make off with another touchdown and a surprise interception, thanks to Rashad's bad pass.

During the next offensive play, Rashad struggles to find an open man. It almost looks like he's tripping over his own feet. He tries to run the ball for a first down, but this fails miserably and he gets tackled. My stomach twists up in a million knots. I sure hope Rashad's not hurt.

"Time out!" Coach Marino bellows. The Pirates group up on the sidelines. This time, they're standing close enough for me to hear everything they're saying. "Rashad, what's going on with you?" Coach Marino demands. He starts rambling angrily. "You're missing throws and tripping over your own feet! We got men wide open and you're not throwing the ball! Come on! Playing like this, you're going to be getting sacked all day! This is not how we're going to win! Their kicker's over there kicking and they got guys over there making plays on the ball. We need to see some of that over here, Rashad!"

Maya Anderson scoffs. "I'm with Coach Marino."

I whirl around and glare at her. "He's trying, okay?"

Rashad removes his helmet. His face is flushed and he's sweating way more than the other guys. "I'm fine, Coach. I...I just..."

"No, he's not fine," Gumbo says. He turns to Mr. du Bois. "Dad, he's still sick and he didn't want me to tell you!"

"Phil! I'm fine!" Rashad hisses. He winces, clutches his stomach, and hunches over. Mr. du Bois puts an arm around Rashad and helps him to stand up straight.

"Nuh-uh. Rashad, I'm swapping you out," Coach Marino orders.

"But Dad!" Rashad whines.

Mr. du Bois shakes his head firmly. "I agree with Coach Marino, Son. You're not feeling well."

Rashad clutches his stomach and glares at Gumbo. "Big Mouth. Watch us lose now."

Gumbo shakes his head. "Dude, have you checked the board?"

Just then, Chauncey pushes his way into the mix and tugs on Coach Marino's sleeve. "Coach, I can play. Put *me* in!"

"Back up! You ain't no good!" Gumbo hisses.

"But he's sick!" Chauncey says, pointing at Rashad.

Gumbo slaps Chauncey's hand down. "Get your hand out of my brother's face! You ain't good! You ain't *never* been good! You can get in the game all you want; my brother will never throw the ball to you."

"Hey, that's enough!" Coach Marino bellows. I shudder. He points at the whole team. "We are a team!"

Just then, Rashad doubles over and gets sick right in the grass.

Chauncey jumps back. Gumbo and the rest of the Pirates, with their backs to Rashad, form a wall around him. I hear a few of them saying, "You're gonna be all right, Ra." Mr. du Bois hands Rashad a clean towel and rushes him over to the bench. Rashad sits down and wipes his mouth with the towel, while Mr. du Bois goes to the water cooler and fills a paper cup with Gatorade. He hands the cup and some stomach medicine to Rashad, who downs both and accidentally locks eyes with me. I look away so he doesn't catch me staring too hard during his moment of shame.

I turn to the bleachers and see my mother sitting there with her mouth fixed in a sad "ooh" shape. Meanwhile, the du Bois family stares down at Rashad in concern. Mr. du Bois waves his hand at his wife, almost as if to say, *He's all right.* "That's okay, Ra-Ra! You're all right!" one of the aunts cheers.

Coach Marino stares after Rashad for a few moments and regains control of the rest of his huddle. He puts our second quarterback, Number Six, on the field and puts Chauncey in as a wide receiver.

As the Pirates take the field, I see Gumbo walking with Chauncey. "You'd better not screw up, Spots," he hisses.

My stomach churns nervously. I'm no football player, but even I know that no one in their right mind would bully their teammate and expect to win a game.

The rest of the game is in shambles, with Rashad out and the other two quarterbacks rotating throughout the game. At the start of the third quarter, the Pirates and the Bulldogs stagger themselves on the line of scrimmage for the play. The Pirates' center snaps the ball to the first quarterback, Number Six, who catches the ball and hustles backwards in preparation for his big pass. Chauncey runs to an opening on the field and jumps up and down. Number Six hesitates with the ball, but then he passes the ball to Chauncey, avoiding a sack.

Time slows down as the ball sails through the air. Chauncey's cleats dance in the grass as he hovers beneath the ball. Surprisingly, he makes the catch, but instead of running to the end zone, he just stands there in the middle of the field, almost like he's frozen or something.

I hear the crowd groaning angrily in the bleachers. From the sidelines, the Pirates scream at Chauncey to run. "Man, what'chu doing?" I hear a few of them yell. Rashad closes his eyes and cradles his head in his hands.

"Chauncey! Run!" Coach Marino screams from the sidelines, but it's too late. The Bulldogs tackle Chauncey.

During the last quarter, the second quarterback, Number 12, manages to move the ball around to the running back and wide receivers. Gumbo scores a touchdown, but the kicker misses the field goal. In the last minute of the game, Number 12 passes the ball to Chauncey, who drops it right when the clock winds down. I turn to the scoreboard and cringe at the glowing numbers. We lost 9-21.

After exchanging a half-hearted round of high fives with the Bulldogs, the Pirates group up for a final word of encouragement from Coach Marino. No one speaks to Chauncey. In fact, I hear a few insults being thrown around. The twins glare at him with menace, like they could beat him up right here. Mr. du Bois folds his arms. He looks livid.

"Listen up, Pirates," Coach Marino begins. "Today was not our proudest performance. A lot to work on in practice this week, but we'll bounce back and make sure we finish this season strong." He nods and wishes everyone safe travels back home.

As the crowd disperses, I watch as Corinne goes to her grandmother. My eyes dart around the bleachers in search of Anita, but I don't see her anywhere. She didn't show.

"Corinne!" I call out. She turns to me and I smile, breaking into a fierce Floss dance. "We're gonna kill it tomorrow on that stage, right?"

The corners of Corinne's mouth lift into a soft grin. Her eyes brighten like the day she begged me to take part in the showcase. "You know it! See you tomorrow, Dizzy." She waves and walks off with her grandmother, leaving me and my mother with the du Bois family. They all shower Rashad with encouraging words, but Rashad doesn't say anything. He stares at his cleats, looking humiliated. I study him sadly. I've never seen him look so defeated before.

Mr. du Bois clears his throat and weaves his way through the family crowd. I'm scared he'll blow up at Rashad over his awful performance, but surprisingly, he drapes an arm around Rashad's shoulders. "Come here, Son," he says, and he doesn't sound angry. He exchanges a hug and a kiss with Mrs. du Bois and leads Rashad away.

Gumbo hustles after his father. "Dad!" Mr. du Bois and Rashad stop and turn around. Gumbo gestures between them. "Everything good?" he asks.

Mr. du Bois smiles and clamps a firm hand on Gumbo's shoulder. "Yeah. I just need to have a quick talk with your brother. Nice effort today, Phil."

Gumbo smiles slightly and high fives his father. He attempts to high five Rashad, but Rashad turns away from him and walks off to the bench. Gumbo frowns and turns to his father. "Ra's mad at me," he says dryly.

Mr. du Bois pats Gumbo on the back. "He won't be for long. You did the right thing by speaking up, Phil." He follows Rashad to the bench and speaks to him in a supportive voice. "Just shake it off, Ra-Ra, all right?" he says, patting Rashad on his face.

Rashad rubs his neck. "Everybody saw, Dad."

"Don't worry about it. Everybody gets sick sometimes," Mr. du Bois says. "But you owe your brother an apology. He was just looking out for you, like he always does." Rashad is quiet and Mr. du Bois continues. "Today was one game. You had a little setback, but you'll be back next week. You've got your brother out there with those good hands, and you'll be making nothing but completed passes, baby. You're *this close* to beating your record and making it to Florida. How close?"

Rashad wipes his nose and holds up his thumb and index finger. "This close."

Mr. du Bois gives Rashad a high five and grips his shoulders. He looks him right in the eyes. "Everybody has an off day, Ra, but guess what? Nobody can beat you. You're number one, and you know why you're number one? 'Cause you work hard. That's why."

"You know it," Rashad says, finally starting to smile.

"My boy." Mr. du Bois taps Rashad on the stomach. "You okay?" Rashad nods and Mr. du Bois smiles. He tugs both of Rashad's ears. "With these big ol' ears. These are *my* ears." Rashad laughs and lets his father hug him. "Nobody thinks any less of you, Son."

Rashad sighs. "Well, what about...you-know-who?"

Mr. du Bois stares at Rashad seriously. "You mean Desiree?" My heart starts pounding like rapid fire as Rashad nods and lowers his eyes in embarrassment. Mr. du Bois crouches down so that he's eye to eye with Rashad. "Nah, Desiree is cool people. If she's really your friend, she won't think any less of you, either, okay? Win or lose, you're still our Number One. I'm sure she feels the same way."

My legs turn to jelly. I take a giant step back. I've just invaded Rashad's privacy. I shouldn't have eavesdropped.

I hustle backwards and accidentally crash into Gumbo. "Whoa. 'Scuse me, Dizzy," he says.

"No, no, no! You're fine!" I twirl the end of my ponytail and clear my throat. "Sorry about the loss."

Gumbo gives me a slight smile. "The du Bois always bounce back." He glances at Rashad, who's still speaking with Mr. du Bois, and clears his throat. "But check this out. I don't think you should come over for dinner tonight. Rashad had a rough game and I know he's pretty embarrassed."

"I understand," I say, because I have no idea what I'd even say to Rashad tonight, anyway. Besides, I've got movie plans with my mother. I smile at Gumbo. "You really look out for Rashad, you know that?"

Gumbo regards me with a serious expression. "I have to. That's my little brother."

My eyes bug out like a frog's. "*You're* the older twin?"

"By three minutes." Gumbo removes his helmet and gives me a wry smile. "You're surprised?"

"A little," I admit quietly. Gumbo nods and I instantly feel bad. "B-but only because..."

"Rashad's the quarterback?" Gumbo finishes. I glance off, completely embarrassed, and Gumbo laughs lightheartedly. "It's okay. Most people think Ra's older when they first meet us because he's so talkative, but he's the baby, and a mean quarterback, too, when he's feeling well."

"Wow. Have you ever wanted to be a quarterback?"

"Nah. That's been Ra's dream since we were seven. He's always had the better arm and I've always been faster, so it's just worked out. Plus, I want to see him beat his record just as much as he does," Gumbo explains. "But he can't do it without me and the rest of our team. We have to know those plays just as well as he does."

I nod. "Do you want to go pro one day like Rashad?"

"Yeah, I'd love to go pro, but I also want to go into business. I'm selling gum and candy 'cause it's easy and a cool way to make a little money, but my real dream is to take over my family's business and expand The Crunch Bowl into something really nice one day."

My mouth drops open with a combination of awe and guilt. I hope Gumbo doesn't think less of his family's restaurant because of my "Sweet Song's" comment. I wasn't trying to offend him at all. "The Crunch Bowl is something nice already," I say.

Gumbo gives me a knowing smile. "Thanks, but I think we both know what I'm talking about," he says, and I cringe. "Rashad and I have been talking to each other about our dreams since we were little. I'm going to do everything I can to help him get to where he wants to be, and when we go pro and make some real money, we'll team up to expand The Crunch Bowl."

I stare at Gumbo, feeling both amazed and a little bit jealous. He and Rashad have such an air-tight relationship that only twins have. It makes me wish I had a twin, too. "Rashad is really lucky to have a brother like you," I say.

Gumbo smiles. "He's lucky to have a friend like you."

I twirl my ponytail and glance at Rashad, who's now standing by his cousins. They all give him high fives and pat him on the back. Surprisingly, Nikita steps forward and offers Rashad a bag of her white cheddar popcorn. Rashad grins and tosses a few pieces in his mouth. As he chews and swallows, our eyes lock and his expression grows serious. I expect him to turn away, but he holds my gaze.

The distance between us shrinks as I offer him a small wave. Rashad gives me a half-smile and walks up to me. "Hi," I say, nervously rubbing the end of my cheerleading skirt.

"Hi." Rashad's eyes glance from his cleats to my face. "Sorry I didn't text you back. I'm feeling much better now."

I smile and poke Rashad in the shoulder. "I knew you'd pull through, Number Four."

Rashad smirks and takes a step back. "Well, I don't want to get too close. My tongue still tastes like vomit, and

I know my breath ain't too far off." I just smile and we exchange an exploding fist bump.

Up ahead, I notice Mr. du Bois emptying the water coolers. He catches me fist-bumping Rashad, smiles, and turns back to the coolers. My face heats up and I quickly turn back to Rashad. "Hey, next week, I'll be cheering 'Do it all, du Bois' for sure." I smirk and flex my pinky. "Me *and* Worm Tooth."

Rashad's dimples cave in as he laughs like crazy. Gumbo glances between us with a half-smile. "What, y'all got inside jokes now?"

I tense slightly. Sharing Worm Tooth with Rashad was one thing, but I'm not sharing it with Gumbo.

"Yeah, it's an inside joke," Rashad says, winking at me. I smile gratefully and he faces Gumbo with a shameful expression. "Sorry for going crazy on you, P. I was a little off today." Gumbo raises his eyebrows, rolls his tongue around the inside of his cheek, and looks away. Rashad sighs and rubs the back of his neck. "Fine. I was *way* off today."

Gumbo cracks up. "You'll be back next week."

Rashad gives his brother a high-five. "You know it."

Just then, Brianna hurries over to Rashad and hugs him by his waist. "Ra-Ra! Ra-Ra!" she yells.

"What? What, Bri?" Rashad mimics, scooping Brianna into his arms.

Brianna speaks in a low voice. "Is your tummy feeling better? 'Cause you, um...you were terrible today, Ra-Ra."

Rashad taps Brianna's nose. "I've heard."

Brianna giggles. "Ooh, Ra-Ra, your breath stinks."

Rashad cracks up, puts Brianna in the grass, and chases her around the bench. As I watch them, my eyes glaze around the field and I see Chauncey walking alone, as usual. I narrow my eyes and see him walking to someone's car. As he tosses his football equipment into the trunk and hops in the backseat, my mind ticks with anger. I don't know who's sitting in that car, but I bet if they were sitting up in these bleachers, Chauncey would get more play time and he wouldn't be getting bullied by anybody, either.

40

The Talent Showcase

Monday, September 23rd, is no day to sleep in.
When my alarm goes off, I immediately text Corinne.

> **Me: Corinne! 2day's the day! Don't 4get ur leggings & black t-shirt!** ☺

Corinne responds two minutes later.

> **Corinne: Thx 4 reminding me!!! See u soon Dizzy!**
> **Me:** ☺ ☺ ☺

By the time I'm all dressed, my mother has a breakfast of pancakes and eggs waiting for me on the kitchen table. I thank my mother, smiling at the memory of our movie outing yesterday. We laughed during the whole film. I think it was the most fun we've had together since the divorce.

"Eat up, dancer girl," my mother says. I thank her for the meal and dig in while she massages my shoulders briefly. "I wish I could be there to see the big show."

I chew a little slower. My mother's only being supportive, but I wish she'd give me a teeny bit of space.

That's when I remember Corinne's mother and how she gives Corinne *too* much space. Corinne would probably give anything for her mother to watch her dance today. I swallow my pancakes and smile up at my mother. "I'll ask the twins to film the dance on my phone, Mommy."

My mother kisses my forehead. "I can't wait to see it."

After breakfast, I throw on my backpack and go to the couch for my plastic bag, which is stuffed with my leggings, black t-shirt, and portable speakers that my mother picked up from the electronics store last night. After double-checking to make sure that everything is packed all nice and neatly, I head outside to the bus stop, where the twins are already standing.

Gumbo notices my plastic bag and raises his sunglasses. "Girl, what's in there?" he asks around a wad of gum. Today it's blue and leaves stains all over his teeth.

I grin and sling the plastic bag over my shoulder. "It's my costume for the talent showcase today." Gumbo nods, but Rashad doesn't say anything. He just takes a huge bite out of his apple and stares at me with his intense eyes. "What?" I demand, tossing my hair to one side.

Rashad swallows the apple. He smirks and rubs his hand near his lips. "You've got something right here."

My fingers fly to my face and I pull off a piece of scrambled egg from my breakfast. "Oh," I mutter. Can't I go one day without being embarrassed in front of Rashad?

"So, Dizzy, what's your talent?" Rashad asks.

I wipe my hand over my face in search of anymore eggs before answering his question. "I'm doing a hip-hop routine with Corinne. We've been practicing all month." My eyes dart between the twins. "How come *you* guys didn't sign up?"

"We can't do other activities during football season. Our dad says it'll break our focus. It's school and football." Gumbo explains.

I nod, suddenly feeling a little silly for being so excited. "Oh...yeah, that makes sense."

Just then, the bus pulls up to the corner. I climb aboard, hand the driver my ticket, and find a window seat near the front. Rashad sits next to me and offers me a plastic bag of grapes. I politely decline. Those are probably for his lunch. "Well, if you guys aren't performing, can you take a video of me and Corinne on my phone?"

"Of course," Rashad says.

Gumbo drops into the seat across from us and smiles. "Yeah. We'll be *your* cheerleaders today."

I grin and rehearse our dance routine in my head. Today is going to be *perfect*.

When we finally get to school, I'm glad to see Corinne waiting by my locker – and she's wearing her new, swirly dress.

My face breaks into a huge smile. "Girl, I absolutely *love* that dress on you."

Corinne beams and does a little twirl. "Don't I look spectacular?"

"Very." I give her an exploding fist bump, relieved that she's showing some spunk since her mother's disappearing act.

The twins walk up to their lockers and drop their backpacks on the floor. Gumbo stares at Corinne.

Corinne takes a step forward and puts her hands on her hips. "Go ahead. Say something stupid about my clothes like you always do," she snaps.

I nervously glance between Corinne and Gumbo. After being let down by her mother on her birthday, the last thing Corinne needs is an insult. My heart races as he removes his sunglasses and clears his throat. "Actually, Corinne, I was going to say that you look really nice today."

My mouth drops open. I glance at Rashad, who raises his eyebrows and stares at his brother with a shocked smirk. He looks at me and I just shrug. Meanwhile, Corinne's hazel eyes blink open and closed like a chameleon's. She reaches up to grab her braids, but she misses and ends up swatting the air instead. "Oh. Thank you, Antwan Philippe," she chirps.

"It's Phil," Gumbo corrects. He grabs the books for our morning lessons and closes his locker. "Good luck in the showcase." He nods at Corinne and heads off to Ms. Hernandez's classroom.

Rashad stares after his brother like he's never seen him before in his life. "Hold up," he mutters, laughing. He smirks at me, closes his locker, and hustles off. "Yo, P!"

I wish could I follow Rashad and hear what he has to say to Gumbo, but then I remember Gumbo's words from Saturday night: Some things have to stay between brothers.

The rest of the morning seems to drag on forever, with Ms. Hernandez giving us all a vocabulary test. Most of these words I've studied, so I'm not rattled.

At noon, the lunch bell rings, and it's officially showtime. Corinne and I race into the girls' bathroom and change into our matching leggings and t-shirts. A few girls standing by the sinks eye us with envy, but I ignore them. We can't help it if we look good.

"Girl, this is it!" Corinne chirps. I grab my phone and wireless speaker from the top shelf of my locker. She bounces on her toes and bombards me with questions. "Are you excited? Are you nervous? Do you think people will like our routine? Do you think they'll *clap* for us at the end?"

I just grin and close my locker. "Come on!" I say. We link arms, strut into The Caf, and find seats near the twins.

Our principal, Mr. Ross, and assistant principal, Mrs. Rizzo, are the hosts of the talent showcase. They take the stage and welcome everyone to the show. Principal Ross glances at his clipboard and introduces the first few acts: a juggler, a deejay, and some kid who performs a stand-up comedy routine. In my opinion, his jokes are dumb, but he gets a few laughs from some kids in the room who know him.

About halfway through the show, Assistant Principal Rizzo introduces a pair of hip-hop dancers from Homeroom 1105. My lunch crawls up my throat.

"Please put your hands together for...Desiree Davenport and Corinne Corelle!" Assistant Principal Rizzo says.

The twins whip around in their chairs to face us. "That's y'all," Gumbo says.

Hands trembling, I drop my bedazzled phone in Rashad's hands. "Promise not to laugh if I look a hot mess?"

"Pony Boots, you'll be perfect," Rashad insists. He and Gumbo take seats in the very front so they can capture the best angle on video. Corinne and I weave through the crowd and over to the stage. It looks so much bigger up close.

I start to climb the steps of the stage, when suddenly, Corinne grabs my wrist. "Dizzy, wait. I'm...scared."

I stare at Corinne with a mixture of confusion and annoyance. "Girl, you'd better come on!" After weeks of begging me to do this thing, she's scared? That's when I remember the drama with her mother. All Corinne needs is a little encouragement. "You can't be scared when you're dancing with a partner."

At these words, the fire slowly returns to Corinne's eyes. She smiles and follows me to center stage. Staring out at the crowd, I can't help but feel scared, too.

My eyes fall on Rashad, who holds my phone in the air. He catches me staring and winks at me, letting his lips lift into a small smile. At this moment, I'm dying.

I notice Morgan weaving through the crowd. She slides next to Rashad and bats her eyelashes at him. Rashad gives her a tight smile, takes a teeny step away from her, and holds my phone higher to focus on me. Morgan glances between me and Rashad. She looks annoyed, but I just ignore her.

I crouch down and get our music set up. Corinne and I break into our routine, hitting each step with power and precision as the beat of Ciara's *Level Up* blasts throughout The Caf. The crowd starts rocking to the beat of the music, causing Corinne and I to dance faster and faster. A few kids in the back jump out of their seats and start dancing, too. Rashad grins as he records us. I accidentally lock eyes with Morgan, who stares at me with a flat look. Her lips are turned up in a jealous way. When our routine is finally over, we take bows in front of a standing ovation.

"They loved us, Dizzy!" Corinne squeals, wrapping me in a tight hug. I hug her back and we walk offstage. The old me would have never had the courage to pull off a routine like that, but the new me is on fire.

"That was so lit!" Gumbo says, giving me and Corinne a round of high fives.

"I know. What else did you expect from two cheerleaders?" Corinne asks, folding her skinny arms across her chest. I smile and give Corinne a fist bump. She's *back*.

"Dizzy," Rashad says. He pats the empty seat next to him, and I smile and sit down. "Girl, you crushed it," he says, grinning. He returns my phone and slaps me a firm high five. I bite my bottom lip and try not to pass out.

"Thank you, ladies, for that wonderful performance," Principal Ross says. "Up next is Chauncey Willis, who will sing *I Can Only Be Me* by David Bruce Whitley."

My heart stops. I completely forgot that Chauncey signed up for this thing. I nervously glance at the twins, whose smiles instantly fade. All I can do is pray to God that Chauncey makes it through his performance peacefully.

The Caf is dead silent as Chauncey takes center stage. The *squeak-squeak* of his black sneakers echoes throughout the room. His arm is wrapped around a boom box, which he places at his feet. He connects his phone to the boom box, and a beautiful piano solo fills the room. Chauncey accepts the microphone from Principal Ross and starts to sing in a soothing voice. His words blend together in harmony as he sings the lyrics of wishing to be someone else, someone better than who he is.

As Chauncey sings, he makes his way around The Caf. He passes each person and sings the lyrics to his song with a lot of passion in his voice. I take a careful look around, afraid to see the different reactions. To my surprise, everyone is captivated by Chauncey's voice, and no one looks hateful. I see faces of astonishment. Even the *twins* look stunned.

"I didn't know Chauncey could sing," Corinne breathes. I just nod because his talent is a shock to me, too. My eyes stay locked on Chauncey as he strolls over to my table. He stops in front of the twins, standing strong as he belts out the final lyric of only being himself.

As the beautiful piano solo fades out, The Caf is silent. Chauncey drops the microphone in front of the twins and glares down at them, his eyes screaming with pain. The twins stare up at Chauncey, but they no longer look stunned. They look furious, especially Rashad. A sudden feeling of dread takes over my body, and before I can even process what's happening, Rashad slowly rises from his chair and glowers at Chauncey with a look that could kill. "You're nothing but a spotted thief," he screams in Chauncey's face, "and you always will be! You know what you did!"

Rashad's steely voice slices across The Caf like a blade. Everyone is frozen, until finally, Rashad grimaces and shoves Chauncey. Chauncey stumbles backwards and starts to shove Rashad back, but then Gumbo grabs his milk carton and dumps it all on Chauncey's head.

I stare at the twins in horror. This can't be happening. Today started off great and now we're back to the bullying? Did the twins forget everything I said about McKayla Arlington?

"Guys, stop!" I exclaim, but Principal Ross' voice drowns me out.

"Excuse me! What is going on, here?" Principal Ross shouts at the twins. He turns to Assistant Principal Rizzo, who immediately nods her head and marches towards the twins.

As the twins get ushered out of The Caf, some girl sitting at a table near mine sucks her teeth. "This boy's a joke," she snaps, flicking her hand at Chauncey. She chucks an apple core at Chauncey, hitting him in the head.

In an instant, The Caf turns to chaos. People start pelting Chauncey with food and trash. Chauncey sprints out of The Caf, not even remembering to take his boom box or phone. A couple of kids try to swarm the stage and grab Chauncey's things, but then Principal Ross orders them to get away and they slink back to their seats.

I hustle after Chauncey. Beyond the screaming and laughter, I can hear Corinne shrieking my name and asking me where I'm going, but I don't even turn around to answer her. Instead, I hurry out of The Caf, down the hall, and finally see Chauncey sprinting towards the boys' bathroom.

"Chauncey, wait!" I cry out. "Are you okay?"

Chauncey turns to face me with fury and despair clouding his eyes. "Leave me alone!" He runs into the boys' bathroom and slams the door behind him. I start to sulk back to The Caf, but as soon as I turn around, I see everyone walking to their classrooms. The talent showcase must be over.

Suddenly, I see Principal Ross weaving through the sea of students. "Has anybody seen Chauncey Willis?" he bellows.

I quickly wave Principal Ross down and point to the boys' bathroom. "He's in there," I say. Principal Ross gives me a quick nod and hurries into the bathroom, while I walk back to Ms. Hernandez's classroom, wondering what will happen to the twins in that office today.

41

The Warning

A half hour later, a very distressed-looking Chauncey interrupts our silent-reading period by returning to Ms. Hernandez's classroom. He sulks at his desk by the window and puts his head down. I stare at the door, waiting for the twins to walk in here, but they remain MIA.

I hide my phone behind my copy of *Bluish* by Virginia Hamilton and fire off a quick text to the twins.

Me: Where r u guys???

Gumbo: In the office. Ross is calling our parents.

My mouth drops open and I catch Ms. Hernandez shooting me a suspicious glare. I clutch my free hand tighter around my book and pretend like my shock is coming from the story. Then I quickly type a response to Gumbo.

Me: OMG. How much trouble r u guys in?

Nobody answers me and I feel sick to my stomach.

For the rest of the day, I wait for the twins to return to class, but they never do. When the 2:30 bell rings, Corinne shoots me a worried glance. "Do you think the du Bois family will still watch you today?"

My throat closes up. I hadn't thought of that. I yank my phone from my pocket and send the twins a text.

Me: Hey guys. Hope everything is ok. Should I still come 2 The Crunch Bowl 2day or...?

Gumbo sends a short response.

Gumbo: Yeah.

Rashad never says a word. Maybe his parents took his phone or maybe he's too embarrassed to talk to me. The vibe is definitely off, so whatever happened in that principal's office today must not have been pretty.

I stand up from my desk and lock eyes with Chauncey as he passes me. He stares me down like he wants to say something, but instead, he just storms out of the classroom. I sigh and leave the room with Corinne, who begs me to show her our *Level Up* video over and over again. "Girl, we were on *fire!*" she exclaims. "Especially you. You killed it!"

"All thanks to you." I start to smile, but then my mind drifts back to the talent showcase disaster. "Too bad our victory was short-lived, though."

Corinne nods sadly. "Well, see you tomorrow." She flounces off to her locker, leaving me by the classroom door. For the first time in weeks, I feel alone. The twins and Corinne are my only friends here in Treeless Park. With one friend living 20 minutes away, and the other two friends getting sent to the principal's office, I don't know what to do.

I gather my books from my locker and ride the bus home in silence. When the driver pumps the brakes in front of The Crunch Bowl, I have no choice but to swallow my fear and walk inside the restaurant. Mrs. du Bois is standing behind the cash register. She smiles at me, but I can tell her expression is forced. She looks exhausted.

"Hello, my dear. Come in," she urges, waving me closer to the register. I smile as she points to the back of the restaurant. "The boys are sitting over there today."

I spot the twins sitting solemnly at a wooden table. Gumbo picks at his fried chicken sliders and offers Rashad a skinny, burnt French fry. Rashad ignores him and stirs his straw around in his strawberry milkshake. He looks lifeless.

I walk up to Rashad. "No vanilla milkshake today?" Rashad stops in mid-stir. He whips around and I force down a laugh as I notice a frothy, pink line coating his lips. "You've got something right here." I draw a circle around my lips.

Rashad quickly dabs his mouth with a napkin. "Hey, Dizzy," he mutters. He shrugs and lowers his eyes. "I know you probably don't want to sit over here."

"Actually, I do," I state with a firm nod.

Gumbo smiles sadly. "Pull up a chair."

I nod and do as he says. For a long moment, I sit at the table in silence, watching the twins eat. My sneakers tap anxiously against the floor. I've got to say something and find out where the twins' heads are, because today ended *wacked.*

"So...how much trouble are you guys in?" I ask meekly.

Gumbo removes his sunglasses and taps them against the table. He sighs. "Principal Ross called Coach Marino. If we mess with Chauncey in school or on the football field again, we're done for the season."

I lean *way* back in shock. That's what I call a warning. "Wow," I moan quietly. "What did Principal Ross say?"

Gumbo doesn't answer me right away. He sighs and scratches his head, like he's embarrassed to tell me the rest. "He saw the hallway video on Instagram. Rashad and I weren't the ones who posted the video, but we *did* start everything, and Chauncey told on us. We're not allowed to participate in any school activities for the rest of the quarter." He pauses for a moment and glances up at me. "Oh, and we'll be in lunch detention for the next two weeks."

"Aw, man," I mutter. "What did your parents say?"

Rashad laughs without smiling. His eyes look really sad. "Our dad is *so* mad, Dizzy." He pushes his cherry to the bottom of his milkshake. "Our parents hate leaving the restaurant for stuff like this. They yelled at us the whole way home. I'm just glad Bri was at school so she didn't have to hear any of it."

Gumbo scoffs. "Oh, you think it's over? You know Dad. Tonight, Bri will hear it all."

Rashad doesn't answer Gumbo. I cringe. "What else?"

"Our parents grounded us until further notice," Gumbo says. "That means no video games or anything fun for the next few weekends. Just school and football."

I nod. Hopefully this puts an end to the twins' bullying. "Well, what about Chauncey?"

Rashad stiffens. "What *about* him?"

"Was he in the office with you guys, too?"

"For a little while. Principal Ross made us apologize to him," Gumbo mutters.

"Well, what made you guys want to ruin his performance in the first place? What were you thinking?"

"He was awful," Rashad says.

"No, he wasn't. Everybody in The Caf was impressed."

"We weren't," Gumbo snaps.

"Fine. Whatever." At this point, there's no sense in arguing with them. "But this whole thing is your fault. You got everyone in The Caf all riled up, and look at how much trouble you got yourselves in! Was it worth it?"

"Doesn't matter," Rashad murmurs. "After what Chauncey did to us last year, he got what he deserved today." My heart rate quickens. This must be what Mr. du Bois was talking about on the phone with Coach Marino. I lean forward and accidentally rest my elbow in some of Rashad's spilled milkshake. Rashad glances at me and then at my elbow. "You've...got your clothes in the milkshake," he mutters.

"I know," I say quickly. I don't even care. "What do you mean, 'what Chauncey did to you last year'?"

Rashad crumples up his dirty napkin and jams it to the bottom of his milkshake glass. "I don't like talking about it," he snaps. He doesn't just sound angry; he sounds hurt, and his voice cracks slightly at the end.

I stare at Rashad in surprise. "But Rashad..."

"Dizzy. Please." Gumbo stares at me with a serious expression. He glances at his brother and shakes his head at me. "Just leave it alone, hmm?" he asks, raising his eyebrows at me. "Come on."

Blinking back a wave of tears, I keep my mouth shut and bury my face in my menu. This is too much. Rashad, sensing that my feelings are hurt, leans forward and clears his throat. I look at him, relieved to see that his eyes look much kinder. "The fried mac and cheese balls with a vanilla milkshake, right?" he asks, gesturing to my menu.

My mouth lifts into a small smile. "How'd you guess?"

Rashad gives me a look. "Desiree Davenport, I know you well," he says, tugging lightly on one of my curls.

I glance off in shame. It's true that Rashad knows me well, but what he doesn't know is how I much I hate bullying. He also doesn't know how invested I've become in his and Gumbo's mysterious beef with Chauncey, and I just can't let him find that out.

42

The Group Project

"I am disgusted" are the first words that slice out of Ms. Hernandez's mouth the next morning.

I take a huge gulp as she paces the classroom, glaring at everyone with her sharp eyes. After the madness the twins started in The Caf yesterday, I'm really not surprised that Ms. Hernandez is coming down on us today.

"Principal Ross told me what happened during the talent showcase yesterday," Ms. Hernandez states. "You all ought to be ashamed of yourselves." Her eyes fall on the twins, who are slouched in their chairs. Gumbo rests his head against his fist, while Rashad keeps squirming in his seat. We all sit in heavy silence until suddenly, a long, loud moaning sound fills the classroom. It sounds like someone's stomach.

The classroom erupts in a fit of giggles. In front of me, Rashad squirms even harder. I bite my lip to keep from laughing. It's him. His stomach must be acting up again.

"Everyone quiet down," Ms. Hernandez orders above the laughter. She doesn't look pleased at all.

Corinne raises her hand. "But Ms. Hernandez, not all of us were part of the food fight."

Ms. Hernandez looks at Corinne, letting her bun-filled head tilt to one side. "Maybe not, Corinne, but none of you did anything to stop it, either." The corners of Corinne's mouth twist up as she sinks lower in her seat. Ms. Hernandez's heels *click-click-click* as she walks to her desk and holds up a black-and-white photo. "Can anyone tell me who this is?"

The words fly out of my mouth. "That's McKayla Arlington."

Ms. Hernandez nods once. "Very good, Desiree. What do you know about her?"

I lick my lips nervously and glance around the classroom. Surprisingly, all eyes are on me. The twins are completely swiveled around in their seats, and Corinne stares at me with a raised eyebrow. Chauncey's eyes bore through mine. I sit taller and share what I learned from Mrs. du Bois last week. "McKayla Arlington was a nine-year-old from Alabama who was bullied by her classmates because of her dark skin." I hesitate, trying to steady the rockiness that threatens to take over my voice. "And she became depressed and took her life."

The classroom is silent. The twins lower their eyes, and I can tell they're thinking about what I said at last weekend's video game party. I look at Chauncey, who's just staring at me.

Ms. Hernandez nods solemnly. "That's right." She holds McKayla Arlington's picture high in the air and walks around the classroom. "A nine-year-old girl took her life because people hated her skin color."

"That's really sad," Morgan comments.

"Indeed, it is," Ms. Hernandez agrees. "But that will not happen at this school." She places McKayla Arlington's picture on her desk and clasps her hands tightly. "I've spoken with the other teachers and Principal Ross, and he's agreed to launch a school-wide case study on bullying."

"What's a case study?" a girl named Cheyenne asks.

"It means you're all going to participate in a group project," Ms. Hernandez says.

The class erupts in groans and protests.

"Ms. Hernandez, why do we *all* have to do it?" Charles asks. He sounds really mad. "I don't even bully anybody! Let the twins do it! This is all *their* fault!"

I hear an angry chorus of agreements. In front of me, the twins sit, motionless. It's like everybody has turned against *them* now.

Ms. Hernandez claps her hands, silencing the room. "It's true: The majority of you are not bullies and never pick on anybody, and now you're protesting this anti-bullying project. Where were your protests when you saw this bullying taking place?" Silence fills the room. "My point exactly." Ms. Hernandez grabs a stack of papers off her desk and hands a sheet to each student. "This is your rubric. You will work together to create an anti-bullying campaign, which you will present to the class on Monday, November fourth."

She holds up a bucket filled with strips of paper. "There will be six groups of four. I'd like everyone to pick a number, which will determine your group. Understand?"

The bucket slowly travels around the room. When the bucket lands on my desk, I pull out a paper strip with the number three. I pass the bucket to Corinne and sigh disappointedly when I see that she picked number five. Leaning forward, I peek over the twins' shoulders and frown to see that they both picked five, too. I can't help but feel a little jealous that all my friends got grouped together.

Once everyone picks a number, Ms. Hernandez reclaims her bucket. "Around the classroom, you'll find easels with the numbers one through six. Please stand by your easel."

The sound of scraping chairs fills the classroom as everyone gets in their groups. I walk to easel number three, which is set up by the door. To my disappointment, I'm stuck with Morgan and two other kids who never hand in their homework on time. What a bunch of duds.

Across the room, the twins group up with Corinne. I look around for their fourth group member, but no one shows up. That's when I spot Chauncey ripping his paper strip into shreds. He glares at the twins and snaps, "Ms. Hernandez, I'm not working with them. I can't stand them."

Rashad glares at Chauncey. "Ain't nobody trying to work with you, either."

Ms. Hernandez quickly steps in between all three of them. "All right, that's enough." She looks around the room. "Someone needs to switch groups with Chauncey."

I expect every girl in the classroom to run to be in the twins' group. To my surprise, no one volunteers. Everybody's definitely mad at them.

That's when my mind clicks. This is my ticket to really get through to the twins about this bullying situation.

I start to raise my hand, when suddenly, Charles steps forward. "Uh, Ms. Hernandez, I'll switch with Chauncey."

Ms. Hernandez looks pleased. "Thank you, Charles."

My forehead starts to sweat. Charles *cannot* be in that group. It has to be me.

"Ms. Hernandez, wait! *I'll* switch with Chauncey!" I blurt out, ignoring the crazy stares I get from the rest of the class. Even Chauncey looks surprised. The twins stare at me, and I can feel the heat of their suspicious eyes burning into my forehead.

Corinne bounces on her toes. "Ooh! Yes, Ms. Hernandez! Pick Dizzy!"

Ms. Hernandez glances at Corinne and turns back to me. "I'm sorry, Desiree, but Charles has already volunteered."

"But...uh...I'll make sure the work gets done! I'll keep everyone on track! Besides, two boys and two girls is a better balance than three boys and one girl, don't you think?"

Rashad gives me a funny look, like he knows I've got something up my sleeve, but I ignore him and keep my eyes locked on Ms. Hernandez. She rubs her chin, like she's thinking about my suggestion really hard. She looks like she's about to say no, but surprisingly, she nods firmly, like it's the best idea she's heard all morning. "I agree with you, Desiree," she states. "And since you seem to be so passionate about this topic, I'd like you to be your group's captain."

I walk over to Corinne, who grins like a madwoman. Chauncey walks to the Group Three easel and stares at me with an interesting expression. He doesn't smile or frown, but his eyes seem to say, *Thank you.*

I smile at Chauncey, but my lips freeze when I feel someone staring at me. I slowly turn my head to the left and my throat closes up. It's Rashad, and he looks me up and down with skepticism. Oh. My. Gosh.

Rashad caught me smiling at Chauncey.

My stomach drops. I force a smile at Rashad, hoping he'll smile back, but he doesn't, and I start to worry that my "brilliant plan" is about to blow up right in my face.

43

Nobody's Fool

The twins don't come to The Caf during lunch today.

At first, I'm confused, but then I remember their two-week lunch detention punishment. As much as I've always hated to see my friends get into trouble, I can't help but feel thankful this time. Chauncey is finally able to eat his lunch in peace, and since the twins were forced to apologize to him, maybe their bullying will end once and for all.

When school ends, we all try to make a mad dash out of the room, but Ms. Hernandez steps in front of the door. "Hold it!" she announces, holding her manicured hands in the air. "I want to encourage you all to get an early start on your anti-bullying campaigns. The deadline is weeks away, but do *not* waste the time. Your outline is due next Monday." Her sharp eyes glance around the silent room. "If you need a place to work, the public library is right around the corner. It's open seven days a week, so I don't want to hear any excuses." She steps away from the door and dismisses everyone.

The twins and I walk to our lockers, with Corinne trailing not too far behind us. "I'm *so* glad Ms. Hernandez put you in our group, Dizzy!"

Gumbo twists the knob on his locker and gives me a curious look. "You sure were excited to take Chauncey's spot even though Charles already volunteered, Dizzy."

My eyes dart to Rashad, who stares at me in skeptical silence. I gulp. "What are you talking about?"

Rashad sucks his teeth. "I saw you smiling at Chauncey, Desiree."

My fingernails clench into my palms. "So?"

Rashad shrugs and raises one of his dark eyebrows at me. "So, what was that about?"

"I was...just trying to keep peace in the classroom."

"You sure that's the real reason, Desiree?"

My stomach turns to knots as Rashad's hard eyes bore through mine. I glance to Gumbo for help, but he looks even more skeptical.

Trying to seem nonchalant, I pretend to be interested in organizing my already-neat locker. "Yeah, that's the reason. Don't you want me in your group, Rashad?"

Rashad looks me up and down in silence. After a brief moment, he nods. "Yeah, I want you in my group. Never mind." He turns back to his locker without another word.

"Let's just get out of here, 'cause The Crunch Bowl is calling my name," Gumbo says, rubbing his stomach.

I shove my books in my backpack. "We're not going to The Crunch Bowl today." The twins frown in confusion, but I keep talking. "We're going to the library so we can get a head start on this project."

Gumbo exchanges a bewildered frown with Rashad. "Hold up..."

"You heard Ms. Hernandez," I state. "We have to make the most of our time."

"We literally have until November," Rashad says.

Corinne rolls her eyes and turns to me. "Some boys just hate to see a girl in charge."

Gumbo turns to me in frustration. "Look, why can't we just work at The Crunch Bowl?"

"Please. Between milkshakes, chicken sliders, and fried mac and cheese balls, you *know* we wouldn't get any work done," I point out.

Corinne's eyebrows shoot up. "Y'all got fried mac and cheese balls over there?"

The twins nod proudly. "It's Desiree's favorite," Rashad states, giving me an impish smile. I glare at him and put my finger to my lips for him to be quiet, but it's too late. Corinne is already staring at me with big, hopeful eyes.

"Ooh, Dizzy, can't we just go for a little while?" Corinne begs. She sounds so hungry.

I groan tiredly. Even though I know how much Corinne wants to eat at The Crunch Bowl, I can't let the twins step over me.

"Not today, Corinne. We have to get started. Our outline is due next Monday," I state. As the group captain, I have to remain firm.

"Well, y'all can head to the library now if you want." Gumbo closes his locker and slings his backpack over his shoulder. "But I'm going home to get some food real quick."

"Word." Rashad closes his locker and follows Gumbo down the hall.

I glare after them. "Hey! Guys!"

"We'll meet y'all over there!" Gumbo calls.

"You'd better!" I yell, but the twins don't answer me. I sigh and motion for Corinne to follow me. "Come on. Let's get to the library before all the good tables get taken."

"Okay," Corinne mumbles. I know she wanted to go to The Crunch Bowl, but she'll just have to wait.

After gathering her own books and cheerleading uniform from her locker, Corinne and I head to the library. I text my mother about today's after-school scenario, and she promises to pick us up at 5:30 p.m. and take us to tonight's cheer practice. Hopefully we can get a good start on this anti-bullying campaign before the evening slips away from us.

Corinne and I make it to the library by 3:00 p.m. It's a cute, little library with work spaces, a computer area, and of course, endless rows of books.

"When do you think the twins will get here?" Corinne asks. She whips out a skinny, white pen and scribbles on the back of her notebook until the blue ink bleeds out.

"Hopefully they'll show up within the next few minutes," I say, but I'm wrong.

At a little after 3:30 p.m., Gumbo finally strolls into the library, smacking on some pink gum. I don't see Rashad.

I frown suspiciously. "Uh, where's your brother?"

"He's probably dipping out on us!" Corinne snaps.

Gumbo sits down across from us and removes his sunglasses. "Would y'all relax? Rashad's right outside."

My left eye starts twitching. "Outside doing *what*?"

Corinne sucks her teeth and flicks her hand in the air. "Whatever. Let's just start without him," she says.

"Rashad's not missing *any* of this meeting. Watch my stuff." I stand up and speed-walk to the exit. As soon as I get outside, my eye starts twitching up a storm.

I can see the back of Rashad's football jacket as he sits on the steps of the library. His head bobs back and forth as he laughs with two other guys who look very familiar. I look closer and realize that they're Dakota Beasley and Derrick Brown: two of the defensive backs from the Pirates football team. What are *they* doing here?

I take a small step back, suddenly feeling intimidated. I hadn't expected an audience, and I've never had to face Rashad around his other football teammates.

Taking a deep breath, I march up behind Rashad. "Hey! Rasha...aaah!" My right foot stomps on my left toe, sending me sailing towards the ground.

Rashad shoots up from the steps and catches me before my face meets the pavement. "Dizzy! You okay?" He stares down at my pink cowgirl boots in bewilderment. "We're gonna have to get you something you can walk in, Girl."

My face feels like it's on fire as Dakota and Derrick's laughter fills my ears. I glare at them and try to blink away the tears brimming behind my eyelids. "I'm...I'm fine."

I grab Rashad's wrist and drag him away from his annoying teammates. His dark eyebrows scrunch together in frustration as he stares down at me. "Dizzy, what's your deal?"

"My *deal* is that you're supposed to be inside so we can start this project, Rashad. Corinne and I have been waiting for you guys for thirty minutes."

"We were eating," Rashad reminds me. I start to respond, when suddenly, my stomach growls. Rashad smirks. "Sounds like you should've joined us, too."

I bite the inside of my cheek in embarrassment. "Well, we have work to do." I try to pull him towards the library, but he's too strong for me.

"Just take some notes on a piece of paper and give it to me later," Rashad says with a laugh. "Phil's inside. Just tell him what I need to do and he'll tell me at home. Why are you making this so hard?"

Rashad walks away from me and goes back to chatting it up with Dakota and Derrick. I stare at the back of his curly hair in disbelief. What is *wrong* with him? Is this the same boy who's been inviting me over to play video games? My friend who called me up when I was crying and held my hand as he led me up the stairs to his family's apartment for dinner?

I clench my fists and walk back up to Rashad. "Look, Rashad, Ms. Hernandez said that I'm the group captain."

"Yeah, the group captain, not my boss," Rashad says. "Why are you tripping, Desiree? I thought we were cool."

"So being 'cool' means that I let you walk all over me."

"Desiree, come on. It's not like that."

"I think it is. If you don't do your part, I'll tell Ms. Hernandez and..." I take a deep breath and force out the rest of my sentence. "You might not be going to Florida this year."

Rashad's expression darkens. He steps so close to me that I can see the peach fuzz on his chin. "You wouldn't do that, Desiree. You know what getting to Florida means to me."

I stare up at Rashad without batting an eyelash. I do know how much Florida means to him, but if he wants to act stupid about this project, then he doesn't deserve to go.

My jaw locks as I place a hand on my hip. "Don't try me, Rashad."

Rashad glares down at me in silence for what feels like an eternity. I wait for him to say something, but he doesn't. His nostrils flare as he takes slow, steady breaths, and I immediately realize that I've got him.

After a few moments, Rashad finally looks away, shifting uncomfortably from foot to foot. He turns to Dakota and Derrick and tells them that he'll see them tonight at practice. Then he follows me into the library.

As we silently walk alongside each other, I sneak a glance at Rashad. He may be my friend who *likes me* likes me, and this amazing athlete who's well on his way to becoming the next Dak Prescott, but at this moment, none of that matters to me, because at the end of the day, Desiree Davenport is nobody's fool.

44

The Meeting

When Rashad and I make it back to the table, Corinne throws her arms in the air. "You guys took forever!" she says.

I ignore her and sit down. My eyes shift over to Gumbo, who's grinning at Corinne with a gleam in his eyes. I look at Corinne, only to find her grinning right back. A second passes before their grins break into loud, crazy giggles.

"Uh...what's so funny?" I demand suspiciously.

"Nothing," Corinne squeals, struggling to calm her laughter. "While you were outside, Gumbo was in here doing impressions of our gym teacher. He's so crazy!"

At Corinne's compliment, Gumbo grins even harder. I roll my eyes. "Let's stop all this grinning so we can get started."

Rashad makes a big production as he sighs, shakes his backpack free from his shoulders, and dumps it onto the floor. He drops into the empty chair next to Gumbo and scoots closer to the table. He looks heated.

Gumbo taps his brother on the arm. "Ra, you okay?" he mutters. Rashad nods silently and lowers his eyes. Gumbo gives me a suspicious frown. "What's wrong with him?"

I shrug. "Nothing. Everything's cool, right, Rashad?"

Rashad narrows his eyes at me and chuckles without smiling. "Sure, Desiree. Miss *Captain*." He leans all the way back in his chair and folds his arms across his chest. "You wanted to lead the group, so go ahead. Lead."

I give Rashad a tight smile. "Believe me, Ra. I will."

Rashad's jaw locks. I whip Ms. Hernandez's rubric out of my folder and place it in the middle of the table. When I ask Corinne to take notes, she sighs and rubs her stomach.

"Okay," Corinne moans. I know she must be getting hungrier, but I need her help right now. I watch as she flips to a blank page in her notebook. She uncaps her pen and scribbles "Group Project Meeting" in her bubbly handwriting at the top of the page.

"Awesome," I state. "Okay, guys, we've got a few weeks to create a solid anti-bullying campaign. I wanted us to meet today just to go over our work schedule and brainstorm a couple of basic ideas. Sound good?"

I offer the twins a bright smile, hoping to get some sort of reaction out of them, but they give me nothing. Rashad sits with a dry expression, like it's literally killing him to sit here and listen to me. Meanwhile, Gumbo looks bored out of his mind. "Let's just hurry up so we can get out of here," he mutters, fiddling with the zipper on his leather jacket.

"You literally just sat down," I remind him.

"Yeah, well, we have football practice tonight and Coach Marino will fry us if we're late," Rashad states.

I roll my eyes. "And Corinne and I have cheer. So, if we just make the most of our time..."

"Hey, Phil!" a familiar voice calls from the front of the library. I whip around, ticked off to find Dakota and Derrick coming at us.

"Can we get some gum?" Derrick asks excitedly.

"How much y'all got?" Gumbo demands. Dakota and Derrick dig around in their pockets and whip out a bunch of quarters. Gumbo grins, stands up, and unzips his leather jacket. "All right, let me show y'all what I got today. Green apple, cherry, lemon-lime..."

As Gumbo goes through every single flavor in his inventory, my teeth clench with fury. I look over at Corinne to see if she's catching this crazy scene, but she's not even paying attention. Instead, she's flipping through a fashion magazine.

"Corinne!" I say. She jumps, causing her copy of *Fashionista Ooh-La-La* to drop right out of her hands.

"Huh?" Corinne asks. Her eyes are wide with shock. "I thought the meeting was on pause."

"Pause? Ain't nobody on pause!"

"I'm sorry!" Corinne stuffs the magazine into her backpack. "There was this ad for Glimmer Glamour..."

I tune her out and turn to Rashad for help. Instead of paying attention, he's paging through a three-ringed binder and looking at pages filled with arrows, x's, and o's. "Um, hello?" I demand, rapping my knuckles on the wooden table. Rashad looks at me and I frown at him. "What are *you* doing?"

"Studying my playbook," Rashad answers. "I've got a lot of work to do to make up for last week's game."

My left eye twitches so hard, it feels like it's about to fall out of the socket. "That's it!" I snap. Everyone is silent. I squint my eyes and point a finger at Dakota and Derrick. "You and you - leave us alone! This is a private group meeting!"

Gumbo sucks his teeth. He takes Dakota and Derrick's money and rewards them with a handful of gum flavors. "Thanks for your business. See y'all tonight," he mutters.

After they leave the library, I glance over at the digital clock on the wall, which reads 4:00 p.m. We're an hour behind schedule and we haven't done *anything*. "Guys, please! Let's just focus, okay?" I beg, holding up the rubric again.

I spend the next 15 minutes fighting to keep the twins' attention. Rashad actively flips through his playbook. When I try to get into our project ideas, he opens a Dak Prescott highlight video on YouTube. "Rashad, come on!" I whine.

"It's on mute," he says. "Keep talking; I'm listening." But I can tell he's not.

Meanwhile, Gumbo keeps getting up to sell gum around the library. I glare at him and turn to Corinne for support, but she isn't much help. "What was the last thing you said?" she asks, her pen hovering over the blank paper.

"Corinne!" I whine. "You're supposed to be listening!"

"I'm trying, but..." Corinne pauses, clutches her stomach, and lets out a huge burp.

Rashad's eyes dart up from his playbook in shock, while Gumbo comes running over to the table, cracking up. "Hey, that was pretty good!" he exclaims.

Corinne tugs on her braids. "Sorry, but I'm hungry!"

I sigh and rummage through my backpack for the mini chocolate chip muffins my mother packed for me. "Here," I say, handing the muffins to Corinne. She gobbles them down and leaves a burp in the air. It smells just like a hot dog.

Rashad looks mad. "Ew! Girl, what'chu been eating?"

"Definitely not fried mac and cheese balls," Corinne mutters, cutting her eyes at me. I just look away.

At 4:30 p.m., Gumbo's phone rings. I glare at him, but he ignores me and answers the call. "Hello? Hey, Dad." Rashad freezes and stares at Gumbo expectantly. Gumbo listens to his father and nods his head. "Okay. Bye." He stands up and slings his backpack over his shoulder. "Ra, c'mon."

Rashad closes his playbook and stands up. Neither he or Gumbo bother to push their chairs in. "You guys can't leave now!" I cry.

"Desiree, we have to," Rashad states firmly.

"We have to get ready for practice," Gumbo adds.

"Nuh-uh! That's not fair!" Corinne whimpers. "Y'all can't just dip out and leave us with all the work!"

The twins ignore Corinne and walk out of the library. My mind wants to call after them, but my mouth is at a loss for words. Some captain *I* am.

"That was a disaster," Corinne mumbles. I frown and stare at the blank page of her notebook. She didn't take a single note! She catches my eyes and frowns. "Sorry I wasn't much help."

There's no way I can stay mad at her. "It's okay."

"Well, we should talk to Ms. Hernandez about this. She might give us some better group members."

"No. Ms. Hernandez can't find out. That'll only make things worse."

"Then what are we supposed to do, Dizzy? The twins won't listen to us!"

"They'll come around. In the meantime, I want to get a start on this project," I glance at Corinne out of the corner of my eye. "You can read your magazine if you want."

I expect Corinne to reach into her backpack and pull out *Fashionista Ooh-La-La*, but to my surprise, she uncaps her pen and leans closer to me. "Girl, what are you talking about? We've got work to do!" she exclaims with a bubbly grin. "And I promise – no more magazines until later."

Over the next half hour, Corinne and I lay out the group responsibilities. We give the twins an easy job of researching bullying statistics and putting their findings onto a poster board.

"Well, what will *we* do?" Corinne asks.

I pause and think about it. "How about an essay? Instead of writing about people who get bullied, we can write about the people who bully and focus on why they do it in the first place."

"That's so smart!" Corinne chirps. "You know what we should include? A poem! I can write one and make it part of the presentation!"

"Yeah." I nod slowly as a wide smile stretches across my face. "That would make our presentation really, *really* pop!" I give Corinne a high five and tell her she's a genius.

At 5:30, my mother picks us up so we can get changed for cheer practice. I try to remember the cheers we've learned, but an anxious feeling brews in the pit of my stomach.

I'm the one who promised that this project would get done, and I'm the one who promised to keep everyone in my group on track. If I don't come through, I'll be answering to Ms. Hernandez in November, and it will not be pretty.

I don't know how I'm going to pull it off, but I've got to find a way to make this group work, for my sake *and* Chauncey's. Failure is not an option.

45

A Dead End

When I wake up on Wednesday morning, I hop out of bed and race through my morning routine. The weather's started to get a bit chillier, so I throw on a heavier jacket with a turtleneck zip-up, but when I walk outside to the bus stop, the twins are nowhere in sight. I panic, because they're always out here first, but then I hear feet stomping down the steps of The Crunch Bowl and the side door of the restaurant flies open.

Rashad hustles outside, followed by a very annoyed-looking Gumbo. Today, he's wearing a gray fleece jacket that's a little too big for him. "What's with the fit?" I ask.

Rashad laughs and shoves his brother in the shoulder. "Bri licked all his gum last night."

Gumbo glares at Rashad. "It's not funny. I caught her in the den sitting in front of my jar. She unwrapped every piece and licked each one, talking about, 'Let me see how this one's gonna taste.'" Rashad cracks up even harder. "You wouldn't be laughing if she'd jellied up your trophies," Gumbo shoots back. Rashad tries not to smile and looks away. "Now, I've got no inventory today," Gumbo says. "And I'm stuck in Dad's old jacket."

"Ooh," I mutter awkwardly. "Why couldn't you just wear your leather one?"

"Because then people would assume I have gum to sell when I don't," Gumbo snaps. "A good businessman never misleads his customers." He whips out his phone, while I chew on my bottom lip. He's not in a good mood at all, but that doesn't stop me from bringing up our group project.

"Well, I need to talk to y'all about our project," I say.

Gumbo glances up from his phone and shoots me an annoyed glare. "Why? We already talked about it yesterday."

"Yeah, but we never went over our responsibilities," I remind him through a tight smile. "Corinne and I are working on an essay and a poem. You guys have to make a poster." Gumbo rolls his eyes and goes back to his phone. Meanwhile, Rashad reaches into his bag and pulls out his playbook. I frown at him. "Rashad? Did you hear me?"

"Yeah, yeah. Poster. I got it," he mutters, but his eyes are glued to the playbook.

I sigh just as the bus pulls up to the corner. Gumbo sulks alone in a window seat near the front, while Rashad drops into a seat by himself near the middle. I start to sit with him, but then he quickly puts his backpack in the empty seat next to him and continues reading his playbook. I freeze. That's weird. We sit together every morning.

Feeling awkward, I hastily sit across from him and lean out into the aisle. "So, Rashad," I start in a cheery voice.

"So, Desiree," he says, mocking my cheerful energy.

I wince. Not even a "Dizzy" or a "Pony Boots" this morning. My jaw clenches. "I was hoping we could, uh, talk a little bit about the poster."

Rashad leans closer to his window. "You just talked about the poster."

I swallow a gulp. "I—I know, but...Corinne and I were thinking that you guys could gather some bullying statistics and make a whole, big thing out of them, you know?"

"Fine." Rashad flips to another page in his playbook and chews on his bottom lip thoughtfully.

My stomach turns. There's got to be something I can say to get him a *little* excited about this project. "Well, you guys can pick the color. For the poster, I mean. Any color, as long as it's bright, you know?"

Rashad exhales heavily. He sits straight up and looks me dead in the eyes. "Desiree, I'm not trying to be mean, but do you mind? I'm trying to study my plays."

I glare at Rashad, angry that he's making my eyes tear up. I look away before he notices the water pooling behind my eyelids. "You *are* being mean." I whip out my phone and sit all the way up against my window so I don't have to look at his annoying, handsome face.

Rashad must sense that he's hurt my feelings, because he sidesteps across the aisle and sits right next to me. "Pony Boots," he says. I face him, relieved to see that his eyes look much kinder. "I didn't mean anything by that. This weekend, the Pirates are up against the Warriors, and their star quarterback is really strong."

I stare at the seat in front of me. Since Rashad doesn't want to talk about the poster, I could care less about the Warriors' star quarterback. "Oh," I mutter dryly.

Rashad stares at me in surprise, like he's expecting me to have more questions, but I don't, and he leans closer to me. "His name's Ian Griffin, and his stats are no joke," he continues, like that's supposed to wow me. "He goes to a middle school on the other side of town, but we'll probably meet up in high school. He could be my competition for the starting quarterback position." Rashad taps his playbook.

"If I'm gonna beat this guy on Sunday, I have to know my stuff inside and out, you feel me?"

I fight the urge to roll my eyes. Rashad might be under a lot of pressure, but I'm still mad that he's not listening to me about the poster. "I get all that, Rashad, but our outline for the project is due on Monday and..."

Rashad turns away from me and returns his eyes to his playbook. "Dizzy, we'll talk about it tomorrow, all right?"

But we don't. For the rest of the week, the twins find excuses to change the subject from the project every time I bring it up. With Gumbo, it's making up gum sales from Tuesday's missed opportunities, and with Rashad, it's nothing but that playbook and Dak Prescott highlight videos. I understand that Rashad had a rough game last weekend, and I know how important football is to him, but that's no excuse for him to brush off my concerns about this project. I promised Ms. Hernandez that this project would get done.

"Well, as long as they know they're *doing* the poster," Corinne tells me on Friday during lunchtime. "What's the big deal, Dizzy?"

I frown at her. "Corinne, you don't get it. I've been listening to Rashad talk about football all week long, but he and Gumbo just won't give me the same respect when I bring up the project. It's like they don't want to talk about it at all."

Corinne sighs. "Well, like I said, some boys just hate to see a girl in charge. Plus, they probably feel under attack with this whole project after everything they've done to Chauncey." I nod in amazement. Corinne's right. "Where are the twins anyway?"

I chew on my mother's homemade chicken salad sandwich and blink tiredly. "Lunch detention. They'll be there for another week." I pause, still thinking about the poster. "I just don't get it. Gumbo said that Rashad really likes me."

"He probably does, Dizzy; he just doesn't want you telling him what to do," Corinne states with a shrug. "Plus, he's probably jealous of how you smiled at Chauncey."

I raise my eyebrows. "How do you know all of this?"

"I watch a lot of old movies with my grandma. Girl, those movies have all *kinds* of personalities. I've seen Rashad's plenty of times." Corinne raises an eyebrow and sips on her chocolate milk. We spend the next few minutes eating in silence, when suddenly, I spot Chauncey exiting the lunch line. Our eyes lock and he stops dead in his tracks. I half expect him to turn away and keep walking, but instead, he does something that surprises me; he smiles.

Time freezes as Chauncey approaches my table, carrying his lunch tray in both hands. "Hey, Dizzy," he says. His eyes, usually so sad and closed off, seem open right now.

I start to smile back at Chauncey, but I tense up when an image of Rashad pushes its way into my mind. Even though he's not here right now, I feel like he's staring right at me with his intense eyes. I take a deep breath, reminding myself that he and Gumbo are in lunch detention right now, so there's no way they can see me. I will *not* miss out on this opportunity to talk to Chauncey.

"Hey, Chauncey. How's it going?" I finally ask.

"Okay." Chauncey rubs one of the white patches near his eyes. "I wanted to say...thanks for, you know, yesterday."

I smile, thinking back to my spontaneous group switch. Chauncey was grateful, but the twins were skeptical. My smile dims as I look at Chauncey. "No problem. People helping people, right?" Chauncey nods, while Corinne just glances between us in amusement. I pretend not to notice her and focus on Chauncey. "Nice efforts on the field last week. Maybe you'll get more action this Sunday, you know?"

Chauncey shrugs. "It's not up to me," he mutters.

My jaw clenches in deep thought as I think back to Chauncey trying to get into the games, week after week. Then I think about how he always walks to that car. "Chauncey, why don't you ever bring any family to the football games?"

Chauncey glances away. "My parents think football is a dead end." His words hang in the air like a bad smell. What kind of attitude is that? I start to ask Chauncey to explain, but he's already backing away. "See you later, Dizzy," he says, and he walks off to his usual table by the lunch monitor.

Corinne's hazel eyes go wide with surprise. "Um, do the twins know you're friends with Chauncey?"

"I'm not really *friends* with him," I point out. "I just don't like seeing him get bullied."

"Well, you'd better be careful, Girl. This whole thing could get really messy," she says. I stare at the table and nervously twiddle my thumbs. Corinne's right. "You really think Chauncey will get to play a lot during the next game?"

"I hope so," I say, but I don't feel very confident. Without any family sitting in the bleachers, he might not get to touch that ball at all.

46

Rashad's Point of View: Redemption

On Sunday, I'm up early. I can't sleep; I've got too much on my mind. Last week I was humiliated in front of the entire field and my boys suffered a loss because of it. I let everybody down, including myself. Today, it'll be different, because I'm fired up and ready to go. The Warriors are going *down*.

I sit up, stretch, and let my eyes glide around my room. My backpack's sitting on the floor by the door. I sneak a glance at Phil, who's still asleep, so I stealthily slip out of bed and over to my backpack. I need to study my playbook. My fingers tighten around the zipper and I pull.

"Ra." My fingers freeze. I slowly turn around and see Phil sitting up in his bed. "Couldn't sleep, huh?" he asks.

Busted.

My ears heat up. Phil is only three minutes older than me, but sometimes, the difference feels like years. "Um...I..."

Phil sort of smiles. "Me neither." He opens the drawer on his nightstand, pulls out his playbook, and holds it in the air. I grin and whip out my playbook from my backpack. What would I do without my twin?

We spend an hour reviewing our plays and footage from our previous games. I take notes on what's worked, while Phil points out how we can improve. Going over all this stuff makes me think about Desiree. My jaw locks with guilt as I think back to how I gave her a hard time at the library last week. I really like Desiree a lot. To be honest, I've been crazy about her since the day we met. But when I saw her smiling at Chauncey that morning during the group assignments, I got mad. I was jealous. Plus, this whole project is rubbing me the wrong way. I don't need to hear all that today.

At around nine o'clock, Mom knocks on our door and calls us to breakfast. We join her, Dad, and Brianna at the kitchen table and hold hands to say grace. Then we dig in. Dad always makes the best waffles and Mom's homemade biscuits are out of this world.

"Mmm..." Phil moans, munching on the food. "Dad, you put your *foot* in these eggs."

Brianna cracks up and turns to me. "Ra-Ra...Phil said 'foot in the eggs.' It's *cheese*."

We all laugh, not at Phil's comment, but at Brianna's. Then Mom and Dad ask us about school. Phil and Brianna do all the talking. I just listen and quietly finish my plate. Every now and then, I glance up and see Dad staring at me thoughtfully. Instead of joining the conversation, I just force a smile and take long sips of my juice. It could use more ice.

I check my phone for a "good luck" text from Desiree. There isn't one, so I sigh and put my phone face-down on the table. I look up and Dad is still staring at me. "So, Ra." He takes a bite of his food and smirks at me. People always say he reminds them of Terrence Howard. "How's Desiree doing?"

Everyone stares at me expectantly. My cheeks are on fire and I know my family can see. Dad raises his eyebrows at me, P stifles a laugh, and Brianna giggles. "Ra-Ra! Your face is turning red!" she says.

"Finish your food, Brianna," Mom instructs, rubbing my sister's face. Brianna does as she's told and Mom smiles at me. "Desiree wasn't here for dinner last week. She's all right?"

I clear my throat and pray to God that everyone would stop staring at my burning face. "Oh, yeah, Desiree's cool," I say, nodding. I'm too embarrassed to share the group project confusion with my parents, so I just stand up and take my empty plate to the sink. "May I be excused?"

Dad stares at me for a few seconds. I can tell he's amused. He finally nods. "Yes, you can be excused."

I exhale in relief. "Thanks, Dad," I mutter, and I hurry back to my room. That was close. I don't feel like answering anymore questions. I gotta stay focused. I need to prepare some words to pump up my team.

A few hours later, Phil and I are dressed in our uniforms and cleats. Mom gets Brianna settled in her car seat, while Phil and I help Dad load up the truck with posters, water, ice, Gatorade, snacks and the first-aid essentials. Dad checks his phone to see if any of our teammates need a ride to the game. No one does, so we all pile in and Dad drives us to the field. I'm nervous, so I busy myself by drumming my hand against my knee. Phil taps me on the shoulder and holds out an earbud. I take it and he cues up a Chance the Rapper album. This is the perfect stuff to get me in the mood.

At the field, Mom and Brianna find seats at the top of the bleachers with our extended family. Phil and I help Dad unload the truck and meet our coaches and teammates by the water cooler. Everybody's chatting and getting a quick stretch in. I find a spot alone and warm up my passing arm, when suddenly, Dad taps me on the shoulder. "Come here,

Ra." I gulp and follow him over to an empty spot near the bleachers. He crouches down so we're at eye-level. "You nervous?"

I force a laugh. "Me? Nah."

Dad gives me a look. "Boy, quit lying." My ears get hot. Between Dad and Phil, I can't hide *anything*. Dad clamps a hand on my shoulder. "Listen, Son. Last week is in the past. Today's a new day and it's a new game. Get out there and do your best. I'm proud of you no matter what, okay? Remember: You're number one." I nod and Dad gives me a double high-five. "Now, come on. Your team's waiting for you."

Taking a deep breath, I follow Dad over to the huddle. Everybody's here now, and all eyes are on me. I give my boys a quick head nod and they dap me up. It feels good to be back.

"All right, Pirates, listen up!" Coach Marino shouts, snapping all of us to attention. "I'm so glad to see you all out here today. Last week, we had a little setback, but we put in some hard work during practice. I'm proud of what I saw. Now, it's time for us to execute. Let's show these Warriors the Pirate way!" Coach Marino looks at me and places a hand on my shoulder. "Rashad, we're all glad to see you back and healthy," he says. I glance around at my teammates. Everyone's looking right at me, except for Chauncey, who stares at the grass. I ignore him and turn back to Coach. "Is there anything you want to say to the team before kickoff, Rashad?"

I turn to P, who gives me a sly thumbs-up. I nod, clear my throat, and stand taller. "All right, listen up, fellas!" I start in a strong voice. "Last week was rough. I wasn't on my game, I made a lot of mistakes, and I let y'all down. For that, I'm sorry." I glance at Dad, who just stares at me quietly. I take another deep breath and continue. "But...today's a new day and it's a new game. I'm gonna go out there and give one hundred-and-ten percent, and I know y'all fellas will do the same. We gotta come out strong, play smart, and push through when it gets tough, y'all hear me?"

"Yeah!" my boys shout back.

"Y'all are my brothers — my blood," I say, throwing a subtle nod at P. "I believe we can win today, but I need your help. Offensive team, be on your blocking game. Receivers, be alert. Good hands today. Defensive team, be out there like tornadoes and let these Warriors know who they're playing against." In the distance, I see the cheerleaders huddling up together. I spot Desiree in the crowd and smile to myself, suddenly feeling warm. I'm empowered. Today, Desiree will see my redemption. "Now, let's go out there and play some football!" I shout at my team. "Where's my d-line at? Y'all ready?"

"We ready!" they shout back.

"Let me hear from my o-line! Are y'all *ready?*"

"WE READY!"

We win the coin toss and decide to receive. Phil gives me a high-five and Dad shakes my shoulder. He's not smiling, but his eyes look really proud.

I backpedal towards the water cooler and accidentally bump into Chauncey. He glares at me and I take a menacing step towards him. "Don't get it twisted, Spots," I mutter. "That pep-talk wasn't for you. I'll never forget what happened last year."

Chauncey narrows his eyes at me, but he doesn't answer. I give him a final glare, walk off, and turn my attention to the field. It's showtime.

47

No Pushover

That Sunday, my mother drives us to the game against the Warriors at Middletown Middle School. I don't feel like cheering for anybody today, since the twins have given me such a hard time with this anti-bullying project. I texted them last night and asked about their progress with the poster, but I never heard back from them. They might be all pumped up to beat Ian Griffin today, but my mind is set on our outline that's due tomorrow, and the twins haven't done their part.

My mother shoots me a worried glance. "You're kind of quiet, Desiree. Is everything okay?" She lowers the volume on the song *I Hear a Symphony* by The Supremes, but I wish she'd turn it up. I like this song.

"Yeah, I'm fine, Mommy," I say. I don't want to tell her anything about the twins avoiding their project responsibilities. Not when she and Mrs. du Bois have become such good friends. It would make everything too complicated. "I'm just thinking about all of the homework I have to finish up before tomorrow," I say.

My mother nods her head. "Well, I'm all caught up with my work, so I can help you when we get home." She turns up *I Hear a Symphony* and sings her heart out.

When we arrive to the field, my mother sits in the visitor's bleachers with the du Bois family, while I group up with my cheer squad. The twins and the other Pirates football players are huddled near the bench with Coach Marino, the assistant coaches, and Mr. du Bois. I see Chauncey out there, too, but he's hanging towards the back of the group. I bite my tongue nervously, hoping that he gets to do *something* today.

At 1:15, the game begins with the Warriors on offense. Just like Rashad said, their star quarterback, Ian Griffin, is no joke. Within the first couple of plays, we can see that he moves the ball around quite well. I hope Rashad is paying attention, since he usually passes the ball to Gumbo.

At the end of the first quarter, the Warriors are winning 7-0. I glance at Rashad, who stares Ian down with a combination of awe and nervousness in his eyes. I can tell that he's thinking about his screwups from last week's game, and I hope his stomach doesn't act up today.

Gumbo grips Rashad's shoulders, like he's trying to encourage him. Rashad nods and gives his brother a fist bump. The twins and the rest of the Pirates' offensive linemen take the field. Coach Marino claps it up. "Come on, Pirates! Let's go! Let's get in the game! No penalties!" he shouts. Mr. du Bois doesn't say a word. He just stands, motionless, with his chin resting on his knuckles. He looks so intense right now. I hope the twins can do something.

Once everyone is staggered on the line of scrimmage, the Pirates' center snaps the ball to Rashad, who catches it and backpedals with the Warriors' defense right on his heels. I'm almost tempted to scream out to Rashad, but then, right before he gets sacked, he shoots the ball from his hand. The ball sails through the air like a bullet and lands right in Gumbo's hands. It's a completed pass, and Gumbo takes off down the field. Using his stiff arm, Gumbo blocks two of the Warriors' defense from catching him. He's running so fast that he starts to stumble, and I'm afraid that he'll fall. There's a collective gasp from our side of the bleachers, but then Gumbo regains his balance and breezes into the end zone. The Pirates' fans go wild.

"Would you look at that! du Bois to du Bois, and it's a 55-yard touchdown!" the announcer exclaims from his seat in the press box.

"Ra-Ra-Ra! Do it all, du Bois!" my cheer squad cries. Coach Marino pumps his fists victoriously, while Mr. du Bois claps his hands so fast, I'm afraid they're going to fall off.

"Let's go, Ra-Ra! Good hands, Phil! Good hands!" Mr. du Bois shouts.

Out on the field, the twins pat each other's helmets and break into a victory dance. Our kicker makes a field goal, putting us on the board with seven points. Thank God. I glance around the field in search of Chauncey and finally spot him standing on the sidelines. He tugs on Coach Marino's sleeve and points to the field. My heart soars just the teensiest bit. Maybe he'll get some good action today, after all.

But I'm wrong. Chauncey rotates loosely throughout the first half, but the ball never comes his way. Meanwhile, Rashad is absolutely on *fire* today. He throws nothing but completed passes to different guys on the team, inching us closer and closer to the goal line at each down. Our offensive line is doing an amazing job protecting Rashad today. He really has no choice but to move the ball around, because the Warriors stay all over Gumbo. Sometimes, Chauncey gets an opening on the field, but Rashad never passes the ball to him. My heart sinks, but I try to smile as I cheer "Ra-Ra-Ra!" for what feels like the ten-millionth time.

At the start of the second half, we're tied 7-7. Coach Marino removes the twins from the game to give them a break. He puts our second quarterback – Number Six – in the game, but this proves to be a big mistake.

During the next play, Number Six's pass is intercepted and the Warriors take control of the ball. The play begins, but the ball is fumbled. Surprisingly, one of our defensive guys recovers the ball and the Pirates are back in control. OMG! The ball is hiked and Number Six is in motion. Assuming that Chauncey is on his game, Number Six makes a quick pass to Chauncey, who catches the ball, but stands motionless on the field. I can hear the crowd screaming for Chauncey to run, but he just ignores everybody. It's like he's stunned or nervous or something. He gets tackled and I nervously glance at the sidelines. The twins glare at Chauncey with pure disgust. Mr. du Bois and the assistant coaches look angry and baffled.

Coach Marino yanks his cap off his head. "Time out!" Eyes bugged and teeth clenched, he points at Chauncey, then jerks his thumb behind him angrily. I almost laugh, but I stop myself. He taps Gumbo and motions for him to take the field. As Gumbo passes Chauncey, he glowers at him. Chauncey just sulks to the bench. I swallow a huge gulp and turn to Coach Robin, who looks very unimpressed. It's a safe bet we won't be making up any cheers for Chauncey this season.

As we advance to the fourth quarter, Coach Marino puts our third quarterback – Number 12 – in the game. Number 12 makes a few completed passes here and there, getting us closer to the end zone little by little. However, the Warriors' defensive line remains strong and prevents us from scoring a touchdown. As the clock winds down, Coach Marino calls another time out and puts Rashad back in the game as our quarterback. I really hope he doesn't try to pass it to Gumbo; the Warriors will expect that and will try an interception. It'll still be a tie, and we'll go into overtime.

At the start of the play, Rashad receives the ball from our center and takes a few steps back. It looks like he's about to hand the ball off to our running back, but surprisingly, Rashad runs the ball himself! Our side of the bleachers goes nuts as Rashad zooms past the Warriors' defense and into the end zone. He scores a touchdown and our kicker makes the field goal, putting us in the lead 14-7. We *won* today!

Coach Marino and the assistant coaches throw their arms in the air in celebration, while Mr. du Bois beams and claps with pride. In the bleachers, the rest of the du Bois family cheers and waves their posters. The Pirates shake hands with the Warriors and return to the sidelines for our post-game pep talk. Coach Marino, the assistant coaches, and Mr. du Bois reward the football team with a round of high fives. Everyone looks ready to take on next week's opponents, except for Chauncey. As usual, he looks glum.

"Listen up, Pirates!" Coach Marino bellows cheerfully. "The season is halfway over. We're at a record of three and one, and today was proof that we are back on track." He smiles at Rashad, who stands taller and looks his coach right in the eyes. "Let's keep the momentum going throughout practice this week," Coach Marino continues, "and you'd better believe we're coming back next week stronger than ever. It's only up from here, baby! Who are we?"

"PIRATES!" we all scream.

As the crowd disperses, I notice the twins standing across the field with their father. Mr. du Bois grips his hands around Gumbo's wrists and grins. "My son with those good hands! That's what I like to see out there, you hear me?" He slaps Gumbo a double high five and wraps an arm around Rashad. "And what did I tell *you* last week, huh? You work *hard*, Ra, and no one can beat you. Who's Number One?"

"I'm Number One," Rashad states. There's a confident fire in his voice. I can tell that he believes each word he says.

I turn away from the twins, trying to make sense of the different emotions I'm feeling. Even though I'm mad at the twins for brushing me off with the project, I can't help but feel happy for Rashad, and I'm proud that he bounced back from last week. However, I also feel sorry for Chauncey. I know he messed up today, but he should have gotten more chances. Rashad got the chance to redeem himself; Chauncey deserved the same.

"Hey! Wait up!" Rashad's voice suddenly rings out from across the field. I turn around and see him approaching me with his helmet in his hand. I panic and glance around the field in search of Chauncey. He's standing by the water cooler and filling his paper cup with Gatorade. If he turns around and sees me talking to Rashad, I'll be toast.

I hastily back up and look around for Corinne, but she's nowhere in sight. Where the heck is she? Before I can even call her name, someone's finger taps me on the shoulder. I whip around and meet eyes with Rashad, whose dimples look extra-big as he grins down at me. "What's up?"

"Uh...I..." My mouth hangs open as I struggle to form a complete sentence. Chauncey takes a few sips from his paper cup and stares out into the field. Thank God he's not looking over here. I turn back to Rashad and shrug my shoulders. "Nothing much. Good game."

Rashad smiles wider. "Thanks. I was on fire today." He swipes one of my pom-poms and twists it around. "Nice cheering. Especially that 'Ra-Ra-Ra' one," he says, smirking.

I glance past Rashad and over at Chauncey. He's throwing his cup away and it looks like he's getting ready to leave the field. Panicking, I reach for my pom-pom. "Can I have that back, please?" I ask in a tight voice.

Rashad stares at my outstretched hand and laughs. "Hey, Worm Tooth's looking pretty good today."

I give Rashad a tight smile. Normally, I'd laugh along with him, but today, Chauncey's nearby and I don't want him to catch me grinning all up in Rashad's face. I snatch my pom-pom from Rashad and breeze right past him. "I have to go."

There's a brief second of silence before I hear Rashad's voice again. "Dizzy!" he cries. This time, Chauncey looks up and stares right at me. Oh. My. Gosh. I want to run, but then Rashad steps in front of me. He looks disappointed, and hurt. "I'm trying to talk to you."

I don't answer Rashad right away. Chauncey is staring me down, and I can't tell what he's thinking. "What, Rashad?" I ask impatiently.

Rashad stares at me in surprise and scratches his head. "Well, are you coming over for dinner tonight? It's gonna be a big celebration." When I don't react, his eyes go wide with worry. "I'll pick you up, same as always, Pony Boots."

My spine stiffens. I'd love to spend another Sunday evening with the du Bois family, but I can't give in. Not after the twins brushed me off this week. I'm no pushover.

"Today's not a 'Pony Boots' kind of day, Rashad," I state. Rashad takes a small step back and blinks a few times. "Listen, I've got too much to do tonight. The outline for our project is due first thing tomorrow morning and you and Phil haven't done anything." I say these last few words loud enough for Chauncey to hear.

Rashad's eyes dart left and right. He looks really disappointed. "But Dizzy..."

"Every time I've tried to bring up the project, you and Phil have just brushed me off," I remind Rashad. He looks like I've just kicked him in the stomach, so I sigh and gesture to the field. "I know that today was a really important game for you, and I'm happy that you won, Ra."

Rashad's mouth lifts into a tiny smile, but his eyes look sad. "So, why can't you come over? You, me, and Phil can work on the outline together."

I glance off. "No. I'll just work on it with Corinne over the phone." I look around the field in search of Corinne and frown when I see her giggling with Gumbo by the bench. Doesn't she care that he's not helping with the project?

Rashad chews on his bottom lip and sways from side to side. "Can I make you a plate and bring it to you later?"

I stare at Rashad and nod my head. Eating his family's delicious cooking *does* sound nice. "Sure, thanks," I finally say. "See you later, Rashad. Great game today." I walk around Rashad, but freeze when Gumbo approaches me.

"Hey, Dizzy," Gumbo says. He glances at Rashad and gives me a knowing smile. "Did Ra invite you over tonight?"

I fold my arms across my chest and look Gumbo up and down. "Yeah, but I'm not coming."

Gumbo frowns in disappointment. "Why not?"

I shrug and glance over my shoulder. "Ask your brother." Gumbo just stares at me, so I force a smile. "Good hands today."

"Uh, thanks," Gumbo says. He gives me a strange look and hustles over to Rashad. I glance past them and see Chauncey walking away from the field, alone. He walks to the same car from last week, but this time, there's a woman standing by the passenger door.

"Boy, get in the car and come on," she snaps impatiently. Her permed bob looks fresh and expensive, like it was just done by a professional at the Pump It Up Hair Salon, and I love her outfit: a red leather jacket with a black turtleneck, faded jeans, and high-heeled, black ankle boots.

"Ma, can you unlock the trunk?" Chauncey shoots back. My heart stops. *That's* Chauncey's mother?

Chauncey grimaces as his mother opens the trunk. He throws his equipment into the cluttered trunk and climbs into the passenger seat. As he and his mother drive off, I stare after them in anger.

I bet Chauncey could be one of the stars of the Pirates football team if his mother were sitting in those bleachers, clapping it up with posters and cheers and chants all for him.

Why does she think football is a dead end?

48

He's Jealous

On Monday morning, Ms. Hernandez collects the group project outlines. I whip our three-page outline from my English folder and hand it to Ms. Hernandez. She glances it over with a pleased smile and says, "Very impressive."

I exchange a relieved glance with Corinne. Last night, we spent hours on the phone coming up with something that we hoped would please Ms. Hernandez. Rashad came over with the food, as promised, and even offered to come inside and help me, but I turned him down. I wanted to stay focused.

As Ms. Hernandez walks off to collect the other outlines, the twins turn around in their seats and face me and Corinne. "Um...what did you guys put in the outline?" Gumbo asks in a low voice. He sounds ashamed.

I reach into my folder, pull out two copies of the outline, and hand them to the twins. They flip through the pages and I clear my throat. "Our responsibilities are listed here, so there shouldn't be any confusion about anything."

Rashad nods quickly and gestures to the outline. "We'll get it done."

"You'd better," Corinne quips.

Gumbo twirls his sunglasses around his fingers. "Are y'all trying to meet up in the library anymore or...?"

"No. We're not," I snap, still angry about last week. "We all have the outline. That's it."

Rashad looks stunned. He leans over to his brother and whispers, "Oh, she's mad."

I purse my lips. You bet I am.

And for the next few weeks, I don't bring up the project anymore. I work on the essay, and I think Corinne makes good progress on her poem. The twins continue to shine on the football field, putting their all into every pass, catch, and rushing yard. They lead the Pirates to victory after victory, but no thanks to Chauncey. He hardly touches the ball during his time on the field. I look for his mother in the bleachers, but she's never there. Instead, she just pulls up at the end of each game to get Chauncey. Rashad continues to invite me over for dinner, and I'm always tempted to say yes, but I hold out and make up excuses as to why I can't make it. Rashad needs to understand that I'm no pushover.

The only bright side I've noticed is that the twins have stopped bullying Chauncey. They return to The Caf, where they have their lunch and mind their own business. Maybe it's the fear of getting in trouble with Principal Ross or Coach Marino again, or maybe it's our past conversation about McKayla Arlington, but there's definitely a change in the air.

"I'm very pleased with you all," Ms. Hernandez says during the last Tuesday in October. "It's clear that you all are taking this project seriously, as you should. Keep it up. I look forward to hearing your presentations next month."

My eyes immediately cut to Corinne. We exchange a wary glance and I shift my gaze to the twins. They appear nonchalant, and I nervously drum my fingers against my desk as I imagine them not coming through with that poster.

"In other news," Ms. Hernandez continues, "your classmate, Chauncey, has an announcement."

Chauncey walks to the front of the room with a plastic bag in his hand. He speaks to the class in a nervous voice. "My birthday's on Saturday and I'm turning twelve, and..." Chauncey pauses and scratches one of the white spots near his nose. "I'm having a birthday party at my house, so..." He lifts his plastic bag and stares at Ms. Hernandez. "I have invitations for everybody. If you're coming, please RSVP by Friday."

Is Chauncey seriously inviting these people to his birthday party? Sure, he's not being bullied *now*, but just a few weeks ago, everybody was laughing when he broke his desk, chanting "Spots" at him in the hallway, and pelting him with food and trash after his performance in the talent showcase.

Then again, maybe Chauncey just wants everyone to see past his skin and like him, and they should. Maybe he thinks that having a birthday party will help him get friends.

Chauncey passes out the invitations. Nobody looks him in the eye or even says "thank you." Everyone just takes an invitation and turns away. These people probably won't even bring gifts. After Chauncey saw me talking to Rashad at the Warriors football game, I probably won't get invited.

But suddenly, Chauncey approaches my desk. Time slows down as he reaches into his plastic bag and unveils a small, white envelope. I can't help but stare at his hand, all white with a few specks of brown, as he drops the envelope on my desk. *To Desiree*, it reads, and it even has a little smiley face next to it. I glance around the room at some of the other invitations. No one else has a smiley face on theirs.

"Thank you," I mouth. Chauncey's calm eyes sparkle gladly as he smiles at me. He drops an invitation on Corinne's desk and she snatches up the envelope like she deserves it. It's interesting how people act when someone throws a party. Free food, good music, nobody wants to be left out.

Chauncey walks along the front row of desks and hands out the last few invitations. As he gets closer to the twins, I panic. How will the twins react when Chauncey gives them their invitations? Will they be shocked? Will they feel guilty? Will they apologize – *really* apologize – for all of the pain and humiliation they've caused him?

But as Chauncey gives out the last invitation, I freeze. His plastic bag is empty, and the twins haven't gotten anything. Oh. My. Gosh.

My face hits the floor as Chauncey strolls in front of the twins, dangling the empty bag in their faces. He crumples the bag into a tight ball and strolls back to his seat. I look at the twins, who stare at Chauncey with wide eyes. They look stunned, angry, and even a little bit embarrassed. Part of me feels sorry for the twins, since they *are* my friends, but when I think about the way they've bullied Chauncey, they really don't deserve invitations to his birthday party.

When school lets out at 2:30 p.m., I say bye to Corinne and meet the twins at our lockers. Gumbo nudges Rashad in the shoulder. "Did you ask Dizzy about you-know-what?" he mutters.

My ears perk up and I look right at Rashad. He glances at me with a nervous half-smile. "Oh...um..."

Gumbo smirks and straightens his leather jacket. "I'll be right back," he says, and he hustles down the hall to sell his hard gum to a group of scrawny sixth graders.

I turn back to Rashad, who nervously fiddles with the knob on his locker. He takes a deep breath and looks at me. "Do you want to go roller skating, Dizzy?"

My eyebrows shoot up in surprise. "Where?"

Rashad opens his locker and I pretend not to notice the 77 he got on his latest English essay. Maybe I'll offer to give him some writing tips one day. "At this place downtown called City Wheels," he says, smiling. "It closed down at the end of the summer, and now it's coming back with a grand reopening. My dad knows the owner, and they're having a free skate night this weekend."

I open my locker and shove my books into my backpack, thinking back to how much fun I used to have roller skating in my old neighborhood. City Wheels definitely sounds like the spot for me. "Wow, that's exciting," I say.

"Well, my parents ungrounded me and Phil, and we're going skating on Saturday. Do you want to come?"

The back of my neck grows hot with guilt as I think about Chauncey's party invitation. I can't disappoint Chauncey. "I'm sorry, Rashad...but I can't make it."

Rashad looks crushed. "Are you still mad at me about the poster? Phil and I are doing it, Dizzy."

"I know. It's not that. It's just..." Before I can even make up an excuse, Chauncey's party invitation slips out of my math folder and lands on the floor.

My tongue feels like a piece of lead as Rashad stares at the invitation. He looks at me with betrayal in his eyes. "Oh, I see. You'll be too busy going to your boyfriend's stupid party."

"Chauncey's not my boyfriend!" I cry, but Rashad just crouches down and shoves more books into his backpack.

Just then, Gumbo hustles back over to us with an easy smile. "Hey. You coming roller skating?" he asks me.

"Phil, you were right. She *does* like Chauncey," Rashad snaps at his brother. "She's going to his party."

Gumbo raises his sunglasses at me. His face is creased with confusion and anger. "What? Ra and I weren't invited."

The hallway feels like it's spinning. "I...I know, but I *was* invited. Besides, Corinne really wants me to go with her. I can't just not show up."

The twins exchange angry glances. "You'd seriously rather chill with *Chauncey* than us?" Gumbo demands.

Rashad slams his locker shut and steps closer to me. "I *knew* you were acting funny." He looks at Gumbo. "That's why she stopped coming over on Sundays. She was probably hanging out with Chauncey from back then."

"Wait a minute! That's not true!" I shriek.

"Yeah, right," Rashad says. "You and Chauncey should just run off together and get married." Hearing the hurt and anger in Rashad's voice makes me want to crawl into a hole, but instead of showing defeat, I stare right into Rashad's eyes and laugh. He glares at me. "What's so funny?"

"You, Ra," I say. "You sound so jealous."

Rashad frowns and takes a step back. "I'm not jealous," he says, scratching his ear. Ah, lying again.

I smirk and fold my arms. "Shouldn't you guys be focused on football, anyway?"

Gumbo sucks his teeth. "We *are* focused, but—"

I cut Gumbo off and smile at Rashad. "Especially you, Ra. This Sunday's the last game before the League Playoffs, and you've gotta know your stuff inside and out, right?" Rashad blinks and glances at the floor. It's obvious that he knows I'm right, so I smile even bigger and bring my act home. "Hey. Who am I?" I do a sloppy backpedal and draw my right arm back, like I'm about to throw a football. Then I do a little dance with my feet.

Rashad remains stone-faced, but Gumbo laughs. "Nuh-uh. She's disrespecting you, Bro."

"That's not even how I look," Rashad tells me, but a small smile starts to play on his lips.

"It's not? How about this?" I grin and do a few more wild backpedals and fake football throws, until finally, Rashad can't help himself. He laughs.

"You're crazy, Desiree Davenport," he mutters. I smile and he gives me the side-eye. "But you're still jacked up for going to Chauncey's party."

My face tenses. "Rashad, come on."

"Look, if you'd rather spend your Saturday with him, go ahead. Do whatever you want." Rashad turns away from me and walks down the hall.

I turn to Gumbo. "Phil, listen..."

Gumbo opens his locker and cuts his eyes at me. "We'll see you on the bus, Dizzy," he mumbles. He grabs a few books from his locker and follows Rashad down the hall, leaving me standing there, alone.

49

Chauncey's Party

The next day, the twins bombard me with reasons as to why I should choose City Wheels over Chauncey's birthday party. Some of their reasons are pretty persuasive, but I remind myself to stay focused on my mission. I still have to figure out what Chauncey did to the twins last year, and attending his birthday party might lead me to some more clues.

"I bet Chauncey won't even have any good food at his party," Gumbo whispers to me during our keyboarding class. After waiting for our teacher, Mr. Johnson, to walk away, Gumbo opens Google Images. He types "City Wheels" into the search bar, and I'm amazed by the pictures he clicks on.

City Wheels is huge, with a shiny, wooden floor, arcade area, laser tag section, and a brand-new food court. My mouth waters in desperation. The skating rink in my old neighborhood looked nowhere near as fly. "Wow...it looks pretty cool," I whisper meekly.

"Dizzy, you should see the *food* they have," Gumbo continues. "I'm talking pizza, hot dogs, pretzels, chicken fingers..." He trails off when he sees Mr. Johnson approaching from the front of the classroom. With crazy cat-like reflexes, he opens our typing exercise again. "I bet Corinne would want to go skating," he whispers hopefully.

I glance at Corinne, who sits near Rashad on the other side of the room. If she knew about City Wheels, she'd wave all thoughts of Chauncey's party away like a bad smell. If she backed out, I wouldn't feel comfortable going alone. "We'd, uh, better get back to work, Gumbo," I say, gesturing to my computer. Thankfully, he doesn't press me any further.

On the bus ride home from school, I expect Rashad to sit alone so he can study his playbook for this weekend's big game. Surprisingly, he sits right next to me. He smells kind of sweaty, since we just finished gym class, and I wrinkle my nose. Rashad notices my expression and frowns nervously. "I stink or something?" he asks, sniffing the inside of his shirt.

"No," I tell him. I put in one of my earbuds and play *Work* by Rihanna. "Don't you have plays to study?"

"I know 'em," Rashad states with confidence. He cuts his eyes at me and adjusts his Dallas Cowboys cap on his head. "City Wheels has an arcade, you know," he says.

I swallow a groan and force a smile at Rashad. "Yeah, Phil told me all that."

"Well, did he tell you about the deejay they have over there?" Rashad asks. He looks me up and down. "I bet they won't be playing any good music at Chauncey's boring party."

"How do *you* know?" I ask in exasperation. Rashad just shrugs. He takes my free earbud and sticks it in his big ear. I cringe. "You'd better not put any wax on my buds."

Rashad sucks his teeth. "My ears are clean." I start to give him a witty reply, when suddenly, my text tone goes off. Rashad's jaw locks. "Is that Chauncey?" he asks bitterly.

My eyes roll to the very back of my skull as I hold my phone in Rashad's face. "It's *Corinne*. She says, 'See you tonight at cheer practice.' We're trying to get to the National Cheer and Dance Championships, remember?"

Rashad shoots me a sheepish glance and lowers his eyes. "Oh. Right."

I sigh tiredly. Rashad's definitely being annoying, but I don't want him to think I hate him or anything. I lift Rashad's cap off his head and put it on my own. "I thought you said you weren't jealous," I say, nudging his elbow.

"I'm *not*, Pony Boots." Rashad scratches his ear.

My eyes narrow. "You know that you scratch your ear when you lie, right?"

Rashad freezes in mid-scratch. "Whatever." I smirk and he yanks the cap way down in front of my eyes. "I'm just saying: If you'd seriously rather party with Chauncey than go skating..."

I lean against the window and take his cap off my head. "Rashad, can we change the subject?"

Rashad gives me a hard stare, and I can sense his disappointment about this whole situation. He finally looks away and pulls his playbook from his backpack. "Fine," he mutters, and I don't hear anything else about City Wheels for the rest of the week.

On Saturday afternoon, I get all fancy in a black turtleneck with a zebra-print skirt, black leggings, and ballerina flats. I slick my thick hair back in a ponytail, which my mother says really brings out my beauty.

At around 3:45 p.m., Ms. Corelle drops Corinne off in front of our place. I grin when I see Corinne waving at me in the swirly dress I got her for her birthday last month. She still looks amazing, and her hair is *so* different.

"Corinne, honey, I love your hair! And the dress looks great on you!" my mother squeals as we all pile into her Audi.

Corinne sits next to me in the backseat and pats her head with pride. "Thank you, Mrs. Davenport!" she chirps.

I sigh and make a mental note to tell my friends about my mother's real last name before this year is over. Corinne keeps turning her head from side to side, like a model, and I marvel at how great her hair looks. "What'd you do to it?" I ask her.

Corinne beams. "My grandma did it special for the party. She calls it her 'stacked do!'"

My eyes stay glued to Corinne's hair, which is indeed *stacked*. Her usual braids are unwound and bound into three balls that shoot up from her head.

I grip my fingers around Chauncey's gift card and check his party invitation for his home address. I share the street number with my mother and she pulls off down the street. As we pass The Crunch Bowl, I can't help but stare.

Corinne follows my gaze and gently nudges my elbow. "Were the twins mad they didn't get invited?" she mutters.

"Kind of, but...they got over it," I decide to tell Corinne. Her hands are empty. She didn't bring Chauncey a gift, although I'm not sure why I expected her to. She did say that money between her and her grandmother is tight.

My mother turns down a street lined with row houses. We park in front of a white house with crooked shutters and crumbling brick steps. The steps lead up to a brown, weather-beaten front door with a golden handle.

My mother unlocks the car, allowing Corinne to bolt out of the backseat. In less than 10 seconds, she's already racing up the steps and working the doorbell like it's a button on a video game controller. My mother shoots me an amused glance through the rearview mirror and I just shrug. I've learned that when Corinne gets excited about something, it's best to let her be.

I follow my mother up the steps, staring up at Chauncey's house with uncertainty. The music from inside is so loud, I can feel the bass to the song *Too Good* by Drake blasting through the windows. My lips purse as I think back to Rashad. Chauncey *does* have some good music at his party.

"I'll be right there!" a high voice calls from inside the house. I hear a few muffled footsteps before the door swings open. Standing before us is a woman whose face looks like it belongs on the cover of a magazine. My eyes dart from her huge eyes to her stylish bob, and I instantly realize that I'm standing in front of Chauncey's mother. As she arches one of her plucked eyebrows and stares down at me and Corinne, I wait for her to snap at us in the same angry tone I heard her use on Chauncey that weekend after the football game. Surprisingly, she smiles at us, showing off a row of pearly-white teeth. "Hello, ladies. Are you here for the birthday party?" Corinne and I glance at each other and nod politely. Chauncey's mother smiles wider and shakes hands with my mother. "Hi, I'm Raquel Willis, Chauncey's mother," she says, running a hand through her already-perfect hair.

"And I'm Giselle, Desiree's mother," my mother says. "What time do you finish up tonight?"

"At around nine," Mrs. Willis says.

My mother smiles. "Oh, lovely. The girls will call me if they're ready to go before then."

As Mrs. Willis welcomes us inside the house, my mouth drops open as I take in the size of the place. There's a long staircase that leads to a higher floor.

As we pass the living room, I look in and see a whole bunch of people packed around a flat screen. They must be Chauncey's relatives. I see two really fat people sharing a couch and scrolling through their phones. Their thighs are huge and the poor couch cushions are just swallowed up and mashed down to a blip. Wow. I'm angry. They're here at the party to eat up food, but can't make it to a football game to support Chauncey? You would think he's got *nobody.*

"Here we are," Mrs. Willis finally says. She stops in front of a door in the back of the house. "The party's right downstairs in the basement, okay, girls?"

Corinne's teeth sink into her bottom lip in excitement. "Come on, Dizzy, before we miss everything!" Corinne squeals. I'm about to point out that we're here on time and have five hours left, when suddenly, I spot something hanging on the wall. It's a framed photo of a muscular man crouched in the grass with a football tucked in his arm. His face is fierce, and he wears a football uniform with the number 96 on his chest. Oh. My. Gosh.

It's the same photo from Chauncey's notebook.

"Corinne, wait," I say, but I'm too slow. She's already dragging me downstairs into the basement. The closer we get to the bottom of the stairs, the more I panic. What if we're the only kids who showed? How awkward will it be to just sit in Chauncey's basement and look at him all night?

But when we make it downstairs to the finished basement, I'm shocked to find most of our class scattered around, and everyone seems to be having a good time. There's a deejay in the corner of the room, and he's bobbing his head to a mashup of all the hottest songs of this year. Pushed against the wall are rows of snack tables filled with punch, chips, dips, chicken tenders, pizza, and cheeseburger sliders. I breathe in the delicious scent, thinking about Gumbo. He was wrong; Chauncey's party has good food.

"Dizzy!" a familiar voice calls within the crowd. I stand on my tiptoes and spot Chauncey approaching from the opposite end of the basement. He's dressed in a loose button-down shirt and a pair of khakis, and he looks the happiest I've ever seen him. "Hey, thanks for coming," he says, glancing from me to Corinne.

"Thanks for inviting us." I smile brightly and hand Chauncey his wrapped gift card. "Happy Birthday."

"Yeah, Happy Birthday," Corinne adds. Her eyes land on the snack table and she takes a few steps back. "I'll be over there." She scurries off and stuffs a plastic plate with every food item on the table. In any other situation, I'd be mad at her for abandoning me, but today, I'm grateful. For weeks, I've been dying to get alone time with Chauncey, and now the opportunity is staring me right in my face.

"So...um...how've you been, Chauncey?" I start off.

"I've been okay," Chauncey says with a shrug, but today, his eyes look bright. He holds up his gift card. "Can I open it now?" I bite my lip and nod as Chauncey unwraps the card. When he sees it, he grins. "Thanks. I love movies."

I smile. "For real?"

Chauncey smiles and nods. "Super hero movies are my favorite." Hearing this takes me back to my first video game-movie night with the twins, when we'd watched *Black Panther* and Mr. du Bois had carried me home. Even though Chauncey *did* invite me to his birthday party, I can't help but feel kind of guilty for showing up. I used to spend my Saturday evenings with the twins; now I'm at a party that they weren't invited to.

"Um, Chauncey? I was hoping I could ask you about something," I continue.

Chauncey starts to speak, but a voice from upstairs cuts him off. "Chauncey! Mema is here!" Mrs. Willis calls.

"All right! I'm coming!" Chauncey shouts back. He turns to me with an apologetic shrug. "Sorry, Dizzy, but I have to say 'hi' to my grandma real quick."

I grimace. "But..."

Chauncey steps back and gestures to the snack tables. "Help yourself to some food." Before I can say another word, he hustles away from me and up the basement stairs.

For the next two hours, I stand by the snack table with Corinne as we fill our stomachs with Chauncey's delicious party treats. Every now and then, I catch Chauncey weaving through the basement, but I never get the chance to stop him and ask about the man in the picture. He's too busy dancing and mingling with everyone else, which I really shouldn't be upset about. After all, Chauncey is finally getting the respect he deserves from our classmates. He probably feels on top of the world right now, and I'd hate to ruin his mood.

At a little after 6:30 p.m., Corinne and I finish off the last of the chips and salsa. Chauncey approaches the snack table and notices the empty bowls. He smiles at us. "Y'all must've been hungry, huh?"

"Starving," Corinne moans, patting her stomach.

"I'll run upstairs and get some more." As Chauncey reaches for the empty chip bowl, my mind ticks excitedly. This is my chance to get upstairs and ask him about the picture.

"I'll help you, Chauncey." I grin, snatch the empty salsa bowl from the table, and follow Chauncey upstairs. We pass the living room and I peek in again. The fat guests are still sharing the couch. Those poor cushions. I cringe to myself and smile at Chauncey as we enter the kitchen. "You sure do have a lot of family," I say to break the silence.

Chauncey reaches into the cupboard and pulls out a party-sized bag of Tostitos. He peels open the bag and shakes the chips into the bowl. "Yeah, but they only come around for, like, birthdays and some holidays. I don't see them too often."

"I feel you." The words slip out of my mouth before I can stop them. I slap my hand over my lips and blink frantically. Chauncey gives me a curious frown, and I bite the inside of my cheek. I didn't come to this party to spill my family drama to Chauncey, but it's too late to backtrack. I've already said too much. "My parents...they're divorced," I admit. "I haven't seen my extended family in months."

For a long moment, neither of us speaks. The only sounds in the air are the lively chatter of the family room guests and the doorbell ringing. I overhear one of Chauncey's relatives opening the front door and saying "hi" to some people, but I don't look out to see who they are.

Chauncey scratches the white spot near his mouth. "My parents are separated," he reveals with a sad sigh. "It's rough, but that's why it's good to do other stuff, like sports. You have something to keep your mind busy, you know?"

I nod. "Can I ask you something? On the first day of school, when we were sitting together in aftercare, I saw this picture of a football player inside your notebook." I take a deep breath and lick my lips. "Who is he?"

Chauncey motions for me to follow him into the hallway. We stop in front of the football picture and Chauncey sighs heavily. "This is my dad, Dizzy."

"Your...dad?" I repeat.

Chauncey nods twice. "My dad grew up playing ball and met my mom in college. They were gonna graduate together, but when my dad got drafted by the Denver Broncos at the end of his junior year, he and my mom dropped out of school to focus on the NFL, but a year after getting drafted, my dad tore his ACL. It ended his career. Since he and my mom didn't finish school, they didn't really have any money, so they moved here to Treeless Park, where they could afford."

"I'm...sorry, Chauncey," I mutter quietly. "How long have your parents been separated?"

"Two years. My mom works as a secretary, and my dad sells used cars. It's not exactly the life they imagined for themselves." He scratches his head. "My parents put me in football to give me something to do, but they don't want me to think about going pro."

"Because of what happened to your dad?" I ask meekly.

Chauncey nods sadly, but then he gets a determined glow in his eyes. "But...I want to prove my parents wrong." He pauses and stares up at the picture again. "I know I'm not the greatest player on the team and sometimes, I mess up, but I really want to get better. I want to go pro one day, like my dad, and I want to make it." I don't know what to say. Chauncey shows up to game after game in the hopes of improving his skills, but never gets a chance, and when he *does* play, he always makes mistakes. "Hey, would you mind bringing the chips downstairs?" Chauncey asks. "I'll be down with the salsa in a few minutes."

"Sure," I say through a sad smile. I go back into the kitchen, grab the chip bowl, and walk downstairs to the basement, but when I make it to the bottom of the stairs, I want to find a trap door and teleport the heck out of here.

"Pony Boots! We made it!" Rashad says, grinning. He slaps Gumbo a high five, and I just want to throw up.

50

Busted

Gumbo reaches into the bowl and pulls out a handful of chips. "Mmm, I love these," he mumbles, shoving the snack into his mouth. "Does Chauncey have any dip for these?"

He and Rashad swipe chips out of the bowl, while I just glance between them in shock. I feel like I'm about to faint. "Wha...what are you guys doing here?" I demand.

Rashad ignores my question. He gives my party outfit a once-over and shifts shyly in his sneakers. They look new. "You look pretty, Desiree," he says.

My face grows hot. On any other day, receiving Rashad's compliment would make my heart do backflips, but tonight, here in Chauncey's basement with Chauncey just a few steps away, I want to disappear.

"Dizzy! Did you get the chips or what?" Corinne cries. She hurries over to me and freezes when she sees the twins. "Um...y'all weren't invited," she says with a raised eyebrow.

Gumbo raises his sunglasses. "I like your hair, Corinne. What'd you do to it?"

Corinne giggles like a loon. "I got it staaaaacked!" she squeals excitedly. Rashad gives her a strange look.

My eyes shoot daggers through Corinne's stacked hair. How can she be so giddy at a time like this? I lock eyes with the twins. "You guys need to get out of here *now!*" I hiss.

"But we just got here," Rashad says around a new mouthful of chips.

I try to shove the twins towards the stairs. "Leave before—"

"What are y'all doing in my house?"

My face feels like it's peeling. I slowly turn around and see Chauncey standing at the top of the stairs. He's holding the bowl of salsa, and he looks livid.

The twins take a few steps back as Chauncey makes his way down the stairs and into the basement. "How did y'all get in here?" he demands angrily.

"Some guy in dirty socks let us in," Gumbo states with a shrug. The air in my lungs feels like poison. One of Chauncey's relatives opened the door, didn't know who the twins were, and led them to the basement.

"Y'all weren't invited," Chauncey snaps at the twins. "Now, get out of my house!"

"Relax. We didn't come here to sit in your dusty basement." Rashad takes a chip and dips it into Chauncey's salsa bowl. After chewing and swallowing, he cups his hands around his mouth and screams, "Everybody, listen up!"

The entire party goes silent. Even the deejay turns the music down. My heart races as I step closer to Rashad. "Ra, what do you think you're doing?" I hiss through gritted teeth.

"Nothing," Rashad answers with a huge grin. He steps around me and addresses the silent crowd. "All right, so, if y'all think this party is wacked..."

"Which I'm sure it has been," Gumbo interrupts with a laugh. He goes to the snack table and grabs a slice of pizza.

"Then come to the grand reopening of City Wheels! They're having a free skate night until nine!" Rashad says.

At the sound of Rashad's offer, every kid in the basement stampedes up the stairs. Gumbo takes a bite of his pizza and shoots a dry look at Chauncey. "You can come, too, Spots, if you want, and, uh, Happy Birthday."

I hastily turn to Chauncey, who stands there, seething. He stomps past Corinne and over to the snack table. Then he slams the salsa bowl down and points his index finger at the twins. "I said, get out of my house!" he screams.

Rashad puts his hands in the air in defense. "All right. We're gone," he says, taking a few steps back. His eyes fall on me, and he suddenly looks hopeful. "Dizzy, are you still coming over for dinner tomorrow after the game?"

My top lip sweats as I turn to Chauncey, who glares at me in confusion. "Chauncey...he's just talking about the, uh, group project," I say, trying to keep the peace.

Rashad frowns in disappointment, but Gumbo steps forward. "Project?" he repeats with a small laugh. He raises his sunglasses at me. "Oh, so you're just gonna act like you don't come over to our restaurant every day after school *and* eat dinner with us every Sunday after the games? Wow."

The basement floor suddenly feels like quick sand, pulling me lower and lower. This can't be happening. My vision clouds with tears as I make out a blurry image of Chauncey's angry eyes boring through mine. I turn away and meet eyes with Rashad, whose brow is creased in frustration. "I thought we were friends, Desiree," Rashad says. He sounds crushed. This is worse than I could have ever imagined.

"We *are* friends, but—"

"For the last time: Everybody out! *Now!*" Chauncey snaps. His furious eyes slice over to me. "You can leave, too."

Every muscle in my body turns to jelly. I feel like I'm dying. "But Chauncey..."

Chauncey just shakes his head. "Not cool, Desiree."

The tears start rolling before I can stop them. I was trying so hard to figure this out peacefully, but I've screwed everything up.

As I wipe away my tears, I catch the twins staring at me in sadness. I can tell that they feel guilty, but I turn away from them and look at Corinne. Her big eyes stare up at me with worry. "Come on, Dizzy. Let's just go," she says. She sucks her teeth and scratches the back of her head. "I *knew* this would get messy," she mutters sadly.

I don't have a response for Corinne, because she was absolutely right.

The two of us follow the twins upstairs. As we weave through the hallway, I bump into Mrs. Willis, who carries a chocolate sheet cake in her arms. The cake is covered with sugar crystals and reads, "Happy 12th Birthday, Chauncey" in yellow icing. It looks so delicious.

"Aren't you ladies staying for cake?" Mrs. Willis asks. Her concerned eyes land on me, and I feel like I'm about to melt. How can I possibly tell her that *nobody* is staying for cake? Everyone's gone, and it's all thanks to the twins.

"Dizzy, come on." Corinne tugs on my sleeve and gestures outside, where the twins stand and wait for us.

"I'm sorry, but...we have to go," I finally mumble to Mrs. Willis. I follow Corinne through the front door and down the crumbling steps.

"So, um..." Gumbo mutters. He awkwardly rings his hands and clears this throat. "City Wheels is just up the street. Y'all can follow us...if you're coming."

Corinne turns to me hopefully, but I look away. Even though I know how much she'd love City Wheels, I'm dying to call my mother so she can just take us home. However, I'd hate to spoil her evening. My mother deserves to relax, too.

Sighing heavily, I give a short nod to the twins. Their eyes brighten and they lead us up the sidewalk. "Y'all are gonna love it," Gumbo says to me and Corinne.

I ignore him, but Corinne walks alongside Gumbo. "I've never skated before," she says shyly.

Gumbo smiles. "It's easy once you get the hang of it." He and Corinne pick up their pace, leaving me to walk with Rashad. I try my hardest to ignore him, but I can feel him staring at me with his intense, light brown eyes.

"Pony Boots..." Rashad begins.

"Do *not* call me 'Pony Boots,'" I hiss in a low voice. A gust of cool wind blows and I wrap my hands around my arms. I should have worn a bigger jacket.

"You cold, Desiree?" Rashad asks. I don't answer him and he starts to remove his football jacket. "Wanna wear my jacket?"

I stare at Rashad in frustration. Why does he have to be so nice to me and mean to Chauncey? It's not fair at all. "No, thank you," I state, looking Rashad dead in his eyes. As the moon begins to rise high above the city, we hold eye contact for what seems like an eternity. Neither of us says another word. Instead, we walk in silence, listening to Gumbo and Corinne chat it up all the way to City Wheels.

51

City Wheels

"What size are you, Sweetie?"

I stare up at the skate clerk, whose voice seems to drown amongst the booming, fast-paced music and the roaring sound of wheels against polished wood. Flashes of neon pink, green, and yellow lights dance around the dark arena, which is topped with a food court, arcade zone, laser tag section, and a massive skating rink. City Wheels is *definitely* out of this world. If you ask me, it's the hottest spot in Treeless Park.

"I'll, uh, take a size five, please," I mutter. The clerk smiles and swaps my ballerina flats for a pair of inline skates. My fingers brush against the black leather. It feels so smooth.

"Dizzy, isn't this is the coolest place *ever?*" Corinne cries, clutching her own skates to her chest. She gazes around the arena like it's a wonderland, and I really wish I could share in her excitement, but with visions of Chauncey's angry eyes embedded in my brain, I can't smile about anything.

"Yeah. It's great," I mutter to Corinne. I take a few steps backwards and accidentally crash into some kid wearing a gold do-rag on his head.

"Whoa, watch where you're going, Girl," Do-Rag says. I back away from him as he hustles over to the boys' skate exchange area, where the twins trade their sneakers for some inlines. My stomach churns anxiously as I watch Do-Rag look the twins up and down suspiciously. I look closer and notice that his eyes are locked on Rashad's sneakers. Part of me wants to scream out to Rashad, but I'm too creeped out by Do-Rag to say anything.

"Come on, Dizzy. Let's put our skates on," Corinne says. She grabs my wrist and tries to pull me towards the rink, but I don't budge. "What's the matter?" Corinne asks.

My eyes stay locked on the twins as they accept their skates and walk to the rink. The entire time, Do-Rag stares Rashad down. I gulp and turn to Corinne. "That kid," I say, pointing to Do-Rag. "He was staring at the twins just now. I think he was checking out Rashad's sneakers."

"What?" Corinne glances at Do-Rag and turns to me with wide eyes. "You gonna say something to the twins?"

I watch as the twins walk to the seating area. They fasten their skates and roll onto the rink. They look ready to have a good time, not get caught up with any more drama. "I'll talk to the twins before the night is over," I tell Corinne.

We fasten our skates and I lead Corinne onto the rink. I try to help her stay balanced, but she's so wobbly that she ends up dragging me down. We agree to skate along the walls, where there are plenty of handrails for Corinne to hold onto.

But after 45 minutes of rail-holding, Corinne stumbles back to the seating area. "Dizzy...I think I'm gonna sit here for a while," she moans.

I stare at her with pity. "You want me to keep you company?"

"No, that's okay. You keep skating. I'm gonna call my grandma, anyway." Corinne whips out her flip phone and gives me a light wave. I smile and roll back onto the rink. I'm no Olympian, but five years of skating around my cul de sac have made me pretty good on wheels.

My legs weave to the beat of the music as I zoom around the rink. Since moving to Treeless Park, I'd forgotten how strong roller skating used to make me feel. Adrenaline pumping, I pump my legs harder, zooming past everyone. I feel unstoppable; I feel like I'm flying, when suddenly...

"Whoa!" My wheels meet a splatter of something thick and red – is it...ketchup? – and I lose control of my skates. My legs wobble and my skates lift faster and higher until I fall and land right on my butt. My face heats up in humiliation as the other skaters breeze around me. I feel like a traffic cone.

"Ha!" a grimy voice cackles from behind me. I glance around and see Do-Rag hunched over with his hands on his knees. He's laughing his peanut-looking head off. "Girl, if you can't skate, get off the rink!"

I glare up at Do-Rag, wishing he'd get away from me. That's when I see Rashad skating over to me. "Hey, leave her alone. Haven't you ever seen somebody fall on some skates before?" Rashad snaps at Do-Rag. He takes my hand and pulls me up. "Dizzy, are you okay?"

"Ooh, Dizzy, are you okay?" Do-Rag mocks in a high-pitched voice. He looks Rashad up and down. "Man, y'all pretty boys think you're all that, but you're really just punks."

Rashad looks furious. "Who are you calling a punk?"

"You." Do-Rag smirks at me. "Girl, you need to be with a *real* brotha, not this Bambi-looking dude."

Rashad clenches his fists and steps closer to Do-Rag. "Get out of my face before I—"

"Before you what?" Do-Rag points a finger in Rashad's face. "You'd better watch your mouth, Pretty Boy. You don't want to catch these hands."

This is all too much. This cannot happen tonight. "Ra, come on. Let's just go," I beg.

Do-Rag glances from me to Rashad. "Listen to your girlfriend, Pretty Boy." His eyes glaze over Rashad's football jacket. "The Crunch Bowl, huh?" he asks, checking out the threaded logo near the jacket's chest. He stares at Rashad with a creepy half-smile and nods. Then he skates away.

I release a huge breath of air that I didn't know I was holding. "Rashad, who was that?"

Rashad sucks his teeth. "I don't know. I've never seen him before in my life."

"Well, when you were getting your skates, I saw him staring at your sneakers."

Rashad stares at me in surprise and glares after Do-Rag with a look that could burn that rag right off his head. He takes my hand and leads me over to the seating area, where Corinne chats it up with Gumbo. They notice our angry expressions and raise their eyebrows.

"What's the matter?" Corinne asks.

Gumbo frowns and turns to Rashad. "Y'all good?"

"We're fine," Rashad answers quickly. We sit down next to each other, and I wait to see if he'll tell Gumbo about Do-Rag, but he doesn't.

Just then, the music in the arena changes to *Let Me Be Your Angel* by Tiffany Evans.

"Okay, all you skaters. This one's for couples only," the deejay announces through the microphone. Tiffany's smooth voice gets louder and I watch all the couples skate by.

Gumbo removes his sunglasses and tucks them into the pocket of his leather jacket. He smiles and extends his hand to Corinne. "Wanna skate?"

Corinne's face lights up like the moon. She nervously tugs at the sleeves of her swirly dress and turns away. "I don't know...I'm not good on wheels."

Gumbo smiles and takes Corinne's hand. "I've got you." He helps Corinne to stand up, links arms with her, and they skate away. Gumbo and Rashad are really cool people when they want to be, but when it comes to Chauncey, they turn into completely different people and I still don't get why.

I stare at Rashad as he watches his brother skate with Corinne. He turns to me and nervously drums his fingers on the seat cushion. "Wanna skate together, Dizzy?"

I slowly turn away. Rashad may have stood up for me in front of Do-Rag, but he crashed Chauncey's party and that wasn't cool. "I don't think so, Rashad."

Rashad looks crushed. "But...I thought you liked me."

I sigh. "I *do* like you, Rashad."

"Then why don't you want to skate?"

I glance off in shame. For the past few weeks, I've been trying so hard to be crafty, but my constant "craftiness" has caused nothing but confusion. It's time to lay everything out in the open. "Because of what you did to Chauncey tonight, Rashad. I know that you and Phil don't like Chauncey, but I really care about him."

Rashad's eyes swirl with confusion. "Why?"

"Well, there are two reasons. At my old school, I was bullied by this girl who was jealous of me. I know what it feels like to have people picking on you for no reason."

Rashad glances from my eyes to his lap. He scratches his head. "Well, I'm really sorry you went through that, Desiree," he starts in a low voice, "but...Phil and I don't hate Chauncey for no reason, and we're definitely not jealous of him. He took something from us, and you wouldn't understand." I just blink, and Rashad stares at me with frustrated eyes. "Just...why do you care about him so much?"

"Well, when I first moved to this city, Chauncey helped me, Rashad. My mom and I had a trunk full of bags that were so heavy. Chauncey walked up to us and offered to help. He carried all of our bags upstairs to our apartment. And he told me that he would've stayed to help us longer if you and Phil hadn't chased him away."

Rashad doesn't say anything for a moment. He clasps his hands together and leans forward. Then he looks straight at me. "Well, I would've helped you, too."

"Why didn't you? I saw you and Phil watching me move in."

"Yeah, but Desiree, you don't get it. Our parents don't want us friending up with people they don't know."

"But...why not?"

Rashad scratches his neck and stares out at the rink. "They don't want us getting caught up with the wrong crowd. Phil's got me, I've got him, and we look out for our little sister. We've got a big family and our football team, and that's who we hang around."

I gaze at Rashad sadly. "Well...why did your mom offer to watch me after school, then? Why was she so excited about me becoming friends with you and Phil?"

"'Cause we talked about you a lot. Our parents thought you were cool and wanted to meet you. If it weren't for that, we probably wouldn't even be friends."

I nod in deep thought and place a hand on Rashad's shoulder. "Well, we *are* friends, and I don't want you to think that Chauncey's stealing me away from you guys or anything like that." Rashad starts to smile, but I remain stern. "But the way you guys bully Chauncey - especially what you did tonight at his birthday party - is wrong, Rashad. What goes around comes around, and I think you saw some of that tonight."

Rashad sucks his teeth. "I wasn't afraid of that dude."

"That's not my point. If you and Phil don't leave Chauncey alone, you could be asking for some real trouble."

Rashad is quiet, and I know he knows I'm right.

Just then Morgan skates over to us and twirls her wavy hair. "Um, hi, Rashad," she says through a shy giggle. She gives me a phony smile. "Hi, Dizzy."

"Oh. Hi, Morgan," I say dryly. Rashad glances at me and raises an eyebrow. He stifles a laugh.

Morgan turns back to Rashad and grins wider. "I love your jacket, Rashad."

"Thanks, Morgan," Rashad says with a blank stare. My body tenses as Morgan starts asking Rashad a whole bunch of questions about football. He sort of smiles as he answers each question, but I don't know if he's just being polite or if he's actually happy to be talking to her.

"I was just wondering if you, um, wanted to skate... with me?" Morgan rambles, nervously tugging on the sleeves of her sweater.

As Rashad stares at Morgan, my heart sinks. Rashad just told me that he and Gumbo don't really make friends with a lot of people outside of school. I wonder if he'll skate with Morgan? He probably will. He's going to get up and skate away with her and the two of them are going to have a grand, old time together, because I told him "no."

"No thanks, Morgan," Rashad states in a firm voice.

My eyebrows shoot up and I immediately look at Morgan. Her face is on the floor. Her dark eyes slice over at me and I just look away. After a brief moment, she skates off.

My eyes narrow skeptically as I stare at Rashad. He catches my expression and frowns. "What?" he asks.

I twirl the end of my hair. "Just 'cause I said no doesn't mean you can't skate with someone else," I mutter softly.

Rashad is quiet for a few seconds. He lowers his gaze to the floor and rubs his palm against his knee. "Yeah, well, maybe I don't want to skate with anyone else right now," he finally says, looking me dead in the eyes. I sit there in surprise, waiting for him to scratch his ear, but he never does. He's telling the truth this time.

For the rest of the evening, Rashad and I sit there together in silence, watching Gumbo, Corinne, and everybody else in here have the time of their lives, and boy, do they skate tonight.

52

The Hard Truth

It's nearly 9:00 p.m. when our free night at City Wheels finally comes to an end. I unfasten my roller skates and watch as everyone gradually clears out of the rink. I keep my eyes peeled for any sign of Do-Rag, but I don't see him anywhere in here. Hopefully he's already dipped out, because the last thing I want to see tonight is Rashad fighting over some sneakers.

Next to me, Rashad leans back and inhales deeply. He blows out, making his lips flap like a braying horse. I'd laugh if I weren't so frustrated with how this night turned out.

"You need a ride home? Our dad's coming to pick us up," Rashad tells me. His voice sounds hoarse. I glance off, feeling kind of ashamed about our mini-spat earlier. The guilty look in Rashad's eyes tells me that he must feel the same way.

"Thanks, but I'm just going to call my mom," I say to Rashad. He nods with a small shrug, and I whip out my phone and dial my mother. She answers after two rings.

"Hey, Baby!" she says. I can hear the faint sound of wheels grinding against pavement. She's probably driving. "Are you and Corinne ready to go? How was the party?"

My hand clenches around my phone. "Uh...it was okay, but we're all at City Wheels," I reveal awkwardly.

"*City Wheels?* What is City Wheels?" my mother cries. Her voice comes through the phone so loudly, Rashad raises his eyebrows and turns to me in surprise.

"Mommy, it's the roller-skating rink not too far from Chauncey's house," I say.

"Girl, what are you doing over *there?*" my mother demands in an even louder voice. She sounds really upset, and I nervously chew on my top lip. How can I possibly tell my mother that the twins are party crashers? I slowly turn to Rashad, who slouches in his football jacket and struggles to meet my eyes. He looks just as anxious as I feel.

"Uh...everybody wanted to go roller skating," I say.

My mother doesn't say anything for a fearfully long moment. Finally, she sighs and I hear her turn signal clicking away. "Well, my GPS says I'll be there in ten minutes," she states. We hang up and I exhale in relief. I hope she doesn't ask me anything else about tonight.

Rashad shifts uncomfortably. "Are you going to tell on me and Phil?"

For a moment, his question leaves me speechless. I could have told my mother that the twins made everyone leave Chauncey's party and come to City Wheels, but that's not exactly true. Everyone chose to leave on their own, except for me. Chauncey *kicked* me out. "No, I don't think so," I mutter. Rashad looks somewhat relieved and I change the subject. "Last game tomorrow before the League Playoffs, right?"

"You know it," Rashad says, but his voice sounds bummed. "You coming over for dinner after the game?"

I grimace. As much as I love the du Bois family, Rashad can't expect me to keep running behind him while he and

Gumbo keep bullying Chauncey. "I'll only come over if you tell me what Chauncey did to you last year," I state firmly.

Rashad stares at me, stone-faced, and then flicks his eyes to the rink. "I told you I don't like talking about it, Desiree. Why do you keep pressing?"

"Because I think talking about what's wrong can help you." I hold out Worm Tooth. "Good friends are real with each other, remember?"

Rashad glances at Worm Tooth like he wants to laugh, but then his face grows serious. "Oh, like you were so real with *me* all this time about why you care about Chauncey?"

I clench my palms. He's right. "Well, if you won't tell me what Chauncey did to you last year, then don't look for me on Sundays." The last part of my sentence crawls out of my lips like a nasty bug, but it's too late to take back my words. I've already spoken, and now, Rashad glares at me like I've just sent a hole through his heart. I tear my eyes away from him and see Corinne and Gumbo skating over to us.

"Dizzy! Did you see me out there?" Corinne chirps. "I can skate now!"

"You were terrific," I mutter dryly. "Listen, my mom's on her way for us."

"That's okay. I already called my grandma. She'll be here soon to take me home."

"I'll wait with you, Butter," Gumbo says to Corinne.

I exchange a glance with Rashad. "*Butter?*" we repeat.

Rashad stares at Gumbo in disbelief. "Since when do *you* give out nicknames?"

Gumbo sucks his teeth. "Since I feel like it. Now, mind your business, with your *Pony Boots* self."

Rashad blinks in surprise, but remains quiet. He chews on the inside of his cheek and glares at Gumbo.

"Yeah, Butter is Phil's new nickname for me," Corinne brags. She giggles and turns to Gumbo. "He says 'cause I was rolling so smooth on these skates like butter!"

Gumbo checks his phone and jerks his head at Rashad. "Ra, Dad says to be outside in ten minutes."

Rashad makes a face at his brother. "I sure hope Butter's grandmother gets here in ten minutes."

Gumbo gives his brother a strange look and then laughs a little. He turns to Corinne. "Can I get your number?"

"Oh, yeah, yeah, yeah, yeah!" Corinne cries excitedly. Her hands flail as she fumbles for her flip phone. When she accidentally drops her phone near Rashad's feet, Rashad looks at it once and turns his head the other way.

Gumbo glares at Rashad and picks Corinne's phone up himself. "What's the matter with you?"

"Nothing. Mind your business, Bro," Rashad snaps, and I cringe. He's really in a bad mood.

After Gumbo exchanges numbers with Corinne, I get the "**I'm outside**" text from my mother. I stand up, smooth out my skirt, and give everybody a small wave. "Good luck in the game tomorrow," I say, mainly to Rashad.

"Thanks, Dizzy," Gumbo says.

Rashad sighs. "I'll walk you to your mom's car."

I rub my arm awkwardly. "Okay. Thanks." I say bye to Corinne and Gumbo again and exchange my skates for my black flats. Rashad walks me outside, and I struggle to think of something to say to lighten the mood. "Next week, I'm competing in the League Cheer and Dance Championship," I remind him in a small voice.

Rashad nods. "Oh, yeah. Good luck. Hope y'all win."

We make it outside and stop in front of my mother's car. I bite my lip. "Well...bye. Have a great game tomorrow."

"Thanks," Rashad mutters. He stares at me like he wants to say more, but he just stuffs his hands in his pockets and silently goes back inside City Wheels. I climb into the backseat of my mother's car and she looks around curiously.

"Where's Corinne?" she asks. Tonight's radio Motown medley is *I Want You Back* by The Jackson 5. I like Michael Jackson.

"She's inside with Gumbo," I say. "Her grandmother's coming to pick her up."

My mother just shrugs and drives us home. I shower, get comfy in my pajamas, and spend some time going over the cheers for tomorrow's game. When I'm finished, I stand in front of my mirror and rehearse the cheer routine for the League Championship next week. Hopefully we'll perform well enough to compete in Florida.

Bzzz! Bzzz! Bzzz!

I glance at my nightstand, only to find my phone spazzing and lighting up. It's Corinne calling me. After she was so giggly with Gumbo tonight, I don't really feel like talking to her right now. Still, she's my friend, and I'd hate to ignore her. I sigh and hit "Accept."

"Hey, Dizzy!" Corinne squeals. "Girl, are you busy?"

"I'm going over the cheers," I tell her dryly.

"Oh, well, I'm home now," she says. "I was just on the phone with Gumbo for almost an hour. Girl, he's so crazy!"

I flop on my bed in frustration. "Well, what were you talking about?"

"Just about how we had so much fun skating, but I think Rashad was a little jealous. After you went home, he was just sitting there, silent." I raise my eyebrows. Rashad must be taking my whole Sunday Dinner-Break pretty tough. "Anyway, Gumbo and I were skating so much, people started making *room* for us on the rink. Dizzy, did you see?"

"Yeah, yeah. I saw," I mutter.

"He was making me laugh the whole time, and he kept telling me how much he liked my stacked hair!"

"Your hair does look nice," I mutter, rolling my eyes.

"Yeahhh..." she says happily. "He said he wants to take me to The Crunch Bowl sometime. I'm gonna ask him if we can go tomorrow." Still too disappointed with how everything ended tonight, I don't say anything. Corinne sighs and keeps talking. "How come you don't sound happy for me?"

"Because Phil and Rashad are bullies," I say. "You know how they used to treat Chauncey in school, and you saw how they ruined his birthday party tonight. How can you just ignore that when we're working on an anti-bullying project?"

"Dizzy, I didn't call you to talk about this."

"Well, you need to hear it."

"Whatever!" Corinne snaps. "You think you know everything, Dizzy, but you don't. That's why this whole thing blew up in your face. Miss Know-It-All was being so two-faced with the twins *and* Chauncey. Maybe you should have just minded your own business!"

I want to fire off a comeback to Corinne, but I can't think of anything. She's right. "Corinne, you don't know what you're talking about."

"I think I *do* know what I'm talking about," Corinne hisses. "I think you're jealous. You just want to be the only one up in the twins' faces, going over to video game parties and The Crunch Bowl. Those people aren't your family!"

Corinne's words slice through my chest like a blade. I know that the twins and I are going through a rough patch right now, but after struggling through my parents' divorce, hanging around their family really made me feel like I'd gained a part of myself that I'd been missing. How *dare* Corinne insult me?

"Oh, yeah, Corinne?" I snap. "Well, the du Bois sure treat me like I *am* part of their family, and I'm trying to help the twins see why bullying Chauncey is wrong!"

"Well, I don't care!" Corinne shrieks. "I'm going to The Crunch Bowl with Gumbo tomorrow after the game and you can't stop me!"

"Well, guess what? The Crunch Bowl is closed on Sundays, so you're not going!" I howl, feeling glad that I one-upped Corinne.

"Ugh!" Corinne barks. "Forget you, Dizzy!" Before I can say another word, there's a low *click* and the line goes dead.

53

You've Got a Deal

The next morning, my mother has to literally drag me out of bed. I don't want to move. My mind is still swirling with the awful memories of yesterday's drama with Chauncey, the twins, *and* Corinne, and the last thing I feel like doing is shouting a whole bunch of cheers in the cold.

Ding!

I nervously check my phone in search of any messages from the twins or Corinne. Surprisingly, I see a text from someone I hadn't expected to hear from at all.

Daddy: Good morning baby girl. I'll be @ ur game 2day. Where is it being held?

I stare at my phone in disbelief. After weeks of longing to spend time with my father, he's finally coming around?

Me: Football field behind the regional high school. 1:15 pm.

Daddy: I'll be there. ☺ See u soon.

The bottoms of my toes curl tightly in the coils of my fluffy, pink rug. I know I should feel elated right now, but a huge part of me is skeptical. The last time my father promised he'd come around, he cancelled at the last minute and I was devastated. I'm not even going to tell my mother about his so-called game debut. He probably won't even show.

I get ready, eat brunch, and drive to the game with my mother. I wince as she asks me more questions about last night. Instead of spilling the drama, I just shrug and tell her I'm nervous to present our anti-bullying campaign tomorrow. My mother offers to listen to me practice as many times as I want. Then she reaches for her phone and plays the song *Heat Wave* by Martha Reeves and The Vandellas. The chorus is actually really catchy.

When my mother and I finally make it to the football field, the bleachers are packed. As usual, my mother sits with the du Bois family and I group up with Coach Robin and my cheer squad. Near the back of the group, I spot Corinne doing toe-touches with Carly Cartwright and Maya Anderson. Corinne's hair is still stacked, and it somehow looks better than it did last night. Ms. Corelle clearly has mad skills.

Taking a deep breath, I clench my fists inside my pom-poms and approach Corinne. Maybe I'll join her toe-touching warm-up and we'll start a conversation, put last night behind us, and get back to being friends.

But as soon as I walk up to Corinne, I regret it. She glances at me, stands up straight, and turns away, like I'm not even standing in front of her. I glare at her, fighting to stop my eye from twitching and tearing up in front of all these people. To my humiliation, my emotions betray me and a couple of tears slip down my cheeks. I wipe them away and freeze when I catch Rashad staring at me from his spot near the football huddle. The back of my neck grows warm with embarrassment. Every time I cry, Rashad always sees me.

Rashad stares at me in concern, like he wants to say something, but then Coach Marino starts talking and Gumbo taps Rashad on the shoulder so they can pay attention. I guess they made up after their little spat at

City Wheels last night. I notice Chauncey hovering next to them, and I wonder how he's feeling this morning after his birthday bust. I look to the bleachers to see if his mother or any of his relatives from the party are here today, but I don't see any of those people.

The football game starts at 1:15 on the dot, but I'm too bummed to pay attention to what's happening on the field. Corinne and I cheer "Do it all du Bois" and "Ra-Ra-Ra," just like always, but during breaks, we ignore each other.

I notice Chauncey loosely weaving through each quarter of the game. As usual, Rashad and the other quarterbacks ignore him whenever he gets open. I feel really bad for Chauncey, especially since I know he wants to go pro, but at least he's not getting bullied on the field anymore.

The only other good thing about this game is that the Pirates win, leaving their regular season record at an impressive eight wins and one loss. Everyone goes wild, laughing and screaming about how excited they are to compete in the Central Jersey League Playoffs, except for Chauncey, who remains stone-faced. I can't really blame him. After all, he barely touched the ball this season.

"Listen up, Pirates!" Coach Marino bellows excitedly. He, the assistant coaches, and Mr. du Bois motion for all of us to huddle up by the bleachers. "This is a huge milestone for our team. Our regular season has officially come to an end. It was your dedication and hard work that got us this far. I want to say a special thanks to all the parents, because we couldn't have done it without your support. Now, it's time to lock in and get focused on the League Playoffs, baby!" He claps, sparking another round of applause from the crowd. The twins look ecstatic and I really am happy for them, but when I think about how last night ended, I don't feel like congratulating anybody right now.

After Coach Marino dismisses everyone and Coach Robin outlines the details about this Saturday's cheer competition, Corinne walks away from me and over to Maya and Carly. I can't believe her. One, little argument on the phone, and now Corinne acts like she doesn't know me? If she's that bothered by what I said to her on the phone last night, then deep down, she knows I'm right.

I stare at Corinne as she giggles with Maya and Carly about something I'm too far away to hear. Suddenly, Gumbo approaches Corinne and taps her on the shoulder. Corinne whips around and grins when she sees Gumbo. She waves goodbye to Maya and Carly and chats it up with Gumbo.

Suddenly feeling lonely, I glance around for Rashad, but he's wrapped up in an intense conversation with his father. My mother speaks with Mrs. du Bois, while Chauncey storms past me without so much as a single glance. I feel so alone, and I wish I could just close my eyes and float away.

"Desiree," a deep voice calls from behind me. I slowly turn around and meet eyes with someone who I haven't seen in over four months. It's my father.

A fiery combination of joy, shock, and anger washes over me as I watch my father stand up from his spot in the bleachers and smile at me. He's gained some weight since the last time I saw him, and for somebody who's supposedly moved on with his life, his demeanor doesn't scream "happiness." As I look closer, I notice that he actually looks pretty sad, like he's missing something important in his life.

My tongue rolls nervously over my teeth as my mother catches sight of my father. She rolls her eyes and turns away from him. My father stares at her with a pained expression. "Giselle," he says, but my mother just shakes her head.

"I don't have anything to say to you, Calvin," my mother states. "Whatever you have to say to your daughter, do it, because she's been waiting to hear from you for a while."

Mrs. du Bois glances between my parents. I can't tell what she's thinking, but her eyes are filled with disappointment.

Time freezes as my father walks around my mother and Mrs. du Bois. I start to smile at my father, when suddenly, I see a woman walking behind him. As my father's hand locks around the woman's, every muscle in my face turns to stone.

"Hey, Baby Girl," my father says, walking up to me. "How've you been?" I don't answer him as he bends down and wraps one arm around my tiny body. The entire time, his hand never leaves the woman's. "I saw you cheering out here today, Beautiful," my father continues. He stares at me with a strange wistfulness in his eyes, like he doesn't recognize me.

My eyes dart from my father to the woman. "Who... who is she?" I ask timidly.

The woman lowers her eyes in shame and offers me a small smile. "I'm Tasha, Desiree," she says. "I've heard so much about you, Sweetheart."

I stare at her smudged, pink lipstick, short, curly hair, and tiny eyes. Why is she holding my father's hand?

"Baby Girl, we need to talk to you," my father says. I don't know why, but I let him and Tasha lead me to a spot near the water cooler. Rashad and his father happen to be standing a few feet away, but I try not to notice them and focus on my father as he struggles to meet my eyes. "Desiree... Tasha is Daddy's girlfriend," my father says calmly.

Every bone in my body turns to rubber as Tasha's eyes sparkle with joy. I haven't seen my father in months. How can he just show up to my game and act like this woman is part of my family?

"Desiree, I want to let you know that Tasha and I are getting pretty serious," my father continues, "and the two of us want to take you to Sweet Song's tonight for dinner."

I can feel my left eye twitching, but I don't even try and hide it. Sweet Song's used to be a place for me, my father, and my *mother*. No matter how much I've missed that restaurant, I'll never go back there if it means eating with a random woman. There's no meal, red carpet, or live band in the world that's worth it.

"Desiree?" Tasha asks. "I...I really hope we can be friends, Sweetie." I don't look at her, but I can overhear her muttering to my father, "Oh, Cal, she's so beautiful." Lady, shut up. Her hand reaches out and strokes my hair. In that moment, I go *ballistic*.

"Don't touch me!" I snap, stepping away from her. At my outburst, Rashad immediately whips around to look at me.

"Desiree!" my father exclaims angrily, but I don't let him get another word in.

"I already *have* a mother!" I remind my father. "You said *you* were coming to the game! You didn't say you were bringing *her*!" I glare at Tasha, who remains silent. I can feel the tears starting to roll, when suddenly, a hand rests on my shoulder. I look up and our eyes meet. It's Rashad.

"Dizzy. Are you all right?" he asks.

My father narrows his eyes at Rashad. "Young man, if you don't mind, I'm talking to my daughter right now."

Rashad's eyes widen in realization as he glances from me to my father. His gaze rests on Tasha, and that's when his expression grows skeptical. He stares down at me with eyes that say, *I'm not going to leave you.* He steps closer to me. "Well, I'm a friend of Desiree's," Rashad tells my father.

My father's eyes dart from me to Rashad, but he doesn't say anything. He must be stumped, since I've never told him anything about the du Bois family, Corinne, or Chauncey.

Just then, Mr. du Bois hustles over to us. "What's going on over here?" His brow furrows as he stares down at me with concern. "Is everything all right, Desiree?"

My father glares at Mr. du Bois. "And who are you?"

Mr. du Bois pauses and stares at my father carefully. "I'm Antwan du Bois: Team Parent for the Pirates football team." He gestures to Rashad. "This is my son, Rashad. My family and I live across the street from Desiree and her mother. Desiree is good friends with my boys. They're in school together. We take care of Desiree in our restaurant every day after school until her mother picks her up in the evenings." Mr. du Bois places a comforting hand on my other shoulder. "We really enjoy having her around."

The suspicion in my father's eyes slowly fades until there's nothing left but shame and even a trace of jealousy. He turns to me like he expects me to deny Mr. du Bois' explanation, but I just stand taller. After what feels like hours, my father sighs and shoves his hands in his pockets. "I'll call you, Baby Girl, all right?"

I don't answer my father. He never calls me.

My father stares at me guiltily and attempts to hug me, but I turn away from him and step closer to Mr. du Bois. Out of the corner of my eye, I can see Mr. du Bois staring at my father in disappointment. Finally, my father nods his head and leads Tasha away. As they walk off the field, the hot anger swirling inside of me bubbles over until I just can't take it anymore. I start to cry.

"Ra, get Desiree some water," Mr. du Bois instructs. Rashad hustles to the cooler and fills a paper cup with water, while Mr. du Bois pulls a clean towel from a nearby duffel bag and wipes my tears. "It's okay, Sweetie," he says quietly. Rashad returns with the water, and I accept it graciously. As the cool liquid washes down my throat, I can feel myself calming down.

Once my water is finished and my eyes start to brighten, Mr. du Bois smiles and tells Rashad to keep me company while he finishes packing up the football equipment. He walks away and I struggle to meet Rashad's eyes. "Thanks, Ra," I mutter softly.

Rashad remains silent, regarding me with a serious expression. He stares after my father and Tasha, who walk hand in hand to the parking lot. Rashad takes my hand and holds it for a few moments. Then he locks his pinky around mine and studies me carefully. "Are you going to be okay?"

I lick my lips and take a deep breath. "I think so. Yeah." Rashad gives me a small smile and I'm suddenly reminded of something very important. "So, our anti-bullying campaign is due tomorrow. How's the poster coming?"

Rashad lowers his eyes. He stares at our locked pinkies and shakes them back and forth. "Honestly, Desiree...Phil and I have kinda been struggling with the whole project."

My shoulders lift in a small shrug. "We all struggle with things that put us on the spot." I poke Rashad in the shoulder and give him a knowing look. He stares at the grass.

"Well, I know you're mad at us, and I'm sorry for acting funny at the library and stuff," Rashad says sheepishly, "but do you think you could maybe...please come over and help us just for a little while?"

I glance between each of Rashad's eyes in deep thought. I know I promised I wouldn't go back to his place for dinner until he told me the truth about Chauncey, but hearing him apologize and admit his struggles with this anti-bullying project shows me that he cares. Plus, after the recent blowup with my father, I'd really love a nice evening with the du Bois family. I need it.

I smile and nod at Rashad, whose face instantly brightens. "Cool," he breathes with a relieved laugh. "Can I pick you up at six?"

"No." I smile and tighten my pinky around his. "Pick me up at seven. I'm eating dinner with my mom tonight."

Rashad grins. "Desiree Davenport, you've got yourself a deal, Girl."

54

Coming Together

My mother and I enjoy a peaceful dinner of grilled chicken, white rice, and collard greens. As I eat, I wait to see if she'll ask me anything about my father. Thankfully, she doesn't, and I don't share a word. Perhaps my mother is angry, or maybe she just doesn't care to know anything.

At 7:00 p.m., Rashad picks me up and walks me to his family's apartment. "What'd you have for dinner?" he asks as he leads me to the traffic pole.

My mouth waters as I relive my mother's scrumptious meal. "Chicken, rice, and..."

"Collard greens?" Rashad finishes.

I give him a shocked look. "How'd you know?"

"You got some in your teeth," he says, snickering. I gasp in humiliation and Rashad stops me in my tracks. "Hey. Go like this," he says, pushing his tongue over a tooth near his top lip. Trying not to smile, I swat his arm, and he laughs as he walks in front of me. Once I know he's not looking, I hastily lick my teeth until I capture the stray collard greens. How embarrassing. "Well, I hope you're not too full, 'cause I saved you some beef patties," Rashad continues.

My mouth breaks into a huge grin. I really missed those patties. "Thanks," I say. We cross the street and my body tenses as we approach the back door of The Crunch Bowl. "Are all the relatives still around?" I ask hopefully.

"Yeah, they'll be here for a little while longer. They've been missing you, too." Rashad smiles and extends his hand to me. Taking a deep breath, I take his hand and let him lead me upstairs. Once we make it inside, I greet Mr. and Mrs. du Bois and reconnect with the extended family members. They all shower me with so many hugs and kisses, I start to wonder how in the world I made it through the past several weeks without their company.

Rashad leads me into the den, and I'm scared that he's tricked me into coming over to play video games, but then I see Gumbo sitting on the floor next to Nikita and Brianna, and they're all hunched over something big and yellow. It's the poster board, and it reads "BULLYING STATISTICS" across the top. I exhale in relief.

"'Sup, Dizzy?" Gumbo asks. He reaches behind him and sticks his hand into a box of crayons, markers, and colored pencils. He pulls out a few different colors and stares at me guiltily. "Thanks for coming over."

I smile and sit down next to Rashad. "No problem," I say, reaching for a red crayon. "Let's get to work."

For the next hour, the twins and I browse the Internet for bullying statistics. Rashad gathers information about the differences between physical, verbal, and cyberbullying, and Gumbo finds facts about how bullying affects people physically, emotionally, and mentally.

When I stumble across a website that lists how bullying causes a decrease in brain volume and leads to depression, Nikita nods. "I believe that," she mutters softly.

We all stare at Nikita as she twirls the ends of her cornrows. "People think it's funny to call somebody big or make fun how much they eat, but...it's not." Her bottom lip quivers, and I realize that she's talking about herself. My heart goes out to her. It sounds like she's being bullied in school.

I can tell that the twins are thinking the same thing, because they stare at their cousin and nod their heads.

When 8:00 p.m. rolls around, the twins and I use our neatest handwriting to list all of the statistics on the poster. Nikita and Brianna add a few stars and squiggles in the corners that make the poster really pop. By the time it's finished, I'm elated. This thing looks fantastic.

"Nice work," Gumbo says, giving everyone a round of high fives. He rubs the back of his neck and looks at me. "Sorry we gave you a hard time with this, Dizzy."

Nikita glances between me and the twins. "Have they been doing you dirty with this thing?" she demands, gesturing to the poster.

Brianna stands up in her little, pink socks and strawberry-print pajamas. "Were my brothers mean to you?" she asks in her best grouchy voice.

I can't help but laugh. "Sort of, Brianna. One brother was a little bit meaner than the other," I say, smirking right at Rashad. He busts out laughing.

Brianna pinches Rashad's arm. "Ow! Bri!" he exclaims.

"Don't be mean to girls, Ra-Ra!" Brianna orders, pointing a finger in Rashad's face.

"Yes, Madame Jelly Fingers!" Rashad pulls Brianna close to him and attacks her face with kisses. Howling with laughter, Brianna throws her head back and shows off a crusty nose. "Whoo-wee! Brianna Chantelle du Bois!" Rashad cries, laughing. "Go ask Mommy to fix your nose."

Brianna just giggles and scurries over to Gumbo. "Did you hear me, Phil? Be nice to girls!"

"Tell 'em, Brianna!" Nikita says. She raises an eyebrow and glances between the twins. "Y'all better treat a sister with some respect the next time she's in charge."

"No doubt," Gumbo says, nodding. "And the same goes for guys, right?"

"Of course. It goes both ways," Nikita says, smiling at me. I smile back and slap her a firm high five.

Nikita is *awesome*.

55

Presentation Day

D arkness surrounds me.
        I'm alone, falling into an endless pit. My arms
and legs are sprawled out as a dreadful feeling takes over my
body. I'm falling faster and faster when suddenly, the twins
and Corinne are falling with me. We're all falling together,
screaming "Chauncey" at the top of our lungs. And then...

I wake up in a cold sweat.

My alarm goes off like an unbearable siren, and I can
hear my mother yelling at me to get out of bed before I
miss the bus. I slowly push my body into a sitting position
and place my hand against my drenched forehead. What a
dream.

I glance at my phone. It's Monday, November fourth,
and it's time to get this anti-bullying presentation going.

Heart racing, I bolt out of bed and speed through my
morning routine. Once I'm all dressed in a frilly blouse and
dark pants, I snatch my completed essay off my mother's
printer. Last night, my mother and I went through the essay
line by line to make sure it sounded the best. In the essay,
I explore the dangers of bullying and why it's so important
to analyze the bully - not just the person *being* bullied.

Glancing over the essay this morning, I'm overflowing with excitement. Wait until Ms. Hernandez hears *this*.

After scarfing down a quick breakfast, I sprint out of the apartment and over to the twins at the bus stop. I grin when I see Gumbo holding the rolled-up poster, but then I think about Corinne. I haven't spoken to her since Saturday night, when we argued on the phone. *Please, oh, please let her come through with that poem.*

The twins and I make it to school on time and grab our books from our lockers. I keep my eyes peeled for Corinne, but she's nowhere in sight. When I follow the twins into Ms. Hernandez's classroom, I glance around, hoping to see Corinne sitting in her spot in the front row. To my disappointment, her seat is empty. "Where's Corinne?" I ask.

Gumbo whips his phone from his pocket and checks his text messages. I exchange a surprised look with Rashad. I know we're thinking the same thing: *So they've been texting each other.* "Butter texted me a few minutes ago," Gumbo announces a little boastfully. "Her bus is running late."

My mouth goes dry. "Late? She...she can't be!"

"Good morning, everyone." Ms. Hernandez shuts the classroom door and turns to us with an eager smile. "As I'm sure you all remember, you'll be presenting your anti-bullying campaigns this morning. Please spend the next fifteen minutes regrouping with your team and be ready to go."

I glance around the classroom as everyone gets in their groups. Even Chauncey is here this morning. Where in the world is Corinne?

Rashad catches my nervous expression and raises his hand. "Uh, Ms. Hernandez? Corinne's running late today."

Ms. Hernandez gives us a sympathetic frown and glances at her clipboard. "I hope she's all right. I'll push your group last, but if she doesn't arrive by then, you'll have to present without her."

My face feels like it's melting right off my skull. What good is our project without Corinne's poem? It won't be impressive enough. She *has* to get here.

For the next half hour, we listen to the first few groups give their presentations. Some of them are actually really well thought out, while others look like they were thrown together twenty minutes ago. They probably were.

When Chauncey's group takes the front of the room, all they do is give a few, dull reasons as to why bullying is wrong. Chauncey doesn't even say anything; he just holds up a flyer that lists resources for bullying victims. What a dry presentation. When you're being bullied and working with three people who never turn in their homework on time, I guess your anti-bullying campaign won't look like much.

Just as Chauncey's group finishes up, the classroom door peels open and I grin when I see a pair of hazel eyes glancing nervously around the room. It's Corinne. Her hair is back to its beaded braid do, and she's wearing her swirly dress, again. Gumbo's face lights up. "Sorry, Ms. Hernandez. My bus was late," Corinne says.

"That's all right, Corinne," Ms. Hernandez says, marking her attendance sheet. "Are you ready to present?"

"Um, yes." Corinne hurries to her desk, opens her folder, and whips out a white piece of paper. It's the poem. I try to catch Corinne's eyes, but she keeps her head down and neatens the rest of her folders and notebooks. I sigh and lead my group members to the front of the classroom. The twins hold up the poster, and boy, does it look snazzy.

"Very impressive," Ms. Hernandez says. She stares at Gumbo and taps the spot near her right eye. "Phil, please remove your sunglasses during the presentation."

Gumbo quickly does as he's told and tucks his sunglasses in the pocket of his leather jacket. Ms. Hernandez smiles, leans forward in her chair, and looks straight at me. I gulp and take a tiny step forward. It's the moment of truth.

"Um...good morning. Heh," I begin shakily. My heart pounds like the bass from a booming stereo system as I stare at my classmates. It seems like everyone's dull eyes are boring right through to my inner thoughts. I grip my hands tighter around my essay and try to tap into my confident side. "I'm Group, and this is my Desiree," I say slowly.

At this slipup, the entire class cracks up, and I just want to disappear. "I...I mean, I'm *Desiree* and this is my *group*," I stammer. The laughter quiets down, but the smirks remain present on everyone's faces, except for Ms. Hernandez and Chauncey, who doesn't even look at me. He folds his arms across his chest and keeps his eyes lowered, like he's waiting for me to shut up and sit down already.

I tense and meet eyes with Rashad, who makes the *Breathe in, breathe out* gesture with his hand. I nod, take a deep breath, and address the class in a much stronger voice. "A bully is someone who uses their words or actions to physically, mentally, or emotionally harm someone else." Ms. Hernandez smiles at me like she knows I'm about to rock the house, so I grin back at her and keep going. "In most instances of bullying, people only focus on the person being picked on, and while that's important, it's not the fairest solution to the problem." I take a step back and gesture to my group members. "For *our* anti-bullying campaign, we not only focused on the victim, but the bully, as well, because all people have reasons for their actions."

My eyes shift to the twins, who stare at the floor with guilt. I hate to see them look so uncomfortable, but they need to hear this.

I read the essay in a strong, clear voice. I discuss the benefits of getting to know the bully, because in order to help someone, you have to know their story and understand why they act the way they do. As I read through the essay, I sneak occasional glances at Ms. Hernandez, who nods slowly and smiles. I smile back, feeling on top of the world.

Once the essay comes to an end, I thank everyone for listening and give a short nod to the twins. They stare at me worriedly, but I wink at them and they hold the poster higher. "Um, for our poster," Rashad begins in a nervous voice, "we, um, listed the different kinds of bullying that exist and...how each one is different from the other."

Gumbo wipes his nose and examines the poster. "We also found some, uh, statistics about how bullying affects people...and how it can lead to mental illness." I smile as he and Rashad take turns going through the poster. They take their time and explain each statistic with genuine detail. The entire time, I notice Chauncey sitting with an angry expression. As much as I'd like for him to appreciate the twins' presentation, I can't blame him for looking suspicious. After months of being bullied and having his twelfth birthday party ruined by the twins, Chauncey obviously needs more proof that the twins have learned their lesson, and he deserves it.

After the twins finish explaining the poster, we all turn to Corinne. Her swirly dress sways against her knees as she takes a step forward and clutches the white paper in her hands. "For the last part of our anti-bullying campaign, we wanted to include something that people would remember," Corinne begins in a small voice. "So, now, I will present an original poem entitled *Bullies, Beware*." Corinne takes a deep breath, clears her throat, and recites her poem:

Dear Bullies,

This poem is for you; you know who you are
I need you to listen, so don't go too far
There is something big that I need to share
So listen up good, because I need you to care
I know that you're angry deep down in your heart
But you can't go on tearing people apart
You used to be friendly; no one thought you were strange
But then something happened that caused you to change
The people you hurt are so sad and blue
I'm worried for them, bullies, but I'm worried for you, too
If you don't stop your actions, you'll be in for a scare
What goes around comes around, so bullies, beware

The last line of Corinne's poem leaves an eerie feeling in the air. The entire classroom is silent. Even Ms. Hernandez is speechless. I sneak a glance at Chauncey, who sits back with his arms folded across his chest. I can't tell exactly what he's thinking, but he looks stone-faced. The twins, on the other hand, stand off to the side looking *very* uncomfortable.

The class applauds as we all head back to our seats. "A job well done," Ms. Hernandez says, smiling at each of us. She hands us our rubrics, and I'm relieved when I see the grade at the top. We got a 96, with just a few points off for failing to make eye contact with the entire class throughout the presentation. I shrug to myself. I didn't want to make eye contact with Morgan, anyway. The project was a success.

As I stuff my rubric into my History folder, I glance to my right and see Corinne staring at me with a soft smile. "Your essay was really good," she whispers.

A weight lifts off my chest. My friend is finally talking to me again. "Thanks. So was your poem," I whisper back. "You're a great writer, Corinne."

Corinne shrugs. "I was inspired by what you said on the phone on Saturday night," she admits softly. Her eyes suddenly fill with guilt. "I'm really sorry, Dizzy."

Although I'm grateful to hear Corinne's apology, her comment about me not really being part of the du Bois family hurt my feelings, but when I think back to how Rashad and Mr. du Bois stood by my side after yesterday's football game, and how kindly their extended family treated me last night at their apartment, I know that the du Bois family loves me, and no one can take that away.

I smile at Corinne and hold out my fist. She grins and we exchange an exploding fist bump. As I glance past Corinne's braided head, I notice something that makes my stomach turn. Chauncey is sitting in the corner of the room, and he's still glaring at the twins. I gulp and look at the twins, who stare at their rubrics with pride.

Corinne and I might be friends again, and the twins may have come through with the poster, but Chauncey still isn't satisfied, and I'm worried that this beef isn't quite over yet.

56

The Eastern Regional Championship

The morning of Sunday, November 17th, is perhaps the busiest day of my life.

I'm nowhere near ready to wake up at 6:55 a.m., but when my alarm goes off and my mother starts shaking my body with the force of an earthquake, I have no choice but to roll out of bed. I do a couple of quick stretches, take a warm shower, and get dressed in my cheer uniform. Today, our boys are competing for the title of Eastern Region Champion at Villanova Stadium in Pennsylvania, and they'll hopefully lead us all to an epic Florida vacation next month. If they're going to win, they'll need all the "Ra-Ra-Ra's" and "Do it all, du Bois'" they can get, and I'll be the loudest cheerleader of them all. My squad and I took fourth place in the League Cheer and Dance Championships, so we're not getting our own Florida trip. Super-bust.

After enjoying a breakfast of scrambled eggs, cereal, and yogurt, my mother and I hop in our car and head to the football field behind the regional high school. We arrive at 8:30 a.m. and group up with every football player, cheerleader, family member, and coach in the parking lot.

I grin when I see a huge, shiny Coach bus that's parked off to the side. When your team qualifies for the Regional Championships, USA Little League Football hooks you *up*.

"Dizzy!" a bubbly voice calls from within the crowd. I glance around and spot Corinne waving at me. She's hovering near Gumbo, who stands next to Rashad and the rest of the du Bois family. After pulling my mother through the crowd and watching her start a light conversation with Mrs. du Bois, I grab Corinne's hands and we squeal excitedly. "Girl, did you see the *bus?*" Corinne shrieks, jumping up and down.

Gumbo grabs his left cleat and pulls his leg back, stretching his quad muscle. "That bus is okay. Wait until y'all see that stadium," he says with a smug grin.

I raise my eyebrows. "You've been there before?"

"Yeah, Girl. We made it all the way to the Regional Championships last year." Gumbo's smile fades and he glances over at Chauncey, who stands near two tight ends who ignore him as they talk amongst themselves. "The Regionals were as far as we got, though," Gumbo mutters, glaring at Chauncey. My heart rate quickens. Wait a second...

"Good morning, Pirates!" Coach Marino announces. He glances up at the crisp, blue sky and grins. "Whew, it's a beautiful day to play some football, isn't it?"

"Yeah!" we all shout back. I glance at Rashad, expecting to see him all hyped up like everyone else, but he's not. His expression is serious and his head is bent over a book called *Winning Through Mental Toughness*, which he goes through with a highlighter. My eyebrows shoot up in realization. Today is the most important game of our season, and with Rashad as our star quarterback, he *really* needs to know his stuff inside and out. I can imagine the pressure he's under right now, so I make a mental note not to bug him and turn back to Coach Marino.

"Today will go down in history as a momentous occasion for the Pirates," Coach Marino continues. "I am so proud of every single member of this team – football players *and* cheerleaders. You all have worked hard, remained dedicated to the sport, and I hope to see the same drive and determination when we step out on the grass this afternoon to face the Pythons. They're a great football team, but so are we, and I'm confident that we'll show those guys the *best* of Treeless Park!"

At this comment, Rashad looks up from his book and stares at Coach Marino. Rashad looks pretty confident, but then he rubs his stomach and I instantly realize he's anxious.

"All coaches, athletes, and chaperones will board the bus," Coach Marino goes on, pointing to the Coach bus. "We'll be departing for Villanova Stadium at nine o'clock on the dot. All families and Pirates' supporters, we ask that you please follow the bus in your vehicles. Thank you all for coming out today, and now I ask that you all please bow your heads for a word of prayer, being led by our Team Parent and sponsor, Mr. Antwan du Bois. Antwan?"

We all close our eyes and bow our heads as Mr. du Bois steps forward. He prays for traveling mercies and the safety of all athletes. When his prayer is finished, I give my mother a quick hug and wave to her as she follows Mrs. du Bois to her car. Amongst the sea of parents flying to their cars, I look around for any sign of Chauncey's mother. Sadly, I don't see her anywhere. Even Ms. Corelle is out here for Corinne. I'm so disappointed. Is Chauncey seriously about to go all the way to Pennsylvania without anybody cheering him on?

I follow everyone onto the Coach bus, which smells brand new and has the coolest-looking fuzzy chairs and miniature TVs hanging from the ceiling. Gumbo sits next to Corinne and starts asking her about any special cheers we've prepared for today's game, while I sit in the window seat across the aisle from them. Rashad walks onto the bus, and I expect him to isolate himself in the back somewhere so he can read his book. Surprisingly, he drops into the seat right next to me, like it's another school day on the public bus. I twirl the end of my hair nervously. "Wouldn't you rather sit next to Phil so you guys can talk strategy?" I ask, making little, choppy movements with my hands.

Rashad stares at me with a smirk on his lips. "Talk what?" He mimics my hand-chops like he's doing The Robot. I swat his arm and he laughs. "Nah, we've been talking strategy nonstop all week." I nod and Rashad gives me a sympathetic frown. "Sorry your cheer squad didn't make it to Nationals."

I give a small shrug, wishing I could forget our mediocre fourth-place performance. Our squad had practiced that routine until we knew it cold, but when we took the big stage, I think we all got a little dose of stage fright. That and the other three teams ahead of us were just better. Thankfully, Coach Robin wasn't too mad and encouraged us all to try harder next year. "At least *you* guys have a great shot at Nationals," I tell Rashad. "How ya feeling today?"

Rashad's eyes swell with nervousness. "Um...well..." He reaches for his ear like he's about to scratch it, and I give him a look. He sighs and lowers his hand. "Honestly, Pony Boots, I'm bugging a little bit," he mutters.

My lips press into a flat line as I nod. "Who's the star quarterback today?"

"His name's Devin Rosenthal and his game is crazy," Rashad explains, shaking his head. "I've been watching his highlights on YouTube. He's fast and has this wild arm and he never misses an opportunity to score."

I smirk and poke Rashad in the shoulder. "Sounds a lot like someone I know."

Rashad sort of smiles, but his eyes still look worried. "I know my plays and everything, but right now, it's all about getting the mental part down, you know?" He looks at me and holds up his book, and that's when I get an idea. Grinning, I reach into my backpack for my phone and earbuds. I offer Rashad an earbud and cue up the playlist I created last night. Rashad gives me a funny look. "What is this?"

"Motown." I point to the album cover of the song that's playing right now. "This one's called *You're All I Need to Get By*, by Marvin Gaye and Tammi Terrell."

Rashad raises an eyebrow. "Who?"

"They're singers from the sixties," I explain. "My mom listens to this music all the time. It's relaxing."

"Hm," Rashad mutters, scrolling through the rest of the playlist. He smirks at me. "Well, I don't want you to think I'm ignoring you, but I gotta study my book, so..."

"I have a book to read, too, Ra." I dig around in my backpack and yank out my copy of *Zeely* by Virginia Hamilton.

Rashad takes the book from me and checks out the cover. "*Zeely?*"

"That's right. It's about a girl who encounters mysteries," I state proudly.

"Oh, so *that's* why you're so nosy," Rashad says with a sly smirk. I scoff with fake anger and he snickers. "I'm just playing." He flips through my book. "So, you like reading, huh?"

I bite my bottom lip and nod excitedly. "Yup. I love all kinds of books. Some of my favorite authors are Maya Angelou, Virginia Hamilton..." I pause and give Rashad a sheepish smile. "Never mind. You have a book to study."

"No, go ahead," Rashad says with a smile. He adjusts his position in his seat so that we're looking at each other eye to eye. "I'm listening." I stare at Rashad, stunned, and wring my hands together. He stares at my hands and sucks his teeth, but he's smiling. "Girl, it's *me*. Why are you all nervous?"

"I'm not," I say, tucking my hands under my thighs.

Rashad rests his fist under his chin, like he's the student and I'm the professor. "So, talk to me."

I sigh. For a second, I'm too scared to say anything, but then I stare at the calm, dimpled smile in front of me and remind myself that this is Rashad – my friend.

"Do you remember when I first came over to your place for dinner and you asked me about my dream?" I start off. Rashad nods and I take a deep breath. "Well, ever since I was little, I've always loved reading and writing, so, one day, it's my dream to become a journalist." My chest swells with excitement, the way it always does when I talk about my dream. "I'd love to solve mysteries and write books one day."

I chew on my bottom lip and meet eyes with Rashad, but he just stares at me. At first, I'm scared that I've just embarrassed myself, but then Rashad smiles and places my book back in my hands. "You are very special, Desiree Davenport," he says quietly.

My face grows warm with surprise and flattery. "Is... that a good thing?"

Rashad nods with a small grin. "Yeah. It's a good thing." He tugs lightly at the end of my side ponytail. "You're one of a kind."

I wait to see if he'll say anything else, but he just keeps smiling at me and eventually goes back to studying his mental toughness book. I open my book, and we read and listen to more Marvin and Tammi for the whole ride down to Pennsylvania.

We arrive to Villanova Stadium by 10:30 a.m., which gives us a few hours to mentally prepare for the game at 1:30 p.m. As we step off the bus and enter the stadium, I'm amazed by how beautiful it all looks. The field is covered in lush, green grass and surrounded by a gorgeous track and tall rows of bleachers. To my surprise, there's a small crowd of people already sitting in the Visitors' bleachers, and they look very familiar. Parked on the first row and right up on the grass is a woman with perfectly-arched eyebrows and a snazzy fur coat. As she checks her reflection in her phone to apply her lip gloss, my mouth drops open. It's Chauncey's mother, Mrs. Willis, and she's out here with all of the relatives from Chauncey's birthday party.

I try to catch Chauncey's eyes to give him a huge smile. To my disappointment, he just shoots me a dry glance and walks right past me. I know that I messed up big time, but deep down, it hurts me to know that Chauncey still isn't ready to trust me again. He probably never will be. Perhaps he'll be in a better mood after today's game. With his family cheering him on from the bleachers, I have a strong feeling that we just might win this thing.

After reviewing today's cheers with my squad and watching the Pirates and the Pythons do a quick warm-up practice on the field, we all gather in the cafeteria for a lunch of lasagna, salad, and bread rolls. As we eat, we're joined by the USA Little League Football officials, who greet us with a message of congratulations. Once all of the formalities are out of the way, we go back to the stadium, and I'm shocked to see that both sides of the stands are packed.

I spot mothers adjusting their winter hats and rubbing their hands together to keep warm out here in this November cold and fathers serving younger siblings Styrofoam cups of hot chocolate. Towards the middle of the visitors' bleachers, I notice my mother sitting with the du

Bois family, who holds up posters, foam fingers, and even a humongous banner that reads, "DO IT ALL, DU BOIS!" in thick, splashy letters. Brianna has her face painted, with the numbers 4 and 24 decorating both of her cheeks in blue and white paint. She bounces on her toes, screaming, "Hi, Phil! Hi, Ra-Ra!" and I smile to myself. It must be so exciting to have two football stars as big brothers. Brianna really is fortunate.

"Ladies and gentlemen!" the announcer's voice rings out through the speakers. "Welcome to the Division One Eastern Regional Championship here at Villanova Stadium. We have a varsity matchup. Please put your hands together for the home team, hailing from Pittsburgh, Pennsylvania, with an undefeated record...the Pythons!"

There's a wild burst of applause from the Home bleachers. It's almost intimidating, since their bleacher section is much bigger than ours. The Pythons' uniforms are a crisp red-and-black ensemble, and their cheerleaders hop up and down with excitement, shaking their pom-poms in the air. I clench my fists inside of my pom-poms and wait for the announcer to call *my* team up in this place.

"And now, hailing all the way from Treeless Park, New Jersey, please welcome...the Pirates!" the announcer cries. This time, *our* side of the field hollers like crazy. My squad and I shake our pom-poms excitedly as both teams approach the center of the field and shake hands. One of the referees performs a coin toss, which the Pythons end up winning. Instead of kicking the ball, they choose to receive. Everyone rises for the National Anthem and the game officially begins.

The first quarter is off to a heated start, with our placekicker making the first move. He sprints to the 40-yard line, draws his leg back, and sends the ball sailing to the opposite end of the field. The Pythons' returner makes a smooth catch and hustles through the grass like a lightning bolt. This guy is almost faster than Gumbo, which makes me feel very uneasy. Our defense must be asleep, or something, because when they finally tackle him, he's only a few yards away from the end zone.

At the start of the second play, the Pythons' star quarterback, Devin Rosenthal, fakes a handoff to one of their wide receivers. He makes a swift pass that sends the ball zipping through the air with this crazy spin technique. Their other wide receiver makes the catch with ease and glides into the end zone like this is just another warmup. Oh. My. Gosh.

"And a perfect throw from Devin Rosenthal for the eleven-yard score!" the announcer exclaims. The Pythons' kicker takes the field and sends the ball sailing through the goalposts, putting them in the lead 7-0. I can't believe this. The game just started and this team is already going crazy.

I shoot a glance at Rashad, whose eyes are wide with shock and uncertainty. He looks frozen, but then Gumbo steps in front of him and starts talking with this intense expression and a lot of sharp hand movements. Whatever he says must ignite a confident fire within Rashad, because he nods and exchanges a double high five with Gumbo. They and the rest of our offensive linemen take the field, and the ball gets turned over to us. Rashad starts calling plays to his linemen. He attempts to make an angled pass to Gumbo near the sidelines, but the pass is too high and the Pythons make off with an interception. Rashad grips his hands on his helmet like he's ready to yank his hair out.

"Ugh, what was *that*?" Corinne shrieks. I don't answer her and try to steady my racing heart by ruffling my pom-poms. The Pythons showed up to *play*. If we're going to win, our team needs to wake up and get serious.

"Take your time, Ra! Focus!" Mr. du Bois shouts from the sidelines as the ball gets turned over to the Pythons. It's our defensive line's turn to try to make something happen.

Sensing the anxiety on the field, Coach Robin orders our cheer squad to break into our "Let's go, Pirates!" cheer. This must give our defense a surge of confidence, because they push through with a strong series of sacks on Devin Rosenthal, forcing the Pythons to give up the ball.

Our offensive line takes the field again, and our cheer squad breaks into the "Ra-Ra-Ra!" chant. Hearing his name shouted from the sidelines, Rashad waits too long for Gumbo to find an open spot, and he's down. There's a flag on the play; it's against the Pythons' defense. Unnecessary roughness to the quarterback after the play is over. It's a 15-yard penalty and an automatic first down for us.

When the next play starts, Rashad takes his time to make sure that Gumbo is wide open before drilling the ball straight for his hands. The o-line does its thing, allowing Gumbo to zoom down the field like a bullet and score a touchdown. That's what *I'm* talking about. Coach Robin orders us to break into a new cheer just for Gumbo, which Corinne is absolutely thrilled about. The cheer goes:

P-H-I-L-I-DOUBLE P-E
Good Hands Phil, lead us to victory!
Goooooo Pirates!

Coach Marino bellows excitedly and pumps his fists like a warrior. Meanwhile, Mr. du Bois laughs and claps his hands so hard, they're probably numb. "Let's go, Ra-Ra! Good hands, Phil!" he yells. Our defensive line is able to keep up the momentum and prevent the Pythons from scoring anymore touchdowns in the first quarter. When Devin Rosenthal fires off a long pass that spins through the air like a torpedo, one of our defensive guys surprises everyone by making an interception and hustling for the end zone. Our side of the bleachers goes nuts as our offensive line reclaims the field. Rashad receives the ball from our center and hustles a few yards down the field before making a sick pass to Gumbo. He scores another touchdown and puts us in the lead. The Pirates are on *fire*.

I shout another round of cheers with my squad and examine our crowd. To my surprise, there's a familiar-looking man walking to the bleachers, and he's heading straight for Chauncey's family. As he sits down next to Mrs. Willis, I take note of his tall frame, broad shoulders, and worn jersey with the number 96 on his chest. Oh. My. Gosh.

It's Chauncey's father.

"Aaaannnddd...that's the first quarter! Pythons, seven. Pirates, fourteen," the announcer says. Chauncey shifts anxiously in his clean football uniform. He hasn't played at all yet. He turns to face the bleachers and freezes when he notices his father. Mr. Willis smiles and points at Chauncey, who grins and points back. He looks ecstatic. My heart races as Chauncey hurries over to Coach Marino and tugs on his sleeve excitedly. He's obviously begging to get put in the game, and I don't blame him. Now that his family – especially his *father* – is out here to support him, he's ready to play some football.

We move through the second quarter in a breeze, with strong offense *and* defense taking charge on both ends of the field. Coach Marino rotates Chauncey in and out of the game, but Chauncey never gets near the ball. On each down, Rashad continues to either run the ball himself or make passes to the other open members of the team. He's doing a much better job of moving the ball around. Unfortunately, the Pythons start to anticipate where Rashad will throw the ball, and they make off with another interception. Just before the quarter ends, Devin Rosenthal hits our guys with a long pass to one of his wide receivers. The wide receiver backs into the end zone and makes a crisp catch, and their kicker makes the field goal. They tie up the score and I grimace. It only took 20 seconds.

"Coming up on halftime with the score at fourteen-all," the announcer says. Most of the crowd gets up to get snacks at the concession stand as the announcer continues. "We'll resume in fifteen minutes, but for now, please put your hands together for the Lady Pythons!"

The Home bleachers section claps it up as the Pythons' cheerleaders perform their dance routine. They're pretty good, and I find myself wondering if *they* made it to Nationals. I make a mental note to check Instagram next month during the week of the big competition to find out.

Once the Lady Pythons leave the grass, it's time for Coach Robin and our Pirettes to show what *we* can do. To everyone's surprise, we perform a flawless routine. I can't help but feel a little bit annoyed with my squad. If we'd performed like this during the competition, we probably wouldn't be relying on the guys to make it to Florida.

When halftime ends, the third quarter begins with our guys on offense. Coach Marino puts the twins on the bench to give them a break and puts our second quarterback, Number Six, on the field. With each down, Chauncey is wide open, but Number Six just won't pass the ball to him. He probably doesn't trust Chauncey based on his past mistakes. I wouldn't. Number Six runs the ball himself, and by the third down, we make a three-point field goal that puts us in the lead 14-17. Sadly, our lead is short-lived. By the end of the third quarter, the Pythons gain control of the ball. They score another touchdown, thanks to their second quarterback, who has the same strong arm as Devin

Rosenthal. Thankfully, their field goal kick isn't good, so they only get six points.

With the score now at 20-17, Coach Marino begins the last quarter of the game with our third quarterback, Number 12. It's a bust, because he takes way too long to decide where to pass the ball, allowing the Pythons' defense to move in. Thanks to Number 12, we're forced to give up the ball. I throw my pom-poms in the grass and yank on my side ponytail crazily. *Do NOT let them score another touchdown!* my mind screams, and thankfully, our defense seems to hear me. They're all over the Pythons' wide receivers, who fail to make it anywhere *near* the end zone by their fourth down.

I glance at the scoreboard and almost rip my ponytail right out of my head. There's only three minutes left in the entire game, and the Pythons are still in the lead 20-17. Forget all of this fooling around with Number Six and Number 12. We need a touchdown, and we need Rashad *now.*

"Time out!" Coach Marino shouts. Thank God! I crane my neck to listen in as the Pirates football team huddles up for a much-needed pep talk. "All right, team! Bring it in! Bring it in!" Coach Marino orders. "This win is still within reach! I have all the faith in this team to bring it home!" He looks right at Rashad. "Rashad, you're back in. You ready? You fired up?" Rashad does a little jog in place and nods his head furiously. Coach Marino grips both hands around Rashad's helmet. "Focus. Eyes on the prize, all right?"

"Yes, sir!" Rashad responds.

Coach Marino nods his head and looks at Gumbo next. "Phil? Get out there with those good hands and catch like you've never caught before. I need you and your brother locked in, understand?" Gumbo nods his head and Coach Marino addresses the other players. "Linemen, I need you guys on your game. Keep that defense away from Rashad and Phil. No penalties. Play smart and play clean."

Everybody nods with determined expressions. Chauncey pushes his way to the front of the huddle and tugs on Coach Marino's sleeve. "Coach! Coach, put me in!"

I notice the twins glaring at Chauncey, but they don't say anything to him. Mr. du Bois just turns his head the other way, while Coach Marino stares at Chauncey in silence. He shakes his head. "Chauncey, I don't..."

"Please!" Chauncey cries, stomping his cleats in the grass. My heart plummets as I glance over at Chauncey's parents. They look hopeful.

Coach Marino's eyes glaze over Chauncey in thought. He glances at the Willis family in the bleachers and wipes a hand over his face. Finally, he looks back at Chauncey and jerks his head towards the field. "You're in as a wide receiver."

Chauncey looks serious as he puts his helmet on his head. The twins glance at each other in anger, while Mr. du Bois stares at Coach Marino like he's lost his mind. "Hey, now, wait a minute. Don't you remember—"

"All right, Pirates! Let's go!" Coach Marino bellows, cutting Mr. du Bois off. He ends the time-out and ushers the offensive line towards the field. I shudder, and it ain't this chilly November air, either. With Mr. du Bois glaring at Coach Marino, I can't help but wonder if putting Chauncey in the game was really the best decision.

The Pirates and the Pythons stagger themselves on the line of scrimmage for the first play. Our center snaps the ball to Rashad, who makes a swift catch and hustles backwards in preparation for his pass to Gumbo.

However, the Pythons block Gumbo's opening. Chauncey runs to a clear spot on the field and waves at Rashad to pass him the ball, but Rashad ignores him and tries to wait for Gumbo to get a better opening. This fails and Rashad gets sacked. My heart sinks. I hope he's not hurt.

"He could've passed it to Chauncey," a man's voice mutters from the bleachers. I turn around, surprised to see that the voice belongs to Mr. Willis. My body tenses as Mr. du Bois glares at Mr. Willis. His jaw locks, but he doesn't say anything and returns his eyes to the field.

During the second down, the Pythons' defense is all over Gumbo again. Chauncey finds another open space on the field, but Rashad tries to run the ball into the end zone himself. Sadly, he doesn't get far and gets tackled. That's the second down and there's only 40 seconds left on the clock.

There's a collective groan from the visitors' bleachers. "What is this boy doing?" Mr. Willis demands, staring at Rashad.

Mr. du Bois whips around with a fierce glare. "Watch it, man. That's my son you're talking about."

"Well, maybe if he'd pass that ball to *my* son, we could make something happen out there," Mr. Willis shoots back, gesturing to the field.

Corinne and I exchange a terrified glance, but there's no time to talk. The third down begins and all eyes are on Rashad. "Here we go! Here we go!" Rashad shouts to his linemen from the line of scrimmage. As the clock winds down from 40 seconds, Rashad receives the ball from our center and prepares for his big throw.

The Pythons' defense tries to sack Rashad, but he hits them with some fast feet and darts out of their path. On the opposite end of the field, I notice Gumbo hustling to the end zone. All Rashad has to do is throw that ball like he knows how, and we'll score a touchdown. We'll win this game.

Time stands still as Rashad shoots the ball from his hand with a force that causes him to land on his back. The ball soars through the air, making a beautiful arc as it travels high above the field. Gumbo hustles after the ball with his legs pumping like a track star. He holds his hands out, and I just *know* he's about to make this catch, but I notice someone else running towards the ball with his hands outstretched. It's Chauncey. He's trying to catch the ball, too.

My body feels like it's being dragged underwater as screams of anguish rise from the visitor's bleachers. Everything feels like it's happening in slow motion. Coach Marino drops his clipboard and yells at Chauncey to stop running, while Mr. du Bois whips his winter hat off his head and throws it on the ground. Corinne and the rest of my cheer squad watch the scene in horror. I can see my mother staring at the du Bois family with worry as they lower their posters, foam fingers, and banner. Mr. Willis shoots up from the bleachers and stares at Chauncey with a mortified expression, but it's too late. Chauncey crashes into Gumbo, pushing him out of the path of Rashad's throw. As the ball bounces in the grass, the clock strikes 00:00 and one of the Pythons lunges for the ball. Rashad's pass is incomplete, this game is over, and the Pythons are going to Florida.

57

The Big Reveal

"Chauncey! What the heck is wrong with you?"
The stadium feels like it's closing in as Gumbo's voice bellows through the air. He stands up and glares at Chauncey, who slowly rises and rubs his shoulder. Instead of answering Gumbo, he just turns away and trudges to the sidelines.

"And there you have it, folks! Your Division One Eastern Regional champions are...the Pittsburgh Pythons, and they're headed to Florida!"

I can hear the announcer's voice loud and clear, but nothing seems real right now. The Pythons won this game fair and square, but I feel cheated and angry. We were *this* close to winning, and now, because of a split-second mistake by Chauncey, it's all over. What was he thinking? Did he mess up Rashad's pass on purpose? No, he wouldn't have. Would he?

The officials take the field and try to begin the closing ceremony, but Rashad doesn't move. He kneels in the middle of the field, whips off his helmet, and slams it in the grass. As he cradles his head in his hands, I see that he's really upset. He must be devastated.

I lick my lips nervously as the officials and referees order Rashad to stand up. He slowly does as he's told, but then he turns to the sidelines to look at his father. Mr. du Bois is wrapped in a heated discussion with Coach Marino. He looks *livid*. Rashad clutches his stomach, slaps his hand over his mouth, and stumbles to a nearby trash can. He gets sick in front of everyone and my heart breaks.

My cheer squad squeals in disgust. "Leave him alone!" I shriek, but no one's paying attention to me. They're too busy watching the rest of the Pirates football team surround Rashad.

Gumbo pushes past everyone and marches up to Chauncey. "Look at what you did to my brother! Are you happy now?" Gumbo screams with pure rage. "You don't belong on this team! That's why nobody likes you!"

My stomach feels it's been hit with a wrecking ball. This can't be happening. Not in front of all these people.

Chauncey glares up at Gumbo and takes a step forward. "It was an accident!"

"Stop lying!" Rashad screeches with a hoarse voice. He wipes his mouth with the sleeve of his football uniform and walks up to Chauncey, his face heavy with fury and despair. "You did it on purpose! You did it to mess me up!"

"No, I didn't!" Chauncey yells. "That's the problem with y'all du Bois! Y'all always think everything is about y'all!"

In that moment, Rashad's eyes flash with anger. He shoves Chauncey, causing Chauncey to stumble backwards. At first, I think Chauncey's going to fall, but he quickly regains his balance and shoves Rashad harder. As Rashad stares at Chauncey in shock, my jaw hits the ground. Chauncey is pretty strong.

"Keep your hands off my brother!" Gumbo shouts, tackling Chauncey to the ground. Everyone cries out in shock as Chauncey tries to squirm free.

The referees blow their whistles, while Mr. du Bois, Mr. Willis, and Coach Marino break up the tussle. "All right, that's enough! That's *enough!*" Coach Marino yells.

"No! I can't stand them!" Chauncey screams at the twins. He starts to lunge for them again, but his father holds him back. "They've been picking on me in school! They turned everybody against me! They came to my house and ruined my party!" He trails off and points at Rashad. "And he never passes me the ball, even when I'm wide open!"

"'Cause you've always been nothing but a scrub!" Rashad screams. "You ruined my completed passes record and you stole our chance at Florida, just like last year!"

My mouth drops open. It all makes sense.

Chauncey's face twists with a combination of pain and frustration. "I wasn't trying to—"

"You knew *exactly* what you were doing," Rashad hisses. He gestures to Gumbo. "My brother and I don't play football just for fun. We need it to pay for college." Chauncey tries to speak but Rashad cuts him off. He takes a shuddery deep breath and I realize that he's trying not to cry. "Making it to Florida would have really opened some doors for us leading up to high school, but you...you ruined it for us again."

My heart slams against my chest. I wish this could have ended differently.

The officials order the Pirates to pull themselves together and shake hands with the Pythons. They do, and we all watch in envy as the Pythons receive a shiny, golden trophy. They pose for pictures and I notice Devin Rosenthal getting interviewed by some of the local news outlets.

Coach Marino and Coach Robin give some half-hearted speech about what a great season we all had and how they look forward to seeing us all next year, but I'm not even listening. Instead, I'm staring at the twins, who sulk on the bleachers. Rashad's face is creased with disappointment as he yanks more grass from the field and sends it sprinkling towards his cleats. His mother and the rest of his extended family look on sadly. I doubt they expected this game to end this way.

When it's finally time for everyone to prepare to board the Coach bus, Chauncey walks away with his family. As they head to the parking lot, Mr. Willis approaches Mr. du Bois. "So, these are the kinds of sons you raise, huh?" Mr. Willis asks, gesturing to the twins.

Mr. du Bois stares at Mr. Willis with a combination of anger and offense swirling in his eyes. He takes a step forward. "And what would you know about raising sons? You've never been to one regular season game to see your boy play."

Mr. Willis looks Mr. du Bois up and down in silence. He nods slowly and adjusts the winter hat on his head. Then he turns away and walks after his family.

Next to me, Corinne sighs sadly and twirls the ends of her beaded braids. "So, I guess you solved the big mystery, huh?" she mutters.

I glance at her and return my eyes to the twins. Rashad catches me staring, but instead of turning away, he holds my gaze with a shameful expression. "I don't think I've solved everything just yet," I tell Corinne. Taking a deep breath, I walk over to the bleachers. "Ra? Can I talk to you?" I ask, wringing my hands with nervous energy. Rashad stares up at me, and Gumbo takes the hint and gives me a sort of sad smile. He stands up and walks off to talk to his cousins, and I sit down next to Rashad.

Rashad glances at me, his eyes hard with anguish. "What's up?" he asks quietly.

My lips part, but no words come out. Finally, I find my voice and meet Rashad's troubled gaze. "I'm sorry about the loss, Ra."

Rashad turns away from me and shakes his head slowly. "I tried to warn you about Chauncey, Desiree," he mutters. "I told you to stay away from him; that he was bad news, and you wouldn't believe me, but I guess you had to see for yourself."

My heart feels like it's climbing out of my chest. "I-I'm sorry," I finally say. "I was just trying to..."

"I know what you were trying to do, Dizzy," Rashad says tiredly. "You were trying to be a detective, and it all backfired."

I chew on my bottom lip and stare at my knees. "Are you mad at me?"

Rashad puffs out his cheeks and sighs deeply. "Not at you, just at the whole stupid situation." He shrugs and looks at me. "But you didn't do anything wrong. You were just..."

"Nosy?" I finish sheepishly.

Rashad's lips lift into a hint of a smile. "Yeah," he says, raising an eyebrow at me. I glance off, embarrassed, but then Rashad scoots closer to me and taps my Worm Tooth. "But...good friends are real with each other, so I'm gonna let you in on a secret. It's something Phil and I don't really talk about." I stare at Rashad in surprise and he goes on. "You remember the first time you came over for dinner and I told you about my uncle Levon?" I nod and Rashad takes a deep breath. "Well, as a kid, he played ball through high school with my dad. My dad was good, but my uncle was great. He was a quarterback for his high school varsity team, and everybody thought he was good enough to go pro one day. Colleges were already looking at him in his sophomore year."

"Wow," I breathe. "Well...what happened to him?"

Rashad rubs his nose. "He got distracted. See, my uncle was crazy-talented, but he didn't want to put in the work to get to that next level. His dad - my granddad - was really strict and wanted him to focus on playing ball, but my uncle didn't listen." Rashad plucks more grass from the field and rubs the strands between his fingers. "During his junior year, he let his friends suck him into partying and goofing off to the point where his game and grades started to slip. He got cut from the quarterback spot and lost his shot at a college football scholarship."

My stomach drops. "Oh, Ra..."

"He graduated from a community college, but he never went pro like he'd always dreamed. All because of some clowns who messed his head up." Rashad turns to me with a pained expression. "That's why our dad doesn't like us friending up with people he doesn't know, and that's why he pushes us to stay focused on the field - so we can finish what we started." He holds his head in his hands. "My dad's sacrificed so much for me and Phil. I want to make it to the pros because...I'd be able to help my whole family in ways I can't even imagine, Desiree."

I place a comforting hand on Rashad's shoulder. He looks at me and I smile. "That's an amazing dream, Rashad."

Rashad shrugs and lowers his eyes. "That's all it is right now - a dream."

"Yeah, but it can really happen. Phil's a great wide receiver and he's so supportive of you, Ra." Rashad nods his head silently and I continue. "You're a great quarterback with a lot of courage and passion, and you definitely have what it takes to go pro one day."

"Are you being for real, or are you messing with me?"

"I'm serious. You really are the best," I insist, poking Rashad in the shoulder. "But it doesn't matter what I think. If *you* believe in you, that's all that matters." I trail off and nod my head. "So many people are proud of your football accomplishments. I know I am."

Rashad regards my words in silence and lets his mouth lift into a half-smile. "Thanks." He pauses and shoots me a playful grin. "Football accomplishments?" I smirk, realizing how funny I sounded, and Rashad stifles a laugh. "You're really cute, Desiree Davenport," he says, and I try not to pass out. He smiles at me for a few moments, but then his eyes grow serious and he stares at the field with a sorrowful expression. "I just wish...*I'd* been the one to help you move into your apartment instead of Chauncey," he admits gravely, and I understand what he means. If Rashad had helped me on that hot, summer day, I would have never cared about Chauncey at all, and Rashad would have never felt like he was losing his friend to someone who ruined an important opportunity in his life, but neither of us can change the past.

We stand up from the bleachers, follow our teammates to the Coach bus, and take seats next to each other near the front. As we ride home in heavy silence, I stare out the window and try to process all of the truth Rashad shared with me, but as I think about Rashad and his uncle Levon, my mind wanders to Chauncey and the excited look he got on his face when he saw his dad sitting in the bleachers. Chauncey was wrong for messing up the twins' shot at Florida. That was just *crazy*, but everybody has a reason for their actions, and maybe, just maybe, Chauncey's reason is that he wants to be the best for *his* dad, too, just like the twins.

58

What Goes Around Comes Around

The next morning, at the breakfast table, I tell my mother everything about the twins, their family, and Chauncey.

My mother sips on her protein shake and listens as I explain everything about the bullying and why it happened. "You should have told me, Desiree," my mother says sadly.

"I'm sorry," I whisper. "I just didn't want to stress you out. We were moving and you were trying to save money so you wouldn't have to pay for aftercare..."

My mother flies up from her seat and wraps me in the tightest hug. "Desiree, we're all we have, Sweetheart. We have to be able to tell each other everything, okay? You can always come to me with anything."

"I love you, Mommy," I say. What would I do without her?

For the rest of the week, I carry her words with me at the bus stop, at school, and at The Crunch Bowl with the twins. Although they don't bother Chauncey anymore, I don't feel closure. Something is missing, but I can't figure out what.

"Maybe it's not for you to figure out," Corinne tells me that Thursday after school. "Maybe you have to let it happen on its own, Dizzy."

I nod silently and wave as Corinne walks to her locker. With cheerleading over until next year, we'll be seeing much less of each other, and I can't help but feel sad about that. I've learned a lot from Corinne in a short time.

To keep myself in good spirits, I make more video game plans with the twins. Rashad arrives to my apartment on Saturday afternoon, and I grin when I see that he's dressed in a tracksuit with a matching sweat band and his new sneakers. "Let me guess. You just came back from conditioning drills, didn't you?" I ask with a smile.

"You know it," Rashad says, giving me an exploding fist bump. "Just 'cause the season's over doesn't mean Phil and I get a break." He waves at my mother. "Hi, Ms. Germaine." My mother waves back and Rashad escorts me down the apartment stairs. Once we reach the door, I grab the knob and start to twist it, but Rashad puts his hand on top of mine, stopping me in my tracks. "Can I ask you something?" I nod and he gives me a curious look. "How come you never told me about your mom's last name until today?"

My lips twist into an awkward shape as I think back to Priya and Tatyana. "Well...my old friends weren't too nice, and I was always embarrassed to talk to them about my parents' divorce. Their parents are still together, and if they knew about my mom's last name, they'd make a big deal out of it, so I guess I was embarrassed to tell *you*, because..."

"Listen," Rashad says, cutting me off. He shakes his head and studies my face with serious eyes. "You don't ever have to feel embarrassed about stuff around me, Desiree."

My face heats up. I don't know how to respond. Since the day I met Rashad, I've always been so worried about being embarrassed in front of him. Now, I realize that he's been looking past my flaws this whole time, like a real friend should. Nobody's perfect.

Rashad leads me out to the sidewalk, where Gumbo and Brianna are standing. Brianna leans on a shiny, pink scooter that matches her helmet, elbow, and knee pads. When she sees me, she drops the scooter and wraps me in a hug.

"'Sup, Dizzy?" Gumbo says. He raises his sunglasses at me. "You ready to get played in *Mario Kart* today?"

I grin and fold my arms across my chest. "Actually, I was planning on beating both of you in *Football Smashup*."

The twins exchange shocked smirks. "Ra, she's got some jokes!" Gumbo exclaims with a laugh. He grins and leads us all up the sidewalk. "Come on. We're going around the corner for some snacks real quick."

Stepping tall in the heels of my pink cowgirl boots, I follow the twins and Brianna up the sidewalk, but as we pass The Crunch Bowl, I see something that makes my stomach turn. There's a few boys outside the restaurant, and they're peering through the glass windows. One of the boys turns around, and I catch sight of a gold do-rag tied around his head.

Oh. My. Gosh. It's that Do-Rag kid from City Wheels.

Do-Rag notices me walking with the twins and freezes. His mouth lifts into a creepy smile, and I immediately pull Brianna along faster. "Um, guys?" I call to the twins, but they're not listening to me. Instead, they're arguing over who's going to get first dibs on the shiny, red controller once we get back to their apartment. My chest tightens as I glance behind me. Do-Rag and his crew are slowly keeping up with us, but thankfully, the twins, Brianna, and I make it to the Get It and Come On before they get too close to us.

Gumbo folds up Brianna's scooter and carries it around the store as we browse the aisles for snacks. I glance over my shoulder in search of Do-Rag. To my relief, he never comes inside, and I let myself relax as Gumbo pays for our popcorn, chips, donuts, and bottles of iced tea. That gum business really *does* come in handy.

After Rashad grabs the snack bag off the counter, I follow the twins to the store's exit and listen to Brianna make up a song about how excited she is to eat her powdered donuts. "Can I have one *now*, Ra-Ra?" she begs.

Rashad slowly turns to me with a tight smile that reads, *You see what I have to deal with?* I just laugh to myself as Rashad tweaks Brianna's nose. "Bri, can we get outside first?" he asks, pushing the door open with his back. He takes a few steps outside and accidentally bumps into Do-Rag. He's got two other guys with him.

"What's good, Pretty Boy?" Do-Rag sneers through a grin. My entire body goes hot as I turn to Rashad. His eyes grow wide with anger and a trace of fear as he glances at the dudes standing behind Do-Rag. "What? You lost your voice, or something? I'm talking to you," Do-Rag continues. He steps closer to me. "I see you've still got your girlfriend with you."

Rashad grabs my hand and steps in front of me. "What do you want?"

"Ra, let's just go," I urge hastily.

"Nuh-uh. This dude ain't going nowhere," Do-Rag snaps. He glares at Rashad and clenches his fists. "We've got unfinished business to take care of."

"Aye, hold up," Gumbo snaps. He steps forward, grabs Brianna, and pulls her behind him. "Ra, who is he?" he hisses, his eyes shooting daggers at Do-Rag.

"Some dude who was talking trash at City Wheels," Rashad answers angrily.

"Oh, you ain't *seen* trash yet." Do-Rag points to Rashad's sneakers. "Take 'em off."

Rashad pulls me close and stealthily slips his phone into my jacket pocket. He puts his mouth to my ear and whispers, "Take my sister and run. Call my dad."

I grab Brianna's hand and take off *running*.

"Phiiiiillll! Raaaaa-Ra!" Brianna screams. The tears are streaming down her face, but I don't even have time to wipe them. She tries to go to her brothers, but I just grab her hand tighter and pull her along faster.

"Come on, Brianna. Come on," I coax, even though I want to scream like a baby, too. What if I'm too late? What if Mr. du Bois can't get to the twins in time?

Moving as quickly as I can in my boots, I stumble towards an alley. However, my foot sinks into a shallow hole in the sidewalk and I crash down with Brianna. She cries even harder and I hear the twins screaming my name. I turn around, horrified to see Do-Rag and his crew roughing them up. They're trying to get Rashad's sneakers.

I gather my strength, stand up, and pull Brianna into the alley. I reach into my pocket for Rashad's phone. There's no passcode – thank God – so I'm easily able to access his Contacts app and find **Dad**. Hands shaking, I dial Mr. du Bois and practically shout with joy when he answers after the first ring. "Hello? Ra?"

"Mr. du B-Bois! It's D-Desiree!" I ramble crazily. "I'm with Brianna by the Get It and Come On, but some boys are after Phil and Rashad! They want Rashad's sneakers!"

"Stay where you are, Desiree. I'll be right there." Mr. du Bois hangs up, and it's just me and a very hysterical Brianna huddled alone in the alley. I hug Brianna tighter, squeeze my eyes shut, and pray to God that Mr. du Bois gets here soon.

"Dizzy?" a familiar voice suddenly calls. My eyes fly open and I don't believe who's standing in front of me. It's

Chauncey, and his father is right behind him. "Dizzy, what are you doing in there? Are you okay?"

I don't respond right away. I'm too shocked. This is the first time Chauncey's spoken to me since almost three weeks ago, when he kicked me out of his house.

"Hey, man, get off me!" I hear Rashad yell from up the street. My ears ring with the ugly sound of Do-Rag's laughter and Gumbo's protests to get away from Rashad. The next thing I know, the sound of a sharp "Augh!" pierces the air. It's Rashad, and he sounds hurt. In that moment, I come to life and stare at Chauncey with pleading eyes.

"Th-the twins..." I stammer, hastily gesturing up the street. "I-I called their dad but he isn't here yet and...you have to help them, Chauncey. Please."

Chauncey and his father run towards the fight. I look on in amazement as Mr. Willis holds Do-Rag's two friends back as they try to swing punches at Gumbo. Meanwhile, Rashad lies on the ground. Do-Rag crouches down and tries to grab Rashad's sneakers, but then Chauncey jumps in front of Rashad and shoves Do-Rag away from him. Rashad watches in shock as Chauncey socks Do-Rag square in his jaw. Oh. My. Gosh.

Just then, Mr. du Bois rushes up the street with a big, wooden stick in his hand. He notices me standing at the edge of the alley with Brianna and rushes over to us. "Stay right here, okay?" he tells me. I nod and watch as he speed-walks to the fight, brandishing the stick high in the air. "Hey! Y'all clowns want a piece of this?"

At the sight of the wooden stick, Do-Rag and his friends sprint off with Rashad's sneakers. I release a huge breath of air that I didn't even know I was holding. It's over.

Shaking, I take Brianna's hand and lead her back to the Get It and Come On. I see Chauncey and his father hovering over Mr. du Bois, who kneels on the sidewalk next to the twins. They're all bruised up.

"Lord have mercy," Mr. du Bois whispers, frantically touching the twins. "I've gotta get y'all home."

Gumbo coughs. "Dad, Ra got kicked in the stomach."

"Let me take a look at him." Mr. Willis crouches on the sidewalk next to Rashad and hands Chauncey a five-dollar bill. "Go into that store and get Rashad some water." Chauncey runs into the store, and Mr. Willis orders Rashad to lie on his back. "Does it hurt when you breathe?" he asks Rashad. Rashad takes a few deep breaths and shakes his head no. "Good," Mr. Willis says. He gently presses a few spots near Rashad's rib cage.

Mr. du Bois looks stunned. "How do you...?"

"I used to play for the NFL," Mr. Willis explains, his eyes never leaving Rashad. "Injuries like these were pretty common, so I'm familiar with how to spot 'em." He taps Rashad's shoulder. "Can you sit up for me?" Rashad winces, but manages to slowly push himself into a sitting position. Mr. Willis smiles and rubs Rashad's back. "Your boy's all right," he says to Mr. du Bois. "No fractures or breaks, but I would still take him to the doctor just to be sure." Everyone exhales in relief. Thank God.

Just then, Chauncey emerges from the store with a few bottles of water. Mr. du Bois quickly thanks Chauncey and takes one of the bottles. He hands it to Rashad and instructs him to take small sips. "How did this craziness get started? What were y'all doing?" he demands.

Sounding very out of breath, Rashad reveals everything about Do-Rag and City Wheels. Chauncey turns away. I know he doesn't want to hear anything about City Wheels. "That kid wanted my sneakers, Dad," Rashad says.

"Sneakers?" Mr. du Bois snaps. "I can buy ten pairs of sneakers, Rashad, but I can't replace you." He points between the twins. "The next time somebody wants to fight you for your sneakers or anything else, give it to 'em, because it's not worth it." He swallows and points to Chauncey. "Whatever beef you have with Chauncey, end it right now. You will respect this young man, because he and his father saved you both today. Now, apologize for whatever happened at his party and thank him."

The twins do as they're told. Rashad stares up at Chauncey with creases of humility and shame on his face. "You really could've been hurt, Chauncey," he says.

Chauncey blinks. "I know, but I wasn't."

Rashad glances from his socks to Chauncey's face. "You didn't have to help us."

"We're teammates," Chauncey mumbles, shrugging.

Gumbo looks curious. "Why'd you push me out of the way when I was trying to catch that ball last week?" He gestures to Rashad. "You messed up our shot at Florida two years in a row, Chauncey."

Mr. du Bois clears his throat. "All right, boys, we're putting that behind us."

"I didn't *mean* to mess y'all up!" Chauncey insists in a pained voice. He stares down at Rashad. "I'm always wide open, but you never pass me the ball. Every week, I never get a chance to do *anything* to improve my game. How's that supposed to make me feel when my dad's out there watching me?" Rashad's face cracks with guilt. He glances up at me, and I know he's thinking about our conversation after the Regional Championships. "I just wanted my chance to contribute, too," Chauncey finishes sadly, "but y'all never gave it to me. I didn't even feel like I was part of the team."

Mr. du Bois studies Chauncey, his expression clouded with guilt. "Well, all of that's going to change right now," he states firmly. Clearing his throat, he stares up at Mr. Willis. "Listen, my boys and I do conditioning drills for two hours every Saturday morning. Some of the other boys come out. It's getting colder, so we'll be in the gym for the next few months." He turns to Chauncey. "We'd love to have Chauncey join us, if he's interested."

Mr. Willis smiles and nudges Chauncey in the elbow. Chauncey looks up at his father, then at Mr. du Bois, then at the twins. I glance between Gumbo and Rashad, whose eyes are calm with acceptance. I know it's too early to celebrate, but I feel like we're moving in the right direction.

Chauncey looks Mr. du Bois right in his eyes and gives a small nod. "Sounds cool." Mr. du Bois holds his hand in the air, and this time, Chauncey doesn't leave him hanging. He slaps Mr. du Bois a firm high five and smiles.

Mr. Willis nudges Chauncey and gestures to the twins. "All right. Y'all shake hands, now."

Chauncey shakes Gumbo's hand. "Thanks for looking out for my bro, Chauncey," Gumbo says. He and Rashad exchange numbers with Chauncey. I turn to Brianna, who's gobbling down her powdered donuts. She's got white powder caked all over her face. Rashad cringes, but stays quiet.

Chauncey pulls Rashad up and they shake hands. "Thanks, Chauncey," Rashad says. "See you on Saturday."

Chauncey nods and I sigh, feeling drained. "Guys, I know we planned to play video games, but you both need to rest. I'll just go home."

"Well, I'll walk you home," Rashad says. "You shouldn't be out here by yourself."

My spirits lift in surprise. Rashad Maurice du Bois never misses an opportunity to let me know that he cares about me.

Mr. du Bois lifts Brianna into his arms and shakes hands with Mr. Willis. "Thank you, man. I really appreciate you stepping in for my boys today. Let's exchange numbers so I can tell you how Chauncey's progressing on Saturdays."

"Sounds like a plan," Mr. Willis says. "And you're welcome. That's how we do around here. It's just us looking out for us."

At this statement, my heart swells with realization.

This is the spirit of Treeless Park, and I really do like it here.

59

Rashad's Point of View: For Desiree

On the Saturday before Christmas, I join my family at the breakfast table and surprise them with a question I've been dying to ask for a couple weeks:

"Ma? Dad? Can I get Desiree a Christmas gift?"

Brianna gasps, showing off the chewed waffle in her mouth, while Phil just smiles and focuses on finishing his plate. Mom and Dad start grinning at each other. "Have something specific in mind, Ra?" Dad asks me.

"I...haven't really decided yet," I admit with a shrug.

Brianna's eyes light up. "Ra-Ra! Get her a scooter just like mine so we can ride scooters together!"

I smile and pretend to think about her suggestion really, really hard. "Mmm, thanks, Boogie, but I'm not getting her a scooter."

Brianna slouches in her chair. "Forget it. Phil, you think of something," she mutters flatly. My sister's hilarious.

"Ra, you could get her a couple of stashes of my gum," Phil says, smirking. "My Q4 profits would go *straight* through the roof."

"And Desiree would be going *straight* to the dentist," Dad says. Everyone cracks up. When Dad laughs, he does a full-on belly laugh that makes everyone join in. Maybe that's where Brianna gets it from. "No, no, get her something nice, Ra," Dad continues. Mom nods in agreement and runs a hand through her hair. My eyes travel to Mom's wrist and I think about Desiree. Looking back, I remember Desiree wearing a bracelet...for a little while, anyway. I wonder why she stopped wearing it?

"How about a bracelet?" I suggest to my parents. They glance at each other and nod.

"We'll stop by the store this evening," Mom says, and thankfully, that's what we do. We enter Treeless Park Jewelers and Dad explains to the sales clerk what we're looking for. Mom warns Brianna not to get her jelly fingers all over the glass. I turn to P, who stands off to the side, texting somebody. I crane my neck and smirk when I see "Butter" at the top of his screen.

"How's Corinne, P?" I ask, smiling.

P glances up, startled, and quickly puts his phone away. His face gets a little red and I raise my eyebrows. P *never* gets embarrassed. At least that's what I thought. "Oh, uh, I... that wasn't Corinne," he mumbles through a forced laugh.

I give him a look. "Liar," I say, and he just smiles and speed-walks over to Brianna. I smirk and shake my head at him. It feels good to bust *him* for once, but I'm kind of disappointed that he doesn't talk to me about Corinne. I want to help him like he's helped me with Desiree. In his own time, I guess.

"Ra, come pick out the charms you want on the bracelet," Dad says. I meet him by the glass and let my eyes glaze over the different options. I smile to myself as I gradually spot the perfect ones. Wait until Desiree sees *this*.

Epilogue

Moving Forward

Regardless of any challenges I've faced, there's always been something about the holiday season that's made life easier. Tonight, I'm having the time of my life at City Wheels, and I wouldn't change a thing.

From my spot in the sitting area, I smile as I watch Gumbo skate with Corinne. She's really gotten a lot better. Her skinny legs wobble as she lifts her black inlines to the beat of a mashup of remixed Christmas songs by Mariah Carey.

I turn to Rashad, who sits next to me and puts his skates on. "So...how have the conditioning drills with Chauncey been going?" I ask.

Rashad raises an eyebrow and stares at me with fake shock. "Hold up. Are we being nosy right now?"

"We are," I say, and Rashad cracks up. I swat his arm and he finally calms down to answer my question.

"Saturdays are cool. You remember when Chauncey straight bopped that kid?" Rashad asks, punching his fist into his hand. I nod quickly. "Yeah, Girl, he's strong," Rashad continues, "and my dad's already talking to his dad about him becoming an offensive lineman next year, so we'll all be putting in work this off-season to get ready."

"That's amazing. What does your mom think about all this?"

"She's glad, especially since she flipped when she found out about the fight," Rashad says, and I just nod my head. My mother reacted the same way and made me promise to never walk around the neighborhood alone for a while. Thankfully, I've got two bodyguards across the street and a third one just a few blocks away. Rashad smiles at me. "I got you something."

My eyebrows shoot up in surprise. "Me?"

"Yes, you." Rashad reaches into the inner pocket of his football jacket and unveils a small, red gift bag. He places the bag in my hand and grins. "Open it."

I open the bag and pull out a note written in Rashad's handwriting. It reads:

To The Amazing Desiree Davenport.

-Rashad

Grinning, I reach into the bottom of the bag and pull out a white box wrapped in a red bow. I open the box and gasp when I see a gold bracelet sporting five charms: a cursive letter "D," a book, a magnifying glass, a cheerleading megaphone, and a cowgirl boot. I stare at the bracelet and struggle to close my open mouth. "Oh, Ra...how did you..."

"My parents paid for it," Rashad confesses, smiling. He fastens the bracelet around my wrist. "But it was my idea, and I picked out all the charms. Do you like it?"

My bracelet sparkles as I turn my wrist back and forth. "I love it, Ra. Thank you."

"It's my way of thanking *you*," Rashad says, his expression growing serious. "You were right, Desiree. I'm sorry for making you feel like you were wrong about this whole Chauncey thing. I was just…"

"Holding a grudge? Being a bully?" I finish Rashad's sentence with a light smile.

Rashad rubs the back of his neck. He looks at me and nods. "Chauncey told us that you were the one who begged him and his dad to help us that day. If you hadn't been there to drag my sister away from that fight…I don't even want to think about what could've happened to her, so, seriously, thank you."

I sit in silence and rub my palms against my knees. "Well, I want to thank you, too."

Rashad raises an eyebrow. "For what?"

I chew on my bottom lip and take a deep breath, thinking back to how sad I was when I first moved to Treeless Park. "For always making me feel like I was part of your family." I glance down at my new bracelet. "This is really special, Ra."

Rashad smiles. "I was hoping you would say that, because I really like you, Desiree, and I wanted to ask you if you'll go out with me sometimes – just me and you?"

The skating rink feels like it's spinning, lifting off the ground, and soaring higher and faster into the sky. Is this real life? I check to see if Rashad is scratching his ear but he's not. He's telling the truth right now.

I bite my bottom lip to keep from smiling too hard and give him a small nod. On the inside, I'm doing backflips, cartwheels, and somersaults all at the same time.

Rashad grins and lets out a relieved sigh, like he was holding it in for years. "Cool." He leans in and gently drops a small kiss on my cheek. In that moment, the air leaves my lungs and I forget how to breathe. Ha! Tatyana was wrong. Rashad holds his phone in the air. "Come on. Smile."

My hands fly to my hair. "Ra, I gotta fix my hair."

Rashad smirks. "Girl, it's in a *bun*. You look good." We lean closer together and he takes our picture. He posts it to Instagram, tags me, and I try not to pass out. Suddenly, I'm reminded of something that happened a while ago.

"Ra, can I ask you something? What was that on the first day of school during attendance with the 'Pony Boots' in the Jamaican accent?" I laugh and nudge his elbow. "You embarrassed me, you know."

Rashad smirks and rubs his neck. "I'm sorry. I was just trying to one-up my brother and I wanted you to like me. I wasn't trying to embarrass you."

Just then, my phone starts buzzing like crazy. I take one look at who's calling me and almost drop my phone.

"Hello?" I answer, putting my phone to my ear.

"Hey, Baby Girl," a familiar voice says. It's my father.

"Hi, Daddy," I say softly. My father apologizes for everything that happened between us *and* for bringing Tasha to the football game.

"I really want to see you during your Winter Break," my father says. "Just you and me, Princess."

I grin as I put my phone closer to my ear. "On the day after Christmas, can we go to The Crunch Bowl? It's right across the street from where Mommy and I live."

"Sounds like a plan, Princess. I'll pick you up then at four o'clock and call you tomorrow. I love you."

"I love you, too, Daddy," I say, and we hang up.

Rashad nudges my elbow. "I'm happy for you, Pony Boots," he says, and my smile grows wider. Everything is finally working out. "So...what do you think?" Rashad asks.

I tilt my head to the side. "Of what?"

"Of Treeless Park. When I first met you, you said you already had friends back home and that you didn't need any friends here."

My body tenses with guilt. "Rashad...I shouldn't have said all that."

"It's okay. A lot of people who come through Treeless Park will judge it because of the way it looks, and they think, 'Oh, it's just Treeless Park. Ain't nothing good coming out of Treeless Park.' But they're wrong, because it's a community of people who *are* trying to build something good and who really care about each other. You cared enough about me to tell me that I was wrong, and I'll never forget that." Rashad stands up, grins, and extends his hand to me. "So, what do you think about Treeless Park? Will you give it a chance?"

As I stare up at Rashad, my mouth breaks into a calm smile. I nod slowly, finally starting to feel whole again. "Yeah."

I take Rashad's hand and stand up. He links his arm in mine and smiles. "Desiree Davenport, welcome to Treeless Park."

We take our turn on the rink, and boy, do we skate tonight.

About the Author

Chental Song Bembry is an author and motivational speaker from Somerset, NJ. As a proud alumna of the illustrious Hampton University, she holds a B.A. in Journalism with a minor in Leadership Studies. She started playing tennis at the age of four and played competitively through high school. Prior to publishing *Desiree Davenport: Welcome to Treeless Park*, she wrote and illustrated "The Honey Bunch Kids" book series. Chental's contributions to literacy have been recognized by Black Enterprise, Ebony Magazine, Essence Magazine, ESPN's *The Undefeated*, BuzzFeed, USA Today, The Ringer, The Cheat Sheet TV, the National Urban League, and Black Entertainment Television. In 2015, she was recognized at the BET Honors as an "Early Riser" and at the Black Girls Rock! awards show, where the former FLOTUS, Michelle Obama, declared her a "Making a Difference Girl." In May 2018, Chental was featured in LeBron James' *Always Believe* campaign during the NBA Playoffs. In her spare time, Chental enjoys visiting schools to deliver an original motivational speech called "Passion and Purpose," in which she inspires children to identify their potential career paths through their interests.

Made in the USA
Middletown, DE
12 February 2020